Other Books in the Vintage Library
of Contemporary World Literature

Aké: The Years of Childhood BY WOLE SOYINKA
Correction BY THOMAS BERNHARD
Masks BY FUMIKO ENCHI
One Day of Life BY MANLIO ARGUETA
The Questionnaire BY JIŘÍ GRUŠA

MAÍRA

MAÍRA

DARCY RIBEIRO

TRANSLATED FROM THE PORTUGUESE
BY E. H. GOODLAND AND THOMAS COLCHIE

AVENTURA

The Vintage Library of Contemporary World Literature

VINTAGE BOOKS   A DIVISION OF RANDOM HOUSE   NEW YORK

An Aventura Original, March 1984
First Edition
Translation Copyright © 1984 by E. H. Goodland and
Thomas Colchie

Library of Congress Cataloging in Publication Data
Ribeiro, Darcy.
Maira.
Translation of: Maíra.
I. Title.
PQ9698.28.I152M313   1984   869.3   84-48043
ISBN 0-394-72214-0
Manufactured in the United States of America
First American Edition
Cover illustration by Melanie Marder Parks

CONTENTS

ANTIPHONY

THE DEATH

"Nobody understands that gringo," says the police chief. "He arrived this morning with a bellboy from the Hotel National and created pandemonium. He is Swiss; I examined his passport. He says he saw a dead woman on a beach up the River Iparana. The Devil to pay!

"People die here all the time, and now I have to concern myself with some woman who died a thousand kilometers away. I sent for you, Noronha, because I know you speak French."

"No, Doctor, only English."

"Never mind. I want you to see if you can find out what the gringo wants. I don't believe his story."

"Could the gringo have killed the woman?"

"What do I know? He said she was fair-skinned and young; as white as he! A dead white woman up the Iparana is something unheard of. Do you believe it?"

Hours later, Noronha gives an oral report:

"I talked to the man, Doctor. I didn't need an interpreter; he found a girl attendant at the hotel who speaks perfect French.

We had a long conversation. Here is what I ascertained. The man is in fact Swiss."

"You don't say! That really is news. As if I hadn't seen his passport!"

"He is a naturalist. That is to say, he came up from Belém with a scientific expedition to film ants."

"Ants?"

"Yes, Doctor, ants. The man is, so to speak, an ecologist-entomologist. He studies insects in their natural habitat."

"What does this have to do with the dead woman?"

"Nothing, he was only explaining how he came to be in such an out-of-the-way place. He really did see the dead woman on the beach. Naked."

"Completely?"

"That's right. And white and less than thirty years old. She died in childbirth."

"In childbirth? Mother of Jesus!"

"The twins were already out."

"Twins! A dual birth?"

"That's right, and they still had not decomposed, no. But there were ants scurrying all over her body."

"This story is building into one hell of an anthill, my friend."

"He, the Swiss fellow, filmed everything but he didn't take any photographs."

"Did you get his film, Noronha? That's the evidence. We need it."

"No, I didn't get it, Dr. Ramiro. The girl explained that it is special color film that can't be developed here, or even in Rio. The man promised to develop and enlarge a few shots of the dead woman and of the site and to send them to us."

Dr. Ramiro rises from his chair and advances toward the subinspector.

"None of that, Noronha! I want the film, otherwise I'll arrest the gringo. Don't you see that there is something wrong with his story? I wasn't born yesterday! Maybe he killed the woman and then thought he'd better come in and report it. Or maybe no one killed the woman, she just died in childbirth. A beach up the Iparana! Is that any place to give birth? And twins at that! What he wants, I know, is to carry away this film of a dead white woman up the Iparana being eaten by his ants. Go back! Get the film or arrest the gringo. He wants to discredit us out there, abroad. I won't allow it."

"Dr. Ramiro, look, this man has permission from the government to go wherever he pleases. I saw it! He has film cans galore. If he wants he could give us any container. And, as you yourself said, he didn't have to report what he saw. If he came it is because the Swiss are like that; they have to tell their father or the authorities anything that is unusual."

"But listen, my boy, were he to disappear with the evidence where would we stand? Suppose we were to find him guilty tomorrow, how would we get extradition papers?"

"You are the one who knows, Doctor. I could arrest the man and confiscate the cans of film and the cameras as well. But it would cause quite a scandal. Wouldn't it be better to get an affidavit from him? A legal statement. In fact he will be coming here at four o'clock to give his affidavit. He is coming with his consul.

DECLARATION

Today, 10 January 1975, the undersigned, Peter Becker, a Swiss citizen of the Canton of Basle, came to this Delegacia to declare, in furtherance of Truth and Justice, what he saw on 26 October 1974 on a beach up the Iparana near the village of the Mairun Indians.

Arriving at said beach early in the morning of said day in the company of a colleague F. Huxley O'Thief and a pilot named Joaquim Quinzim, Becker saw the following: on the beach, approximately twenty meters from the waterline, lay a young white woman in a supine position half naked, her body painted with streaks of black and red forming lines and circles. The said woman had her legs spread, and between her thighs could be seen a double fetus; I mean, two male embryos still enveloped by the placenta and tied to their mother by umbilical cords. He verified that the woman was dead—cold body, rigor mortis—as was also the case with the fetuses. He also verified that she had bled during childbirth. He verified that on her forehead there was a small scar from an old wound, now a cicatrix. And, moreover, that her face, hands, and legs were marked by striated scratches, some of which were partially infected. These latter considerations prompted him to assume that a crime might have been committed. However, he wishes to say that it was not only for this reason that he sought out competent authority to whom to make the present complaint—correction, communication. He does so as a result of the extraordinary nature of his encounter with that white woman who had died while giving birth to twins on a deserted beach near a village of wild Indians. To complete this communication, the deponent declares that he and his companions met the Indians referred to above. They themselves approached the beach, probably on hearing the noise of a motorboat that stopped there. He believes that this was the case because the Indians manifested greater surprise at seeing the corpse than at seeing the strangers. They howled, attracting a great number of men and women who came running from the village about five hundred meters behind the sandbanks. On arriving, the Indians gathered around the body, commenting excitedly in their own language of which the informant understands not a word. At a certain moment, the indigenous women began to pull their own hair, weeping and lamenting in a great show of feeling. One of them, upon finding (the informant does not know where) the jawbone of a piranha, started to gash her face and legs with it until they bled profusely. The other women, following her example, took the mandible and lacerated themselves as well. Perhaps an hour after this savage reaction, some men came with a hammock into which they put first the stillborn embryos and then the deceased, and returned in the direction of the village. The informant and his companions remained for some time on the beach trying to obtain more information, but only the children paid them any attention and they knew nothing about the Brazilian language. Later on, when they went to the village, the body was no longer there. According to information given by Sr. Quinzim, who had dealt with those Indians before and who could understand them, the corpse had been taken to the Indian cemetery adjoining a former village some three kilometers to the north.

This being all that he has to declare, the deponent puts himself at the disposal of the Brazilian authorities for any additional information, whether in person or through the good offices of Sr. Max Piaget, consul for Switzerland, who is also signing this document.

"It's a nasty case, Dr. Ramiro. What are you going to do?"

"I've no idea, Noronha. Gringos only serve to give grief. Who ever heard of a story such as this? And why the Devil did he have to come and make his complaint here, in my backyard? I know he flew direct from Naruai to Brasília, but he could have waited until he got to Rio to tell his story. And you, Noronha, what are your ideas? As far as I'm concerned there's no crime to investigate: the woman simply died in childbirth. As do so many others. Could she be Swiss?"

"What we have to do is close this case, Doctor. The best thing to do is to make a copy of the declaration and send it on as an official communication. I don't know where to. Perhaps to the National Indian foundation? In my opinion . . ."

"That's all we need: what do they have to do with this? Or do you think the Indians killed the gringa and then fell into that pagan lament just to confuse the Swiss man?"

"Not at all! Let me send it to the Ministry of Justice, to General Cipriano Catapreta. I'll do a good job of it and put the case into the hands of someone competent to handle it. To discover as well whether the Indians are the culprits. Only the Ministry-General can make anything of this. The Civil Code declares that the Indians are immune, like madmen, minors and married women—that is to say, irresponsible before the law, innocent."

"I want to see how this will end. What we don't want is to be left with a hot potato in our hands. What a relief that that consul signed as a witness."

"Send it on, Noronha! And write that I made the consul sign so as to make him responsible if, at any moment, we discover that the Swiss is guilty. Doctor of Ants. How ridiculous! What he was doing was poking around in the interior, searching—of course—for some mineral. I'm not so dim as to suppose that the ants of Brazil are so important that an expedition would leave Switzerland just to film ant heaps."

Dr. Ramiro turns his chair around as if intending to get up to bring the conversation to a close. Noronha understands and starts to leave.

"You are right, Doctor, absolutely right."

ANACÁ

The Great House of Men is teeming with people, like ants. Men, women, children. Alive and dead. All the Mairuns are here. The living, in surprise, are standing or sitting and are looking at the old chieftain who is crouching before the guide of souls in the exact center of the enormous hut. The dead enter and depart, flying in circles that rise from the Great House to the heights of Heaven. They are visible only to the eyes of the guide of souls, sitting on his bench with an eagle's head carved at both ends.

All are here. They gathered at the Summoning of Anacá, the chieftain. He must have something very important to say! Never, except at momentous ceremonies, may women and children enter the Great House of Men. Never. Today everyone is here, the children too. The dead are also present, as always, but today in greater number, entering and departing rapidly.

"Yes, I summoned, you," said the chieftain in a low voice from where he was crouching, staring at the ground. "I have danced the Coraci-Iaci many times. I have sung the mare-mare many times. I have eaten many pacu fish and I have drunk much caium, cassava beer. I have fucked sufficiently. I have enjoyed more than my share of laughter. I am old. My hour has come, I am at the end. Yes, I'm going to leave you now, without a chieftain. My orphans. I need to die so that a new chieftain may emerge and grow."

The guide of souls makes a muffled buzz with his maracas and starts talking to the dead.

"Yes, it is so, my family, but wait. Yes, it is the chieftain Anacã who speaks. It is he. He says he will die today. He goes, yes, but not now, not here, it will not be now. He will die at your sunset, at our sunrise.

"Look, Anacã," says the guide of souls, turning toward the chieftain, "it is your father, my uncle Uira, of the Carcaras. He is saying that he is going to arrange a hunt for you. A great hunt for white deer in the high grass of the savanna." The chieftain replies: "That's good, we shall hunt together again. With him I shall see the midnight sun."

The chieftain rises, carrying his bow and two bamboo arrows in his right hand. In his left hand the *tacape*, a sacrificial club, his weapon and symbol of authority. He stands for a moment in front of the guide of souls who also rises and takes from the neck of Anacã the ceremonial flute made of a jaguar's shinbone and ties it to the central column of the hut.

Anacã looks around, resting his eye on the face of each man, each woman, each child. He starts to circle the interior of the hut along the wall, looking always at each and everyone directly in the eyes. So he bids farewell to all the Mairuns, without words, and departs in silence through the door on high that he never used in life. They all stand still listening to his footsteps as he walks outside and makes a slow circuit of the Great House. Then they hear farther away, his pacing in ever diminishing circles on the dancing ground. It was as if he wanted to cover all the ground he had walked on during the century of his life.

Everyone remains in the Great House, silent, some sitting, some squatting, others lying down. The children sleep. Only the faint sound of the rattle of the guide of souls. It is like the buzz of a bee, barely audible, but in the silence of this night it sounds like a scream. All the Mairuns are there, huddled together, as if to warm each other. Only around the Oxim, who is sitting near the door of the lower end on his haunches, is there a void of reserve, of disgust and fear. The dead fly in circles in the air entering and departing, all of them wanting to speak at the same time to the guide of souls. But none of them says anything. They also know that the beelike buzz of the rattle demands silence.

In the vast world of the few living Mairuns and of the multitude of those who have lived and died, the news spreads. The chieftain Anacã has decided that on this night of the living he will lie down to sleep as usual, only to awake near dawn, half dead/half alive so as to see the light of the black sun shining.

It is morning. Anacã, lying dead in his hammock, is waiting. Around him are his people of the Jaguar clan. Except Avá, his successor, who went away a long time ago and never returned. The corpse of Anacã, recumbent in the hammock, glows, wrinkled in a sunbeam shining through a hole in the thatched roof. Today, all day long, the Sun will watch Anacã, and the eyes of all the Mairuns will also be fixed upon him.

At last, the guide of souls arrives with another man of the Carcara family, his nephew Teró. The two of them lift the chieftain from the hammock and lay him on a new mat on the ground of the Great House. There and now they paint him carefully, fine striae of annatto-red dye that run uninterrupted from his throat to his feet. His face is painted with bluish-black juice of the unripe genipap, except his eyes, which are covered with shells, highly polished, sparkling white.

Jaguar, the great nephew of Anacã, crouching there at one side, holds in his lap a woven grass basket bearing the feather ornaments belonging to the old chieftain. One by one he selects the most beautiful and hands them to the guide of souls who places them: in the ears, pendants; in the hole in the lower lip, a labret; on the head, a diadem of golden oriole feathers; on his throat, necklaces of snail shells; round the waist, the arms, and the ankles, belts, bracelets and fringed ankle bands.

Anacã is once again being made visible in the dignity of his office as chieftain, realized by the colors of the paint and all the feathers. At last, when the sun is at high noon, he is carried to the dancing ground. There, in the exact center, he is laid on a mat with his decorated black bow and two reed arrows to one side. On the other side, as if reposing, is a war club also ceremonially adorned with its caparison of cotton tufts, its long shaft braided of the finest straw, its handle enlivened by filaments of scarlet feathers.

The men of all the families of the clan of the blue honey creeper relieve each other as they open, in the hard-beaten earth of the dancing ground, a grave for Anacã. They work slowly, using stakes with fire-hardened points that resound as they wound the earth, marking a lugubrious rhythm. They open a grave, long, perfect, the exact length of the body of Anacã which is lying there to the side, but a grave that is only a palm and a half deep, and is clean and smooth as a coffin. The excavated earth is crumbled by hand, by small boys, until it takes on the consistency of a fine powder, and forms a mound on the side opposite where Anacã waits.

At the end of the afternoon, with the light of the red disc of the sun growing in the horizon, Remui, the guide of souls, comes to bury the chieftain, Anacã. All are here, but only the men of the family opposite and complementary to the Jaguars, only the Carcaras, occupy themselves by lifting the corpse and depositing it in the grave.

Anacã rests there now, where he will rot, and the guide of souls examines everything critically. He corrects the painting smudged in one place and too shiny in another. He rearranges, as they should be carried, the bow and arrows on one side and the ceremonial club on the other. Finally, he adjusts the ornaments on the head, the body, the arms, and the legs. Seeing that everything is in perfect order, he steps back a few paces, turns his back and sits down in the correct ceremonial position. All the men sit also waiting for the sun to set. When the red orb touches the horizon, Remui rises almost with happiness, approaches, and fills both hands with the pulverized earth and lovingly deposits it on Anacã. Each man in turn approaches, fills his hands with earth, and helps to cover the dead body of the chieftain.

At this time, when still it is neither day nor night, in this the final hour of the chieftain Anacã, the women arrive, all together, bearing on their heads huge gourds of water, pure, crystalline, from the Black Lake. Each of them approaches and slowly pours her water on the mound of earth that covers Anacã. Gradually the earth levels off, sinking and becoming mud that in the following days and weeks will be transformed into the ooze of decomposed flesh.

Anacã is buried. Soon he will die. Life must now be reborn.

ISAÍAS

All men are born in Jerusalem. Was I? I shall be a priest, a minister of God in the Church of Our lord Jesus Christ. But am I a person? No, I am a no one. It would be best were I a priest. That way I would be able to live in peace and perhaps even help my neighbor—if my neighbor would allow an Indian who is shit to bless him, to hear his confusion, to forgive him.

I realize I have a complex: obsessive, paranoid, or schizophrenic? I don't know. In fact, no one wishes me ill because I am, or because I was, Indian. They take it into account. Many even find it affecting: "A converted Indian?" Almost always they are astonished: "Are you going to be ordained?" And finally all wonder: "Will you dedicate yourself to becoming a missionary?" At this point they ask: "Will you return to your own people?" They want to say, "to your tribe, to your savages." Will I? Or will I not return? Belgians or Dutch can catechize Indians. Spaniards, Italians, and even North Americans can proselytize in Italy, in France, in Brazil, wherever they like. But I, a Mairun Indian, can I be a priest? Never! Even in Brazil, would I be taken for an Indian all the time? No! There it is different. Many people look Indian and wander all over without anyone caring. Many even boast that their grandmother was captured with a lasso. Especially if they are dark. But it is different with me. No grandmother of mine was captured with a lasso. I am myself a savage. I am my grandmother.

Father Ceschiatti is worried. He is the best confessor and spiritual guide that I could ever hope for. He had never seen an Indian. He had never seen a mission. He had never left here, Rome. This is why he understands me. To him I am not an Indian; I am the Indian; I am the generic Indian, neither better nor worse than anyone else. It is as he says: "To be Brazilian, Congolese, Mariun, is it not the same? You are Mairun as I might be Congolese." But it is not the same. He tells us: "You are Mairun as I am Genoese, as our brothers in the Order are Italian, German, Brazilian. He says that I am Mairun (and I am) as that Congolese to whom he refers has the misfortune of belonging to a certain tribe in the Congo. He does not know, but I very well know that, if the time should come for there to be a Congolese nation, the Mairuns there would continue to be Mairun, that is to say, not Congolese, not one!

He likes to say that I want only to restore my pride in being Mairun so as to make me feel that I am an offering from my people to the Church of Our Lord Christ. To serve where it would be most useful to propagate the faith. He insists that there is nothing extraordinary about me: every man, he says, has his roots, whether they be in a Genoese village or a New York borough or in a little tribe in the interior of Brazil. What he does not understand is that I have more than my share of roots. I am full! His village is part of a nation; it is a borough or a town or a suburb, and, as such, it can even be forgotten because it is part of a whole. With us, the Mairuns, it is different. My village is not a part of anything. It is a people unto itself; that is to say, a tribe with its little language, its little religion, its little customs destined to disappear. He replies that it should not be like that and adds: "The Mairuns are one aspect of humanity, one of the faces that our Lord God gave to man. An aspect that being also He, must survive." But I ask, "Survive for what? And how, since they are dying out?" They (myself included) are (we are) now only two hundred, counting the old ones and the children. Which is to say if they (we) grew greatly in number, within a century they (we) would be at least two thousand souls lost in a nation-state of millions and millions. So what is that? Is it worth the trouble?

Everyone who leaves the village will become someone like me; that is, nothing. Those who remain there will only inherit the bitterness of being Indian. Like me, they will try to scrape their faces to disguise the tatoo, those two wretched little circles burnt right beneath the eyes. It is high time that these fools stopped branding the children. My marks are barely visible. In their place there are only scars. Everyone thinks they are burns that I never had.

The other day I dreamed about myself: I was a handsome man, a priest, and I had long hair like Christ and the hippies. But, as a Mairun, I had on both sides of my face the distinctive tribal marks. I was proud of myself, relaxing. But it had nothing to do with living and struggling. I was ready to die for love of God and Father.

What I need, I am sure, is the character to confront life, to play my part whatever it might be. In the end, to be a Mairun or a Brazilian, white, black, Indian or mixed-blood is of no importance to me. My corruption, my mistake, is that I can never forget this, neither by day nor by night. That I can only brood on, suffer, and endure these absurdities. I need to meet in faith acceptance of and self-confidence in my image and my essence. For this I need to pray even more. But I am praying less every day and with less faith. My faith is diminishing. Am I praying for that which cannot be given to me? I have no right to hope for miracles. Are there still miracles? Perhaps there never were. And in the miracle that I am asking for, what is it? It is for God to transform my very substance, to make a Genoese or a Congolese or a Brazilian or any kind of man. It is not God's problem. It is mine. I must accept myself as I am so as to be more respectful of His work in me. Little work of shit, may God forgive me.

When Father Ceschiatti hears my tortured worries he nearly loses patience. It is not that he considers my sins of anxiety serious, my desires for punishment (they are not). What irritates him is the negative quality of my supposed virtues that Father Vecchio found so edifying. He used to say: "My son, when I was your age my flesh was ardent. It was enough for night to fall for me to panic. I knew the torture would begin all over again, that the Devil would once more prowl over my body to drive me mad and make me ejaculate. You are different, you control your instincts with the power of faith. You even wish more temptations upon yourself so as to overcome them with prayer." The truth, however, is with Father Ceschiatti; my virtue is negative, more an offspring of weakness than of strength.

But not even Father Ceschiatti is right. He also does not understand me. It is not a matter of weakness or strength, but of an entirely different order of things. It is about uncapitulated sins—the sin of not accepting oneself as one is, of not consoling oneself for falling outside of a viable oneness such as that of the Genoese or the Germans. And the sin of envying the capacity to be indistinguishable from the others. To be equal, in spite of all possible differences—thanks to an essential identity—is what I yearn for. I rack my brains thinking about this. And I make no headway. How can I say, Father Ceschiatti asks me, that I am not accepted when I have been here in Rome for so many years at the expense of the Order; when the Order has in me the fruit of forty years of religious instruction; when out of love for 'us', the Mairun tribe, so many Fathers and Sisters have been there, all these years, suffering fevers and hardships? What can I say to him? "Thanks!"?

I writhe in the grip of this obsession as poor Father Vecchio in his youth tried to calm his sexual drive, but the more he persisted the more he would become inflamed and the more he would ejaculate. Once, in the church, he told me, during the Holy Mass, at the most sacred moment. Everyone has a cross. This one is mine; I will bear it with the help of God.

Every day Father Ceschiatti advises me: "It is urgent for you to overcome this obsession so as to make yourself ready, finally, to take Holy Orders." I am lacking nothing else, only the certainty that I am a priest of Our Lord God and the courage to say so to Father Ceschiatti. Not during my conversations with him, but in the hour of confession. I cannot! When I kneel there, certainty vanishes. I think, I feel, and I know that my place is on this side, kneeling and weeping, never on that side, listening, understanding, forgiving in the name of God. But God and the Virgin must help me. Tomorrow illumination might arrive. Perhaps even today, who knows, at the evening mass.

My day will come, I know. I will emerge from it transfigured, walking among men as one who bears with himself divine blessing, having forgotten my face, liberated from the mad idea of my spurious nature. I am a child of God. In Him I am a man, any man. In Him I am a person and not only a Mairun, or even worse, a Mairun convert, civilized, transplanted, fugitive. Fugitive, but bearing, carrying, if not the outward appearance, the essence. I am Mairun, an unfortunate. This is the irreducible truth that hurts me like a wound. I am Mairun, I am of the Mairuns. Each Mairun is the Mairun people as a whole. More so than an Italian is Italy, or a Brazilian, Brazil. It is so because we are threatened with extermination, and it is necessary that our people should survive and thrive in the last of us.

This is the only command of God that completely moves me:

that each people retain its identity, with the face that God gave it, whatever the cost. Our duty, our destiny—what to call it?—is to resist, as the Jews resist, as the Gypsies, the Basques, and so many others. All are improbable but alive. Each of us improbable people, is an aspect of God. With its own language that changes with time, but that changes only within limits. With its customs and peculiar ways that also change, but change in a similar fashion, according to its own spirit.

In the future, I don't know when, someday, those among us, the improbable ones who survive will have their opportunity. For what? To be sure I don't know. But I feel it is one of God's designs. It is He who decrees what we shall be and that we shall remain the same.

I am going to say this to Father Ceschiatti, inverting his argument. Yes, my confessor, we the Mairuns are an aspect of God, our Creator, worthy of being an aspect of Him, so we have a mandate to preserve ourselves in all the singularity of how He had made us. What is the consequence of this mandate for me? I who am Isaías of the Missionary Order and, at the same time, Avá of the Jaguar clan of the Mairun people? No, never. This ambiguity is far away from me.

At last, everything is clear. In truth I was only acting, am still acting a script that I have learned. I am not, I never was, never will be Isaías. The only work of God that can come from me, burning my mouth, is that I am Avá, heir to the chieftain, and that I am beholden only to the Jaguar people of my Mairun nation.

JUCA

After many years Juca disembarks at the Mairun port. He knew of the death of the old chieftain and so returned. Anacã had inspired fear in him. Fear arising from respect. Also he had threatened him: "If you set one foot in this village again, you will die." For Juca this was not merely a threat, it was a curse, a promise of calamity. He had never come back.

He barely sets foot on the beach when he yells: "Hey, my people, I'm back!" He unloads two kerosene cases that, at the top, contain tobacco cut in pieces and blocks of rapadura sugar, and, from the middle on down, bottles of fiery rum. He walks toward the path behind Boca and Manelao who are carrying the cases. He advises:

"Look, Manelao, I don't want you getting involved with the women of my family. No! These Mairuns are sly. Making them work is as difficult as catching a jaguar with a fishhook. I must do it. Their hour has arrived. They are my family. They need to produce."

He walks exuberantly, exhorting the two men. At times he stops, looking at the beach on one side and the village on the other, looking at places along the old trail where, as a child, he ran about. He walks leaning to one side, lower on the side he carries his revolver. He has a cripple leg. Along the road, he keeps meeting Indians who are going down to the beach. He greets them in Mairun and tells them to return to the village. "We're going to the Great House of Men, you come too. Today there's going to be a celebration. I've brought presents for everyone." No one listens. Even the children veer off, staring into the distance, so as not to pass near the three men who are coming up. Juca is not dismayed. He addresses everyone in a loud voice, greeting and telling them to go up to the Great House. In a low voice he says to his men: "These fucking half-wits, sons-of-bitches, they think they're people. Primitive shits. They're going to have to deal with me, though."

He arrives, finally, at the circle of huts of the half-deserted village. He looks inside one of the huts and then goes straight to the Great House. There are a few men sitting there fixing arrows and rearranging ornaments. Juca delivers a discourse in Mairun:

"My family, you are ingrates. Here I am. I've returned. Who

is going to weep for me according to custom? I'm a powerful chief now, a boat trader. Let's celebrate. Let's have a party today for my return. All right? I know the whole world is sad about the death of Anacã. I am too. But he died a while ago, and we are still alive. You have wept enough for him. No man was ever buried as he was. Never. When it comes to burials, no one can match us. It is our tradition, ours, of the true Mairuns. Ours, of the Mairun with blood like mine. Well, Panam of the House of the Jaguar, wasn't she my mother?"

He pauses to draw breath and to study the effect of his words. The Indians remain seated, attending only to what they are doing. It is as if no one were talking there. The big river trader starts up once again:

"Now we must begin a new life, my family. You need many things. You need Rand rifles, Matao machetes, Jacare hoes, Mossoro salt, Sol matches, Union scissors, knives, and fishhooks and nylon line and yet more things. I have all these things. It is only a matter of wanting them. It is only a matter of working. But now I'm not going to barter only for dried arapaina fish, no. Now, I want otter skin—not of the giant river kind, of real otter, the little one, the lustrous one. The lakes are full of them. All you have to do is draw your bows and bring them to me. But aim carefully so you won't damage the skin. Kill them in the head or the neck, the back is sacred."

He stops again to take note. No effect. The cases are on the ground at the feet of Manelao and Boca, the only ones listening to his discourse. Juca continues his speech:

"Just today I brought you some presents. Here I'll leave all I've brought. Look, the best Braganca tobacco, good rapadura sugar from Vizeu and a little rum from Creciuma, strong as fire. All are presents. I'm not charging for anything. Later I'll be back to settle the account of the skins. For each skin, I'll give a good present."

Teró enters the hut calmly and goes up to Juca. He stops in front of him and says in good Portuguese,

"Juca, go away! Go away with your things, now! Anacã

told you never to come back, or you would die. He is dead. But his word lives on. You are talking here, but you are already dead. Go die where you wish."

"Threatening your cousin, dear relative? From where did you get the idea I am afraid of Indians, you son of a bitch?" Juca replies with a hand on the holster of his revolver.

"No, it is not a threat. Anacã did not want to see you. Neither do we. If you don't take that rubbish away, we'll throw everything in the river along with you, right now."

"Throw my merchandise away? No one will, never. I'll kill the first man that puts his hands on anything of mine. And listen to this! I will return. You'll see! I will return soon. You're proud of being under the protection of the government. Isn't that right? It's your shitass Elias bragging that he'll call in troops in aircraft. He never will, you know. You'll see, I'm going to Brasília, and I'll return as agent of the FUNAI post. I'll kick that thief out. Then the tune will change. Don't waste time waiting. You'll see!"

Then four Indians enter, two at each doorway of the Great House, with harpoons for catching giant arapaima fish. Teró closes calmly,

"Good bye, Juca. Don't come back again. We don't like to see you. We become sad. We are vexed."

"What kind of a joke is this, my relative? I came only to be kind."

"Go away, Juca, go away from here!" The harpoons, even without being aimed, threaten, intimidate. In an instant the load is on the heads of Manelao and Boca. Before leaving, standing close to the door, Juca makes an obscene gesture with his arm. But he bows his head and departs quietly. On the way back he says,

"These fucking half-wits will pay for this. I'll return to take care of them. So many idiots, stretching out in their hammocks, and I with no one to hunt otters. I'll show them, with the help of God and Senator Andorinha, I'll take their pride down a little. Primitive shits! Let's go, Boca, son of a bitch. And you,

Manelao, let's get going; you too, unfortunate pig. I'm not paying anyone to loaf at my expense, no. A few shots up your ass
from my revolver will heat you up, you good for nothing vaga-
bonds."

Thumping along from side to side he continues the insults all
the way to the river, the beach, the boat. They embark and head
down river.

"Turn the motor off, Manelao. Why waste gas going downstream? The current is carrying us along nicely. Today I'm in
no hurry, there's no work. We're going to wait and see what
those stupid layabouts produce for us. We'll stop at Corrutela. I
want to see if those cowboys without a herd will decide to work.
I need to talk to them. I have to find a way of getting them to
do man's work—such as hunting animals for their skins. They
refused the load of rum and tobacco that I sent them. Why? At
least they'll have to pay for what it cost to send. I need to see
what they're up to. If I don't take care of this river, no one will.
It's not inconceivable that those disgraceful primitives are in col-
lusion with that gringo of the launch that sprays water all over
and travels like the wind."

The boat drifts with the current in the middle of the channel.
To keep her riding the current without yawing, Boca puts at
the stern, in place of the motor, a great Mairun steering oar
with a blade like a rounded shovel. Hours pass, the sun is setting. Exhausted, Boca begs,

"Boss, where's my herb?"

"Don't kill yourself with weed, you fool!"

But after a few minutes he tells Manelao to take the oar for a
while and rolls a joint for Boca. And he sends Boca to smoke it
in the bow.

"I want to smell the smoke from there."

"Do you see, Manelao? Those half-breeds in their huts,
Indians kidnapped from childhood, are never without herb.
They smoke more than they eat, the rascals. But let him smoke.
We're not in an hurry today. The current is carrying us along

well. We'll go through the Long Stretch tonight; by day I can't bear to see the length of that endless straight."

The boat advances in the midst of a moonless night. The sky is full of stars; the black river sparkles with little waves propelled by the wind. Boca, back from the bow, takes the steering oar at the stern and keeps the boat in the current, always in the mainstream. The joint between his lips has gone out, and he murmurs:

Iparana, paraná-panema: Ipanema.
Iparana, paraná-d'agua
Panem-panam: barbuleta
Barbuleta Azul—Panam-oui, panam-oui, ouii
Tanajura, Tanajura, bunda mole, bunda dura.
Ica, ica: pipoca do Para. Para.
Belém, Belenzao. Belém pai-d'egua
Mariquita piriquita, piriquita dela
Mariquita mija de pe, chue, chue . . . e
Mariquita de Belém, puta, meu bem
Tanto dente, Mariquita banguela . . . ela
Belém. Belenzao . . . Belém . . . de quem?

Boca takes the oar, relights his joint with a homemade lighter cupped in the palm of his hand, takes a few drags of smoke, and proceeds:

E Belém bom, Puta, tanta puta
Puta, Putada. Deputado, deputada
Mariquita puta banguela. Mija piriquita, mija nela
Mija na tabua. Taboa. Taboado, tabuada
Vamos dance nhô? Xereco-xeco, xeco-xeco, xeco-xeco
Te mato, negra descarada
Negra relaxada, regacada, reganhada
Boca, o Boca. Eu, eu! Boca, booo . . . oca
Juru-Boca. Jurui-jurujuru
Petium-Petum. Petum-petim. Petim

Para pararaca jararaca
Perereca, eca, eca,
Cedroi-iiiui. Inaja, tracaja. Mija?
Para papa chibe. Chibe bom. Bem bom: bombom
Tucupi, tucupi. Tacaca ... caga
Tucupi, tucupi pipi. Tacaca caga
Tacaca no-tucupi

Boca, the oar secure in one hand, the joint between his lip, continues to eat shrimp in pepper sauce all through the night, while the boat is carried along by the current through the Long Stretch. Juca and Manelao are snoring on the leather bundles.

They awake as night ends. First Manelao who makes a noise awaking Juca. They converse a little while watching the banks to see where they are. It is almost the end of the straight. Manelao gets up, balancing himself on the gunwale and orders: "Boca, get away, I'm taking over." He takes the oar and sits in the stern, steering the boat along the current. Boca goes and curls himself up to sleep at Juca's feet, up in front, where the cargo is. Some time later Manelao shouts,

"Hey, Boss, why don't you tell us that story again, the one about the Skull-Bag?"

"I'll tell it now. Boca can't do without that story, can you, Boca?"

"That's right Boss, but not at night. In the dark it frightens."

"None of that, you are afraid by night, by day, at any time. You're going to hear the story again, Boca. But before telling it, I want you to grab there, your face, there. Go on! Grab your face, beast!"

Boca cringes. Juca jumps on him; the boat rocks, but Manelao steadies it by swaying from side to side. Juca pushes Boca to the bottom of the boat, grabs him by the hair, and pressing his fingers on his face says, "Look good, Boca, here under your cheeks, right here, do you see it? Do you feel it? What do you have here? It's bone isn't it? Your skull! Boca's skull! Why are you afraid of a skull? You are a skull, beast. You are carrying a skull inside your hide. But you have more skull than most people, Boca!"

Juca feels Boca's face, his forehead, his head, and starts to say lugubriously, "You are all skull, a walking skull. Any day now, Boca, you'll die. Then your flesh will rot, Boca, this here, look." He grabs Boca's cheek, pulls and twists it, scrunches his mouth, rubs his nose.

"All your flesh is going to rot, Boca. Then your skull is going to appear all white and gleaming. Yes, Boca, a big skull all yours. Prettier than you are now, Boca. You were never handsome, were you, Boca?, but after you die, your skull is going to be lovely. I can already see you in your whiteness, Boca. Yours skull walking around here, gleaming white in the darkness of the night."

Boca, crammed in the bottom of the boat under Juca's feet shakes and grumbles, while Juca, possessed with devilish glee, continues:

"Let's get to the story, Boca. Here we go! You don't remember it, do you? Let's see if you remember the story of Skull-Bag. Don't think it's a make-believe story or talk for the sake of talk. No, it really exists. It walks past here. It is looking for people with skulls like yours to beg a nice, compact one, a few borrowed bones. In this case it has the shape of a woman. She will not be beautiful because within there are only a lot of loose bones rattling, truc-truc-truc. She moves by little hops, doesn't she, Boca? She hops along, going proc-proc-proc. Every time her feet land on the ground her legs double over like empty pants. She is always making that muffled sound, chuc-chuc-chuc-chuc. It's her bones, knocking, there inside her, one against the other. She doesn't need solid ground to walk on, no, Boca, she walks on air, she flies. She can fly anywhere. Also, she can walk on water. She could come to your side now. Right now, do you see, Boca? Open your eyes, stop being frightened, you shit. She could arrive at any minute, do you hear me, Boca? It's a sack made of wrinkled skin, and it's full of bones. It has the face of a woman, the shape of a woman. There she'll be; she's going to ask you for a few little joints. She'll come any minute now, Boca. You'll see, she's coming! Did you see, she's coming? 'Oh Boca,' Juca says, doing a malicious imitation; it's her, Boca, she's talking to you: 'Little Boca, little Boca, a joint, a little joint, don't you have one for me, just for me, for auntie, your auntie?' It is she speaking and dancing all over you and rattling truc-truc-truc." Juca talks, rapping Boca's body with his hands and feet. "It is she who is coming, rattling chuc-chuc-chuc. I'm only preparing you, Boca, preparing you for the encounter. It could even be that the Skull-Bag wants to marry you. You'll be delighted, Boca. She comes flying, leaps, and falls on top of you—chac—like that. . . ."

And he abuses Boca's stomach with his hands and feet. "This is how she'll fall on top of you, the legs and the hands screaming 'Boca, Boca, my nephew, my little nephew, now I'm your wife, your little bride!' "

Juca and Manelao laugh helplessly at this story, repeated night after night for Boca, who always ends up terrified.

ÑANDEIARA

Anacã rots underneath the dancing ground, watered every evening with the waters of the Black Lake. He rots and oozes a sweet stench, penetrating, horrible. Its presence seems to depend on the direction of the wind, blowing from the dunes of the Iparana toward the clearing in the forest. It is not a stench of the decomposing meat of a dead animal or of a disinterred corpse. It is a smell as sharp as the point of an arrow, as light as a feather, as penetrating as a bamboo splinter. And always, eternally present, in the nose of everyone. Even in the midst of the forest, hunting, fleeing from it, it stinks, and is borne on the skin, in the hair, God knows where.

Every evening the women come in a file carrying jugs of water on their heads. The guide of souls also goes to look and to help. Sometimes he speaks with Anacã. Yesterday he was saying: "Here we are, Anacã. We are not sending messengers to other villages inviting them to your feast because there are no other villages. Only this one, as you well know. But we are all here, all the Mairun people, the living and the dead. Maíra and Micura are also coming here with their mischief."

Today he relates some news to the old chieftain. "Look, Anacã, here is something good! Our Avá, my son, your nephew, the Uruantaremu who must become chieftain, is about to return. He was taken away from here by the alien sorcerer many years ago, do you remember? Well, yes! He is about to return. He will come, bringing us everything, in a white boat as big as the Great House. Do you believe it? How strange. Perhaps it is for the good. Perhaps it is for the worse. Who knows? What I doubt is that he'll get here; there are many evil spirits loose. But it is good to know that Avá has freed himself from the mill that was grinding him. He is free, but he is alone. Very alone."

Thus the Mairuns heard, from the chatting of the women, that Avá was returning. He had left as a child, that is, he was carried away by a missionary, a great giver of presents, very jovial, a talker.

"It was for the best, now we shall see," says Teró to the men gathered on the dancing ground. "Yes, it was good, because he is returning now and bringing with him the best things from the world of the white man."

The weather has ceased to change. Azure days have finally arrived. The sky is completely blue, all clouds having been washed away, and the mosquitoes have already disappeared. Anacã had chosen the best weather in which to die. The best, as much for the joys of the festivity as for the sadness of the weeping and for the despair that would follow. The happiness of summer is already in everyone, in everyplace.

At the Black Lake, each beach begins to welcome its annual

occupants. White herons and their blue sisters twist and untwist their long slim necks, and, elegant and svelte, they prance on their sandspit. Rosy spoonbills with carmine cloaks, ruffled feathers, are coloring their beach. Jabiru storks, scratching the silt with their long beaks, are poised, with joy on one leg, every bird in its place. Scarlet ibis dart from here to there, painting the bushes. Teal and tree ducks invade the tremulous water, licked by gusts of wind, eating minnows, and conversing by quacking at each other. Long-legged lily-trotters hop and scurry on the floating bogs, frightening everyone with the golden spurs on their wings. Brown-black cormorants with yellow throats descend in flocks, extending their necks and wings as they perch on half-submerged islets. Migrant flamingos disguise their ungainly ways under a display of scarlet plumage.

When someone arrives at the edge of the lake, there is great commotion. First the nearest birds that can see, look, become startled, and take flight in fear. Then the others, as the news and the fright spread further and further. The noise of wings flapping resounds in the trees, creates an echo, and returns and is reflected on the face of the water in a mocking gesture. Now it's not only the lake; the treetops are speckled with white and pink, carmine, grey and brown. Beautiful, beautiful.

The entire forest has awakened after the months of winter. It has freed itself from the heavy soaking rains. Now flowers are blooming. Explosions here, there. Fronds coming into being, some dressed as for a gala, in celestial blue and scarlet; others in monkish habits ranging from silvery white to bishop's purple and on to the saffron yellow of Buddhist robes. The splendor of the colors of the fronds boldly sets ablaze the deepest greens, the light greens, the green greens, the moss greens, the limestone greens.

The birds are singing in a glorious cacaphony. Toucans with yellow beaks and golden throats whistle and dance pirouettes over the highest treetops. Above them, in the sky, flock the bluest, the reddest, the yellowest birds of all, the great macaws, flying in pairs, jealous, conversing. Soon bands of loquacious warblers arrive. Then the red-fan parrots, proud of their collars and of their insults to the gossipy parakeets.

Within the forest, whistling at dawn and running on the ground, are the great curassows whose greenish-black feathers have a metallic sheen. Minuscule hummingbirds, each of its own color, circle, stop for an instant in the air, then fly off again, coming and going, tracing straight lines of color in the air. On the highest branches brilliant turquoise honeycreepers are hopping. At the summit of the treetops that reign over the green sea of green forest the hangnest orioles are screeching and extending their tails to show Maíra the sun-yellow of their secret plumes.

At the edge of the water, chestnut-colored horned screamers cry viu-viu-viu, proclaiming their virginity, armed as they are with double spurs. Rusty hoatzins with dentated beaks and sharp pointed wings swing their crested heads from side to side, uttering discordant cries and making a mess around their perches in the thickets of mucca-mucca. In the darkness of the forest, self-contained and silent, the squawking of the falcons is suddenly heard, filling animals and men alike with dread. Bellbirds clang their hammers on sheets of iron. Motionless musical wrens, red and black enchanted sorcerers, sing their melodies to the shadowy forest.

In the village as well, under the burden of the odor of the death of Anacã, exultation in the joy of living returns. On the dancing ground, at all hours, young men of diverse clans practice throwing lances of javari palm at straw dummies. Others are wrestling, preparing for the competitions to come.

Every morning and every evening we dance around the grave of Anacã. Old dances, almost forgotten, that none of the young people have seen are danced again by the men and the women of each clan. The Coatis, always discreet to the point of being timid, because they are the last to arrive today, have to dance the whole morning. All are enchanted by the circular dance in which men and women are dancing, marking the rhythm with sticks, and blowing enormous gentle flutes. Couples are dancing together, lowering and raising their heads; the woman one step to the rear, holding the right shoulder of her man with her left hand. After a few turns, two Coatis want to stop, but no one will allow them; everyone begs them to continue. A little later, the people of all the clans, intermingling, are dancing the dance for couples to the music of the Coatis. In the end even the little boys and the little girls are dancing too, beating the ground with their little feet and shaking their little heads.

"This dance," say the Coatis, "is the one we learn from our cousins on the other side of the world who are people like us. It is they who fix the walls of Heaven that have been breached by floods."

The Great House is filling up with good things to eat for the feasts to come. Baskets of sawari nuts. The hanging jars are countless, full of finely ground cassava flour. A profusion of baskets with farina. The grilled meat of various game begins to accumulate, and cantles of sun-dried arapaima fish. Still more will have to be provided by the hunters and fishermen if all the people attending the great feasts during all of the days to come are going to be fed. Today the guide of souls has four enormous widemouthed pots rolled into the Great House. They have just been molded and fired by old Anoa. They are authentic, huge as they used to be in the old days, and hollowed out as they should be to allow for the proper fermentation of cashew wine. All are exquisitely painted.

Great will be the ceremony for Anacã. And it must be so, to recuperate the happiness and strength that we lost with his death. Already we should have danced the Coraci-Iaci, but we cannot. It is the solemn dance of the Jaguar, the dance of the chieftains. Without a chieftain, how could we have danced it? When shall we sing again the mare-mare of the Coraci-Iaci, watching the dancers balancing huge whorls of palm fronds on their heads?

Soon the guide of souls will tell us what we will dance today. We are all here on the dancing ground, waiting for the dance of the evening. Already it can be seen that there is going to be a ritual because Remui, the guide of souls, has brought out his double-head stool from the center of the Great House and is sitting in his place. Leaning against the wall of thatch of the Great House looking straight in front of the setting sun, the guide of souls gives the signal. With a flute made from a jaguar's shinbone he calls forth a man from each house. They emerge conversing and walking rapidly, each over to his own side. The news runs from mouth to mouth. It is the Ñandeiara! It is the Ñandeiara! Each child who can talk will now know his name and will now receive on his face the mark of the gaze of Maíra-Coraci the Sun, the coraci-maa.

The women begin to arrive and seat themselves, with their children held between their legs, on the side of the guide of souls. They sit in a preordained order: on the right, the people from the side of on high who are oldest; on the left, those from the side of below who are more recent. Together, they form a long half-moon having as its center the grave of Anacã. Two young masters of ceremonies, one from the House of the Jaguar, the other from the house of the Falcon ceremoniously seat themselves upon their own legs in front of the women. One of them has on his knees, gripped by both hands, a harpoon for catching arapaima: he is Jaguar of the House of the Jaguar. The other carries a spear for hunting jaguars: he is Naru of the House of the Falcon.

The children already grown, the girls and the boys, the men and the women, are there looking at the guide of souls, at the circle of mothers, at the masters of ceremonies solemnly pointing their weapons, and at their helpers who are sitting to the side and are busy keeping a hot fire going.

With each phrase from the flute of the chieftain, played by the guide of the souls, a woman rises with her son or her daughter, on this side then on that, and leads her child to one of the masters of ceremonies. Those from the side of on high go to Jaguar, those from the side of below, to Naru. The mother sits in front of the master holding the child firmly between her legs and looking behind her toward the guide of souls who then pronounces the name of the child: a boy, Toi; a girl, Manitza. Everyone repeats, shouting, Toi, for Toi! Manitza, for Manitza!

Directly the master of ceremonies takes two pipe-nuts, well dried, and puts a burning ember into each nut until its circular opening is incandescent, then applies both of them simultaneously to the bones on the eyes of the child. This way, by fire, are created two perfect circles that, when healed, will be indelible brands. It is the coraci-maa, the solar mark of the Mairuns. The mother, holding the child firmly by the arms and legs, then leaves with it to console it at home.

The evening comes to a close with a dance conjoining the jaguar and the falcon, reminiscent of the Coraci-Iaci, but without the grandeur. It is a dance that is sung, sad and joyful, denying death and affirming life, reintegrating the world.

In every house a child is crying and touching his mark with his finger. Each of them repeats with its mother the name it has inherited from a great-grandmother: Jaru, Jaru. . . . The mothers and aunts laugh at those who cry, pointing to their own marks and those of others.

"Now you are of the people, my son. You are a Mairun. Now you are of the Mairuns: those who eat cassava cakes, who like pacu fish, who laugh with gusto. Come on, you must laugh too!"

The older ones lovingly recall old stories of those forgotten great-grandparents who will survive, incarnate in the children. They recount their stories so that each will know who was the last Toi or the previous Manitza, and all the others. Putir, the old Jaguar, had been a hardworking woman, very lively and a joker. Jaru, of the House of the Pacus, had been a quiet man, who hardly ever said anything, but when he laughed in peals, as only he could, the whole village resounded. The Heron Tuim was the most expert hip shaker ever among women. She knew how—she was a noble public whore and beautiful.

ALMA

In the reception room of the convent, a fair, slender woman leans over the nun, explaining:

"It wasn't a thoughtless decision, Sister Petrina. Nor a hurried one. I thought about it intensely. Speak to Father Orestes, my confessor. He knows what a sinner I was. Now what I most want is to serve God." ("Holy Virgin!") For the sake of charity, Sister Petrina. . . . I know that God does not need me. It is I who need him. I also know that the Order is not the place to straighten out anyone. But I beg you, Sister Petrina . . . allow me to go with the French sisters. (Another one, my God!) I need to, Sister Petrina. I need to so much. You know the works of my father." ("I know them.") "Look at the name he gave me, Sister Petrina: Alma. That gives a measure of his spirituality. A spirituality I was not worthy of until his death. Now, I want to recuperate myself. I want to fulfill, in the service of God, all of his advice that I never heeded. He died, as you know." ("God bless him!") He died, confident that I would rediscover myself, that I would return to the faith. In truth, I never lost it entirely, Sister Petrina. I was very confused, my mind was in a whirl. Now I've found myself. I don't aspire to much, Sister Petrina. All I want is to give through a mission testimony of my love for God." ("So many people here. . . .") "I know, I know what you are thinking. But try to understand, Sister Petrina, I can't do anything in the shanty towns. God cannot exist among so much hunger, sex, and drugs. It does little to rekindle faith in me. It is my refuge, my hope. But I don't want only to enjoy a state of grace. I don't want only to rehabilitate myself in the eyes of my dead father." ("Of God, my daughter!") "Yes, of course, in the eyes of God. I want to be a

soldier in the army of Our Lord." ("Mother of God!") "I want
and I need my life to have a mission that will redeem me. After
years of confusion and pride, I arrived at understanding through
analysis." ("Psychoanalysis. . . .") "Yes, Sister Petrina, psychoanalysis. You don't believe in it, I know. It repels you. But I
say to you with humility, I learned a lot, a great deal. What I
want is to serve the Lord. Each person has his own way. This is
mine, now. I need your help, your understanding, your charity. I
don't want any glorious sacrifice. Nor to martyr myself. But I
can no longer endure this city where I was born and reared. I
need to go far away. This is why I got the idea. I want to go to
the Mission on the Iparana. My place is there, Sister Petrina."
("Our Lady of O?") "Yes, but with the new congregation with
the sisters. Someday I would like to enter the Order, if I deserve to. Not like you and the others, who are saints." ("God
in Heaven. . . .") "But I say to you in all humility, I learned a
lot. I want a mission of service with the French nuns, Sister
Petrina. If I had to I would work as a teacher, a cook, a nurse;
I would look even after children. In truth, I don't know anything about the sick, nor about teaching. Still less about cooking. But I have completed a course in psychology at the Catholic
University. I realize that I have studied little, but I learned
something. And I've read a lot, perhaps too much." ("Too
much. . . .") "It's true that I'm confused, Sister Petrina. But
I know that for me there's no other way out. For the sake of
charity, help me. I only beg that it be soon. It is not impatience or haste, no! Perhaps it is anxiety. But it would be a
genuine anxiety to suffer another suffering—to suffer for love
of God. I can't stand any more. It has cost me dearly to find
myself, but now I know, I have certainty and urgency. A certainty that I've gotten from analysis, thank God. ("And from
faith, my daughter?") Yes, Sister, exactly. Faith, security, and
charity. Now I know what I can give. And I know what I can
give with a new spirit of Christian charity: friendship.
("Mother of God!") "I beg you with all my heart to help me,
Sister Petrina. I will make the necessary preparations with ut-

most diligence. I will face any sacrifice with pleasure, especially if I have a solid hope that I won't be denied what I desire. I want to go to the Mission, Sister Petrina. To live my new life there. With people who need me, who need my devotion. I have read everything about the sisters, about what they are doing to create a new House in Brazil." ("This is still being studied.") "I'd like to know if I can see them, if I can speak with them when they arrive. Even if it's only to teach Portuguese. They don't have to know. Look, I was educated at the Catholic University, and I speak French fluently. Excuse my vanity, but I know enough to help them in the initial phases. I know they will arrive any day now." ("So the papers say, my daughter.") "No, Sister Petrina, don't deny me your help." ("I'll speak . . . to Mother Superior.") "Oh, everything is going to depend on her help. I need her as a soul needs God." "Enough, Alma.") "Oh! Sister Petrina, I have grown through your words, I have learned much from this conversation. I only want you to concur with me that there are many roads to God. One can start from faith and purity and arrive at his service. Someone else can start from worldliness, joie de vivre, deceptions, even analysis. This is my case, this is why I have begun so late, twenty-three. Father Orestes helped me a lot. Sister, please speak to him. He knows that I want to rise from sin to virtue by way of service to God." ("Yes, my daughter, that could be.") "Oh, Sister Petrina, for the sake of charity, don't dissuade me. Don't give me your final word now. Not yet, for the love of God. I know you won't shut the door on me. I beseech you. No, Sister Petrina, I don't want to press you. You said you are going to speak to the Mother Superior. I'll wait. I only beg that you'll receive me once more." ("More so than we, Father Orestes can help you. . . .") "He has already done all that he can for me, Sister Petrina. But I will speak to him. I will listen to his advice. I will also ask him to come and see you, Sister Petrina. Not to intercede for me, but to inform you, with his authority of a confessor, of the solidity of my decision and of the extent of my need. I know the French nuns are about to arrive . . . I know."

A nun knocks at the door and enters, summoning Sister Petrina to a meeting in the cloister. Alma asks for her blessing and goes out into the garden, into the square, into the city no longer hers.

NONATO

In compliance with the decision of His Excellency the Minister of State for Justice, General Cipriano [Catapreta,] I designate Major Nonato dos Anjos, a Cavalry officer, attaché at the ministry office in Rio de Janeiro, to u dertake a special mission detailed as follows:

1. To proceed, with the greatest urgency, by normal means of transport, being authorized by this document to make the necessary requisitions for passage, to the Indigenous Post of FUNAI on the River Iparana.

2. There, in the neighboring Indian village, in the Mission of Our Lady of O, and wherever else may be indicated, to investigate the truth of the facts narrated by the illustrious Swiss scientist, Peter Becker, in accordance with the annexed copy of his declarations made to the police in this city.

3. Regarding all the facts observed, verified, and proved, the designated officer will present, to this ministry, a detailed report assigning criminal responsibility to the person or persons guilty (if that should be the case) of the death of a white woman on the banks of the Iparana River on 26 October 1974.

Major Nonato dos Anjos will be entitled to military pay and to travel expenses for the journey, which cannot exceed, the period of forty-five days. At the end of the mission he will present

*an account of any extraordinary travel expenses that will not
exceed the total allowable compensation.*

Give this your attention and comply with it.

DR. ARY CORVEIA
CHIEF INSPECTOR OF CRIMINAL INVESTIGATIONS
DEPARTMENT OF FEDERAL POLICE

JAVARI

Each evening the grave of Anacã is watered once more. The
water seeps through the crust of dried clay to the bottom. To
the flesh, dead and corrupt, that is disintegrating, softening, and
rotting. The odor that rises is very fine, very sharp, very sweet.
An ominous reek. At noon it seems visible, highlighting the
mirage of the forest inverted in the sky. The gusts of wind do
not wash the air; they only recirculate the stench and make it
more concentrated. Never before was Anacã, the chieftain, more
present and dominating.

Even he, dead as he is, must be disturbed, because today we
cannot dance the Coraci-Iaci, the dance of the chieftain. The
men and women of the new clans were spinning about the
whole night, not knowing whether to continue or not.

In spite of everything, as much as is possible, the ceremonial
feast is going through the prescribed cycle of dances, rites, and
competitions. This morning all the clans are on the dancing
ground, men and women, old people and children, forming two
circles of nervous spectators around the young men competing
at 'javari' with long rhomboid spears cast with the aid of throwing sticks. Supporters from on high and from below reunite and
intermingle; people from various houses, oblivious to clan divisions, applaud and encourage the contestants.

Jaguar and Naru are winning because they have triumphed in almost all the contests and did not let anyone catch up with them. The javelins, in spite of having their points blunted with balls of cotton, injure severely, especially when they hit the thighs. A hit in the trunk would be terrible, but a throw would be the pride of the contestant and his clan. Each lancer, consecutively, offers his body, as an unprotected target, to his adversary. One may dodge only from side to side or defend oneself with a bundle of sticks held in the hand, and this after the spear has been thrown. Now Jaguar and Naru are contending between themselves to decide the championship. Neither can reach the other; the Jaguars and the Falcons are, for now, reciprocally invincible.

It is afternoon. At last the time has come for hand-to-hand wrestling and enthusiasm is rekindled: huca-huca! It begins with the entry onto the dancing ground of all the men who propose to compete. They come painted red with annatto, white with pipe clay or blue-black with genipap juice, according to the colors of their houses. They keep their knees protected with cotton rope; they wrap cords around their arms and legs to display musculature and to arrive at the shape they would have if they were perfect.

The first to jump into the circle opened by the spectators is Iacumá of the Heron clan, growling provocatively. He is a mature man, a famous competitor, many times a champion. The other contestants watch and dodge. No one is keen to accept the challenge. Iacumá makes a complete circuit of the dancing ground, on his hands and knees, growling, challenging. Suddenly Diaí, of the Pacu clan, jumps into the center of the ground, bellowing. Iacumá advances towards him and the two confront each other like jaguars, snarling. Twice Diaí flings out an arm to grab Iacumá, who evades him. It is Iacumá who grabs him. There they are, the two of them, face to face, kneeling on the ground with their arms entwined, violently banging heads, one against the other.

The winner is the one who throws his adversary or merely

touches him behind the knee. Iacumá and Diaí struggle for a long time, getting tired, stopping, grappling, disengaging, grappling some more without the contest being decided. Excitement mounts, it is evident that Iacumá, the older of the two, is tired.

Will Iacumá lose? They grapple again; the struggle grows harder each time. Diaí frees an arm and tries to get the leg of Iacumá in a hold. But it is he who is thrown. Everybody shouts, "Iacumá, Iacumá! Herons, Herons!"

Iacumá, half stooping, circles the dancing ground without growling. He delights in his victory. Diaí jumps up, brushes off the dust, and disappears.

The contests follow their usual course. The leaps and growls of competition, the acceptance of the Challenge, the total locking of shoulders, arms, and heads, and the sudden decision, impossible to foresee. Aipá of the Pirarucus against Emeri of the Coatis; Emeri wins. Náru of the Falcons against Tupé of the Leaf-Cutting Ants; Náru wins. Epecui of the Pacus against Guiacá of the Tapirs, Epecui wins. Murá of the Snails against Tuxá of the Turtles, Tuxá wins. And later, Epecui beats Emeri, and Tuxá beats Náru. Finally, Tuxá beats Epecui but, exhausted, is beaten by Iacumá who is champion of hand-to-hand wrestling once again. "Iacumá, Iacumá! . . . Herons!"

All the mature contestants have now fought. It is time for the younger men, who, although without challenging the champions, are also painted and ready, waiting their turn. The first to jump into the dancing ground is Jaguar who enters screaming, challenger that he is. Everyone looks at Iacumá who has finished a hard struggle and is exhausted. Will he risk his championship against the youth of Jaguar? Jaguar's penis is not tied up; he wrestles painted and adorned, but dressed in pants to hide his nudity. The old chieftain, Anacã, had not wanted to bind the penises of Jaguar and the other youths of his generation, although much time had passed since they were supposed to have been tied.

"Let them wait, let the wait," he would say.

All the young men of the Mairuns are waiting for their chieftain, the new chieftain, to tie up their penises, transforming them into adults.

Iacumá does not budge. He seems not to sense everyone's anticipation. They look, then toward the Falcon, Náru, of the family complementary to that of the Jaguars, the brother-in-law of Jaguar himself, but Náru also does not advance. Jaguar completes his circuit, stands up for a while and begins another, snarling even more defiantly. He wants to fight. He is about to stand up again after his second circuit when an adversary emerges. He is Maxĩ, a burly youth from the new house of the side on high of the Herons. All mouths gasp, every chest constricts. A Heron is confronting a Jaguar. Will Maxĩ beat Jaguar? They are the same age; Jaguar is well known for his daring, for his strength and his courage, but Maxĩ is an unknown. A struggle begins as never was. They lock arms and heads, straining every nerve without moving. Suddenly Jaguar throws himself on top of Maxĩ in a hold that is almost always decisive and of which he is a master. Maxĩ recoils, and quickly both are moving backward, moving forward, always interlocked, without yielding a millimeter. They continue intertwined, struggling, sweating. Now they turn and turn, always in the same direction and in the same place. They pause, confront each other, disengage, are in a clinch again unexpectedly, and they begin to revolve in the opposite direction, to revolve and revolve without leaning. Maxĩ, in a supreme effort, tries to force back Jaguar's head. Now he has his chin on the other man's back and is gripping him at the same time with all the strength of his hands. But Jaguar remains upright and at the same time does all he can to move Maxĩ to the side where he seems to have the weaker leg. In a supreme effort, Jaguar, emboldened in trying to end the contest, steadies himself on his toes and lashes out again like a spring, trying to suspend Maxĩ in the air and then fall on top of him. He fails. Maxĩ, almost suspended, uses the instant when Jaguar is off balance to twist him a little toward his weaker side. Both fall, but Maxĩ's touches Jaguar's knee joint. He wins! There is a moment of incredulous hush, and then the shout, "Maxĩ! Maxĩ! Maxĩ! . . . Herons!"

Jaguar rises and, acknowledging his defeat, quickly leaves, while Maxĩ, still on his knees, commences his round of glory, circling the dancing ground, roaring now but without the note of challenge. And then is heard the cry of Iapsã, who breaks through the ring of spectators and, running, advances toward her son. Standing next to Maxĩ she puts her foot on his chest, forcing him to lie on the ground and to surrender completely to her. Iapsã then opens her own thighs and with both hands tears off her wrap, spreads and displays herself, shouting, "He came out of here! He's my son! I gave birth to him! I gave birth to him!"

All mouths repeat in unison, "Iapsã! Iapsã! Maxĩ! Herons! Herons!"

Other young men measure their strength, but by now no one is paying much attention. They are like everyday exercises, announcing in their way the champions of the future.

All the people, who during the day had intermingled for the contests, now begin to separate. For entertainment those of the side on high band together—the Ants, the Coatis, the Herons, and the Pirarucus—and pit themselves against those of the side below—the Pacus, the Snails, the Tapirs, and the Turtles. The great wise ones of the Jaguars and the Falcons are not involved in this account. Certainly so as never to lose.

Without premeditation the gathering of men is arranging itself, with discipline, on the side of sunrise and of sundown, to watch the dusk. So returns the order of all the days of the Mairun people, united but divided into halves by marriage and for marriage, and divided into the houses of their clans. Whoever looks on this from outside, how will he understand? Only we, those from within, can know. Even so, only more or less. The Mairuns are a deep and secretive people.

AVÁ

From up here, withdrawn in my void, I see my Mairun village through the haze of a sunny afternoon. It is a circle of houses ringed by two roads of beaten earth. One passes in front of the houses: that's the inner road. The other, passing behind, is the outer one. From each house runs a little path to the dancing ground where the Great House of Men is situated.

The whole village has the form of an enormous cartwheel with its axis at the Great House. The spokes are the paths from the houses, and the studded rim, the two circular roads with the houses in between.

From up here, flying toward it, I see, engraved in the earth, protruding from the forest surrounded by tiny plots of land, the village where I was born. The houses are enormous baskets woven with branches still green and flexible, that are then covered with satin-tail grass. The largest of them, the Great House of Men, was for many years the point of reference for Father Vecchio who never rested until he built a chapel even larger. But the Cross could never compete in grandeur with the ornament of the Great House: two tree trunks, whole and dried, with their roots outside, attached to the summit.

Now it must be darkest night in my village. In the houses everyone is asleep in hammocks slung between poles in the walls and in the central masts, forming the little groups of each family. The hammock of the man is lowest; above it is the woman's; and above hers, the childrens'. Below them, and to combat the chill of early dawn, burns a little fire of twigs that barely illuminates the ground.

In a few days I will be there, sleeping in the Great House where the men without women live. The hammocks are slung in an order that reproduces inside, in a way, the order by which the clan families arrange themselves outside. Always, there are a few men awake, some together with others, conversing, regardless of the hour. If it is a night with a full moon and a man can see another's face, many will squat together there all night laughing and telling tales. If it is not, some will always find a way of seeing each other to converse, to laugh and to rub against. We the Mairuns are the ones who laugh. Laughing is our mode of being, of living. I need to relearn how to laugh. Among us, a hard, serious face is offensive to everyone. Each person who passes someone frowning looks at him and smiles sweetly, trying to soften the rigidity of his face. We are the ones who smile with the teeth of the true Mairuns, white, big, and good for laughing. Mine are not, unfortunately for me.

Any day now I will see my sun, this my old Maíra-Sun, glowing like a sheet of metal perfectly brilliant, in the water of the Iparana. I will see the half wheel revealing the outlines of the village, of its environs of new and old clearings, and of the vast forests of the Black Lake.

The people of the village go to the river along a tortuous path that seems to delay itself in curves amid the tall grass as if for fear of losing itself in the sand dunes. There on the beach, aligned one next to the other, will be many canoes made from the bark of the locust tree. Each will contain paddles of rounded wood and the long arms of the crutches. Some will also have great steering oars and poles as well as creels and other fishing gear.

Many irregular trails made by bare feet cut through the dense bush of partly burnt clearing toward entrances to the great forest. It extends for many leagues, silva et virgo, without there being any clearing larger than that of my little village.

Arbor una nobilis:
Silva talem nulla profert
Fronde, flord, germine:
Dule ferrum

Dulce lignum
Dulce pondus sustinet
Flecte ramos, arbor alta,
Tensa laxa viscera,
Et rigor lentescat ille
Quem dedit nativitas:
Et superni membra Regis
tende miti stipite

My forest is a world of tall slender tree trunks, growing out of the clear ground, rising and rising to create foliage only up there at the summit. Light enters there only in rays where a bolt of lightning felled a tree, but the forest directly closes over those wounds. Its natural light is a green penumbra, as somber as in a Roman cathedral. Only twice a day is there noise: at sunrise and at sunset. Then the chorus of howling monkeys leaps from branch to branch, making an unreserved uproar, and all the feathered creatures sing or coo and flap their wings either from fear of the night to come or from early morning joyfulness. These are the two masses sung in the virgin forest: that of the morning and that of the evening.

All of us Mairuns are much afraid of seeing night fall there in the forest. If this happens, we sling our hammocks one next to the other and we keep the fire going, terrified, waiting for time to make its slow journey through this dark tunnel that is a night in the forest. Hours of dread are always realized when someone recalls a frightening story of men asleep in the forest who lost their souls and became animals and lived as animals forever after.

From up here, looking not out there, but here within, into the depth of my own being, I see my world. It is here now when my Mairun village breathes as it did and as I saw years ago. I view it and review it in every detail, I see it from impossible angles as in the composition of the most ancient bands and of the clan families. An invisible line divides the village into two halves, that of the rising sun and that of the setting sun. Each has its clans that seek wives or husbands in the opposite band.

This division of the village in halves reflects the divisions of the world as we know them, always divided in two: day and night; light and dark; the sun and the moon; fire and water; red and blue; and also male and female; good and bad; ugly and beautiful. One band of the village is of the day, of light, of the Sun, of fire, of yellow. It includes my Jaguar family, among others. The other band is nocturnal, crepuscular, lunar, aquatic, blue. It includes the reciprocal families, like that of my brothers-in-law the falcons, of the carcaras, and of many others. One band says of the other that it is effeminate, bad, and ugly. It has still not been decided whose defects these are. But to me, in the depth of my being, it appears that it is they, those of the other side who are womanish, ugly, and bad. If this were a matter to be discussed, I would have many arguments to prove my thesis. Except for me, all of us of the Rising Sun are the most beautiful, the strongest, the best at everything, except for me.

From up here, from outside, far from my little Mairun world, now half-forgotten, I enjoy and suffer recalling it, as I have during all these years. Still I am astonished: why are our people, so simple in all matters, so strongly attached to coherence? Why so much desire for organizing things and for arranging them in symmetrical order? The village expresses on the ground ideas that we carry in our heads: the band of the Setting Sun and the band of the Rising Sun, the side on high and the side below, the outer road and the inner. But not only in the village. In this, as in everything else, we are this way. We live divided according to rules of yes and of no; of heat and of cold; of luck and of hazard; of life and of death; of joy and of pain; of raw and of cooked; of the mouth and of the rectum; of the penis and of the vagina; of the head and of the naval; of blood and of milk; of semen and of saliva; of the nude and of the clothed; of silence and of speech; of the root and of the branch; of skin and of the bone; of animal and of vegetable; of game and of fish; of laughter and of tears; of the clitoris and of the glottis. When we speak of one, there is the other, offered like right and left, front and back, demanding attention, and, if it is the case, pleading its part.

But it is in the village, in its shape and its organization, where the duality of our spirit expresses itself more completely. First in the two bands: the one over there, of my brothers-in-law, and the one here, of my sisters. These bands exist in space and can be seen. They are the Rising Sun and the Setting Sun, when one is looking from the Great House of Men. But they also exist inside us. Every Mairun, upon meeting another, knows at once if the Mairun is from here or there, if that Mairun can be copulated with or is tabooed, is a brother or a brother-in-law. By day or by night, wherever we are found, our tendency as Mairuns is to arrange ourselves in space in the same way that we live in the village.

But a person from over there is not a stranger. No, a person from over there has nothing in common with this feeling of mine that here I am only a Mairun, that I am marginal, that I am lost and alone in this alien world. As to the Mairuns of all the bands and families, I am of them. And they are with me so as to form together a powerful we that protects everyone.

It is true that I and my Jaguar people form a small, exclusive we. But we are weak, incomplete, and aware that we exist, in fact, within the oneness of the other "wes," all relatives. When I think of my opposite clan, the Carcaras, I see it as my complementary reciprocal. It is there, among them, that I am going to look for my woman who will bear my children. It is there, among my brothers-in-law, that I will have my closest friends. That woman and those friends will be all the more mine precisely for being of a nature different from my own. They are the ones I need so as to form together a we that is vigorous, fecund, and complete.

Another place where dualities are plainly visible is the Great House of Men. It is rare for all the Mairuns to meet there, but when that happens, on the occasion of some ceremony, my small people start arriving and sitting anywhere, apparently, like the faithful of the six o'clock mass at the Church of the monastery. But not at all! Each one sits in what he knows as his own place. The very ground of beaten earth where we dance is also a place of prescribed positions. There everyone has a place for watching and for participating in ceremonies, or simply for day-to-day life. That ground is the center of the world, the fixed point around which everything revolves, everything happens. There on that straw bedding of the dancing ground of my village all matters that are really important are decided. It is there that the Sun rises, runs its course, and sets every day, in the sky of that dancing ground. It is from there that each of us, sitting in an appointed place, can see the Sun setting everyday.

Soon I will be there, to the right of my father, the guide of souls, to the left of my old uncle, the chieftain Anacã, right in the center of the semicircle of men seated in position to see the day die. Around them, women will serve food in black calabashes. Who knows? Some grilled pacu fish with yam and elephants' ears. Dogs and other pets yawning and stretching lazily. Every day we will re-view the great solar wheel, the red face of Maíra, which for half the year can be seen in front until it descends beyond the Iparana, like a brazier, above the most distant forest. Those depths of the setting sun are for us the side of the living savages whom we know, the Xaepes. Further still, in lands unknown, on the same side, will be the mythical savages already confused with phantoms.

The opposite side, where the Sun rises, is the corrupt side from which comes invasion, sickness, whiteness. It is the side where I am now; it is the side from which I am going away, returning.

For me, my Mairun village, during the many years of my exile, existed only within me, in my memory. It was a void in time, way back in the past, that I would revive daily, recollecting it in every detail so that it would never disappear or die within me. Now, my Mairun village is also a void in space, but there before me, in the future.

XISTO

The day is ending in the small town of Corrutela. The people returning from the fields, from the corrals, from fishing, are gathering in the shade of the little church. It is an old chapel, built by Father Vecchio. It is no longer open. Nowadays nearly everyone is a *believer*.

There squatting is the mystic *beato*. Each person arriving approaches to listen, first standing, later also in a crouch. The men patiently chewing tobacco or smoking their pipes. The women nursing their babies and watching the older children playing nearby and scolding them. It is this way every evening, always on the shady side of the closed chapel.

Xisto speaks in his slow, hoarse voice with a strong Ceará accent. He speaks softly like someone who is thinking deeply and courageously. Much of what he says has to do with things within himself, some think. But almost everyone assumes that all is written or is in accord with the word of the Prophets. Occasionally, Xisto will explain the relation between his work and the Holy texts. He has two offices there in the little town of Corrutela: to preach to the living, to pray and sing with them; and to wash, lay out, and bury the dead. The rich and better-off people pay for a coffin. The poor, buried in hammocks, don't pay for anything. Charity almost came to an end with the Brotherhood of the Rosary which used to give graves and coffins to its members.

Corrutela also has its priest. A gringo who comes every other week in his motorboat to preach and sing. Even then, when he is there, Xisto talks more and, it seems, with more wisdom. At least with greater clarity because the language of Mr. Bob is gnarled. The pastor himself enjoys listening to the sermons of the black prophet.

Xisto rerolls the cigarette Tonico the carter gave him. He licks the straw, lights up and begins his discourse.

"This world has mystery, everything here is enchanted. Even old Calu there, washing clothes and scratching herself. Even old Izupero, who works day and night at his job shoeing hooves. Even they have mystery. There is one who gives orders, it is the Lord. There is another, who gives counterorders, it is the Devil. But there is also one who is to come, the Enchanted. No one knows who he is. It is not God or the Devil. It is a person created by us, one of us. I, who knows? Not even I know. God exists and has the power to command until the end of the world, but he also suffers. He who has the power is the boss; he can command everything save his own destiny. The destiny that He made, that He designed for me, for you, for everybody, He also designed for himself as well. I will never understand it, never. And I should; I have eyes to see, ears to hear, and up to a certain day to unravel the tangle. But what I see is far less than what I don't see. And what I understand is only the tiniest speck of this great world in which I am entwined. There are so many things that are not understood. Simple, quotidian things, but full of mystery. What is there to say about the complications?"

Xisto clears his throat, takes a drag, looks slowly around at the faces of almost everyone, and continues to speak in a measured tone.

"Who can say what trees are profuse in seeds? Who knows how to explain the power that makes a seed grow, pulsating, under the ground, sucking substance to extend roots, to branch, to grow leaves, to effloresce, to bear fruit producing more seeds to repeat the process. It is destined, it contains within itself its little rules, but full of force and wisdom. One says how a leaf should be. Another speaks of flowers, their shape, their aroma, and their color. There are also little rules for the fruit with its taste and poison and ability to generate seeds to start everything all over again. It's the same with things that are even simpler, like our noses. Look at my nose. It was small when I was a boy. It grew, filled out, but it grew always according to a rule, as if within a mold. The seed is not master of its rules, of its destiny. Nor is the nose master of its form. This is how life is in Corrutela. No one is master of his own rules. Not God, not the Devil."

Xisto stops talking, looks at everyone in turn, and rests his eyes momentarily on Perpetinha, who is trembling. They are all waiting for him to ask her to begin a song. Nothing. He continues his address:

"Here, in Corrutela itself, people are born every year, live as children, grow up, marry, fornicate, give birth to people, then get old and die. All in accordance with the rules, with fate, with destiny, and all intermingled. One to marry the other, the other to murder one. This one to marry him and that other to die at his hands. Guilt. Whose is the guilt? Who can save the killer? Who can undo the predestined marriage?"

Tonico the carter ponders, looking round. He asks himself what gives the sacristan Xisto the strength and wisdom to say things that nobody had thought of?

Inspiration, does it in fact come spontaneously from inside him, or did a gift from God give him the wisdom of the revealed word? He speaks better, clearer than many priests of the church who have studied at seminaries. The awful thing is that when he begins to talk he forgets to pray and sing. He even gets annoyed if someone complains.

Xisto continues: "I see so many impossible things happening and so many inevitable things not occurring. I used to think there were no rules. Today, I know that everything has its rules, common sense, and destiny. The Enchanted is the master of destiny. He speaks through our mouths. Everyone, without meaning to, goes about saying, without knowing, one thing here and another thing there. I go about listening, go about seeing. Only by thinking I go about regulating things without wishing to. It is not the Devil, an apparition; nor is it God, a sanctity. It is people created by us. I, one of you sitting in this circle. Why can't you, I, anyone be the Enchanted. Why can't it be you? Who is it?"

The *beato* lowers the tone of his voice, murmuring rather than speaking: "I am full of doubts. My doubts grow every day. I don't know anything about what will happen, and for a long time I didn't know anything about what had happened. Nowadays I find my hand involved in present deeds. The hand, the will. Common sense is not destiny. It is the rule of the Enchanted. Look at Mr. Nono, he died, he left Mrs. Aninha to lead the life of an old widow, hidden away. Time passed without my seeing Aninha, without my thinking of her. The other day I thought, not only thought, I saw. I saw her image with her goiter more swollen and her wart bigger than ever before. I knew that vision was killing the old woman. I knew that my pity for her, that she was still alive, was too strong for her to endure. Next morning, I sat right here on this spot, warming myself in the sun, waiting. I knew that the first person to pass by would give me the news. No one passed by, but the bell started tolling for the dead. I was frightened. I had seen no one enter the chapel. But I though, it must be the Host-licker Donga. I waited. She had to come see me, she had to order from me the grave and the coffin. Then she offended me, saying that it was a pauper's death and wanted credit. And she continued: 'As for my own, don't you worry yourself, Sr. Xisto, I still belong to the Brotherhood which will pay for my burial.' 'I'm not thinking about that, Mrs. Donga, death awaits all the living,' I said, then went on, 'But my death will come long before yours. It's you who will have to bury me.'

"I myself shivered when I heard that word-voice issuing from my mouth. I would have been foreseeing my own death, asking for ruination. No, I knew it wasn't so. It wasn't I, I knew it wasn't I. There's no duplicity in those sayings that come from our mouths, from deep down there, without our willing it. It is the talk of the Enchanted. It comes out with such force that no one can keep quiet, that is, without breaking down and dying on the spot, ruined.

"You have heard, now think. Mrs. Aninha, the vision I had of her, was it not a death summons? That utterance, the an-

nouncement of my death, is quite clear. Is it not as clear as day?
I comply with a rule, with common sense, with destiny. But
without praise and without blame, or even innocence. From it
comes the command for good or for ill. Death, when it is time
to die. Happiness, when it is time to be happy. It is that which is
written. I comply with the law, the law that issues from within
me. Who knows about destiny? Not I, no one. Only the Enchanted knows. And he speaks when he wants to, through my
mouth, through your mouth."

Ze da Tropa looks nervously at Tonico the carter, as if to
ask "Is he touched in the head?" Taking courage, he clears his
throat and opines: "It's the hour of the psalm, Sr. Xisto. The
sun has set."

"The psalm does not have an hour, brother. Today it is the
heart of man that speaks. Today I am confessing my misdeeds
for all the world to hear. Not all, only those need listen who
have sinned and are guilty. Whoever has a pure heart may leave;
he does not belong here in the midst of the sinners."

Ze shrank back, spat, and passed Xisto a cigar he had just
rolled, as a peace sign.

"And don't think, Sr. Ze da Tropa, that I am telling you
anything new. The people know, they know or suspect. When
they speak of the evil eye, omens, sorcery, misfortune, adversity,
it is about this that they are talking. Without knowing what it is.
The bad thing here is that when one comes with understanding
to unravel one thing from another, right away another comes
who doesn't see anything, wanting to sing. Singing has its time!
Today we need courage. A lot of courage to think about the
mystery. And a lot of fear to know that good and evil are
interwoven. Sometimes good is born from evil. More often
good results in misfortune. Whoever looks for advantage must
accept both good and bad alike. If I don't control what I do or
what I think, neither for myself nor for others, how can I
know where God is? The source of truth, is it to be found with
the wish to be twisted? Did I kill Mrs. Aninha, or was it the law
that shook within me, making me have a vision? And was it for

good or for ill? It was for the good, perhaps, if she had arrived at her hour. It was for the worse, perhaps, if she was not prepared to die with a clean spirit. But who can absolve anyone? And if I were to tell her or such people what I have dreamt— Look, here comes the misfortune, prepare yourself, brother, the hour of your death is at hand—they would be struck down there and then from pure fright. No, I keep it to myself, I purge it in my breast, all alone. Well, brothers, let's stop now. Let's sing. Sister Perpetinha, begin the Song of the Holy Men."

Xisto recites a verse from memory, in a raucous voice:

Ah, this sinful nation
A people burdened with iniquity
A backsliding race
Corrupters of children.

Then, he lowers his voice to a murmur:

They have blasphemed against the Lord of Israel . . . of Israel
They have forsaken the Lord, their God . . . their God

Perpetinha raises her tremulous voice even higher:

Shout, o ye gates . . . ye gates
Cry out o ye city . . . ye city
Thou, O Philistine, tremble in every limb . . . every limb!

Xisto recommences his discourse: "Nothing in this world is eternal, only God and the Devil. Everything passes, what is good and what is bad will also pass. None of us will remain, nothing will remain. But one thing remains. It is sin. This is definite. You sin today against the law, the sin remains there, throbbing. You purge it through penitence, through the hope of pardon, but it remains there, testifying. When the hour comes, the true hour of the Last Judgment, it will be there denouncing you. When God separates the just on one side and the sinners on the other, what will count is that sin, weighing on the scale of perdition. Everything passes, everything ends. Save sin. You can be just and pure. But, like me, you can be burdened by sins already sinned, by past sins that no water can wash away."

Xisto pauses for a moment and presses on: "I know that the padre says that he hears confession, gives penitence, and pardons. Could that be so? Does he wash away the sin, the sin against the Law of God? The sin of those who fall into temptation? No, sin can never be washed away. No, guilt is guilt and God is the judge. God alone. The Devil is the collector."

SUCURIJUREDÁ

The men of all the bands set out on a journey far from the village. Only the women and children bear the sharp stench of Anacã, incensing the air. Some go up the river or down the river to fish for arapaima with harpoons, or for pacu with bows and arrows. Others search for suitable backwaters in which to stun fish with toxic plants, by far the easiest method. Others prefer also to fish with arrows and harpoons in the Iparana by caves, forming a network of waterways through which only a Mairun would wind his way without getting lost. Still others venture into the forest to hunt furred or feathered game. They will return, the fishers as well as the hunters, only when their baskets brim with the dried flesh of fish or game.

The young men are also leaving today. But they don't go alone, and they don't go to hunt or to fish. Theirs is another obligation: guided by Teró of the Falcons, they seek an enormous *sueuridju*, the biggest anaconda in the world.

In their canoes they paddle for a whole day up the Iparana. From there, by way of a connecting branch, to the Black Lake which they cross, slashing the water with their paddles, making all the birds take flight, with a trac-trac of drums. They sleep and then move forward up the Rupi creek, through the green tunnel of trees, thick with foliage, leaning out over the water. It is harder work than to paddle in silence, pushing away branches and vegetation blocking the way and pulling out tree trunks cutting the channel from one side to the other.

They continue always forward, attentive to the gestures of Teró who goes in front leading the way for the file of three canoes. They arrive, at last, at the place where they believe the giant snake is to be found. But it isn't there. They advance, searching keenly from one side to the other. The risk is not small that the snake will see them first and lash out at one or two of them. They see plenty of game hidden in that wilderness: deer, capybaras, a tapir, and two anacondas. But not being of the size that they were looking for, Teró leaves them behind.

It is in the middle of the afternoon that they happen upon the anaconda, almost confused with the tree trunks and vegetation. It is visible only to those who know what to look for, its greenish-black scales, placed in rings along its back, its yellow belly stained with great dark blotches. It is partly coiled on a trunk, slithering. But it's not looking for food; just below its throat a bulge protrudes where the skin is stretched and the scales part. It must have been a deer or some other large game that it had killed, crushed, and swallowed. Now it is slowly digesting it, enjoying the taste and swallowing the juice.

Noticing the three man-canoe animals coming up the channel the snake supports itself better around the trunk and alertly raises its head atop its extended body. No one says a word. With gestures, Teró orders the eleven men to jump out all at once and to surround the anaconda from all sides. It watches suspiciously, stretching and constricting its neck, swaying its trifid tongue, and asking itself what little animals are these? A little before they were three centipedes in the water, now they are a swarm around it. At a whistle from Teró they jump in concert and grab the great snake by all parts: the head, the throat, the body on its various ringed welts, and the tail that it was uncoiling, wanting to strike a few blows.

Now they struggle against that living muscle, difficult to restrain, extremely long. It is an elastic tube that constricts and swells, recoils and expands. Sometimes it arches itself, lifting the men in the air, and then it straightens out and hardens, throwing them on the ground. It draws strength from the men securing its head to deal blows to those holding its tail, making them dance astonished. But they all keep a firm grip, even as she throws them in the air or on the ground.

The great snake hisses unceasingly, solely from fury, but it surrenders in the end, almost immobile, trembling. Teró then releases the tail, shouting at Jaguar to release the belly and to go secure the tail. Teró moves forward to grab the throat of the anaconda, right behind the head where Maxĩ is, and releasing the snake, Maxĩ stands in front of it, astonished. Teró shouts ordering him to offer his face to be bitten by the anaconda. Maxĩ wavers for an instant, but quickly pulls himself together and sticks his chin in the monstrous mouth that gives a firm bite of a rabid dog. Maxĩ retires bleeding, and, while thinking about caring for his wound, he hears another shout from Teró ordering Jaguar as his substitute to go receive, in turn, the bite.

So, one by one, the young men pass in succession from the tail to the head, each of them offering his face to receive the mark of the truth of the anaconda. Once bitten they immediately go hold the snake in place of the companion whose turn it is. So, from start to finish, the snake continues to be held in place, maintained almost immobile, by more than twenty powerful hands.

All have been bitten. Now it was a matter of how to let the anaconda loose, as it was still alive, testifying in the forest, with its shame, to the daring of the Mairuns. They say that such a snake never again descends the creek to cross, gloriously, with its back arched and supple, the mirrors of the water of Black Lake.

At a gesture from Teró, all release the snake, jump back and separate, running to the creek. The anaconda has neither the opportunity nor the time to coil itself around someone to crush him, nor to knock a man down with a lash of its tail. They return to the canoes, still bleeding from the slashing bites. Proud, they let themselves bleed.

Dusk is falling, but they have to paddle downstream for some hours more, entering the night, before camping at the mouth of the creek. Teró smiles with contentment. The young men paddle, silent, serious, circumspect, with a feeling of the importance of what they had achieved. No one washes the dried and co-agulated blood from his face. Still in silence, they sling their hammocks one next to the other, each with its fire burning underneath, against mosquitos and curupiras; thieves of blood and of Mairun souls.

Tomorrow and the next day, they will have to paddle on, camping twice more, before at last entering the village on the morning when they are expected. They lose sleep, hearing Teró tell stories of previous snake-biting rituals, in which all kinds of accidents had occurred, including one in which a snake had died from so much fury and humiliation. The worst was a blow from a tail that almost ripped the backside off the guide of souls who, while still a young man, had gone for his bite, the cicatrix of which he still has on his face. Each generation tells and retells stories, speaking of its snake as the biggest of all.

"Yours, this one of ours, was average. I have seen bigger," says Teró.

"None of that," says Jaguar. "Nothing of nothing, old man. This one is the mother of all snakes. There is none bigger!"

The greatest feat ever told there, and never equalled, was that of one generation which, while returning from the snake-biting rite, decided to hunt and still managed to arrive within the prescribed time, everyone bearing something: one carried a deer, another an elk, another a tapir; all were bringing meat for the village. The story inspires Jaguar, and they decide to re-peat the effort. But it has to be done within the two and a half days remaining, muses Teró. That's how it will be, Jaguar

promises. They arrange a fire hunt in a space in the forest that
had been cleared by a previous fire, no one knew when, close to
the Black Lake.

They awake while it is still night and watch daybreak as they
are already paddling. In the afternoon they beach the canoes
on the shore of the lake and head together toward the far end
of the clearing. There Teró prepares a torch of dry straw
soaked in resin for each man. He lights a fire and waits for the
wind to blow in the direction of the lake. When it is time, when
the gusts are strong, they light the torches and run first to one
side, then to the other, as Teró directs, to form the great circle
of fire that will lick and expand as it burns brush and scrub.
This way they set an enormous trap of fire that will close on the
beach near the canoes in about an hour.

There, on their return, the men rest from their trek and wait
for the game with their bows and arrows ready to fell whatever
comes. The animals around the clearing, seeing the fire approaching them from all sides, try to escape, furiously scurrying here
and there. But they end by fleeing in the direction of their
only way out along the shore of the lake, right where the hunters are waiting. Emerging are deer, stags, anteaters, half a herd
of elks, labba, coatis, snakes, agoutis, armadillos, a spotted jaguar,
two ocelots, and even a black puma. It is a lustrous huge black
cat, enormous, with silvery blemishes on the velvety darkness
of its sable fur. It leaps out of the fire and smoke and looks
for an instant at the men who are just as surprised to see it
and are marveling at it. It leaps once more, then, unexpectedly,
upon the waters of the Black Lake. Jaguar and Maxĩ enter the
water in pursuit of the jaguar but soon come out. There in the
water, swimming faster and better than they could, the jaguar
could easily have finished them off with a swipe from a paw,
breaking their necks. They return to the edge to see where the
jaguar would emerge. They go after it, in spite of the warning
given by Teró pleading for them to let the jaguar go that had
already gained its freedom.

Teró of the House of Falcons who are masters of living jaguars, could very well have given an order instead of begging. If anyone was entitled to kill that animal, it was he. But he saw that it was impossible to prohibit his son from engaging in this adventure, and indeed, despite everything, Jaguar went ahead with his new, inseparable friend, Maxĩ.

Their companions wait happily until the end of the afternoon and then anxiously all night. At dawn Teró decides that they will all go home carrying the enormous load of butchered game to be dried there. In the village they could perhaps organize a group, if need be, to go search for Jaguar and Maxĩ. They put the three canoes in the water and embark, paddling through the Black Lake. They paddle day and night to arrive early in the morning of the appointed day at the Mairun landing.

Teró blows through his conch the tune announcing the arrival of a hunter with game. On the beach the young men are painting themselves, rearranging their ornaments to best effect; they lift entire carcasses of game and follow the trail to the village, singing. The people there, who are just arising, are happy at their encounter on the dancing ground. There, seeing an impossible feat repeated, they are going to mount an enormous barbecue. And Jaguar, they asked, and Maxĩ?

The following day is one of apprehension, but no one says anything. Only the guide of souls remarks to Náru that perhaps they should ask Teró to return with a party to look for them. But why? Would it not be an affront, perhaps, to presume that they are not capable of taking off on their own to carry out properly what they set themselves to do? Neither Remui nor Teró takes any initiative. Seemingly all they care about is grilling the huge mound of meat, eating bits, drying the larger cuts, and mashing certain portions with farina and banana. All to make sure that this would be the finest of food for the great days of the coming major festivity. But no one stopped listening, searching in the wind for welcome news of the return of Jaguar and Maxĩ. What has happened to them?

Only three days later, as evening approaches, one hears the

coarse sound coming from the flute with which Jaguar and
Maxĩ are announcing their return. They came on foot from the
skirts of the high forest. Jaguar in front, seen from afar seems
enormous and deformed. Everybody stares apprehensively.
What has happened? As he comes closer he displays and dis-
simulates uncommon stature and blackness. He is entirely
covered in the hide of the puma. On his head he carries the big
bloody head of the panther. On his arms, the skin of the forelegs and the paws armed with claws. On his back, with the
enormous black pelt gleaming, the hindlegs and the tail are
being dragged, scratching the ground. That is how he enters the
dancing ground between the double file of amazed men and
women, adding another potent smell to that of Anacã and the
roasting meat. It is the special scent of the great jaguar, strong
enough to make one sneeze, and the stench of the semiputrefac-
tion of its fresh pelt.

The guide of souls suddenly appears in front of Jaguar who
prostrates himself directly upon seeing him and hearing the low
but urgent sounds of the rattle and flute. Commanding him with
his eyes, the old guide of souls makes Jaguar approach Anacã's
grave and kneel there. And he begins to speak in a voice low
and powerful:

"Anacã, it is Jaguar who is here, in front of you, your
grandnephew Jaguar. He has brought the puma, the black panther. He has brought it for you, brother of the living jaguar. Its
life is of the falcons. They must be the ones to kill it. For this
reason, here is Teró, who now will let the blood of the puma
flow. The claws, to be sure, will be a crown for Jaguar. The
teeth will be a necklace for Jaguar, but the hide, that is for the
House of the Falcons. The shinbones will be a flute for
the chieftain to come."

Jaguar rises, divests himself of the black skin, puts it on the
ground, in front of the grave, and sits in the ceremonial position. Teró slowly approaches, kneels on the side of Jaguar, takes
into his hands the skin, soft and fresh, holds it up, makes a ball
of it, twice buries his old knife in its folds, killing the puma, and

rises to his feet. He stands before Jaguar and begs, "Help me." Jaguar also rises, and the two of them, father and son, take up the pelt in all its grandeur, and with it they cover the grave. The head is set where Anacã's head was, on the side of the Rising Sun; the tail, where his feet were, toward the Setting Sun. Teró then says,

"The great tiger belongs to Anacã today; in it he will rest this afternoon and all night. Tomorrow I will occupy myself with it."

The guide of souls ends the ceremony with a happy trill from a small ocarina made from a calabash. The men and the women all approach to stroke the pelt, enormous, black, lustrous crescent marks. Revived there, in the center of the dancing ground, is a puma immense as the night, arms and legs outspread, with its curved claws and its mouth full of yellowing ivory fangs, enormous, on the tomb of Anacã, the former chieftain of the Jaguar clan.

In the afternoon everyone happily follows Jaguar and Maxĩ who walk in the direction of the beach. Maxĩ begins to tell there, in that moment, a story that he continues telling throughout the whole day and that he will never finish telling in all the days of his life.

Only he cannot tell it sitting down quietly. He tells it standing, pacing, gesticulating; it could be on the beach, on the dancing ground, or even inside the Great House of Men, but he needs space. When he begins, everyone knows, it is necessary to grab the dogs by the legs and to open the scene in which he is going to relive his past.

Telling his story, Maxĩ speaks, shouts, jumps, dances, snarls, and bites. Now he is the great cat standing on its paws, terrifying. Then he is Jaguar armed with bow and arrow, or extended as he throws a javelin, pure nerve, muscle, and eye. In one instant Maxĩ jumps from tiger to man, and back again from man to jaguar. Sometimes he succeeds in being at once both man and jaguar. Jaguar and the jaguar are confounded in each other.

He tells how they had followed the puma for an entire day, never seeing it but guessing its presence from its rumbling and its tracks, now here, now there. Who was hunting whom?

He tells how the puma, on the following day, confronted them, standing on its hind legs and growling, killer that it was, but fled when it saw its own death in the eyes of Jaguar.

He tells how the black panther then defended itself against a gigantic bamboo arrow that would have opened its chest, with an instantaneous swipe of its paw that smashed the arrow to bits in the air.

He tells how, later on, Jaguar wounded it badly, twice, with barbed arrows that remained in its flanks, swaying to and fro without success in drawing blood.

He tells how Jaguar, in total silence, worked all night without pause to make a spear from the heartwood of a palm tree, its point sharpened with a knife and hardened in fire.

He tells how, finally, he caught the scent of the puma, betrayed by its stench, and found it hidden behind a clump of Attalea palms, all curled up.

He tells how Jaguar then confronted the enormous puma that approached him, rapidly and silently, on its four padded paws, quickly, to unleash upon him a mortal leap, snapping his neck off and drinking the still hot blood.

He tells how the puma stopped, motionless, on seeing the spear that Jaguar was brandishing in the air, extending his arms, and forming a great, moving circle.

He tells how, within reach of the tormenting circle but a pace or two away, the black jaguar stood on its hind legs and extended its forelegs, snarling, growling, swaying its head from side to side, biting the air, now this side, now that.

He tells me how he shook with fear at the deadly fury of the tiger, unleashed upon Jaguar with each swipe of its giant paw to shatter the menacing lance.

He tells how they advanced toward each other, the big cat standing up, growling, full of menace, fatal; the man, silent, offering and withdrawing the spear, standing firmly on his two feet, resolved not to turn and flee in terror.

He tells how they advanced slowly, step by step, Jaguar and the puma, one toward the other, until the puma firmly grabbed, with its two paws, the spear that Jaguar was offering, and sunk the hardened point in its own chest, exactly where Jaguar wanted it.

He tells how the puma bled from the depths of its chest, yowling with ferocious fury, an unintentional suicide, accomplishing the will of Jaguar.

SERVICE

Here I come, Lord, to serve you. To serve you with my soul and my body, in sorrow and in pain. From the world I want nothing and want everything. That is what I beg now: the opportunity to purge my sins with pain, the satisfaction of suffering for the love of God. I would like to be martyred, my Father, to testify through my flesh, before your eyes, as to what a redeemed winner can do, to show what the love of God can do through me.

No one believes in me, not even I myself. At times, I less than anyone. My vague and distant family knows little about me. But they know about my problems—of the asylum—and like Philistines they regard me, asking, in astonishment, why such an obsession over the love of God?

Fred, of whom I am fond and who is fond of me, doesn't understand anything. He reduces my conversion, my desire to serve, to delight in suffering to redeem myself for the death of my father for which I blame myself. Psychoanalysis without sanctity is wisdom without sentiment—presumption. It can help one who is totally lost to find himself, to support himself as he is, in light of any occurrence. But it does not allow anyone to transcend and realize himself as a creation of God: always virginal and innocent in His eyes, whatever one's faults. Only faith and service to God can give us this capacity, can give it to me, will give it.

There in the Mission, with the sisters, I will finally have the peace I never had, steeped in carnal passion, weighted down with the love of my sacrosanct father. He saw in me only kindness and purity. Oh! my poor father who is in Heaven and who, perhaps, can see me from there! Never, my father, never, will I fall into searching for your essence in someone else as I did so many times over without realizing it: mea culpa, mea maxima culpa.

Not having a mother to love, nor a brother to teach me how to be a better person, nor friends, for years and years I had only my father. I concentrated on him entirely. We lived off kindness and presents, on his part, and off that anxiety and anguish, on mine. Not even his death freed me.

With quiet surprise, as if it were an offense, he witnessed the ripening of my body, the onset of my menstruation, the swelling of my breasts, my outbreaks of acne. He waited for me every night, silent, with the black rosary in his hand, so that together we would kneel in prayer before the oratory of my mother. He guessed my first kiss, and suffered. He guessed, too, and suffered in anticipation when I slept with Queco, and then with others and others and others. He never said a word. But he told me just the same in a suffering tone as he whispered the rosary. Oh! My father!

My major suffering was to see him waste away from illness! The skin losing its tone, the eyes their brilliance, and he, weakening, with belabored breathing and fever. Even more it pained me to see him becoming each day more wrinkled, ugly, and old. He suffered, too from an obsessive preoccupation that I not be the one to wash him and change his clothes. That is why someone was always there to do it.

I suppose—or so Fred convinced me—that it was this love for my father that led me to go out after old Edmundo for a foolish affair. He was the owner of the pharmacy across the street from our house. He gave injections to my father, with taciturnity and circumspection, and he would slip it into me, saying filthy things in the voice of a radio announcer and pretending to teach me the greatest secrets of lovemaking.

After many others came Fred. He, too, was older than I; he, too, was a father figure. He knows this better than anyone. He knows it so well that he wants to add additional thrills by imagining that he is my father and my son, and by fucking me as if I were his mother and his daughter. He has never wanted to leave his wife for me. His love has always had this limit. But he is generous in giving me things: the apartment, the car. Generous also in understanding. Above all during those confused years when I sought, through intimacy with so many, to create a world of tenderness and invented happiness. I used to take off the clothes and the shoes that Fred would give me and dress as simply as possible, to the point where I discovered in the simplicity of simplicity a more refined sophistication. I vested and divested my body in an endless gift. I was as searching, through relations first with one, then with another, with nearly anyone, to be a person among people, one among the others, to practice living together. All in vain. I would always end up in Queco's bed, trying to help him fuck me without being able to.

I gave Fred much grief, much more when I got on drugs. First it was weed, which taught me how to delight in my palate, to feel what touching can give, to fall in love with suffering and enjoy total love. But the time came when all of this gave me no more than a distant image of what I was searching for. Then came acid, which renewed my sentiment of myself, enflaming, once again, my whole body, completely opening the pores, setting my hair on end, moistening my mouth and my intimate I. I was entirely resplendent. After that came heroin, and with it madness and institutionalization. And Fred, once more saving me until I found myself. Had there been shocks? Had there been fright?

Something happened at Pinel. Something that affected me deeply. There in the depth of my being something broke. It was then that this necessity surged up within me, to retrace my steps, to regain the lost road. A very simple thing that my father had shown me, pointing with his finger and holding out his hand to guide me. But then I was not capable of seeing or of feeling: faith.

Everything began with a wish, a strange desire to sit in church once more and to smell the odor of incense rising in wisps of smoke toward Heaven. A desire to hear the organ resounding in the nave. I would remain there for hours on end. How many times did the caretaker have to touch my shoulder to say that she was about to shut the church? It was she who one day led me to Father Orestes. He came one evening and talked to me right there; he asked whether what I needed was not a good confession. I didn't think so that time. I said no. But I spent the whole night confessing to myself, telling God what I thought of myself. Since then, I confess and take communion daily.

One day there fell into my hands a message from God, his Word, the one that was going to save me. It was that newspaper article about the nuns. The nuns whom I am going to search for now. The nuns who are going to save me. The nuns who are going to find me already there, living among the savages. The nuns who ask for nothing and have no wish to convert anyone. Only to participate in the lives of the Indians, for the love of God. If one day there should be a miracle of conversion it will be because God wants to turn that tribe into a Christian community, without innocence and without sin, for the love of God and his own will.

I am going there to wait for them, in spite of everything.

Above all in spite of the words of Sister Petrina of the Sacre Coeur Convent, who is so harsh with me. Still, her words resound in my ears: "You will gain nothing, you will gain nothing by going there. It will do you no good, really. The only door to the Order is in France. Were they to accept anyone here, it would only be to send that person there. There you would have to undergo training. The Order would take you in only after completion of the rites, after the act of consecration. Only then would it decide where any sister is sent. The sisters are trained only there, there in France, only there. Exclusively!"

Father Orestes said that is how it is. It could be. But what will the sisters do if I get there before them and offer myself in complete surrender? Here I am, to do obediently anything you want. Here I am to serve you, wherever and in whatever capacity. I am not begging for anything, not even for the glory of being a nun, I desire only to serve. I want only to live among you, as you will live among the savages. For this I'm going.

INQUIRY

I have decided to record in this notebook the observations from which I shall compose my report, to H. E. the minister, on this mission with which I have been entrusted: clarification of a presumed crime that occurred in this district, the victim of which (I have just ascertained) is a person by the name of Alma (I still don't know her surname) who had arrived here from Rio de Janeiro. I myself arrived yesterday at the Edward Eneas Indigenous Post of the FUNAI, founded nearly forty years ago by the then S.P.I. with the objective of giving assistance to the Mairun Indians, recently pacified. It is run by Agent 17, Sr. Elias Pantaleao. He lives here in the company of his wife, Dona Creuza, in a house with a hipped roof, adobe walls, and a flagstone floor, the only decent building in the entire vicinity. Sr. Elias is a man of about fifty, having been a functionary of the S.P.I. for more than twenty-five years, and he has previously served in many other posts. He is an affable person but clearly inadequate for the job of leading Indians to civilization. He must be a "believer" in religion, because before meals he takes a pack of cards from a drawer, the Bible (part of it, naturally) is transcribed on the cards; he deals them out and solemnly reads one or two verses.

From what I have seen up to now, he lives like a rancher with the post's herd of cattle at his disposal and three men in his service to look after them, milk them, and to work a modest clearing. As to the Indians, here at the post there are only three families, very interbred, of whose children (five) Dona Crueza is the teacher, (adding her salary to her husband's salary). I will not delve into this further because my mission is not to judge officials of FUNAI, but only to investigate the crime that concerns me.

Sr. Elias began by telling me that he had prepared a report on the matter that was ready to be sent to his director. Later he effected a modification: he had only the intention of preparing such a report. In fact, he knows nothing about even the fundamental facts of the case. He volunteered, however, that he was acquainted with the deceased woman who had been brought to the post for the first time, by the ex-Indian, Isaias Mairun. Subsequently, she came several more times, alone or accompanied by groups of Indians. She always came in search of medicaments which Dr. Noel of the H. A. S. (Health Assistance Service) periodically supplies to be distributed gratis to the Indians. She had not been, however, assigned as a nurse or in any other capacity. Neither was she recognized as a missionary. Her presence in the village was a matter of fact. She simply arrived, having been brought by the aforementioned Isaias, an ex-seminarian who had been waiting to be ordained as a Catholic priest but who had impulsively made a last visit to his native village, and ended up abandoning his religious vocation.

The aforementioned seminarian had met the cited victim, named Alma, in Brasília, or Rio, and they had traveled together to the Iparana. It was apparently her intention to devote herself to missionary service together with some French nuns who have still not arrived in the region, but who are expected. Concerning the relationship between Alma and Isias, the agent could only remark, in a confident way, "they were acquaintances—who knows if they were friends? They were hardly lovers."

The facts supplied by Sr. Elias are evidently precarious. He does not know for certain when she arrived here (therefore he was unable to verify if the stillborn twins were conceived here or somewhere else). Nor does he know how or why she died, whether it was a natural, accidental, or criminal death. His only information concerning the twins was what I had already provided him with. Everything indicates that this man lives confined to the post, knowing nothing of what occurs in the village —two leagues upriver—except what the savages themselves see fit to tell him.

He is also an impostor, according to what I have been able to observe and verify. At first he sought to show me he could speak the Mairun dialect, addressing a few phrases to the Indians who live here. Their perplexity and their replies, in abominable Portuguese, made me distrust him. I proved the matter by asking, in their dialect, the names of certain things, and I could see that Sr. Elias had lied. An incompetent and a liar, both serious defects. But affable, he as much as his wife Dona Creuza, who never ceases to complain about the headaches she suffers, about her isolation in this bush, about her anxieties concerning her son who is studying in Minas, and above all, about her married daughter and the grandchildren she hardly ever sees.

The fare they have given me is modest but tolerable. Yesterday morning we had coffee with milk and some biscuits from Para, as hard as corn, called crackers. Today I was able to have the curd that I had asked for, and Dona Creuza prepared some sweet cassava cakes which eaten hot with fresh lard are a substitute for bread. For dinner they have served chicken from among the few they raise (in cages elevated from the ground to protect them from the opossums) and dried or fresh meat from the cattle of the post, which they slaughter from time to time.

I asked Sr. Elias why the cattle had not been given to the Indians to raise themselves, knowing very well that I was touching on a delicate matter. The man explained it and his explanation failed to convince me. According to his story, the Indians are still in the age of hunting. If they were given cattle, they would kill them all the same day. To them, a calf or a cow or a steer is game to be eaten straight away. He then added (with some justification) that if the three hundred or so head of cattle at the post were distributed among the Indians, there would be less than one for each, which would leave them in the same poverty.

I asked him why he didn't hire Indians instead of backlanders for work at the post. His defense was amusing: "Major, do you want to have me prosecuted? Don't you see that we can't employ the Indians without falling into the condition of their exploiters? This has never been done at any post because it would lead to the worst of consequences." He then delivered his strongest argument: "It is also important to have some backlanders working here, to serve as a model and example. How will the Indians ever learn new work techniques if we don't teach them?" As his final argument, he concluded: add the fact that we cannot depend on the Indians for any regular work; they would come one day then miss three. Under these conditions, who would look after the cattle and cultivate the land?

From what I can see, the thing is well contrived and justified purely so that the Indians remain in the village as Indians and the agents in the posts as their remote tutors. The result is that the Indians will never assimilate or appropriate the uses and the customs of civilization. But also that the officials of FUNAI will not lose their employment as bureaucratic-landholders milking the national treasury.

Returning to the theme that concerns me and about which I will state my opinion, let me here outline the established facts:

1. The dead woman, by the name of Alma, was a native of Rio de Janeiro, white, she must have been under thirty years of age, tall, thin, and rather unattractive. ("I wouldn't call her pretty," said Sr. Elias. "She was really a lovely person," said Dona Creuza.)

2. She lived for several months with the Mairun Indians, and left the village to die, without having had the opportunity, as far as is known, to establish contact with any Brazilian.

3. She died on the 26th of October last year, according to the deposition made by the Swiss scientist, on the beach referred to by him, and everything indicates that she died giving birth to twins of the male sex.

4. Did she die from the parturition itself (I still must investigate this) or from a related incident, still unknown? Who would kill a woman giving birth?

5. Under these conditions, the only suspect, for now, is the ex-Indian and ex-seminarian named Isaias, who brought the woman here and cohabited with her in the same house in the village, identifiable as the House of the Jaguars, as Sr. Elias has informed me.

In light of these facts, what remains to be done is the exhumation of the corpse to proceed with an examination of the body of the deceased to verify whether the wound on the head constituted the cause of death. This is what I will do tomorrow or later with the help of Sr. Elias. Taking advantage of the opportunity, I will visit the village for an inspection, and I will be better able to investigate some of the facts with the Indians themselves. Did someone kill that woman, and if it was not this Isaias, was it one of them? And if it was one of them, it will be as if she had not died, because, according to what I have been advised, the savages are not responsible before civil law. But would this apply to the said Isaias, who suddenly decided to return from abroad when he was on the verge of being ordained? Sr. Elias thinks that the legal immunity of the Indians is relative, not total: they can be judged and punished for their crimes. However, he alerts me that the judges are always inspectors of FUNAI, and that the punishment is mandatorily administered at an Indian post, maintained for this purpose. Can it be true? Does this seem reasonable, or even credible? Especially if the code of immunity were applied to the said Isaias. He would thereby be converted into a privileged Brazilian. With the prerogative to commit any crime or outrage without being subject to the arm and rigor of the law as he should be.

JURUPARI

Anacã still resides in his decomposing flesh and in the untouched marrow of his bones. Only at the end of the funeral rites will he liberate himself as a spirit to become integrated in the world of the dead. He is still the chieftain of the Mairun people. Even in death, he commands with the will inscribed in tradition, the contribution of everyone to the realization of this final task: his ceremonial funeral.

In this way, a man comes to an end even as life is being renewed. Anacã dies so that the Mairuns can be reborn. At the same time that his flesh, watered every day, is dissolving in death, his people are being reborn in the rites that rekindle in everyone the joy of eating, the happiness of singing, the pleasure of dancing, the courage of daring, the joy of copulating.

The ceremony is approaching its climax before coming to an end. During the following days no one will attend to anything but this. All the dances that were rehearsed, all the matches that were trained for have been danced and fought in the last few days. For hours and hours we danced proudly, painted and adorned. Gleaming wrestlers, decked out in their ceremonial ornaments, elegantly tied with cords and distinguished with bells, fight, reliving the Mairun traditions. Every noon, after the morning dances, and every evening before nightfall, we all of us together eat on the dancing ground of the village.

At last, the best part of the festivity begins: one whole day, a night, and half the next day we drink the cashew brew that has been foaming so vigorously in the rundlets half buried in the ground of the Great House. We start drinking early, after the howler-monkey dance, and by midday we are already running the risk of becoming confused. We can still recognize brothers and sisters on the dancing ground, in the sunlight. But soon night comes and more and more brew. Much attention will be needed for father and daughter to recognize each other. Only sons and their mothers, I suppose, and perhaps uncles and their nieces, will be certain to identify each other. Only those perhaps, but nothing is certain. What is most probable is that soon no one will be able to guarantee anything in the midst of this world where everything spins and spins, while right becomes left, day becomes night, what is up comes down, what is outside goes in, joyfully, and what is inside goes out, vomited.

Spun with the force of the piss of God, the wheel of the feast spins and spins. The feast is now the wheel of life and reaches everything: the stench of the chieftain, Anacã, the piquant aroma of good food, and the frothy aroma of the cashew brew. The red of annatto, the blue-black of genipap juice, and the yellow of all the macaws and hangnest orioles. The taste of meat and the taste of fish. The sister and the sister-in-law, the uncle and the father-in-law, the daughter and the daughter-in-law. The whistle and the snore. The disc of cassava bread and the little ball that is sawari nuts. The belch and the fart. The vomit and the shit. The blood and the milk. The semen and the sweat.

The spinning wheel spins and turns. Everything revolves around this, the navel of the world: this, the Mairun dancing ground with Anacã the chieftain buried at the center. Only he is fixed in that world that spins and turns, turns until it's spinning. The day revolves in the pit of blue sky of the immense beyond. In the far heights, Maíra and Micura drink cashew brew, whirl and dance, fall down drunk, sing, and roll around laughing. Everything whirls overflowing from the depths of the sky, the stars, falling as if drunk, whirling without an axis on the bluish panther skin of God the Father. There below, in odorous space, the living spirits of the dead wing and whirl, drinking cashew brew and waiting for Anacã. Even the unweaned spirits of the sweet and piercing graveyard stench revolve and croak drunkenly.

So it was that during a day and its night the world spun, gyrating, and this morning it continued in the gyre, spinning in a swirl until there sounded in the village the whistle—fiiiii . . . of the living flute, startling everyone, followed suddenly by the thundering boom of the end of the world—ummm . . . what could that be? And again the terrifying rumble—ummm . . . what could that be? Is the world about to end? Fiiiii . . . ummm. . . . There they are closer, the whistle and the roar. The flute whistling and the ferocious beast bellowing, together, without a pause. The voice of a fish? Yes, they are the evil spirits. It is the piping guan, the flute of the Juruparis. Here they come, the horrifying ones! Are they coming to the feast to whirl? No!

On the dancing ground, panic spreads among the people not fully awake from their drunkenness. It makes everyone run, fall down, get up, and stagger dizzily from one side to the other. Here they come, the horrifying ones! And they come ululating like sirens. They come from the depths of the water, from the world below. They are the water Juruparis, far older than mankind. Prior to Maíra-Poxi. Who knows how long they have existed? They are the people of the depths, the Jurupari of Maíra-Monan.

The men rush into the Great House. The women, frightened stiff, flee and fall, shrieking, gathering their children so as to hide inside their huts, with their eyes shut tightly. In every house, fear possesses all. The women and children crouching with their backs against the walls, their faces turned toward the center of the house, with their eyes shut tightly. Terrified. Mothers clutch their children, children their mothers, mute from fear. An assault by the Juruparis is the most frightening menace of all. A woman who looks at an ananga will be raped until she dies, torn apart by its enormous wooden member.

The children will be turned into evil spirits.

The whistle of the living flutes and the ululation of the bellowers of Maíra whistle and rumble and growl, become louder each time, nearer each time. Are they going to enter the village? They are already here! There they come, everyone senses them, hearing the din of their rush between the House of the Falcons and the House of the Turtles, and from there to the dancing ground. Now they circle the Great House of Man, howling all the while. Will they attack the Great House or not? Now they are wheeling into the circle of houses. Now they divide into two groups; one runs in one direction around the back roads, the other takes the front road. They circle running and howling and digging their claws into the thatch of the houses that crack and crumble.

Terror grows in each house. Each woman clutches her child closely, shuts her eyes more firmly, thinking—it's now, it's here! No, they have gone ahead! But here come the others in the back: they're here, now! At once, they break into two houses simultaneously, huts of the Tapirs and the Pacus, dragging down walls and entering through the holes.

The evil spirits fill the house with their horrendous presence, the fetid smell of decomposing mud from the bottom of the river and the sinister rustling of their straw garments. From the mothers, blinded by their wish not to see, they tear away the more fully grown children and drag them outside. Going from house to house they take one or two youngsters who are seized by three or four evil spirits rustling their straws, roaring and roaring with the solar rhomb. The mothers, their faces buried in the ground so as not to see, defend as best they can the smaller children who are choking from fright. Excited, the girls cry, scream, wet themselves from horror as their knees shake, while they lean toward the ground, covering their eyes with their eyelids and hands.

The boys, captured and carried by the evil spirits, are dragged outside, kicking and screaming, to the riverbank. There they are thrown into the center of a circle of evil spirits who dance, holding hands, whirling and whirling, merging and roaring, but punishing severely any boy who dares open his eyes to see or who tries to escape.

When the boys who have been kidnapped are all in the moving circle of men-cat-fish, all of a sudden the dance and the rumble of rumblers ceases, provoking a palpable silence. Then, two of the evil spirits enter the circle; they take hold of one boy and carry him, kicking, before a masked one who is standing, waiting. When the boy is close, the evil spirit who is waiting starts to shout at him: "Open your eyes! Open!" While doing this he removes the blue mud from his face and says, "Look closely idiot, I am your uncle Náru, not an evil spirit. There are no evil spirits. The Juruparis are extinct. Those who exist now are we, real men, Avaetes."

The fear and fright of that boy and of the others vanish gradually and are transformed into perplexity. The circle of evil spirits breaks up, and each man allows himself to be identified, removing the woven structure covered with blueish mud and shaped like a catfish head, and undoing his straw skirt. The boys look half thunderstruck. One of the brighter ones takes the bellower, sees that it is a wooden shingle carved in the shape of a fish and attached to a string, and he swings it round his head, making it roar—"I'm a Jurupari!" he shouts, exploding from joy.

When all the little boys calm down, Náru gathers their attention. He tells them to sit around him on the sandy beach, and he explains calmly:

"Look well, you must learn this: Now you too are men— little men. From today on you will live with us in the Great

House of Men. You are going to learn properly to loose an arrow or throw a harpoon. We are going to teach you to hunt and fish. Pay heed, from now on none of you will ever go into the houses of women. Only if you are very hungry and need to eat something during the day or in the future when you are grown-up, when you marry. Even then, you will go only at night to see your woman. Apart from this, single or separated, you will live with us in our house which is the Great House of Men. There a woman never enters, nor children. Only we, the real men, Avaetes."

In the houses, the women remain agitated. The fear and the fright of being raped persists. The children are whispering nervously, asking the whereabouts of their stolen brothers. Where is Petin? Where is Xita? Where is Uri? Where is Pai? Where is Oti? They end by falling asleep, disconsolate.

At dawn happiness returns as the first rays of sunlight hit the dancing ground, the chorus of the Avaete dance, sung by the men, begins, and everyone runs to look. There they are, the stolen boys, sitting in a semicircle around Anacã's grave. Each of them, perfectly painted, with his head covered with a tress of flowers and with bracelets on his arms, waistbands of beads, and little bells on his ankles to mark the rhythm of his first dance as a grown man. Every mother, every sister looks on with fondness and loving memory at the son or little brother who, proud, hardly looks at them: women! Little by little everyone joins in the Avaete dance which takes on a ritual disposition. In the center of the dancing ground, revolving by themselves without leaving their respective places are children in a ring who, a few days before, had received their names and the sacred marks of coraci-maa. Around them, dancing in a larger circle, are the little boys who came to know the evil spirits. Next, dancing in the opposite direction, the circle of those who bear on their faces the fresh scar from the bite of the anaconda. Each of them holds hands with a girl from the opposite band, his best-loved girlfriend. And at last, encircling all the others, holding hands and singing the old chorus of the Avaete, the mature people dance. Keeping always to this arrangement we all dance until nightfall, when we sit in the Great House for the big feast.

The Great House is cluttered with hammocks on all sides. One for each man. Sitting astride or reclining, but always with their feet on the ground, the old Avaetes and the recent converse, leaning toward each other, even as they are served with loving care by their female relations: each one's wife, lover, former lover, mother, aunt, sisters and cousins, daughter, niece, granddaughters, great granddaughters. Each will come here to serve, smile, eat together, even for a short while. Regardless of how many women a man has—whether his sister or his mother-in-law—he will expect them all, one by one. Regardless of how many men had been lovers of one woman, today they all are remembered, cared for, attended to, and loved.

On the floor of the Great House numberless little fires are sparkling, heating up meat, cooking pepperpots, making tisans red hot that are then distributed to all sides. Very slowly, after much delay, morsels are produced, little by little, nice and hot, colored with annatto, in the bottom of black calabashes for the delight of the loved ones.

Oh! Remui, my he-man, don't you remember your lover Anoa, of the Turtles? Eat some of my peppered turkey. Is it still the way you like it?

Hi, papa, it is I, Pinu. I've brought a little stewed midubim for you. Notice how tasty it is.

Falcon Remui, eat more slowly, my old man. And see if you can resist drinking some of this, some of this cassava brew the mangaba juice. We have to eat until tomorrow after nightfall, advises Moita.

Grandfather, I am Mbia, daughter of Uruantapia. I've brought you a little paste made from roast and smoked labba. It's a delicacy, grandfather, with a lovely aroma.

Uncle of mine of the Mairuns, it is I, Inima, little Falcon uncle, drink some of the cajá nut porridge of mine.

Father, wake up, you've eaten too much. Don't fall asleep, father. You need to stand up and stretch your legs, have a look round, then a bit more to eat. Here's my little granddaughter Putir who has brought some guava drink for you.

Remui, old fellow, it is I, Iuicui, I've brought you something from the old times: turtle liver with kill-Devil peppers. You'll love it.

The old guide of souls, Remui, sits, leans back, lies down, sleeps, wakes up, and consumes food and tenderness.

Ah! Anca, my beautiful lover of so many years ago! It's good of you to remember me.

Pinuarana, my little daughter who is already a grandmother, it gladdens me to see you happy like this.

Moita, my little old woman, sit here and eat with me, woman. Must I always go looking for you? Why do you disappear, evading me?

Mbia, my granddaughter, who has given me the pleasure of seeing once again my grandfather Uruanta in my great-granddaughter Uruantapia.

Be careful, girl, don't forget: you are raising a Jaguar, the future chieftain of the Mairuns. Careful. Put strength into his marrow.

Oh! Inima, most beloved of my little Falcons, are you fucking my grandson Jaguar too much?

Putirtai, my pretty great-granddaughter, am I the first man you are serving? Or did that little ocelot Mbia, your mother, make you serve that great jaguar, Jaguar, first?

Inincui, dear sister, they say you are ripening into a beauty, is that true?

On through the night, the day and the next night, we eat, converse and laugh; we eat, we drink, we walk about, we shit; we eat, we drink, we belch, we spit, we vomit, we converse and laugh; we eat, we make love, we dance, we fuck, we sleep, we drink, and we vomit; we eat, we shit, we piss, we fart, we talk, and we listen: we eat, we walk about, we make love, we sing, we dance, we fuck, we sleep; we eat, we drink, we shit, we piss, we cry, and we laugh.

It is a feast of game and fish, of cassava cakes and farina, of tapioca and corn mush, of cassava wine and cashew brew, of meat and manioc porridge with cassareep sauce and pepper. A feast of the mouth and of the nose, of our mouths watering as we are eating and smelling the flesh of animals of the forest, the water, and the air. A feast of delight in chewing and swallowing foods that are salty, peppered, sweet and peppered, sour and peppered, a feast of seeds, roots, fruits, and leaves. Some foods are mixtures of fish and plantain; others are cooked in pots of brownish clay. Many are roasted or broiled over a barbecue of hot charcoal.

The wheel of the Mairun feast gyrates. Maíra and Micura will be there too, making love to the girls, eating, shitting, and laughing. It is certain that the spirits of the dead have also descended to see and watch the joy of the people who eat, dance, sing, and laugh.

Now the men are emptying the rundlets, conserving in their drinking vessels what remains of the cassava wine for them to drink on the dunes of the Iparana. Today, many marriages have been made, unmade, and remade.

THE RETURN

Here I am at last, in Santa Cruz, waiting to go forward, returning.

O God of Rome who illuminates me not
O God of Heaven who seest me not
My God, whom I invoke in vain
My God who refuses my offering
Give me the lost self that I would be
Give me the dignity of a Mairun face
Give me the tranquility of a Mairun soul

Only God, the omnipotent, can help me . . . if God, the omniscient, wants to preoccupy himself with me or whomever he wants me to be.

I am not a soldier returning victorious or vanquished. I am not an exile returning with nostalgia for his roots. I am the other in search of one. I am the result of this struggle to remake ways that have undone me.

I left as a boy; I return as a man. But I am full of disgust with the taste in my mouth. I am consoled only by the thought that the round village is there awaiting me—my little Rome. . . . Perhaps it will not be in the same place, but it will certainly be within the great circle of the Iparana. The people of each clan, inside each house, will have changed. Many will be old. Some will have died during these years and will be visible only to the old guide of souls. Many, born since, will have become men and women. How many sons has my sister bestowed on me? The old chieftain Anacã, my clan uncle, is he still alive? Who will now tie the knot of shame on the members of young men? Is the old guide of souls, Remui my true father, who begot me in the womb of Moita, still alive? Is my old father still carrying out his charge as guide of souls, seeing and talking to the living and the dead? Remui, mystical guide of two communities, genuine high priest of Maíra-Coraci, the Sun, how I long to see you again. My brothers and my sisters, so many of them, of the band of the Yellow Rays of the Rising Sun, what has become of them? My in-laws and step-children of the Blue band, how are they? Who will be waiting for me to be my wife? Who will carry in her womb for the band of the other side my seed of guide of souls?

I am coming back for them; I am returning with a desire to recover a mode of living together that I should never have disrupted. How will they see me? Let it be at least with the same deep tenderness with which I shall regard them. Looking with sweetness at the old age of those whom I knew as mature. Looking with pleasure at the boys of yesterday, the men of today.

Looking with love at all the new people who know nothing of me.

Since I left when I was very young, but thick-boned and covered with firm flesh, they will seek in me a stature I would have had but for all those respiratory problems caused by harsh Roman winters. If it were not for my memory telling me I am who I am; if it were not for so many memories linking me to what I was, I would not recognize myself in this squalid, hunched-over man returning home. Except for the memory that binds us together, what do we have in common? My past could be that of someone else. I have realized the most improbable of my possibilities. I have nothing to do with the boy I once was, or almost nothing. Even less with the man I am to be. I am only an ardent desire to return and to be a little of what I could have been had I not strayed so far.

God the Father, Creator of Heaven and Earth
God the Son, Jesus Christ our Lord
Dying on the Cross, at the wish of the Father, to save us
(To save those of us who would have been saved without Your
  holy blood)
My poor Angel of Darkness, I serve as a rebel against the Lord
Our Lady: uterus of God
God my father, Mairun: Maíra-Monan
(With your huge swelling phallus growing under the earth, like
  a root for all women)
God the Son: Maíra-Coraci, luminous Sun.
Micura, Your fetid brother: gamba-opposum
Mosaingar: man-woman, womb of God
God the Father, God the Son, fallen Archangel
Holiest Mary, Lily of the Lord
Maíra-Manon, Maíra-Coraci, Micura
Mosaingar: mother of the Twins of God
My God of so many faces, I who believe as much as I
  disbelieve.

I pray to each one and to all, I pray and beg in a humble way:
Not to arrive there if not through Your goodwill
No more than to arrive there, if this is Your will
But, if I arrive, that I may be one among all.
Indistinguishable. Undifferentiated.
Unmistakably a Mairun Indian within the Mairun people.

I know well I am raving again with these, my confused prayers. It pains me to think of the hurt they would provoke in old Father Ceschiatti, always full of horror and sadness when I repeated to him one of my crazy invocations. It would hurt me too with a profound feeling of sin, of disaster, of frustration. Today it doesn't matter. I know at last, that today and forever I shall pray like this.

I am two. Two are in me. I am not I; within me is he. He is I. I am he, I am we, and so we have to live. The old confessor will never again have to wait before Mass for me to empty myself of my ego. I too will never again tremble from fright at that hour of truth, the ancient truth, the truth of others. Now I shall live with my own truth, my own muddled truth. God in Heaven, my father and my uncle. God is God and Maíra. Maíra is God.

This is my rod of return to the Mairun, the people of Maíra. There is my position, my place. There I am a man of the band of the Rising Sun: of those who, sitting at the back of their houses at dawn, watch the sun rise. I am one of those who follow with respect its great orbit in the immensity of the sky. I am one of those who sit together every evening, there on the dancing ground, on the other side of the Great House, to watch the sun go down. I am a Jaguar, of the clan that provides the chieftains, of those who never kill a jaguar but who require a pelt from each man who wants to be very much a man. Especially from him who wishes to sleep with one of my sisters, with a Jaguar. I am the reciprocal of the Falcons who live on the other side of the village, behind the Great House. From our house it is impossible to see theirs. From their house it is impossible to see ours. But they and we form a unity, a true we, that deeper we of those who know they can neither live nor die without the other.

There, I, Avá, am the brother, the uncle, the brother-in-law, the father-in-law of a great many men and a great many women. With them I shall live knowing, just by looking at them, who is who, where they come from, what they expect of me, what I am capable of doing, and what I should do in relation to them. Walking through the village among the women or sitting in the Great House flanked by other men, I shall discern and distinguish their nature, as Pacu, as Tapir, as Turtle, as Coati, knowing thereby whether she or he can or cannot marry me or another, or whether it would be tabooed, prohibited, incestuous. Each of them will recognize me as the chieftain-heir, Avá, of the Jaguar house, the direct descendant reincarnating Uruanta, the ancient chieftain, brother of my grandmother Putir who will be reincarnated in the grandson, yet to be born, of my sister Pinu.

All of that I am going to relive. All of that which I struggled to keep alive in me, but which could not live save in memory, now will be relived. All of that tomorrow will be pulsating as life there in the village, for me and for all. There, I will see her, that blue Falcon destined to be my wife.

I will also see and, who knows if I will remember, in the darkness of night on the dancing ground, a public woman. How I would like to have one lying with me here tonight, voluptuously caressing and writhing next to me. They come from the new clans, from those that arrived later. That is why they live on the sides above, the space that the wheel of the village opened for them, who knows how many centuries ago. They are in a certain way inferior. No, perhaps they are not inferior. It would be better to say they are wilder. They are still being tamed. It is said that they entered the Mairun world as prisoners of war. But being a very brutish and cowardly people they could not be eaten. So they remained there, continued to live there, and intermingled with us. One day they learned to form clans like us. Later, it is not known when it could have been, they integrated themselves into the village.

But the situation of the new clans is very special. The guide of souls, guardian of the word, who talks with the dead, never speaks with their dead. It is as if they die definitively, once and for all, here on earth, when they die. There is an important ceremony which they are not allowed to see. They wait until it's over, camped in the bush. Only at night do they enter the village and remain there to watch the very end of the ceremony, but they walk about and look with discretion, as if they were not present. We pass among them and do not see them. Only toward morning do they take their revenge, defeating our champions in hand-to-hand combat. For this they train year round. They are the best wrestlers.

But what I remember are the women who have come from these new clans. They are chosen from among the prettiest girls to participate in the initiation ceremonies of the Mairun youths, two or three each generation. Once declared public women they cannot take husbands. At the conclusion of the ceremonies, they are the most beautiful, the most attractively turned out, because their beauty is the pride of all the Mairuns. They remain for years with a cascade of hair down to the chin, and they flip it back in a most bewitching way. The other women wear bangs.

In fact, they are more feminine than the ordinary women and maybe even more Mairun. Not allowed to be taken as wives, they are as if suspended in the air. Because they make themselves desirable to all men, they are nobody's women. They are everybody's women. They are women unto themselves. Fucking other women does not provoke jealousy in any Mairun women. To the contrary, many wives give their husbands a knife or an ornament, saying, "Go look for Meda, she is so lovely and will be tender with you." Perhaps one night I will have to cover Meda. Meda will be no more. She was older than I, and today she must be ancient.

But other public women will still be there, waiting for me, women who like to fuck and who know all about love. They have their art. Other Mairun women also like to fuck, but their only trick is the glory of keeping, inside them all night, a hard prick that never comes. This is not true of the public women. They know how to make a man spend all his spunk, how to make a man come all night inside. Will I be able to service an ordinary Mairun woman, staying inside her for the entire night? I need only recall my long nights of anguish lying on the cot of the convent with a near painful erection and my conscience burning with guilt. My prayers to the Virgin Mary to help me, to bring me succor, to make me flaccid. I am erect, now and here, on my bed in this pension, as I yearn for a woman. Why am I not going out into the streets to be with a local woman, a carioca? No! I don't want a stranger. And I don't want to come again in my hand or in the sheets. I am saving myself for my Mairun Falcon.

QUINZIM

Juca is worried. He is inspecting the boat noticing that some of the planks that had been well nailed are loose. He even grumbles about scratches on the ancient hull. But his attention is not on the boat. It is on the oblique conversation he is having with Quinzim, bullying him.

"Then the gringo didn't give you anything? He didn't give you a bean? Be careful or I'll turn you inside out, you little shit. I'm not going to pay you anything, not on your life. I rented the boat, and I received a fee. I told you that I would pay you your daily wage. But you've taken too much time; you took the money from the gringo and now you're hiding it. Another thing: I want to know chapter and verse of that story about the white woman dead there on the beach. It has been very badly told. Come on, Quinzim, I want to know all the details."

"Yes, Sr. Juca," Quinzim begins, "as you wish. The men were moving very slowly, staring at the bank the whole time for termites' nests, or ant heaps. I never saw them searching for minerals with that box with dials that isn't a clock which you told me to keep an eye on. I watched very carefully, day and night. If one went out I stayed with the other because I couldn't follow both of them. But I carefully watched what they took with them and what they brought back. I also had a good look at what they had in their boxes, cans, and bags. Samples of minerals? Powder? Stones? Nothing like that, nothing."

"You're trying to make me out to be a fool, aren't you, Quinzim? An idiot for thinking that the gringos want one thing when what they really want is something very different. You piece of monkey shit. You're nothing but shit. Tell me what I told you to tell me. Tell me what you did and how much money you wheedled out of them. Now come clean, you son of a bitch."

"It was just as I've told you, Boss. The men, that lot, were traveling very slowly, without caring if the engine failed."

"And what about that outboard, Quinzim? Are you also going to tell me they carried it to Naruai?"

"That I don't know, Boss. I only know what I saw: the motorboat arrived at the beach at Ibepora. There, close to the airstrip at Naruai. That's where the personal belongings of the dead woman were. I helped the gringos to unload their cargo, and with it the engine. They themselves carried it all to the ranch where they were going to spend the night to take the plane the next day. I returned at once, paddling the boat to here, in Eurebá, to hand it over to Sr. Pio. I then came to wait for you, as you told me, Boss."

"Tell this story straight, Quinzim. Speak like a man, you dog. How did it go?"

"It was just like that, as I've said, Sr. Juca. We traveled look-

ing at the banks from one side to the other. They, stooping
down to look at the ground, looking in front of those sandbanks
on the beach to see if there were any ant heaps there. Principally of those ants that make so much noise, and of a similar
kind capable of great migrations and that have strong jaws, and
of bush ants. They also liked the red and black leaf-cutting ants
and the very big black kind with the terrible bite, the tocandira.
We stopped for two days in Buritzal. Three more in Araverum.
In sum, five days of digging and digging. We worked like mad.
They wanted to dismantle everything so as to discover the trail
of the ants, their little dens, caverns, and underground nests. It
was necessary not to destroy anything, to leave the little by-
ways neat and clean, not to meddle with them. They would put
a glass contraption on top and wait for the ants to return at
their ease, watch the queens, the workers, the soldiers. White
maggots in a hornet's nest, their food moldy. Everything was
filmed by day and night with the use of a light. I had to look
after the generator and the motor to provide juice for the
spotlight. I also had to do some fishing for them and for myself,
because all they ate came out of tin cans, and it gave me serious
diarrhea. It was without end. It's not your fault, Sr. Juca. No! It
was easy. But my daily wage, if you'd like to pay it, that would
be fine. As you know, I'm not doing too well, and the woman
and children are badly off. The only food they have is what you
know about, which you yourself left at the house, and by this
time, for sure, it must be finished. Now, Sr. Juca, all I'm asking
you for is to take me back home and then give me a little hand-
out, whatever you see fit."

"I'm not giving you anything," thundered Juca, "you are a
lousy sneak, Quinzim. You want to take advantage of me. Do
you think I've swallowed that story of working for the gringos
day and night, regardless of your own chores, regardless of your
contract, just for love of their green eyes? Where is what they
gave you? Manelao, do you buy this? And you, Boca, even
though you're an idiot, would you take a contract like this?
Well Quinzim, not Boca, it seems I don't owe you anything, you

son of a bitch. If you'd told me what they paid you, I'd have
discounted it. You didn't tell me that. You didn't tell me because
you got more than what I owed you, you thief. And I warn you,
I'm going to get to the bottom of this. I will still find those shitfaced gringos, you'll see."

"Well, you are within your rights, Boss."

"How many days did you stop on the way up, Quinzim?"

"Only there at Corrutela, where we stopped more than a
week. The gringos met a black man there who knows all about
ants and about the Bible."

"Boy, what kind of tossed salad is this, ants mixed up with the
Bible?"

"Exactly that, Boss, I'm telling you the man is named Xisto.
He came from Crateus. He used to be a corporal; now he lives
there with the cowhands, praying and singing with a Bible in his
hand. He is the sacristan of that other gringo, that Mr. Bob with
the speedboat."

"Then has Bob stopped bothering with the Indians? Is he
starting to convert the backwoodsmen?"

"Yes, Boss. He goes there every month, bringing things. He
distributes booklets, and directs prayers and singing."

"What about the ants, man?"

"It was just as I said, Sr. Juca. The black man, Xisto, knows
everything about anthills—where they are most abundant, the
name of each, how each variety of ant lives, where they work,
everything. He says that even in their kingdom they enslave the
blacks. He talked a lot with the gringos; I sat there listening,
amazed. Later we left for the savanna to look for anthills, to dig
them out and photograph them. We also lost three days while
the gringos palavered with Mr. Bob. They stayed as guests in the
tin house. Not me, I slept by the boat. I wasn't going to be
frightened off by the Xaepes. . . . From there we went straight
to Naruaia. The gringos didn't want to stop at the Mission. We
passed there with the sun at ten o'clock and they told me to
keep on going. That's the truth, Boss, the absolute truth. You've
got to believe me."

"Believe you, Quinzim? That'll be the day!"

"You'll find out some day soon that all I've said is the truth, Boss. The gringos gave me only this flashlight without batteries, a pair of blue denims, and this striped cotton shirt I'm wearing. And these five cartridges here in my hand that I asked for, I don't know for what. If you want, it's all yours. They didn't pay me anything, Sr. Juca. I swear by my mother's soul. But let it be as you wish. I ask you to take me down there back to my home. I'm very worried; I left my woman and children with one hand in front and the other behind. But have it your own way, Boss."

"I won't take you, Quinzim. My boat is not for barefaced liars and swindlers like you. And if your family is that bad, leave it and start another. Women are for making babies and yours is worn-out. Now that you look so sharp, with those shiny shoes you've got—you didn't mention them, but the gringos gave them to you, I saw those shoes on the feet of one of them—with all those new clothes, it will be easy for you to find a woman. In Ibepora, right near Naruai, there are plenty of women all the time. Dóia, for instance, the widow. Help from me, forget it. Beat it, Quinzim, I don't put up with any shitfaces on my boat, especially shitfaced bastards who want to squeeze money out of me with phony sob stories. Isn't that so, Manelao? But first, you shitface, repeat every detail of that story about the beach. Was the woman dead? Was she killed? Was she really white, and young? What was she doing there, with my Mairun people? With whose permission? FUNAI's? Was she a missionary?"

"I don't know, Sr. Juca. I only know she was dead. She died giving birth, to stillborn twins. It also seems that she was young and not something to throw away, no, Boss. Pardon me for saying so, dead, defunct as she was and spread open, she was a pleasure to look at. Fair hair, all hairy down there around her private parts. Her body was plump, her breasts swollen, the big kind. She was lovely. Now, that she was killed: it was the gringos who said that, when they were talking among themselves. They found a lump on her head and some bruises on the temple, also on the neck, but none of those could have been fatal to a woman like that. She died giving birth, there on that beach. The Mairuns say that she had been in the village for quite some time, more than a year, living with them."

"No, that couldn't be! That's impossible!"

"It's so, Sr. Juca. When you passed through the village more than a year ago, she had already been there for some time, living with them." ("Was she really?") "She was there, Boss. She was brought by Isaías, that one who was to be a priest, but she was not his wife, no, Boss. She belonged to no one. This is what I was able to make out. But, as you know, I don't speak the dialect, and the gringos like to gossip about anything. You yourself are the only one who could go there and find out what was going on from those people."

"I know, you fool. And I'm going there, right away. How was it that they received a white woman in the village, got her pregnant, and then abandoned her on the beach? These savages have no mystery for me. That shit Isaías, I still can't make him out. I expected to have a bishop for a cousin, and the pig comes back to live as a savage. It's all a lot of bullshit. Beat it, Quinzim. I didn't like your story, not by a long shot. But don't go far; I'm not giving you room and board, because I'm not stupid enough to look after a coward like you. But I want to know your where-abouts, and I still want to hear every scrap of that story before I go down to Belém. Don't play the fool, Quinzim, thinking you're going to get away with something. You owe me a debt, and I'd go after what's mine even in Hell. You know, my repu-tation isn't a nice one, and there's a reason."

"As you like, Sr. Juca. All my life I've worked for you, ever since I was a boy. Now you doubt me. So be it. But tell them to give me a fishhook, Sr. Juca. A fishhook, a line, and a box of matches, so that I can fish and eat."

"Not even that, Quinzim. Your account with me is closed. Here, only Dóia has credit. I keep more than a hundred families of shitheads alive along this river besides her, and the one to tie me down has yet to be born. It's a time for ripening nuts, Quinzim. A time of plenty up there on the sandbanks, a time for fat turtles, a time for custard apples. Go into the savanna, no lack of food there. Or, do you know only the foods of the forest? Don't worry, the jaguar won't harm you. Not with those four cartridges of shit that you wanted to give me—just show them to him, and he'll run away. All you have to do is show them. Get lost, Quinzim. Let's go, Manelao, this guy is already dragging my ass."

MANON

The drizzle of the night flattens the dust on the dancing ground and washes the atmosphere so that the stench of Anacã is left stronger and more pervasive. It continues to intensify, impregnating everything: pure and sweet. Now it smells blue as well. Who knows why?

The ceremonial is nearing its end. Everybody is asking when there would be another funeral like this. Who is going to live—thinks Teró of the Falcons—who is going to die like Anacã? When would another Anacã come? He lived a long life. It was he who united the Mairuns. Previously, we had lived dispersed, isolated in little villages lost along the beaches of the Iparanã after the slaughter caused by the plagues brought by the Europeans. It was Anacã who brought the people here, to the forests of Black Lake. He pacified enemy groups. He fused dispersed clans. He even restored those shattered clans on the verge of disappearing. Never again will there be anyone like Anacã.

Today, finally, Anacã will be wept for and buried. He will die, at last; for himself, for the Mairuns, for the whole world. The ceremony starts in the morning, very early, when all the people come to sit, forming in an enormous semicircle on the far side of the Great House, to watch for and assist in the rising of the Sun. In front of all of them are Remui, the guide of souls, and Teró; and directly behind them the heralds, Jaguar and Naru, in ceremonial office.

At the center of the circle, easily distinguishable, with his back to the sun, stands the old guide of souls. On his head he wears the greatest of all his headdresses. It is made of feathered arrows that emerge from his head upwards, sideways and backward, forming a sun with rays. It is so big that even when he is sitting he is taller than Teró, who is standing right by his side, carrying on his back the outspread skin of the black puma. Behind him, also wearing tall headdresses, but of lesser presence, are Jaguar and Náru. Jaguar with a headdress of yellow feathers from the tails of golden orioles, mounted like a small sun on a cane framework. Náru with a headdress made from the feathers of hyacinth macaws. In addition, both are wearing labrets, bracelets, and all their other ornaments. They are splendidly painted as well: Jaguar all ruddy with scarlet annatto; Náru, blue-black with the juice of the genipap. The old guide of souls carries only his enormous solar diadem, Teró only the glistening black pelt which contrasts with his body whitened with pipe clay. The great wheel of the Mairun people watch as with the deepest piety, Coraci the Sun is born in front of them, enormous, red, gleaming, out of the gigantic headdress of Remui, the guide of souls, turning the sky blue and coloring the world. The guide of souls then stands up and walks, casting an enormous shadow in front. He walks alone, beneath his giant headdress, to Anacã's grave on the other side of the dancing ground. There, he sits down in his place, in the ceremonial position, to the right of the grave. Teró, Jaguar, and Náru also stand and walk slowly. The two youths sit on the opposite side. Teró remains standing behind the guide of souls. Only then does everyone else rise to regroup around them but now, on the side of the setting sun, forming the great circle of all men, women, and children of the Mairun people.

See everyone in place around him, the guide of souls shakes

his rattle and trills his tiny ocarina; then he hangs both ceremonial instruments around his neck, completely spreads his
arms to their full extension, brings them slowly together, joins
his hands, palms downward, and lowers them, digging into the
soft earth of the grave. He buries them together, slowly, and
begins to break through the crust of mud, shoving it to the
sides. Below this he uncovers a bed of dark, soft mud with an
intense terrible smell. He works now to remove with his hands
that slime underneath, draining with a gourd the thick greasy
and greenish liquid in which the bones of Anacã had separated.
The skull begins to appear gray on the bottom of the grave,
shining in the morning light.

The guide of souls pauses for a moment, wipes his hands clean
on some green leaves, takes his flute from his neck, and trills
again, softly. Everyone stands rigid, attentive, to hear his voice,
low and solemn:

"Anacã, my chieftain, Anacã, today is the day of your
death. Soon your final hour will arrive, Anacã. The hour to
die, definitively, for us. Your feast is nearing the end. We have
danced all dances except the Coraci-Iaci—you know why. We
have held all the contests including the javari. We have eaten
much meat, we have eaten much fish. We have drunk much
cassiri. Your hour has finally arrived, Anacã. For this we are
all here."

Having finished speaking, the guide of souls begins to remove
the bones from the grave. First he takes the cranium in both
hands, empties out the liquified material inside, wipes it clean
with manioc leaves, and puts it to one side on a new mat. Next
he removes the great bones of the legs and arms and pelvis. The
two heralds then begin to help, lifting out and cleaning
the smaller bones of the vertebra, the ribs, the rounded bones of
the feet and hands, and the phalanges of the fingers and toes.

The whole skeleton now gleams on the mat to one side of the
mound of muddy leaves. The guide of souls then stands up and
returns to the Great House. The people disperse. On the dancing ground, only Jaguar and Náru remain, gathering the last

little bones which they take rolled up in the mat to the river. They return hours later, bearing the bones, now whitened by so much scraping and cleaning with sand and water.

The guide of souls, seated on the double-headed seat, sounding his rattle, receives the clean bones set on a new mat. He then calls by name, one by one, the oldest men from each house and gives them the large and small bones. He himself keeps the skull which belongs to his people, the Carcaras, the Falcons.

The men, women, and children of each clan, sitting together in the corner of the Great House that corresponds to them, begin the delicate task of embroidering, with loving care, the large and small bones with minuscule colored feathers, overlapping as in the plumage of a live bird. To facilitate the completion of this magical work, the women weep to the rhythm marked by the rattle of the guide of souls. Now they murmur softly, a plaintive, mournful song. Now they sing a high wailing lament. Now they wail with choked cries, awash in tears.

At a certain point, when the decorated bones shine throughout the Great House like jewels of blue, red, and yellow feathers, the rattle of the guide sounds again, in a new rhythm. The women all stop crying and some of them, the Jaguars and Falcons, walk to the center of the Great House. There they take scarring instruments, teeth of dogfish set in triangular scraps of gourd, and with them proceed to rasp their faces, arms, and breasts, scratching the skin to form an array of fine lines. As the instrument is drawn down, lacerating, what appears at first are simply the white lines. But soon they darken and suddenly shine as red drops, and finally blood runs down the face, the arms, and the breasts. All the rest of the women cry with greater agitation, always to the rhythm of the rattle of the guide of souls.

The mourning is brusquely interrupted by another trill from the guide, and the women who had been standing, bleeding, return to their places. Then the men from the same two clans come to take their places. In turn they take up the scarring implements to bleed themselves. Each of them slashes his skin deeply without saying a word, while sisters and nieces, wives and daughters, from the diverse clans dispersed through the Great House lament, tearing out their hair by the handfuls, weeping and wailing from pain and emotion.

At a new signal given by the rattle of the guide of souls, all the mourning ceases again, and with it the sacrificial scarring and the desperate tearing of hair. Then the old guide pronounces, breaking the silence,

"Anacã is dead here on earth. May he live in the world of Ambir."

Once again he starts to play the rattle in a light, almost joyful rhythm continuing as the clans bring the embroidered bones, feather jewels, and show them with pride to the guide of souls and to each other.

The skull is resplendent in the blues and greens of rare hummingbirds. The long bones of the arms and legs and the shoulder blades shine transfigured, some in the feathers of the royal-sceptered, golden-breasted toucan; others in the red and heavenly blue heraldically striped tail feathers of a bird known only to the most deeply initiated Mairuns. The thick and round bones of the pelvis and spine sparkle in evanescent fields of purple and carmine or glitter in electric colors over off-whites or sparkling blacks. However many bones compose a human body are shining there, scintillating for a moment, illuminated in ineffable colors in the hands that are displaying and delivering them, radiant, to the old guide of souls. He touches the velvet of the feathers overlapping like those on a bird, divines the significance of the delicate gradation of tints and tones, and places them lovingly into a basket of the whitest straw that stands at his feet.

When the deliverance is over, the guide of souls carries the basket of feathered bones outside the Great House by the lower entrance and thence to the trail leading to the Iparana. He walks slowly under the evening sun that throws behind him his elongated shadow and the shadow of his enormous ceremonial headdress. He is already walking along the Iparana path when all the men, women, and children issue from the Great House to accompany and overtake him.

At the beach, Remui enters a canoe full of flowers where Jaguar and Náru are already waiting, one standing at the bow, the other at the stern, each with his navigating stick. When the guide of souls sits in the middle with the basket of bones between his legs, Teró, aided by others who position themselves in front of him, comes with a mast of aroeira, recently cut and stripped of its bark, placing it at the bows in the form of a cross.

The canoe descends with flowers and, containing the basket of decorated bones and the recumbent mast, goes forth, pushed by the poles Jaguar and Teró thrust down the riverbed.

Soon and gradually dozens of canoes carrying the Mairuns are launched, accompanying the funeral. They navigate slowly upriver by means of poles and paddles, up to the opening that leads to the Lagoon of the Dead. They enter, frightening the birds that take off in search of refuge in trees nearby. From there the egrets, spoonbills, and herons watch the arrival of the ceremonial canoe that pauses in the middle of the lagoon to await the others. From these, various men enter the water, swimming with their feather adornments, to retrieve the mast from the canoe of the guide of souls. They then dive with it to drive it into the riverbed, planting it firmly in the Lagoon of the Dead. It rises now above the waters and above the whitish-green floating islands of scraw bog, this mast that bears, tied to its tip, the straw basket containing the feathered bones of Anacã. It is the cleanest, the most beautiful, and the tallest of all the masts of the Lagoon of the Dead.

The canoes withdraw slowly, are paddled backward, so that the Mairuns can continue to see before them the mast of Anacã. The opaque moon rises, veiled in the night that now approaches.

HOMILY

THE MEAL

The fair young woman, tall and slim, is filling out a form at the Hotel Continental: Alma Freire, single, missionary, born in Rio de Janeiro, arriving from Rio. She inquires about the National Foundation for the Protection of Indians and takes a taxi there. On her return she asks the porter how to get to the Air Express office to book a passage to Naruai.

The thin dark man registers at the same hotel: Isaías Mairun, single, seminarian, born in Iparana, Matto Grosso, arriving from Rome. He inquires about the missionary order's house and goes there by taxi. Later, he also asks about taking the plane to Naruai.

The porter points at Alma and says: "That woman is also going to Naruai." They introduce themselves: "Alma . . . Isaías." Sitting in the small lounge next to the bar they drink coffee. Alma is wearing a long-sleeved gray blouse and a long dark skirt. Isaías a black suit with jacket over an ecclesiastical shirt.

She: "Are you Protestant?" He: "No, I'm Catholic." She:

"Are you a priest, then?" He: "No, a seminarian. Are you a missionary?" She: "Not really. I want to, though. I'm preparing for it. That's why I'm going to Naruai, on Monday's plane." He: "It's the only one, they say." She: "Excuse the impertinence, but are you against taking orders?" He: "No, I'm not against anything, no, Madam. Nor in favor."

The waiter serving the coffee asks: "Is Madam the new delegate, the wife of Dr. Espinola?" She answers energetically: "No, God spare me. I'm not a delegate, or anybody's wife. . . ." The waiter insists: "Everyone's asking me for the woman delegate."

They resume their conversation.

"Are you then nearly a priest?"

"An eternal seminarian, that's all."

"May one know why?"

"No, I myself don't know, Madam. Miss. What I mean is, Miss, that's my affair."

"Could I perhaps be of some use to you?"

"Oh! There are so many things. . . . It depends on what you want to help me with. I have an appointment now, Miss. Later I shall be at your service. After all we are both staying at this hotel till Monday and traveling together to Naruai. We will have other opportunities to talk."

They rise to leave, conversing until they get to the elevator. Isaías: "Are you going to stay at Naruai? Do you know the place?" Alma: "I'm going farther, to the Mission of Our Lady of O." Isaías: "Then we shall have plenty of time to get to know each other. I'm going there too."

At dinnertime, Isaías sits down in the restaurant and orders just as Alma walks in and approaches him. "Good evening, Father Isaías, may I sit at your table?" He agrees with a gesture. As Alma sits, she asks: "You have been away a long time, haven't you?" Isaías explains that he has been in Rome, completing his priestly and theological studies. Alma remarks: "You speak with an accent but you have a Brazilian manner, so I figured out that you must have lived abroad. In Rome? I've been there twice. But I was a different person then. If we had met, we'd have had nothing to say to each other."

Isaías inquires with surprise: "And now we have?"

"I, at least, have a lot to say. If you will be so kind as to listen to me."

"Why not! I will listen most attentively, but I don't know that I can be of any use to you. So many years away; so unprepared to help."

"Much more than you may think. But I owe you a personal explanation. I am not going to the Mission at the invitation of the fathers. I am going to offer myself there, at that very place, to demonstrate my desire to serve. I am going to ask them to let me serve in any way I can. My only wish is to wait there for the French nuns who are going to the Mission."

"This is something new. Up to now we have had Italian sisters and a few Brazilian ones, but French nuns?"

"It has to do with a new House that's being founded, Father Isaías. But to return to my problem. I was telling you that I am going to the Mission on my own. I am without the consent of the Order. I am doing this in the hope of making them respect my egoistic desire to put myself at the service of God."

"Excuse me for saying so, Dona Alma, but you are using very grand words: egoism, love, service, God."

"You must forgive me, my enthusiasm sometimes gets the better of me."

During dinner, a page comes to ask Isaías if he is the new secretary to Senator Piaba, from Maranhão, of the ARENA party, and insistently inquires: "Isn't he around somewhere? I'll get a good tip if I deliver this letter to him." "No, I tell you it's not me!" Isaías repeats annoyed, facing Alma once again: "I don't think you are well informed. I have never heard of volunteers in a Mission. Missionary work needs people who have been chosen and who are well prepared. People who are solid. Missionary work isn't wearing a halo. Missionary work is malaria, insect bites, routine. And discipline. It serves God as each day the sins of yesterday are purged—our own and those of others. With hope but without urgency."

"For a missionary you seem rather lacking in ardor, Father Isaías."

"I'm not a priest, Dona Alma, as I said, I am only a chronic seminarian. I have many doubts about being ordained. I am not even sure that it is my true desire. I live in a trance, Dona Alma, if you will forgive the confidence."

"I think I can help you, Father Isaías. Your faith, ancient and battered, needs my modern faith built on hope. We can help each other mutually. You can consolidate in me my vocation as a missionary. I can strengthen in you the courage to serve the Lord."

"Now, Dona Alma, we are both making rather grandiose pronouncements. To begin with, you have been asking, apparently, for my help. Then you also want to help me. I am actually afraid that neither of us can help anyone. As for myself, I must tell you that I, too, am going to our Lady of O without an invitation. But I would like to propose something to you: why don't we abandon this convoluted conversation and talk of simpler things?"

Isaías then speaks of his amazement at this new city, constructed so rapidly. "These modern people seem like the ancient Romans. Everything is strange to me here, stranger than Rome. You see, I left my village when I was a boy, for the Mission. I passed my youth shut up in a seminary in Old Goiás without family or friends, living the same life as the fathers and the sisters. In Rome, for years I lived in similar isolation. Today, on my return, I look with fear at this enormous new world, full of people from everywhere. What kind of country are they making?"

"You spoke of a village, Father Isaías. What village?"

"Oh, I still haven't told you. I am Mairun, a Mairun Indian."

In spite of Alma's exclamation of surprise, which he finds

humiliating, he continues to talk throughout the dinner. Afterward, they leave and walk across the spacious lawns until they
reach the viaduct; they pass below it and continue along the
esplanade of the ministries. Together they see and feel, almost
without comment, the weight of the enormous deserted city.
This Brasília at its most solemn, with its tall white buildings
projected on a sky of fire. They walk for hours, on the grass
and on the asphalt strip along the great avenue, looking silently
at the cathedral while holding hands, at the scattered buildings
of the Ministry of External Affairs—the Itamarati—and at the
Three Powers Square with its grand palaces. They return,
cutting across the thicket behind the ministries. It is already
late at night when they reach the tower. They sit in the dark,
turning to look at the city with its moonlight reflected in the
sky. . . . Isaías, again absorbed in his own thoughts, inquires:

"This is perhaps the Anti-Rome? I learned to think of Rome
as being the city. In Rome, the archetypes of all styles, at least
of Western styles, were born and remain. But there is nothing
of Brasília there, not even a hint of it. Will Brasília be a new
creation, the new style of a new man? What is being announced
here? A canon? The canon of civilization burgeoning in the
jungle?" He asks Alma if she also perceived Brasília as the city.

"Not at all! Brasília is Oscar's joke and Lucio's fantasy. They
complied with Kubischek's request, 'I want a city that baffles
the imagination!' He got it! Brasília baffles everyone. You, too,
are stunned by it, aren't you?"

Isaías is silent again, rekindling his self-inquisition.

"What do I know? I only ask if this monumentality is solid, if
it is going to endure. Is Brasília capable of maturing so that one
day it will have beautiful and moving antiquities like the Roman
ones? Or is it only a Martian encampment destined to grow old
and dwindle away? They say that our tropical climate is not
propitious for lasting works. It is true our climate intensifies
life, but it renders it more voracious, more fugitive. Here in
Brasília it is not like that. This climate is of a desert, cold and

dry. The people are beginning to blossom. The forest is this fragile bushlike glass. Here, almost anything can be created to endure. It must endure."

"For me, this is the new Eternal City."

"And yet why should it last? No one builds a house thinking it will be a monument. The terrible thing about Brasília is that it was born old. Only its clothing is new. Looking into these apartments, one sees the same classes as there are in Rio: civil servants, bureaucrats, worried only about their pensions, their salaries, and their retirement to Rio. No one is born here. No one loves it here the way one loves Cosme Velho in Rio.

"And yet you've left there, to seek other horizons. For me, Brasília signifies a great deal. I doubt if a similar world exists anywhere else at all." And he continues trying to put his astonishment into words.

"Brasília today is like the Rome of the Popes who built the Holy See for those who would view it with eyes of the past. It is necessary to wash ones eyes to see Brasília. Or perhaps, Brasília, upon being seen, washes our eyes."

"No, Father. Brasília is a display of fireworks. It only sparkles. It lives and grows because there are no mines in California that can compare with that national treasury when it comes to finding gold. The salaries alone that they pay out here would buy I don't know what."

Isaías, self-absorbed, agitated, searches for himself:

"Brasília returns me to the Mairuns, to our myths of creation. What is most sinister has a place here. Brasília is the Mairun world transfigured. The worst of our world is here converted. Does it thrive? This region where the Iparana rises is for us a kind of hell; it is the mouth of the subterranean world: the abode of Mairahú. Here the only residents are supposed to be enormous black dogs with gigantic mouths, guardians of Maíra-Monan, my Father-God—ingenuous, ferocious, capricious. It frightens me to think that the abode of Maíra-Monan is now exactly the navel of Brazil. Any Mairun would have advised against the construction of a new capital in this place.

For us, everything good must exist down by the mouth of the Iparana, where Ivimaraei, the Earth without Evil, our lost paradise, lies—the lost kingdom promised to those who are desperate beyond hope. Let's go back, Dona Alma, it's late. We have a long way to go."

They descend from the Tower bumping into couples gently caressing each other in the dark corners of the landings. They return in silence, each one self-absorbed, submerged and reduced within themselves, with delight and disgust. Alma thinks about the strange experience of passing hours in the company of a man who doesn't feel obliged to show signs of desire for her. She surprises within herself a disposition to be provocative. No, she thinks, that business was right for the other, not me.

Isaías wonders about the significance of a woman who goes and a man who comes along the same road. They need only pass each other and continue ahead. But it seems that the encounter will be prolonged. Tortuous? Before departing from the Tower they stop for a moment in the esplanade to look, once more, at the great arch-axis of the city resplendent in the light.

MAIRAHÚ

Nanderuvuçu ou petei, pytu avytepy añou ojicuaã

In the beginning, only the eternal bats flew in the infinite darkness. Then came our Creator, the Nameless One, who, alone, discovered himself as such and waited. When the hour came, he joined his hands into a conch, blew his breath into it, opened his eyes, and shot from them a thin beam of light. In the twilight of that serene gentle breeze He went about inventing creations.

He began by making highlands and lowlands and supported them with shores. Then he opened rivers and lagoons. Next, he put into the new waters the first creatures, the juruparis, his favorites. He gave them the jacuí, the living flute, so they would have music; he also gave them fish for fishing and even land so they could eat to their satisfaction. The juruparis themselves are fish above the waist and human below. It was also to them that the Nameless One gave the night that slept at the bottom of the deepest waters. They are evil, perverse, wicked.

The Old One created in turn the curupiras who are around there even today, hidden in the forest. They are incomplete people. One is missing a leg, another has feet turned back to front. This one has only one eye, that one has eyes out of place. Their occupation is to eat the souls of those who get lost at night in the forest. They are ill-omened, dangerous, treacherous.

Only after making the juruparis and the curupiras did the Old One learn to create real people, whole people. He then created our forebears, the Mairun Ambir. But he made them without any badness whatsoever. They were neither men nor women; they were all equal. They didn't have ass holes; they ate and vomited through the mouth in order to eat again. But they each had a vulva with teeth like the mouth of a piranha which was only good for fucking with the Creator. Their prick was a snakeroot that grew under the earth. It sufficed to knock three times on the ground for the prick of Father-God to emerge there, hard and ready. Whoever coupled with it received and gave pleasure to the Nameless One. Only afterward, they had to urinate into a pot. After five days, that urine would have fermented, creating a small child the size of a minnow that grew slowly in the water they poured over it every day.

It was also Mairahú who created all the animals. He drew each animal in the sand, elaborating it with great care until he liked it. He then blew his breath on the design, and the animal would rise in amazement. He then frightened the animals off, dispersing them: Shoo! Shoo!

But they were not animals like those of today. All the creatures lived in villages and spoke their own language like human beings. To each of them the Old One gave a present to be proud of. The king vulture received fire; the deer, salt. A little blue bird, the honeycreeper, won pepper; the toad, tobacco. The tayra became master of honey; the spider, of cotton; and the macaw, of annatto. Each good thing was given to one animal who would not share it with anyone.

That world of the Old One was not very good. There was neither day nor night, only twilight. And there was little food. There were neither men nor women: they were all equal. The worst was that the Old One liked to play cruel tricks on his creatures. He wanted only to amuse himself, but the little people suffered badly. Sometimes he sent a flood that would inundate everything, and the people, the animals, and the curupiras had to struggle to avoid becoming frogs. At other times he caused fire to rain; the trees and the thickets would burn. The people, animals, and the curupiras suffered horribly. But things were always good for the juruparis who lived in the water. Through floods and cataclysms of fire, the juruparis were always all right, watching from the midst of their lagoons and laughing heartily at the sufferings of the little people. Back then the Old One nearly lost his breath from so much laughter. The noise of each cackle became thunder and lightning. It filled the hearts of those little people with dread.

THE LIPS

The Douglas DC-6 flies low in the morning mist above the high hills of the Iparana. At times, it sinks into air pockets, alarming the passengers who are jolted violently. It flies almost empty: Isaías and Alma occupy, by themselves, the whole aluminum bench welded to one side of the fuselage. On the other side is the family of a postal official going to Cachimbo.

Alma wonders why she is frightened when she is not afraid of death. Twice I've tried to kill myself, she recalls, but this flight will be the death of me. Not the end of the existence I have known until today, but a brusque, brutal interruption. Why do I feel so much dread?

Her fear is enormous, above all when the aircraft, passing through clouds, shakes and vibrates like a tin can bumping along a stony road. She watches Isaías beside her, staring through the oval window at the little world of the savanna below, with its stunted vegetation dirtying the fields. She is irritated by his tranquility. Poor devil, she thinks and almost says, that little mosquito face shows no sign of fear. Does it ever? Why, dear God, am I following him? But I'm not following anyone. With him or without him I would still be here in this damned creaking plane.

It begins to rain. The raindrops falling on the fuselage make a terrifying noise. The steamed glass prevents him from seeing anything outside, and Alma is irritated even more when she sees Isaías staring at an invisible landscape. We are flying through a cloud, she thinks; any minute lightning will strike this shitty aircraft. Her fear mounts, and she grabs Isaías's arm. He throws her a glance and quickly turns back to the hazy vision of the grayness below.

I wish the rain would stop, Alma sighs. I don't want to die now. Or here. Or in a crash below. She looks at the quiet children, fastened to their seats on the other side, and feels ashamed. Could they know that I'm dying of fright? Of course, when I'm weeping with desperation. Why am I not praying, my God? I never pray when I need to.

Strapped to the bench, pressing against the seat belt, terrified, she awaits the next jolt. If she could get out of here she would travel by foot across the savanna, she consoles herself. It might take one year or it might take two, but it would be better. What difference would it make, Alminha? It is necessary to accept death when it comes, she tells herself, and replies, but I can't, I don't want to die now. What I must do is stop thinking of death and disaster. Positive thought: everything will be all right, everything will be all right. We are going to get out of this. But I can't . . . my whole body aches, and now this, my God, this nausea. Ahhh . . . I've vomited in the aisle. Everyone will see what I had for breakfast. Why should I care? Shit on anyone who is disgusted.

The aircraft reaches, at last, the end of the turbulence, and continues to wing through the tranquil morning. But Alma is still terrified. Her blind fear has unleashed an anxiety that now persists. Today has given me a taste of my last day. It is a premonition. The weather is better. But it's a trick. Behind this fair spell is the reality of my death. There won't be a tomorrow. And I will have died for nothing, gratuitously, without deserving my death. Why do I have to be so theatrical about everything? Today is a day like any other, and I am flying. The aircraft is swaying a little. The whole world is calm, the children are tranquil, are even smiling and eating biscuits. . . . Dear Lord! What a horror! I'm going to vomit again. Now this taste of bile in my mouth.

Isaías gives her a bit more attention, then turns again to watch at the earth below; he is sad and pensive. Alma broods: to die isn't what's worst, it's this anxiety of waiting for death. Worse still is this bitter taste in my mouth and the queasy acidity in my stomach. I could die soon, everything could explode all at once —I, this plane, the world. Finishing with me, finishing with everyone, finishing, too, with this horrible shit.

"Isaías, say something!"

"What, Alma? We are approaching. You are going, I am returning."

Although the muscles of her entire body are tense, Alma forces herself to admit that the plane is now flying smoothly. It even seems pressurized instead of that old tin can from Air Express. Perhaps it was good to have been afraid, she thinks; fear has made the moment more valuable. What a serious moment of shit! But more valuable for what? Let me think about something else.

What is Isaías feeling? He has hardly said a word during the whole trip. I think he is more frightened than I am. That fixed stare down below is a pretense. But he hasn't vomited. What can he be seeing? His soul has flown through the window. It must be crouching down there under one of those tiny little trees or on the bank of that creek, testing the water with a finger to see if it is cold.

Isaías, hidden within himself, hums: "Pan-ge lin-gua glo-ri-o-si Cor-po-ris my-ste-ri-um."

He is sad, ugly and sad, poor thing. No one would ever think he was an Indian. No one would imagine an Indian so thin. The only thing alive in him is his burning look. He seems calm when he speaks, but it is only self-control. It is a defense. In truth, he is as much in despair as I am. No, he is disillusioned. So what? Disillusioned or desperate, it comes to the same thing. I see him clearly now: he is a tiny bit of a man, insignificant. It's a good thing he is the way he is: there will be no temptation. We will be like siblings, marching together in fraternity. He to recuperate, I to find myself. Words, more words. Instead of feeling, of living, I talk, I proclaim. Nor am I capable of thinking on my own. I know only to worry myself sick over this confusion of intentions and wishes. What is certain is that I am standing in front of a new door, a new door that will open for me. But open on what?

Oh, My God, this flying contraption will be the end of me. It's creaking again. I wanted a simple life, without anxieties, without contradictions. What I've wanted is so simple. I want to be a person with a name, a face, always the same; today, tomorrow, every day. The same for me, for the whole world, always. But a person that others see and consider necessary, a person who needs others but who always helps. That is all I ask for. What a fright! My God! Spare me this, My God! I have to . . . no, I don't have to do anything; I'm not going to suborn God. But this fear, this fear will finish me off. And now the children are eating again, chewing and chewing. I can't help myself, I'm going to vomit my intestines, my stomach, my liver, ahhh . . .

Isaías gives Alma more of his attention, trying to distract her: "I don't think we'll be late in arriving."

He leans over to examine his pocket watch hanging on a chain, and he shows her the time; it is almost eleven o'clock. Alma, clutching his arm, begins to calm down. But not her stomach, which is still spinning, empty, in spasms of nausea.

What an awful flight, my God, and in Your service. I need to think about serious matters. Here I go—where? I know there are. . . . What I will no longer do is go to bed, eyes closed, anyone who comes my way; nor, my eyes open, with one or a few. But I'm not frigid anymore. And I have not yet taken a vow of chastity. I am going to have desires. I must think about this. I need not give it up. I can give of myself in another way, to give out the kindness within me. To mean something to the others. Not exactly that, not that kind of surrender, as in Rio. For months I thought it was important to gain spiritual strength through the most contrite prayers in preparation for the hour when my faith would be put to the test. Later, I understood that I myself would have to search for my own challenge. This is what I'm doing. I cannot fall back into the old life of offering myself freely. Manecilla was my nickname. Sure, it was Nara's wickedness, but I must admit that Manecilla was what I was. Now I know that to give or not to give is not a program for anyone. The problem is to find a cause in which I will be strengthened, a cause that has a sense of mission. Not to gratify me, but to allow me to serve. And, above all, to avoid at all costs returning to that solitude. To arrive at this, there is no other road but communal human life, profound and true. I could even see giving myself to someone if that were the case, if it were spontaneous, if it didn't compromise me. Even to this mosquito face here; if he begged me, I'd accommodate him. But it is necessary that this not be important. Or, on the contrary, that it be important to the cause.

Hold on, I must be mad, daydreaming like I used to back in Rio. What I need to do is invent a new mode of being: proper, just, the good mode of life. No of living with him (God help me!) but with everyone. Not that I want to be an example. I didn't come into the world to be a model. I have no originality whatsoever. But I'm not made of iron either. What I want is simply for the whole world to love me, even if this world is a little world of shit. This is my weakness. My soul expands or shrinks, fills up completely or empties itself, depending on how I am treated. If I am just given the time of day, I will almost burst from joy and goodwill. But if no one pays me attention I teeter on the edge of annihilation. I only want to be seen and treated as a person among people, to live with them, to give and to receive, in an agreeable way. There can be a grain of suffering because that is a part of life. But it should be suffering that is necessary, not the futile anxieties of endless anguish, of bottomless depression. I must not fall into that again.

Here I am in this flying contraption, burning to free myself forever from depression, tedium, self-loathing. But will I have the strength to do so, my God? I have to. Behind me is the old life already lived and wasted, worthless. I have no past because I don't want any part that was mine. But I have a future, that which I am going to create with my hands and my heart, beneath the light of God, our Father. This faith that lives within me is now telling me that it is worth living the life of God's little creatures, like me, like him.

Isaías leans toward Alma to mention that the plane seems to be descending. They look out. Naruai must be that tiny, red rectangle, remote, drawn on the savanna, with a small shed to one side. He had been expecting a small city. She too.

Alma controls the nausea provoked in her by the descent and continues to brood: I had the courage to leave that world behind. Now I must have the courage to face this one. I am going to open that door come what may. I know what lies behind me: it is a world of people devoid of souls who offer their bodies as compensation. As for me, that is over: no more extended arms, offered bodies, giving and begging. Now I'm going forward, with the nuns or without them, in search of a new life.

And what if no one here needs me? No! That is impossible! My
God, could there be someone in this wilderness, this vast and
empty world, who would refuse my offering? Refuse it as useless, unnecessary? Perhaps. No! Will there be a place for me?
There has to be! Where there is so much poverty, hunger,
helplessness, two hands are welcome help. But is there hunger
here? Perhaps not. I am two hands and a mouth. What are two
hands worth? It depends. But not all hunger is hunger for bread.
Isaías himself is here, so ugly and so shy. He needs understanding and affection. With him (who knows?) I might be able to
realize my better self. Through him, I could learn to be useful.
They could let me live among them and accept me, and I could
learn to become necessary. Here or anywhere else. But let it be
here, my God, because this is the place I have chosen.

The plane lands, bouncing along the bumpy strip, and taxies
toward a thatched shed. The pilots peer out of their cabin,
muttering:

"Antão is not here. Could he be sick?"

"It's the first time he has ever failed to show up," replies the
sergeant, "and today, when we have brought him passengers."

The old Douglas stops at last in front of the shed. The fuselage
rumbles, the motor coughs a few times, and the propellers finally come to rest. The sergeant rolls the back door of the
cockpit open and, looking at Isaías, says jokingly:

"The city of Naruai—we've arrived!"

Outside only three potbellied little boys who dart happily
from side to side of the plane can be seen. Isaías and Alma disembark, jumping from the door to the ground. They take their
suitcases from the sergeant's hands; they walk away and stop,
looking from left to right, searching for someone.

"Hey, priest," the sergeant yells, "move off with the girl to the
edge of the strip, we're going to take off. We have to get to
Cachimbo early, and this airstrip is kind of short. The house is
about three kilometers further below, on the bank of the
Iparana. Those little boys will show you the way. Good-bye!"

"Thank you, sergeant. Have a good trip!"

THE RIVER TRADER

The glory of the sun rising from the water. The Iparana, a gleaming band of light, incandescent, gilding the brown sand of the beaches. In the forest, on both sides, it is still absolute night. Quinzim, abandoned there alone, advances toward the beach with his back to the boat, the sun lighting up his face. He does not want to turn around. He does not want to see the motor which he hears buzzing, propelling the boat beyond the dead water, to the current, and from there to the long reaches of Pará. He guesses Juca's intention: he will leave me here at Ibeporã in the place of Antão the pal who had disappeared in the lagoons while searching for others. Traveling in the boat are Juca, Manelão, and Boca.

Manelão: "The savages fucked the white woman till she died. Shameless shits."

Juca: "No one knew about her, and they hardly talk about the return of Isaías. Anything can happen in this Iparanã of the Indians. I didn't even know. So, my relative returned, bringing a woman for others. Who can understand their stupidity? I have to take a look. I don't like stopping at the village; I might quarrel with my relatives. But I have to keep tabs on what is going on along this river."

Manelão asks Juca to explain how he is related to the Mairuns.

Juca: "It was my father who tamed those savages. People used to say that he worked for FUNAI, which back then was called the S.P.I. It was he who pacified the Mairuns. They were all very wild. That's the way it was; it's all written down somewhere. But they only pacified them, pacified them and let them run wild. It was my father who was assigned by the government to live near them, to take charge and calm them down. He grew

old, living there where the FUNAI post is now. In those days
there were no shops or stalls, not even a river trader, because my
father would not allow it. Those were the orders from Colonel
Rondon. But then the S.P.I. was closed down. My father then
realized that this effort was not civilizing anybody and that he
too was lost. He used to bring merchandise and give it free to the
Indians, because they didn't know how to make anything. It was
afterward that they started producing. My father got rich and
the Indians as well. But then there was a crisis and they lost
everything. My father had a store full of balata but couldn't sell
any of it. The crisis was ugly. He died, but he left behind him a
Mairun woman with a big belly. She was Panam, my mother. I
was brought up in the village as an Indian. But I knew; Panam
kept telling me every day that I was a white. I left as a boy to
accompany a boat trader, Toninho, father of Miss Coló. It was
he who started me out in life. When my luck improved, after
the death of my patron, I sent someone to look for Panam. She
didn't want to come; I had to bring her by force to give her
treatment. She was very sick; she died in my house. She is
buried there in Creciuma with an adobe urn on top of her
grave. Every other year I have it whitewashed."

Juca lights a cigarette, takes a drag and continues with relish:

"At that time there were countless Indians around there.
Every day of a voyage you could see a village on one side or the
other, on that Iparanã of the Indians, as it was called. Each village had more than twenty houses in two circles around the
Great House. Already, in the time of my father and of my
boyhood, this had started to decline. What finished off those
Indians back then was measles and influenza, then gonorrhea and
those other illnesses which they still have. Once upon a time,
they were robust; they didn't even know what a toothache was,
and the villages were full of children. It was a joy to see them,
they say. But they were wild. What my father did to tame them
after years of skirmishes was to appear suddenly, naked as the
day he was born, in the midst of a group of Mairuns, taking
them completely by surprise. What a fright! Seeing a little man

with nothing—naked, unarmed—there in the middle of them, the
Indians arrived and would have their first parley. From then on
my father could go there even clothed, and later armed, because
the news soon ran from village to village. But the Indians tell this
story their own way. According to them, it was they who
tamed my father, with great difficulty. Through him they got
to know other whites who weren't coming to attack, shoot, and
kill people."

Boca: "Then you yourself are a half savage, aren't you, Boss?"

Juca: "What savage, you little turd. You're the savage, stolen
as a boy by the Epexãs. Fool, don't you know that what counts
is the blood of the father? There you are, trying to be people
you're not, even though on account of your father and mother
you're an Indian and an Indian you'll be. But I have Mairun
blood, yes indeed. I even have rights according to their law
which is matriarchal, and Elias agrees. I even believe that I am
the true Mairun chieftain, because our family, the Jaguars, is the
one that always supplies the war chiefs. The position has now
been assumed by the so-called Isaías, who was carried away by
the missionaries to be a priest and who has now come running
back. But he wasn't good enough to be a priest; he'll be hopeless
as a chieftain. The new chief ought to be Jaguar, my nephew.
But he is still too young for the office. Since Anacã died, Teró
has been in charge, but that is not in accordance with the law.
They need a chieftain by right. I could demand my rights,
planting myself flatly in the village with some good men, well
armed, if I had the backing of the government. But I don't want
to hear about that. Especially now that the Indian population
has dwindled, and FUNAI in Brasília decides everything. Now
being Chief isn't worth shit. After all, I'm not a savage: my
father was a white man and the mother just a sack in which
the semen of the man grows. The best job nowadays is to be
agent of a post, like Elias; he gets a salary every month from the
government, and doesn't have to do anything. Nor do they
want him to do anything. As my friend advises: I can't, I
shouldn't interfere in the customs of the tribe. But the Mairuns

have about had it. In less than ten years they'll vanish from sight, without leaving a trace. That great world of theirs will come to an end, disappear. Only those will remain who can get out of the village in time and become productive."

Boca: "And their wealth, Boss, the money they've collected, where is it?"

Juca: "They didn't have any money. What they had were plenty of utensils, cloth, and bead ornaments which my father used to bring for them. Nothing was left, because these idiots have the custom of burying with the dead everything that belongs to them. Supposedly so they can use it in that heaven of theirs, that other world. But what's for sure is that no one can collect that way. And, even if they did, those savages wouldn't know what to do with it. When the good times ended, wealth remained only in the cemetery. The cemeteries are full of rusty old sewing machines marking the graves. Buried with the remains are those fat, blue porcelain beads, a kind you don't see anymore. Once, some time ago, I got hold of a few of these and went to the village to try to sell them. But the Indians didn't want even to look at the beads, thinking that I'd disinterred them. They started calling me Panema, the ill-fated one, which is why I quarreled with Anacã. It was a lie: I had bought those little beads in Belem; they came from other Indian cemeteries. The wealth of my father's time ended with the crisis and the dying out of Indians and animals."

The boat arrives at last at Prainha after hours and hours of travel. The three men walk to the tumbledown hut of the old Mister that the Xaepẽs had set fire to years before. Boca lights a fire to grill a fine catfish hooked by Manelão. They drink a beverage made from manioc flour sweetened with rapadura sugar provided by Juca, and the talk continues.

Juca: "In the good times, in the beginning, what my father bartered for with the Indians was a weak kind of rubber yielded by those trees down below. They collected it by chopping down the whole tree and letting the milk run out on the ground where it coagulated. Later on, this trade slackened, and business

turned to turtle egg oil and egret feathers. Here, at that time,
flocks of snowy egret would darken the sky when they flew
overhead. They've disappeared. I don't know if it was an epi-
demic, like what happened with the Indians, or productivity
that did it. For a long time then plumage was the best merchandise on the Iparanã. It was exported in bulk, I don't know
for what. The feathers had to be clean, showing off their natural
whiteness, and had to remain attached to the skin. Especially
those fine quills from the nape. Only the Indians knew how to
catch and treat the white egrets. They killed them with arrows
with small stones as points so that the birds were knocked out
and did not bleed. Then they peeled off the skin complete with
feathers and quills, using a sliver of bamboo as a knife and
blowing to separate the skin from the flesh. Before the egrets,
the best business was in turtle-egg oil. There used to be a great
number of turtles, and countless numbers were exported. At the
beginning of summer, which is when the turtles produce, the
Indians kept paddling up and down the river waiting for the
turtles to emerge from the water onto the beach to lay their eggs.
They then collected all the eggs and killed the turtles, opening a
hole in the shell to take out the balls of fat they have there. The
eggs and the fat had to be cooked to purify the oil which was
then put into kegs. It was all leaving, exported. At first to be used
as fuel in lamps, they say. Then, in my father's time, the oil was
exported for Chinese food. What's for certain is that they exhausted all that was easy and lucrative. For us, nothing remained
but alligator skin, and now it's getting scarce. And an occasional
otter or ocelot pelt, and you know to what great lengths I have
to go to collect these. What could make us some money is
dried arapaima meat which those lazy Mairuns can produce in
quantity when they have a mind to. If that idiot Elias didn't stick
his nose in everybody's business I could put this bunch to
work."

Boca: "In spite of this, you must be rich, Boss: three boats,
two Johnson outboard engines, a shop there in Creciuma and
Dona Coló, a lovely woman."

Juca: "More respect, you son of a bitch. Dona Coló is a dried out arapaima, I know. But she is my woman, so have some respect. But me rich? Get out of here! You backwoodsmen only think I'm rich because you've hardly ever left the Iparanã even for a trip to Belém. You don't know the world. If you knew Rio, Brasília, or São Paulo, you'd know a little about life. You'd know what it means to be rich. The way we live is a disgrace. Compàred to the rich there, even I am shit, like you are compared to me. What I make in a year, one of those assholes could spend in a day in one of those fancy hotels full of beautiful whores. But that won't go on for too long. The price of skins is rising. I'm going to work like mad this year; I'm going to make that bunch of monkeys on the riverbank wonder why they were born if not to come up with the otter and ocelot pelts I want. This is the second year that I've fattened those fools with provisions. Those who know how to hunt are going to have to produce. I'm giving them a little time, but I'm through with gentleness. I'm going to lean hard on them. Are you listening, Manelão? Hard! Sure they can't pay all at once, but I'll go up and down again and again until these bushmen of the riverbank see it's time to deliver the otter and ocelot pelts. I'm going to pull my feet out of the mud, Manelao."

Manelão, who was cooking, fills a calabash with tapioca pudding, peppered and rich with fat, adds some yellow slices of catfish, and hands it to Juca. Sitting on the sand they eat with gusto. Manelão takes out of his bag a little tin flute and begins to blow a little music having the effect of a lullaby. At the same time, Boca is slinging the hammocks between the blackened stakes of the broken-down hut that had belonged to the Mister, and he murmurs, disgruntled, "One day those Xaepẽs will finish us off here. Why the stupid valor of sleeping here, begging for arrows to be shot at us? I, who am not so brave, nor much else, I'm going to sleep in the boat."

MAÍRA

One day, Ambir the Old wanted to experience his creations. He belched and hurled the belch into the world so it could become his son. The belch circulated lazily through the air, navigating the darkness and looking at the little things that were hotter and were throbbing, alive, there below. It then saw, in the midst of the twilight, some larger beings that stood out, that were imposing.

They were scattered trees. The belch descended on one of them and penetrated its trunk. From inside there, it began to test how it feels to be a tree. It lowered itself by way of the roots, and along with them it consumed earth and drank water. Afterward, it took an erect pose, with the trunk standing tall, proud of itself, rising and branching out. It circulated with the sap and felt, there at the top, the great fronds of innumerable leaves fluttering in the wind.

For a long time Maíra enjoyed that state of being with branches and leaves, the feeling of being a tree. He liked it. Especially the palm trees which rise so erect to open into fans at the very top. It gave him pleasure to spiral his way up the trunk, feeling the pain of the scars left by so many fronds that had died to enable the palm tree to grow and yield coconuts.

From that great mantle of forest He caused the birth of another, and then more and more. So he could have a keener feeling of the world of the trees. So it was that he made the great forest which grew and grew. Maíra was now the savage jungle covering everything with countless trees. Through them he experienced soils of different tastes, the cold of subterranean waters, the song of the rivers, the tranquility of the lagoons, but above all, the air and its sputtering breezes. For eons Maíra grew greener and greener, feeling the world as a forest and making the forest grow all over the world.

The son of the Old one, still unborn, multiplied itself this way, for the first time, like a tree or forest. Later, they say, he experimented with various other beings, but he always returned to the great leafy being that gave him the most pleasure: the forest. With the forest he extended himself, hurling more fronds into the air, more trunks toward the sky, and more roots into the ground.

The son of God was there, dispersed in the forest, when one day he saw passing close by our ancestor, Mosaingar, who attracted his attention. Maíra liked him and wanted to see the world through his eyes. He descended, dressed himself in the skin of Mosaingar, and, deep inside him, he made a hole for himself, a womb. There, seated, he perceived the symmetry of the right and left sides with everything duplicated but different, inverted, of that grandfather who would become his mother. He felt at first the strangeness of that body of smooth skin, devoid of hair but hairy in places. Then the feet, also naked, without shoes, thick-skinned, gripping the ground with the toes spread apart and flexible. He admired the two legs, supporting by themselves the body, erect and slim. He liked the two arms extending into opposite hands that opened into agile fingers and ended in nails without the aggressiveness of claws. With pleasure he tested the amplitude of the chest with its respiratory bellows.

Enchanted, he then discovered the mobile head with its openings for seeing, hearing, smelling, and tasting. He stopped there more fully to enjoy Mosaingar through her senses. Through the eyes he saw the darkness of the world, the absence of color. Through the ears he heard and recognized the noise of the wind rustling in the forest. He also heard the distant music of the Juruparís, coming from the bottom of the waters. Through the nose he smelled stenches and fragrances, all of them faint. Through the skin of Mosaingar he felt the hot and cold waves of the world. He then experienced, with pleasure, how the body as a whole works, knowing how and where each of its innumerable parts functioned. Finally, he gradually savored, with the whole mouth, the pleasure of eating things of all tastes. The only thing he disliked was the aftertaste lingering in his mouth after he vomited. He ended by feeling the entire body again, from the tips of the outspread toes to the bristly hair, from the grainy texture of the tongue to the dentulous vulva. He believed that it was well made. He recognized that Mosaingar was the finest creature of the Father-God. But there inside, he also thought that it could perhaps be improved.

Then Maíra begged Mosaingar to be his mother, who would be able to pick and taste all the fruit directly in front of her. Ambir the Old was annoyed. He said no, and beat his belly protesting:

"A son still unborn does not speak."

Maíra too was annoyed. He grabbed the viscera of Ambir and started pulling them again and again to make him obey. Finally, Mosaingar, unable to stand the pain, picked that fruit for biting, chewing, and swallowing. Mosaingar recognized that it was good, that it could be eaten.

Soon thereafter, Maíra wanted to experience the shape and essence of a flower. It was a very difficult thing to do. Mosaingar said no, he did not eat flowers. Maíra answered that he wanted to see not eat. Mosaingar said no, he would not wear out his eyes looking at a flower. Maíra said he wanted only to smell. Mosaingar said, "No, I don't smell flowers." In the end, Maíra again had to force Ambir, pinching his tripes until he picked a flower to admire and smell. So, only by using Mosaingar's eyes and nose could Maíra smell the flower. He liked that.

Maíra was involved in getting to know the world of old when he saw, running through the bush and making funny faces, a little animal: that stinking little opossum Micura. Maíra found it amusing; he liked it and immediately thought: "Here is the one who will be my twin brother."

He called with all his strength for the opossum to enter the hole in the belly of Ambir. But Mosaingar did not want Micura to enter; she tightened up, closed her legs, flexing the muscles of her thighs. Poor Micura, complying with the will of Maíra, struggled and struggled. Mosaingar was screaming no, beating Maíra in the stomach and biting Micura with the piranha teeth of her cunt. Maíra lost patience and had to break the teeth from inside to allow his brother to enter. At last, Micura found his way in and liked the sweet warmth inside. He remained there curled up, looking at Maíra and Maíra looking at him.

The two stayed, conversing and growing. Sometimes they quarreled. One day Maíra complained that the world outside was too ugly, too dark, too sad. Because of this he wanted to return and live in the abode of the Nameless One. He continued grumbling and lamenting and started to cry, they say. Micura would listen, curled up in his little corner of Mosaingar's womb. Afterward he said, "That world outside there is mine. I have no other. I'm going outside to live in it. I'm going to do whatever I can. My abode is here. Back there, there is nothing. I don't cry; I fight."

Maíra stared at the little warm creature all curled up at his side; his brother and his son. He admired that courage to live, appreciated it and thought that perhaps he could improve on the creation of Maíra-Ambir. Then he related to Micura that he had often set out for the outside in a variety of guises. He never set foot on the ground. It wasn't worth the trouble—so many things to do, so many things to change. For what? It was not amusing. Back then he had been alone. Now he was not: he had a brother, and that world of Mosaingar was perhaps worth the trouble. It could even be amusing.

"Shall we be born?"

He made a complete turn in the uterus of Mosaingar who crouched with pain, thinking it was time to give birth. Mosaingar placed her hand on her belly and asked: "Child of I don't know whom, am I about to give birth? Think well: you will be born without a father. I never writhed on the prick of God. How are you going to be born if you are not the child of the Nameless One?"

Maíra replied from inside: "Look, Mosaingar, our mother, don't be concerned. You are going to give birth to twins. We are not the children of God. We are the parents of the human race to come."

Maíra and Micura were born like people—the Mairuns. Maíra was very innocent; he played with the little boys in the village like any other little boy. He performed prodigious feats without meaning to, because he didn't know his own powers. When he was vexed and would say to his little companion, "Get away from here," that one would really make a rapid exit; he would disappear entirely. If in a game of animals Maíra said, "I'm a guinea pig!" he would turn into a guinea pig there and then. When the children said, "Let's play anteaters," directly Maíra would change into an anteater, happy and talking there before them. But he remained himself within, because later he would once again become what he was. The older children, noticing this, began to be frightened. With foreboding they saw the twins and saw their power grow. They would ask: "What will become of us when those two are adults?"

Some, the most timorous, always talked about this, commenting every night on the risk they were running. "Did you see that? Today he turned Micura into a hummingbird that flew around the entire dancing ground pecking at the little boys. If he were to decide one day to turn into a jaguar, what would become of us?"

They wanted to free themselves from Maíra and Micura as the only way of saving themselves from a great danger. At first they tried a strong poison to knock Maíra and Micura out, so they could cut them up and disperse the parts far from each other. But the potion took effect only in Micura, and Maíra quickly cured him, making him vomit.

They then decided to take the twins on a hunt and leave them in the middle of a herd of peccary to be slashed to bits; it would take a long time to put them together again. But the twins were the ones who amused themselves: they mounted two wild peccary and drove the entire herd through the village.

What confusion was caused by the pigs, entering homes and
knocking things over and biting people. Finally they encircled a
man and ate him. Only then did Maíra send the peccarries back
into the bush, saying, "Now this one is finished. And it was
good. He was the one most in favor of doing away with us."

Without meaning to, out of innocence, Maíra had created
death.

They all stood there, looking sadly at the remains of the man
torn to shreds by the tusks of the peccaries, still quivering with
the desire to live, but never to be put together again. Some
started to cry. Maíra watched, preoccupied. Then he began to
laugh a little and burst into a belly laugh. And said, "Now let
us laugh together, brothers. To laugh is good." Micura began
to laugh with Maíra; the contagion took hold and everyone
fell into helpless mirth.

After that time, no one ever tried anything against Maíra again.
But his life was becoming more difficult, because they asked
him for all manner of things, as they were too lazy to make any
effort themselves. Finally, Maíra and Micura couldn't stand it
anymore. They left, walking that way. They finished growing
up while traveling and getting to know the world. At times
they would meet a person or an animal who, recognizing them,
would beg for something. They would give it, but always with
malice. To some who wanted to be beautiful, Maíra gave white
skins but made them very smelly: they are the Europeans.
Others who wanted to tan their skin to a nice golden brown,
Maíra turned black as a brand.

THE MOUTH

They walked for hours. Isaías carrying the big suitcase on
his head. Alma dragging his valise. The other big suitcase

jounces on the heads of the two bigger boys. At last they see the river and, over the dunes, the cabin.

"It's Chico Remo's house. He has lived here for many years," Isaías remarks. They proceed, looking at the thatched hut. As they approach it, Isaías sees an old black woman grilling fish, and he salutes her: "Good afternoon, Auntie. Where is my friend Chico? I am Father Isaías from the Mission."

"Blessings; come nearer, Father. Chico is with God, dead and buried. It's been years. My man now is Antão. Do you know him?"

He doesn't; but soon thereafter Antão arrives, carrying an agouti. He is a Paraense with a thin neck; he has a big head and is quite a talker.

"Good day to everyone. I wasn't expecting a soul today. When I saw the plane land, I came running. I was out all night looking for otters in the backwater up there, but I had no luck; I managed only to get this agouti."

They introduce themselves; Antão already knows Isaías by name and by word of mouth.

"I'm a native of Para, Father, a man who drinks cassava beer. I was brought to the Iparanã as an employee of Sr. Juca. He is my boss. I've been living in Ibeporã for so long that my son by Dóia is almost four years old. He's that little one over there." Antão raises his voice and shouts: "Hey, boys, take these suitcases inside." He turns back and asks the visitors for their hammocks.

"Mine is in the valise, and Dona Alma's must be in one of the bigger cases."

"And what of the Mission, Father Isaías? Why are they lagging so much? They are not usually late. Those fathers are always here when any of their people come. They are usually here hours before with the motor already running."

"Well, yes. I'm worried."

"Only this little case, Father?" Antão inquires, opening the valise to take the hammock out.

"Yes, Antão, I travel from afar, but I travel light."

"How many years has it been since you left here? Everyone speaks of the Indian who went running all over the world throughout the foreign countries of the priests. What seems to me to be missing are the two marks, father Isaías. They say you are a Mairun. What did you do to erase them? Nobody is supposed to succeed."

"It's just a fact of life, old Antão. Here, the marks will be revived, you'll see."

"May God watch over you, Father Isaías. Why do you need them now that you are a priest. There'll be a great feast at the Mission to celebrate your arrival. It's a pity I can't go; Juca has made things rough for me. Will the launch come later today to pick you and the lady up? Why is it so delayed? Maybe the radio isn't working." Isaías snatches at this excuse: "Ah, that must be it. The darned radio!" Antão is even more apprehensive: "Then we are in a bind, Father. I've already told you that Juca has made things hard for me: I won't even be able to row you to the Mission. You and the young woman will have to wait here until they come from the Mission to pick you both up (God knows when). Or until another motor boat comes up or goes down (which is very unlikely). Things are not looking good."

"Then I'll have to wait? No, I can't stay here all that time. Do you have a canoe you could lend us, Antão?"

"There's always the one from the Mission that is used to transport cargo and is towed by the launch in situations like this. The leaks have to be caulked and the shelter put in place. But the river is swift; going down the side channels with a little help from someone you might take three days, five at the most. Don't tell me, Father Isaías, that you still don't know how to row? Or to seal a canoe or thatch a new shelter? I don't doubt it. And the lady, judging from her airs, is incapable of being any help on a voyage. You'll see, she'll be like one of these new nuns arriving; they don't even know how to sit properly in a canoe."

Alma, sitting on a wooden mortar made from a tree trunk, looks at the blackness of the grime on the old straw of the hut.

Antão is slinging the hammocks in opposite corners of the little house which has only one room; in one remaining corner is his own hammock, in the other, those of the children, one above the other, with mosquito netting. Having slung the hammocks, he goes back to talking about Juca:

"That man disembarked here last week and behaved like a wild animal. He abused me in vile language and almost dislocated my boy's spine with a kick in the backside, the poor thing. It was a real brawl. Now he keeps company with Manelão who is cross-eyed and quiet. But who looks at people with that wandering eye of his, gleaming with a powerful desire to do evil. Look, Father Isaías, this Juca talks like a mad man, and I have to put up with it. What can I do? But it's his bargaining that fucks me. You figure it out. He forced on me this .22 single-barreled rifle and six boxes of cartridges; two pairs of pants for me; the mosquito net that I've put over the boys' hammocks; some pieces of cloth with thread and a needle for sewing, which I won't let Dóia touch. He also left six bottles of Viseu rum, a meter of Braganza tobacco only to tempt me; some boxes of matches; a dozen fishhooks of various sizes; and this spool of fishing line which looks like monkey tripe but is unfortunately useful. Figure out how much all of this is going to cost me?"

"It's true, Antão, you're in a mess. A debt like that can't be paid off in a year, not at Juca's prices."

"That Juca spoke clearly: 'I want payment in the form of otter and ocelot skins even if your old woman Dóia has to give birth to animals for you to kill.' I'd like to clear out of here, you know, go downriver, but I'd only fall into his hands. And the Air Express plane only takes poor people out of here to die in the hospital.

"So I'm in a real mess with no way out. I've just been tracking an ocelot but couldn't find it, the one that was taking Dóia's chickens. I set a trap for it, but it got away with its skin. Forget about otters too; I've never seen one. Dóia, who has been living here fifteen years and more has never seen one either. But that

Juca says I have only to go deep into the forest, by the side of the lagoon, to find them. Everything is easy as Juca sees it. With otters just sitting around waiting to be taken by the handful. But only if the hand belongs to that twisted devil himself.

Antão pauses a moment, sighs in agony, walks round the room moving things and setting them straight. He begins again, distracted:

"Can't you save me, Father Isaías? You could if you took the Mission into account. You who are a Brazilian are not ashamed to talk to a backwoodsman like me. All you'd have to do is pay my debt to that Juca. I would serve you for the rest of my life, Father Isaías. Save me, Father, save me! Let that be your first good deed on your native soil."

Antão nearly breaks into tears.

"Calm down, Antão, get a hold of yourself, man. I have nothing, believe me. Unfortunately, I didn't bring anything with me. Nor can I get anything. I am returning as I left, with empty hands. I am returning to the Mission like anyone else. I could ask the Superior to assume some of your debt, as a form of assistance, but only he has the power to do anything.

Antão remains deep in thought, worrying; then he says, slowly and bitterly,

"Better not, Father. It would be better to say nothing about this. That Juca is an arrogant man, and you are weak. Look! I know the Mission has never shouldered the burdens of anyone. Their Holinesses care only for the Indians. We, who live on the riverbanks, see those fathers only in the distance. But you know the law on the Iparaná: a debt is a debt and must be paid without assistance. I must either pay or die. I can't pay, neither can I flee. If Father Ludgero did not accede to your request and then spoke to Juca, I would truly be a lost man. Don't say anything, Father Isaías. Father Ludgero has never wanted to help anyone. I won't be the exception. Everyone has his own fate. Let it be as Juca wants."

Calmed down by his own words, Antão starts planning:

"I think I'll go camp at the edge of the lagoon with the whole

family like my pal Pio. That's the only way that I'll be able to
pay off this debt. The worst thing is that .22; it fires a nothing of
bullet. One needs the aim of an archangel; if it doesn't hit the
animal in the eye, it's a wasted shot. If I only had a shotgun or
one of those Belgian .44s. But this piece of shit . . . ! You see, I
hunt with it carrying a bow and arrows on my shoulder, because if I were to meet a jaguar or a herd of peccary, with this
thing I'd be fucked."

"That's enough of that, Antão; anger doesn't help anyone,"
Isaías says, worried. But Antão continues:

"That shameless Juca told me not to forget to piss down the
barrel of the .22 as we did with the old .44s. He said that if you
piss the shot wobbles, and, instead of tearing the flesh of the
animal to bits, it makes the animal fall dazed, right there at our
feet. And how much will he charge for this peashooter? I'm
going to need a passel of skins to pay for the .22 alone."

Antão rests a little, wipes his brow, and asks, in a preoccupied
tone,

"And weapons, Father, did you bring any? Or hooks and line,
match, salt? I didn't see any in your baggage."

"No, Anatão, I brought nothing. I thought the people at the
Order there in Brasília would have alerted the Mission. I hoped to
find the launch here, and so I didn't come prepared. Now, I can't
go back. The thing to do is to go on, alone with the woman."

"But not even we, who've lived on the riverbank so long,
travel like that, with one hand tied to the other. I'll look
for a hook and a few yards of twine for you and a box of
matches as well. And a bow, can you manage one?"

"None of that, Antão. Forget the bow and firearms. If it
comes to killing, I am the one who will die, a victim of either
men or beasts."

Silent and perplexed, Alma listens: What a world this is, she
thinks, enormous, savage, belonging to no one or to one man
only, that Juca, the all-powerful. She starts walking with Isaías
along the beach. They take their shoes off to dig their feet into
the sand and feel the coolness of the water.

She is even more surprised when Isaías tells her that he is related to Juca. There you have it, she theorizes, it's the off-spring of an Indian and a white fulfilling his destiny by punishing the savages on his mother's side of the family, as Professor Moreira used to say. Isn't that an expression of the will of God? It has been that way for centuries. First along the seacoast, then further and further inland. Now it is here on the Iparanã. It will advance tomorrow to wherever there is virgin forest in which whites and Indians fight and intermingle. The few offspring who make it become villainous murderers like that Juca. Isn't it time to put an end to it? Why doesn't the Mission do something? And what about FUNAI? Isaías tries to explain:

"This is another world, Alma. The Mission brings a new message, not a new order of things. It prays: it does not colonize; it does not reform. That's up to FUNAI. It guarantees the Indians a tract of land forever on the right bank of the Iparanã. It gives some protection to those who stay in the villages. There the Mairuns are more or less secure. What they can't do is leave, or they will fall into the hands of one of Juca's bunch or someone else of the same stripe. The Mission also is always sheltering some Indian or other for a short period of time."

Alma is hardly consoled by what she hears. She can't believe it.

"Look, Alma, this is the service of God you had so much to say about a few days ago. The Kingdom of God on the Iparanã is this. Perhaps your Carioca slum is better, don't you think?"

"No, Isaías. My place is here. I don't know why. I don't know for what. It is impossible for me to turn back, nor do I want to. That world behind us has no room for me. Perhaps it does for you. Didn't you say they offered you a position as a teacher wherever you liked? I too could have been a teacher, of psychology or whatever, but I didn't want to be. Nor do you. Our place is here. I am going to find myself. So are you. You are going to submit. You are going to take Orders. You are going to run the Mission. Didn't you hear Antão say that a Brazilian priest is needed?"

"We are only now beginning to enter the mouth of the forest; you still haven't seen anything. I went away a long time ago, but I know each curve of the Iparanã, of my Mairun people. This dilapidated shed is the same one I used to see back in Rome whenever I thought about my return. The only new thing is the airplane. Previously, we went on horseback, traveling for weeks to get to Goiás Velho from here. I knew that here time had stopped, as if waiting for me. I knew that from here I would walk in either the direction of the Mission or that of the village. We have a long road ahead of us, Alma. It will be hard work. Be patient. Don't wish to solve every problem that you see."

They return to the hut. Isaías wants to tell Antao that, in spite of their being alone and helpless, they will go on.

"That's up to you, Father. If I were in your place I'd wait here a week for the plane. I'd put up a sign on the field for it to land, and I'd fly back with it. Later, I'd return properly equipped or with everything arranged with the fathers. Now, if your wish is to go ahead, I will help you a little. At least with something to eat. My advice is I don't advise it. Your being alone with the girl in the mouth of this great world of God and the Devil, I don't advise it."

"Understand, Antão, we have to make this voyage, it's urgent. What we need is the canoe and your help in caulking it and putting up the shelter."

"The canoe is over there. I'm going out at dawn to hunt; you go with the boys to search among the rocks at the rapids for stuff to stop the leaks and for the resin they know about. When I return I'll bring some bushrope and some wild plantain leaves to thatch the shelter. Late tomorrow everything will all be ready. Day after tomorrow, you and the girl will be on the river, if that is what you want."

In the hut, Alma opens first one suitcase then the other. From the first she takes a dress which she gives to Dóia. From the second, she takes a long knife to gut fish. Antão looks at the knife, Alma looks at Antão. She hands the knife to Isaías:

"Keep this. We'll need it."

"So you're really going on a voyage such as this," Antão says, "without anything. The only help you might get is from my friend Pio, at Eurebá, two days downriver, but he is in the jungle. Aside from him, there are only those sons of bitches, the Epexãs, who are good for nothing and never help anybody. They hate us. It would be better to keep your distance from them and not stop. Not even that Juca wants to have anything to do with them. They are the most wretched race of mankind ever seen. It is said that if they could eat covertly, without running any risk, they'd butcher Christians and eat them roasted."

THE MASS

The Mission of Our Pregnant Mother of God: lime-washed white walls; floors of cedar boards, precisely cut and well scrubbed; roofs of sun-drenched tiles; white cloths hanging to be bleached by the sun.

A time that is ancient dry, Attic—with clipped wings and blind eyes—ceaselessly spills its impalpable sand. It interweaves the countless days and nights of missionary life with long drawn-out hours.

Nothing happens or fails to happen in the observance of the daily ritual. Repeated without pause, the forms of worship belong to the hours, the words to the daily rite, the meditations to the prescribed penance. Everyday time affects only the priests and the nuns who are slowly but inexorably aging.

For some, the time of carnal affliction and dread has long passed. Now, their fears are recondite heresies concerning how to love the Virgin Mary more and more. For others, whose flesh still burns, there is the ever-present fear of the voracious moment that suddenly consumes and corrupts the virtuous continence suffered for so long. In those who are at peace, the tranquil flesh calms fervor and zeal. In those of warmer blood, quivering flesh enflames the spirit with missionary zeal.

Two arduous, daily exercises—inducing groans and perspiration—preserve a clean soul within the body. Sermons, prayers for the living and the dead, supplications, chants and exorcisms cleanse the souls, iron them out and starch them stiff like the white coifs of the nuns' habits. Abundant ablutions, suds from soap and water, dilute the lasciviousness of the body. The light intimate apparel of the sisters and fathers are washed separately from their black and secret soutanes and clerical garb. Not an atom of sweat, foot odor, semen, catarrh, vomit, blood, excrement, menses, urine, tears, nothing animal can remain. No secretion, nothing may be permitted to besmirch these angelical vestments.

The soda that ate the tallow in the miracle of soap-making also cravenly eats all the dirt, all the smudges, all the filth. Nothing must remain. And if something does, the weekly boiling with lime and ashes will wash it out, will clean the garment.

In the cloisters, swept free from even a speck of dust, the fathers assiduously hone their long razors, firmly stroking the leather strap with the cutting edge. On the other side of the cloisters, the sisters persist in making the stone sing with fine tonsorial scissors. The priests shave, scrape their hairy faces every holy day. The nuns lop and clip immodest hair that grows ceaselessly, and they comb it into smooth locks separated by straight lines of chalk.

Priests and nuns, outside the cloister, on foot, standing or walking, masks of faces and bare hands, fluttering. Modest and indiscreet they peer out, blankly, frightened, from within the obscurity of their vestments, with faces and hands like those of black turtles. They walk as if endlessly measuring the corridors with their paces. They salute and bless each other, crossing themselves reassuringly.

The gaunt ones righteously exhibit the leanness resulting from their facile fasting. The fat ones can barely hide the sacrifices of their wretched abstinences in the flaccidity of their loose flesh. Each and all see themselves, judge themselves, and pardon themselves.

"Here comes poor Father Bento, hiding his well-stuffed paunch. May God help him to control his appetite and free me from my lack of it."

"There goes that dry stick Sister Ignes with her gallant addiction to winking her left eye at me. May Our Lady give her strength to achieve virtue and give me patience and modesty."

Dry ashes of lives, without honey or salt. Hard lives, with blind affections and clipped desires. Suffering servants of God, forbidden to be themselves, dressed in mourning because they cannot die.

All the forbidden tenderness flourished in secret is watered in silence through frangi-pani, myrtle, Arabian jasmine and white lilies. Hidden and transparent—among the official flower beds of roses, canna lilies, and carnations—they make the night lovely with their flowers and scents.

In the twilight of dawn, in front of the high altar of God the Father, little Father Ludgero says the great Mass. Every day, he delivers as a sacrifice the body of our Lord.

Asperges me, Donine, hyssopo et mundabor:
lavabis me, et super nivem dealbabor
Miserere mei, Deus. . . .

The happiness of the salt of the living and the sadness of the funeral oleographs are well guarded in closed glass frames above the sacrificial altar, awaiting the hour. Now, only the Mass, sung in a hoarse voice from a deep baritone, leading the singing of the nuns, the boys and the girls—only the mass resounds and echoes:

Sanctus, Sanctus, Sanctus	*Hagios o Theos*
Dominus, Deus Sabaoth	*Hagios ischyros*
Pleni sunt coeli ey gloria tus	*Hagios athanatos*
Hosanna in excelsis	*Eleison imos*

At the same time, in front of the smaller altars, the lesser fathers humbly implore, in murmured masses, forgiveness for sins they have not committed; bless the bread, the wine, and the work; and drink contritely the blood of Christ.

Confiteor Deo Omnipotenti
quia peccavi nimis
cogitatione, verbo et opere
mea culpa, mea culpa, mea maxima culpa

When the time comes, the body of the Lord, white as starch, is put into the fleshy mouths of the supplicant nuns.

Audi, filia, et vide, et inclina aurem tuam
et concupiscet Rex decorum tuum
Ecce Agnus Dei
Ecce qui tollit peccata mundi
Accipite, et manducate ex hoc omnes.
Hoc est enim Corpus meum
Accipite et bibite ex eo omnes.
Hic est enim calix sanguinis mei
Domine, non sum dignus
ut intres sub tectum meum
Benedictus, qui venit in nomine Domini
Hosanna in excelsis.

In the silence of death and incense, the servants of God contemplate the mystery.

God is God. Light is light.
Giver of life. Giver of death.
Creator of the visible and the invisible.
Begetter and begotten. Savior and Redeemer.
The hand is the Father who sacrifies and delivers His Son.
We are the children who save ourselves, bleeding,

Offering, once again, the body of the Son of God.
Spilling, once again, his Holy Blood.
We eat Thy Flesh. We drink Thy Blood.
We announce Thy Death.
We proclaim Thy Resurrection.
God, my God, is dead: until he returns to judge me.
God, my God, is alive: look and await.

Per ipsum, et cum ipso, et in ipso,
est tibi Deo Patri omnipotent: in unitate Spritus Sancti,
Per omine saccula sacculorum. Amen.

Converging prayers, resplendent waters, razors, scissors, penances. Lime and lye. Repentances. Each one performing his task reconsecrates souls, resanctifies bodies already sacrificed to God. He attends to everything from above. Perhaps He is moved and approves, who knows?

MAIRAÍRA

Maíra discovered the full extent of his powers while playing with Micura one day on the beach. Each of them was holding up a handful of glowworms for illumination, but the light was very weak. All the same, Maíra drew, right there in the sand, a stingray with its sting and all. In the penumbra he became distracted and stepped on the drawing. He got such a sting! From this, he understood that he could make anything.

"I am Maíra," he remembered, "I am the belch of the Father-God. He, Ambir, now has a name: it is Mairahú, Father of Maíra. My son will be called Mairaíra." He then started to discuss with his brother, Micura, what they could do.

Maíra: "The world of my father, Mairahú, is ugly and sad. It is not a good world for people to live in. We can make it better."

Micura: "Won't the Old One be offended?"

Maíra: "Probably you are right. It is better to do nothing."

Micura: "Nonsense. There are some little things we could do."

Maíra: "Let's go then and take what they have from those who have and give it to those who have not."

Micura jumped from joy: "Yes, let's go. First is fire. I have been feeling very cold, and I'd very much like to eat a good barbecue."

Fire belonged to the King Vulture who rules in the great village of the vulture people. They ate only maggots from carrion, toasted on hot embers. They didn't need much fire. They used it mainly for light to discover the carrion and for heat to warm their naked bodies when they divested themselves of their feathers to play like humans.

The plan the twins worked out for stealing fire was to kill a big deer, a very big deer, leave it to rot and breed abundant maggots, and then send some of the stew to the King Vulture with an invitation to come and stuff himself with the rest. They did this. Maíra drew an enormous stag, puffed so as to bring it to life, then killed it. When it was good and rotten and full of maggots, Maíra and Micura sent a blue-winged macaw, the bird that speaks the most languages, back to the King Vulture. They remained hidden under the carrion to grab the double-headed king when he dug in. They did this. When the King Vulture was firmly in their grip, Maíra yelled:

"Keep calm, my King. Don't be afraid. I want only fire for my little people. They go about cold. Everything they eat is raw."

But a terrible row began because both the King Vulture's heads started replying, speaking at once, one saying one thing, the other, another. Maíra couldn't understand anything. Then one of the heads of the King Vulture turned to the other and engaged it in a private conversation. Time was passing, Maíra didn't know what to do next. Then he had an idea. He told Micura to take hold of the voluble king. Maíra himself raised his hands and turned each of them into a vulture's head with beak and all, and so he was able to talk back hard to the two heads of the great King Vulture. Only by so doing was he able to get the king to order that fire be brought, but the King Vulture still wanted to trick Maíra by supplying fires which burned with very little heat and gave little light, but fortunately Maíra tried each one out. He tested them one by one.

"No, this one won't do; it's not the fire we want. No, neither is this one the fire we want. No, nor is this one the real fire." At last they secured the fire they wanted and struck a bargain.

Maíra: "You vultures are going to have plenty of carrion to eat. Your big chief with the two heads will have only one in the future, so he won't be able to trick people anymore. But the head that remains will have this red and white diadem I'm giving it now."

King Vulture: "Keep the fire, oh, Mairuns. But make plenty of carrion for us."

Maíra and Micura went around the outside world taking and redistributing everything good that had been appropriated by one animal only. They took the honey from the tayra, the fierce little honey bear, and Maíra made it increase in calabashes for the people to eat until they were satisfied. Micura said:

"No, that's not right. If those shameless Mairuns don't have to work for it, they'll get lazy. Maíra, put the honey in a hollow tree or at the bottom of a termite hill and encircle it with bees and hornets." He laughed and said:

"Whoever wants to eat sweet honey is going to run into difficulties; he'll have to work to get it!"

After this, they took red annatto from the red-winged macaw, black genipap from the curassow, the secret of preparing salt from ashes from the deer, and from the honeycreeper they took pepper seeds. This was all done so that the Mairuns could paint themselves and eat with enjoyment. They also took tobacco from the toad, because Maíra was very fond of smoking cigars. Micura liked smoking even more, but said its proper use was in sorcery. They stole the cotton shrub from the spider, and Maíra improved on it so that it grew balls of cotton, ready for the Mairun to use.

"No, that's not right, brother. That way the old women will have no work to do. That's bad; they'll get very lazy. Let's make it a seed with a small tuft of cotton inside. Whoever wants to can pick it, twist the thread, and make yarn for weaving a hammock or a baby sling."

Maíra did this, and that's how Mairuns can carry their babies in slings and sleep and fuck in hammocks, which is very good.

From afar, Mairahú, the Old One, watched that confusion with disgust. He thought his son was getting bad advice from the false brother he had invented. He couldn't let the things go on as they had developed, or the whole of creation would be ruined. He shouted from there above:

"Hey, belch of mine, listen here, stop indulging in new fantasies. Let well enough alone and see what happens.

Maíra recoiled and sank under the weight of the voice of the Old One. Later, when he had recovered from his fright, he thought perhaps the Old One was antiquated. He no longer knew what was good for his own creation. Micura agreed and added:

"It is His envy; everything is better now. To speak the truth, that world is no longer even His."

"That's it!" said Maíra with great emphasis, speaking harshly. So he decided then and there to bring about some sweeping reforms.

THE TONGUE

Between the river and sky, the canoe runs swiftly under the sun atop the mirror of the water; a moving black point in the immensity. The beaches hide themselves in a haze in the distance. The forest is a dark belt on the horizon. At times it projects an inverted image of itself in the sky: a mirage.

At the stern, Isaías is guiding the canoe along the stream, letting the current do almost all the work. Alma, under the thatched shelter, grips the gunwales. She has still not found her balance.

The canoe runs in the water, the sun rises to the skies. With a new lease on life, Isaías smiles. His infancy as a canoehand has been reincarnated. The same river, the same sky, the same paddle: "This boat made of planks doesn't glide along like my Mairun dugout." On the bottom lay the bow and arrows belonging to Doia's boy. ("Take these, Father, you may need them. Send me another for the little boy.") A child's little bow, perhaps I can manage it. To one side, a heap of grilled fish, wrapped in their own black crust of burnt scales. They are almost indistinguishable from the cassava tubers baked in their husk. This is all that we have to eat. And this is what we are going to keep on eating. This is what I could pull out of the river. Will I find anything? There is only an abundance of water, sky, and light. Isaías, bewildered, smiles brilliantly:

"What's the matter? Are you laughing like a lunatic?"

"Not me. What is to become of us in this world so great and small?"

"I'll tell you this. It couldn't be worse than the other."

The little canoe descends the Iparanã of the Mairuns. Sitting on the stern thwart, Isaías keeps the steering paddle submerged in the water. Sitting before the shelter and facing him, Alma precariously balances herself toward the bows. Her head is wrapped in a nightgown.

"It would be better for you to face forward or to sit under the shelter. Otherwise, you'll roast yourself in this sun. A bad sunburn is about the only thing we lack."

"Don't be ridiculous, I can't talk to someone whose face I can't see. Try to explain to me better why you think you don't have the strength or the ability to change things on this Iparanã."

"You don't know what you're asking of me," Isaías replies, convinced that neither he nor anyone else could make a difference to the order of things on the Iparanã. At least I know what I can't do, he consoles himself. How could I, ex-Isaías, now Avá but not yet actually Avá, pretend to aspirations that eluded St. Francis with his innocence and goodwill, St. Thomas with his faith and wisdom, St. Ignatius with his resolution and astuteness, and St. John of the Cross with his passion and charisma? "Your sin is vanity, Alma. You want to take from God something neither St. Teresa of Jesus nor St. Rose of Lima ever achieved. We are aimless little souls, expiating sins we don't even know, in this world without pity. And here you are, asking for miracles."

"Save your stones, Isaías. It's worthless casting them at me. Tell me, what is it you want to do here?"

"Me? One thing only: to live the everyday life of the Mairuns. To eat grilled or boiled fish that I've caught myself, with now and then if I'm lucky a little meat. My desire is to live among my people once again, and with their help to cleanse myself of this oil of civilization and Christianity that has permeated me. I didn't like lying to get this canoe, even less doing it to unfortunate Antão. How many more days, how many more months will have to pass before I won't ever again have to play your game: to lie and lie in accordance with the rules of your world?"

"My world? I have nothing to do with it. I am against it as much as you are, perhaps more. I only want to know why you don't want to change it."

"But that's precisely it. No one can change anything. If there is to be a change, it will come naturally. Slowly, very, very slowly. And the only changes I can foresee, those that I see coming, are for the worse."

"What pessimism, Isaías! How can you live without hope? Here, now, you are talking like a different man. I never realized you were this way, so lacking in faith."

"Don't kid yourself! I have faith all right. But my faith is devoted only to this simple yet difficult thing which is to live once more among my people. There I will do whatever they expect of me. I ask only that my pessimistic views don't come to pass just yet. I ask that civilization advance a little more slowly, not reaching there just yet. I know very well that we, the Mairuns, exist only because the Brazilians have in fact never been in the Iparanã. On the day they become interested in doing so, the Mairuns will be finished. It pains me a lot to think this, and it hurts even more to say it, but so it is. Our viability is improbable, and does not depend on us. Perhaps it depends only on God. Perhaps even God cannot save us. And you there, asking me to create, to bring something into being. I am not Maíra, nor even Micura!"

"I can't go along with such inertia, Isaías. It is necessary to react. Perhaps the solution does not really lie in saintliness or miracles, but neither does it lie in disillusionment. One has to find some efficacious way to take action. Don't give up, man! That Juca fellow, can't you find a way of finishing him off?"

"Juca? You want me to get rid of him? To kill Juca? That would be easy. But a week later, five boat traders would be quarreling over the domain of the Iparanã. Forget any notion of finishing off Juca. As if he were the guilty one. I also think he's not the problem. He is the solution, yours and the Brazilians'. We Mairuns and the Epexãs don't deal with Juca. We know that the best thing that he and all the whites can do for us is to stay out of our lives. To leave us in peace. Our problem lies elsewhere, and I have yet to understand it fully. Our problem is that of a little Mairun David, almost helpless, fighting a civilizing super-Goliath. The possibility of our winning is nil. But neither will we be defeated. We shall continue, century after century, more and more embittered with our disgust at ourselves."

Alma ceases her interrogation. Quietly, she thinks: I embarked for Naruai thinking that here I would achieve a solid truth that would rule my life. I thought the problem would be to live in compliance with it. I see now I was searching for some minor personal truth. But I don't regret it; coming here was useful; it was good to uproot myself from my useless existence. But I am also useless in this world of his. Useless for anything. If even he is useless, dispensable, what can be said of me?

Isaías rekindles the conversation: "You yourself live by saying that living is complicated. It is, as you well know. What I want isn't easy either. It seems as if I am coming back to be only what I effortlessly would have been had I remained. What you want to do seems more complicated to me. You want to remake yourself spiritually so as to reform the world materially. Think hard about this: Aren't we asking too much? No one has ever succeeded in achieving all that."

Alma does not reply. Outwardly, she tries to look into the depths of her soul. She thinks: I am tired of planning things. Now I am going to rely on intuition without the necessity for reasons or for faith lest it ever fail me. I'll plunge into things come-what-may. Right now, all I want to do is to proceed in this adventure or misadventure, regardless of what happens. If it ends in nothing, I will have lost nothing and will be free of the compulsion to search for my essential self in my innermost being and other nonsense from back in Rio. How futile all that was! The chatter among women, to discover ourselves, we would say. The chatter between men and women, to interact with equality. It's enough to make you sick. None of it was of any use.

Running around all over the place in despair until I couldn't stand it anymore. At the right time I put an end to that without putting an end to myself. I was tired, tired of myself and of trying to save the world, conspiring but with no possibility of success. I was tired of the awful fear of confronting, with my mangled flesh, the fangs of ferocious dogs. I was out of control. All of this served only to rid me of inhibitions, to make me an easy lay, and to get me hooked on drugs.

I went to kick the habit in that hospital, and from there I came here. But I'm very different from him; I don't have a past or a future that owes me anything. My past has neither a present nor a future. I'm as free as when I was born, free to do anything that enters my head. The only thing I cannot do is go back. I can't imagine what I'll do here. But I'll find out. I know my road ahead: to descend this great river with Isaías in this worthless canoe, hungry, staring at the waters without end and the two lines of forest without beginning. Everything the same, exactly the same as on the day of creation. I'm going on: Trust in God and keep your step firm! Don't they say that a path is cleared by treading? There I go, after myself.

Most likely concerned by Alma's silence, Isías strikes up a conversation.

"I don't understand you. Where is the humility and meekness of the little nun-to-be? What do you want? Where are you headed with this mixture of anguish and impatience? You seem starved, hungry for something in a terrible way; I can't imagine for what. But at the same time you seem forever sated with everything; again I can't imagine with what. Do you have to get into such deep waters in order just to become a psychologist? Are you all as twisted as this? Doesn't anyone in your circle want simply to be a mother to her family, content to realize herself by nursing her children?"

"Don't be naive, Isaías; what's so simple about that? Is there anything more twisted than being the mother of a family? Than taking care of whining sniveling children all day? Than waiting for a husband to come home at night to argue and quarrel and then to do the same old slam-bam without any desire? They can only endure this because they are doped. Long before Pavlov, men discovered through practice the conditioned reflexes for domesticating women. Nobody escapes from feminine servility. The domestication is like that of hunting dogs and race horses. Only, it's so trivial, so lacking in importance, so vulgar, that nobody even notices, or escapes it."

"But you did, it seems to me!"

"Oh, sure. All I did was dive deeper and then exaggerate my new role, that of antiwoman. I now had a new out. I learned, for example, to fuck men the way they used to fuck me."

"Is this a confession?"

"Don't be ridiculous. We're just talking for want of something better to do." She shuts up but continues to confess within herself: I started trying to invert roles. I soon saw it wasn't worth the trouble: I would always be the one to end up getting fucked. As abstinence was of no use, and as I have neither a talent for lesbianism nor a taste for fingering myself, I stopped. I had a breakdown, I was into drugs, and even more vile, I abandoned myself. I ended up there in the hands of those male nurses whom I need to forget. When I came out, what saved me was a return to faith, faith that vanishes even as it appears. My God, I'm desperate again; for what? Sated yet hungry, he says rightly enough; it's a terrible mixture. Why don't I learn to live simply? Not as the mother of a family; wife and bearer of children; but just as a person? But perhaps htat problem doesn't exist, outside of my own confusion. All that I ask for is so simple! Why can't I achieve it? Why doesn't anyone?

Isaías, gripping the handle of the paddle at the stern, has also dived deep within himself, speculating, inquiring. Will I become the chieftain? How? With what strength? But how to avoid it if old Anacã has died? How did he die? I know that there is no other man of my generation in the clan who is his nephew. There is no alternative: if I return, I have to assume the position. What I could do is run away and never go to the village. But if

I disembark there as a Mairun, to live there, anything can happen. The succession will have been decided without recourse. From the very start they could treat me as the new chieftain instead of a chieftain-to-be. And there will be no way to dissuade them. For me, to turn it back would be impossible, unless I come to them as a priest. What I must do is clear things up in my mind, ask the old fathers at the Mission to tell me all that has happened lately so that I can anticipate what will happen when I arrive. And reckless Alma, what am I going to do with her? The Mairuns will take her for my wife. Will that be a good thing? Will it be a victory to bring a young good-looking white woman into the village? Or will it be considered a betrayal of the Falcon women from whom, according to tradition, my wife is to come? If I were going there as a reformer, with the illusion of leading the Mairuns to civilization, it would be good to take her. But that's not why I'm going. I'm going to Mairunize myself as much as I can. To that end she is an obstacle. I have to find a way, a way that will be obvious even to her, of showing that I have nothing to do with her, nothing at all.

Isaías withdraws the oar from the depths, allowing the canoe to balance itself in the current. He needs to rest his arms, numbed from having to maneuver the oar for hours on end in the water. He continues to brood: stuck here, within myself, descending this my Iparanã, far in a remote and different world, I feel as I used to feel lying on my cot in my cell there in the Roman convent. Is it because I carry within myself the hole into which I recoil and sit with pleasure, a refugee inside me, alone, meditating? That must be it. But it's also spiritual and physical fatigue. I just can't anymore. I need to take refuge once again in that hole, that redeems me so that I may babble once more, playing with them, the old litanies.

Ave Maria stella
Dei mater alma
Atque semper Virgo
Felix caeli porta

Ave Maria: rosa mistica
Ave Maria: mater castissima
Ave Maria: mater inviolata
Ave Maria: mater annabilis

Salve redix, salve porta.
Ex qua mundo lux et orta
Gaude Virg gloriosa
Super omnes speciosa

Salve Maria: sedis sapientiae.
Salve Maria: virgo virginum
Salve Maria: virg genetrix
Salve Maria: vas spirituale.

"What's that?" Alma shouts, terrified. Isaías is frightened, controls himself, looks carefully, and reassures her: "It's nothing, really. It's only an Epexã canoe hiding from us at the edge. Don't look over there, we're going straight ahead.

THE MEETING

I am noting here some news of an auspicious nature. A local merchant just arrived at the Indian post and had lunch with us. He is somewhat crude and foul-mouthed, as is the case with many of our best backland people. As compensation, however, he is a man endowed with an evident sense of objectivity and a notable capacity for action. These qualities practically make him the opposite of Elias. All of this adds up in him to a spontaneous predisposition to assist me in my investigations into the truth regarding the crime that constitutes the object of my inquiry. During two hours of conversations with him I learnt

more about the Indians and about this district than in days of
talking with Elias.

He calls himself José Jaguar de Oliveira; his nickname is
Juca. He is a crony of the agent and, though he says this with
modesty, he is the only electoral representative of Senator
Andorinha in this region. Being the only one, he is more, much
more, than a common electoral representative. The arrival of this
man lifts my spirits.

His father was the true civilizer of these lands. First, as a sub-
officer of Marshal Rondon; later, as a powerful dealer. For many
years he lived in this same place which was then a large village
with hundreds, if not thousands, of Indians and backwoodsmen,
and which functioned as a busy commercial center. The slump
in rubber and other tropical products, the revolution of 1930,
and, above all, the death of his father contributed to the mis-
fortunes that befell the Iparanã.

It is sad to think that this lovely region was once so much
more valuable to Brazil and to civilization than it is today. Now,
the only civilizing forces in this vast area, first, Sr. "Juca" de
Oliveira and the workers contracted to him who take from here
and export products worth several million cruzciros a year;
second—though far behind—Elias who represents the federal
government here through FUNAI and whose activities we have
already appreciated at their true worth; third—but in an honor-
able position—the Catholic Mission of Our Lady of O, which has
struggled here for forty years to convert the Mairuns and other
Indians, and whose work has borne good fruits; and, finally, various little Protestant missions nearly always led by North American clergymen. These appear and disappear fleetingly, without
leaving visible signs of their teaching.

It remains for me only to note that today I had a futile interview with the aforementioned Isaías. He is a weak, decrepit,
little fellow, contrary to the image I had formed of him, which
was that of a real Indian. He was more or less forced into my
presence by Elias. He didn't want to discuss anything with me
and refused to give me any information. He refused obstinately,

with eyes lowered and chin against his chest, and with hostility toward me, Elias, and Sr. Juca. When I told him that even if I didn't have sufficient evidence to convict him, I had enough to indict him, he barely raised his eyes. When I stood in front of him and shouted; "I'm going to arrest you yet, you little fraud," he only said, in a clear voice: "Let it be as God wishes."

He said nothing more, nothing about the dead woman, or about himself, or about the birth. What to do? I can't return empty-handed; I must go back with something concrete. If I don't obtain proof in the next few days that the death was the result of an accident during childbirth or whatever (though it must be concrete), the only thing left for me to do will be to arrest this ex-father, ex-Indian, ex-person as a suspect. Back in Rio he'll have to talk; of that there's no doubt. Who is in a better position to judge? I won't accuse him. But I believe he is the only one around here who could be the culprit, and therefore he should be indicted. Above all because he owes the Brazilian government, the Brazilian state, Brazilian justice some explanation which he obstinately refuses to give. I have offered him ample opportunity to comply. I asked him for complete information about any of his dealings with the deceased woman that might throw light on the motives and circumstances of her death. Information which I would convey faithfully and clearly. Well, he has refused. His fate is now in his own hands.

MAÍRA-POXÍ

Maíra had always thought that the world of our Creator, the Nameless One, wasn't of much use. Without wanting to, he found himself imagining and inventing in his mind the world as it ought to be; a world good for his favorite people, the Mairuns of the Iparanã; a world that was truly a joy to live in.

One day he decided that the hour had come. He began the work of reforming the world by bringing together all the Ambir people who existed and dividing them into two groups—those over here and those over there. He ordered those over here to build a very large hut that would become the Great House of Men, and he showed them right there how to construct it. When it was ready, Maíra went inside, sat on the ground, and tapped the ground three times to cause God's prick to emerge. When it rose in front of him, as hard as it could be, he cut it off at the base with one stroke, grabbed it firmly, and thrust it between the legs of those who were standing around. At the end of this task, all were now men with their own pricks, and they went out to fuck the women there outside on the dancing ground or wherever they liked. What a feast of copulation it was.

Maíra and Micura, who also had their own pricks, joined the fucking with great glee. The festivity lasted what remained of that morning, the whole afternoon, and continued late into the night. By midnight, many men were exhausted. Some of them were weeping because their pricks hurt, having been hard for so long, and sore from so much fucking. Micura complained that his prick was in a sorry state. But Maíra, who had yet to fuck even half the women there, said no, they should keep going.

When dawn broke, Maíra called all the men to the dancing ground and showed them a mat covered with little snakes of many colors. They were coral snakes he had collected and stuck into the meshes of the little mat. Then he started calling each man. He showed each a coral snake, killed it then and there, and squeezing it from the tail toward the mouth, skinned the snake still nice and fresh. He tied a knot with the skin on the tip of each man's prick, above the glands, so that the head could be kept soft and hidden inside it's hood.

Then the women came grumbling that Maíra had given the men pricks but had not given them anything. He decided to create something for them too. That's when he invented the uluri-covering forbidden to men, and the sense of shame. He showed the women how to plait one from the underbark of certain trees and the most fashionable way of wearing it over the cunt. He also taught them to feel very ashamed if they were without an uluri. On the same occasion he taught men and women how to choose one another for love, that is to say, with lust and jealousy. In that way, he said, no one will be the way I was last night when I wanted to fuck all the women all the time. Each couple will last as long as desire and jealousy keep them together.

Micura then suggested another urgent reform: it is necessary to open assholes in men and women so that they need no longer vomit all their excrement through their mouths, but will be able to shit instead. Maíra agreed and started calling the people one by one. When one came in he told him to get on all fours and held him tight. Micura, approaching from behind with a well-sharpened firebrand, bore an arsehole right in the middle of his rump. It hurt, they screamed; they bled a bit, but they left content; now they could shit!

When they had finished remaking the Mairuns so that they could fuck, eat, and shit with pleasure, the twins taught them how to lay out the village, with the Great House of Men in the middle, the dancing ground to one side, and the circle of houses surrounding everything. It was then that Maíra invented sin. He divided the village into halves, one half was the side of sunrise, the other, the side of sunset, and he ordered that those in one band should marry those in the other. He organized families and taught the proper words to differentiate relatives. Chiefly: fathers and uncles of fathers-in-law; brothers and cousins of brothers-in-law. All of this so that people can communicate without isolating themselves. Since then each one of us has had to seek a mate far from the house. There it is forbidden; it is incest!

From up above, Maíra Ambir looked down with rage at the disaster his son was making of creation. But what really provoked his wrath, it is said, was the fact that he had been castrated and was unable to fuck anyone at all. He bellowed in the voice of a chief giving orders and in the strongest words:

Mairahú: "Maíra-Poxí, you big shit, listen to me."
Maíra: "Speak, Mairaíra, my son, I'm listening."
Mairahu: "I am your father, respect me."
Maíra: "Without me you would not be a father."
Mairahu: "I am the one."
Maíra: "I, the other."
Mairahu: "The other is nobody."
Maíra: "I am he who is."

After this tough conversation, Mairahú and Maíra never spoke to each other again. The war of the world had begun. It wasted all of ancient times with ceaseless struggles and continues even today without respite. It is a hard battle in which Maíra confronts Mairahú so that the world may remain as it is.

THE GULLET

Isaías takes off his shirt, offering his naked torso to the sun and wind, and puts more force into the strokes of this paddle. The canoe flies in the river, the sun flies in the sky. The cool water of the Iparanã, sparkling, shines on the blade of the paddle.

Alma and Isaías are alone in this immensity. He recalls myths and recounts old stories:

"Here, behind those black dunes, was the village of old Aruá. All Mairuns can tell stories about him. He was an avaeté, a real man. They say he was the first to see the white men. He thought they were a tribe like ours and was curious; but his warriors who approached them wishing to speak were killed. Aruá saw then that these animals were fierce and quarrelsome. What could he do to get closer to them? He carefully prepared an attack, lost one man, but succeeded in capturing a boy whom he carried back to the village where he left him until he learned to speak the Mairun language well. Then, Aruá went out again with his warriors and the boy to tame the whites. He surrounded the camp of a group of them who were searching for diamonds in a mine, and he trapped them there for a long time, hungry and thirsty. Sometimes he gave them a little something to eat, but always very little water. At last, when the whites understood that Aruá didn't want to kill them, the whites agreed to talk. They laid down their arms and talked. They exchanged tools for food and water. Aruá managed to make peace with them. It's not as if the little boy had helped much. He was a member of a distant tribe, the Urubus, and did all he could to poison those first relations. Poor Aruá, he had no way of knowing that the whites were not a tribe like ours or like others that occupy a single riverbank, or two at most. He didn't know that they were the first of a whole world of people, an inexhaustible anthill, occupying the entire earth, insatiably swarming all over the globe. In the following years, more and more started arriving. They continue to surround us to this day. They have already taken possession of the side of sunrise; someday they will take the forests of the sunset. Then we will be reduced to an islet in a sea of whiteness. So it must be, but it hurts."

Alma, who in the first days had been enchanted watching the river, saying that this was a great place for tourism what with all these great beaches of golden sand, now is quiet, vapid in spirits. She doesn't leave the shadow of the shelter. There, angry and embittered she complains:

"Isaías, I'm sweating. Sweat is running down my back, my breasts, my thighs. This hot breeze is killing me. Can't we pause on the bank for a while and jump into the water?"

"No, Alma, we can't. It's more difficult to navigate at night so we must take advantage of the rest of the day. I want to stay here in the middle because this channel is carrying us along nicely."

"Then talk to me, Isaías. Tell me something! How did it come about that all these Mairuns living along this endless river disappeared?"

"Ah! But they haven't disappeared. According to our beliefs, they are still around here as spirits. Only they are transformed. That fat leaf we call mixu is a white deer to them, which they hunt. A white deer to them is our thick green leaf. Only a guide of souls, like my father, can see and talk to them."

After a pause, he proceeds in a sad and serious tone:

"The truth is they were finished. We are finished. Sickness was what probably killed most of them off; then work. It cost a lot for the Mairuns to learn to take refuge in their own way of life. To accept nothing. To avoid all contact. At first, they all wanted to become Europeans. Later on, each new generation wanted to leave the tribe to live with the whites. At last, we learned that there is no place for us in the European world, except places where not even animals could subsist. If life is difficult for a man like Antão, for us it is impossible."

Alma breaks in, wanting to understand, but Isaías continues:

"Many died and are still dying of disillusionment. This is but something peculiar to us Mairuns. We can die when the desire to live leaves us, when the joy of life ceases. A Mairun can lie in his hammock and say: 'I will die today' and will in fact die. It is not that he commits suicide, drinks poison. No. He dies because he wants not to live. This happens to many people: men who have lost children or women who are distraught at losing a brother or a child. All kinds of people who, seeing the end of the way of life they have enjoyed, and seeing the emergence of a way of life they abhor, become disillusioned and decide to die. I feel within myself that I too could make that decision. I too could make my heart stop, I don't know how."

Alma doubts it:

"I really don't think you could, Isaías. You're no Indian, don't kid yourself. You are as civilized as I am."

He insists that there are at least two modes of knowledge.

"One is what I feel, the other is what I learned in all those years. I've read a great deal—ethnology, psychology, theology. But all the things I learned form a kind of spiritual garb, a superficial cape, loose, slack. Within me, like a kernel, is my perception of the Mairun world. It is my deepest root. It is the seed. It is that which, in making me a man, makes me at the same time a member of my tribe, the Mairun people. This perception is my essence, my being. From it emerges a kind of wisdom that is different from the others, which cannot be spoken or communicated. It can only be lived. It is that which tells me I could die if I want and decide to. And what's more, it's impossible to teach something to anyone else. This feeling . . .

"Please, Isaías, what baloney! You should be able to come up with something better. You say that I'm all tangled up, but you're the complicated one, my friend. You make more difficulties for yourself than I've ever heard of!"

"I'm not joking, Alma. I'm speaking seriously. I'm talking about what I feel."

"Poor thing! I know. You weren't born, you were established. You are Mairunity itself."

This little wretch doesn't even know that she has guessed correctly. I was indeed established. She has probed the truth better than she thinks. I never did have an ordinary life. When I was a boy in the village, I was already chieftain-to-be. I was being prepared to take the place of my uncle Anacã, who for his part took the place of his uncle, Uruantã, and so on from one to the other back to the first Uruantã. The Mairuns can recite a list of more than twenty chieftains, giving for each the place where his umbilical cord and his skull are buried, that is to say, where he was born and where he died. My misfortune was mumps, which interrupted my destiny. Father Vecchio came, to cure me and right away he said that he couldn't treat me there in the village, so he took me to the Mission. I remained there. But here, too, I was not treated like the other boys. I never played with them. I had to endure the fathers praying over me day and night. Above all, Father Vecchio. His efforts were made not to convert but to reshape my soul. Put through that mill, I ended up wanting, desiring, aspiring to be a missionary. I felt I had been born to be one, that God needed me. In this state, I traveled to

Goiás Velho, to São Paulo, to Rome. I now returned devoid of everything.

"Yes, I was Mairunity. Now I am any Indian whatsoever."

"What was it that stripped you of everything?"

"What do I know? But I'm not yet entirely emptied. I still feel contaminated by those ideas, sullied by those preoccupations. I feel impure in the Mairun sense, impure as raw meat that has not been bitten and ritually purified by the sorcerer.

Alma tries to eat a piece of stale boiled cassava tuber and a bit of grilled fish, complaining that it is impossible to chew the scorched thick skin.

"That's what gives the fish its taste," explains Isaías, "it's like salt."

"It's disgusting, absolutely disgusting!" snaps Alma; but she goes on eating it.

At last, they beach the canoe because Isaías wants to take advantage of the remaining daylight to caulk a hole that has opened between two planks. He is wary of tackling the rapids with a leaky canoe. In a furious current, that crack could open up and flood everything in an instant, shivering the boat apart and dashing the pair against the rocks.

After removing the shelter, he cautiously turns the canoe over. He gathers some tow, melts the rest of the tar, and carefully calks all the spots that might be likely to leak.

Alma goes off to have a look around. She walks into the forest which begins right there next to the beach. After only a few steps she feels nearly lost. She walks a little further in what she thinks is the direction of the shore, but she gets even more disoriented when she doesn't find it immediately. She knows that she is close to the shore because she has not walked more than a hundred meters. But in direction? Where is the river? She feels bewildered in the middle of the forest of tall, thick tree trunks with foliage spreading out high above her. The ground she treads is covered with a thick soft mantle of dead leaves. She starts to call Isaías, humming Isaías! Isaías! as if she were playing. Then she shouts in a serious tone, Isaías! Isaías! Finally she shrieks hysterically, Isaías! Isaías! It is only when she stops shouting for a moment to control herself that she hears him answering from one direction: "I'm coming! I'm coming!" When she sees him, she is ashamed of herself.

"What's this all about, woman? You are next to the river but you are frightened? Couldn't you see where you were?"

"Yes, but it frightened me."

They return, walking slowly. Then both are startled violently by a screech coming from up there in the branches of the trees. It is a band of howler monkeys that had never seen people before and were attracted by Alma's screaming. They have come to find out what the noise is about. Leaping from branch to branch they are less afraid than curious to see the source. The old males guard the front and the rear; in the middle are the females with their little ones suckling or riding their mothers' backs. Young monkeys of all sizes are jumping and shrieking all over the place. The most terrifying snorting comes from the old and cunning leader of the band, an enormous, bearded howler monkey showing off, coiling his tail around a branch and holding on with his feet alone. He swings his body in the air and screams a syncopated shriek by tapping his mouth with his hands.

Alma watches, motionless. She has never seen so many animals together: wild animals, monkeys. Enormous monkeys, shrieking and howling. She is even more astonished when she feels a soft blow on her head. She smells the stink of turd and then sees the monkeys shitting into their hands and throwing it at her. Isaías is some distance away, out of range.

Alma runs to the beach as fast as she can, throwing off her clothes to the winds, and jumping frantically into the water. She wants to wash herself, she urgently needs to wash that slippery nastiness, that disagreeable taint of vile-smelling monkey turd from her hair and body. First, she swims impatiently, diving, kicking her legs, and rubbing and smoothing herself in the water with her hands. Then, partly clean and having calmed

down a bit, she sits on the beach and scrubs herself with sand
and leaves. But soon she returns to swimming and diving, scrub-
bing herself again, sniffing the tufts of crushed leaves as she
searches for traces of the persistent stench.

Isaías, upon returning, remains hidden in the tall grass nearby,
watching her without disclosing his presence. He could perhaps
have come closer, revealing himself and staring as much as he
wanted to. But instead he takes an obscure delight in furtive,
stolen, shameful glances. It is the first time since he was a little
boy that he has seen a woman bare, naked, stripped. It is the
first time in his life he has seen the pubic hair of a woman and
everything revealed. The muscles of his thighs and of his arms
are quivering as if he were suffering a cramp. His throat constricts from anguish. It is not lust, perhaps, but perhaps it is.
Desire strangled by surprise and fright. A man and a woman,
alone on an immense deserted beach.

THE WORD

Xisto, squatting by the wall of the chapel, is praying today as
he does every afternoon. His voice is hoarse, his accent, strong:

"My brothers, here we are again for our evening prayer. I,
with my mouth and my words; you, with your ears and your
understanding. Here we are, my brothers, once again. In front
of us we have the Holy Bible, our salvation. But we also have,
and we need to have, in addition to faith, perspicacity. Without
perspicacity, who can be saved? A perspicacity with substance,
with judgement; a perspicacity without perfidy. Our Lord God
abominates all indignity."

He rests a while and continues, admonishing:

"The mischievous One is right here, on the loose, in the
midst of us. But God will save us. We have the book in hand

and faith in our hearts. We also have Perpetinha, who, with her fine virgin voice to call upon God, praying, entreating. Her mother, Mistress Gueda, is always there at our beck and call. But not Master Cleto. He is an old believer, but his love is now for his cows. They eat grass the whole year round. They give birth to provide him with more cows. He believes he is their fat shepherd, that he shepherds the herd. What foolishness! It is they who shepherd him. They go on eating God's pastures and multiplying on their own to enrich him. But there is Mistress Gueda to pray for him and Perpetinha to sing. But can one pray on another's behalf?

"As for me, I don't think so. Each of us is alone. Each of us must pray with his own mouth and heart. Each of us has something to expiate. Each of us must save or lose himself. There are those who think my words are impertinent because I spoke the other day against the rich. Still I continue to preach against them; I acknowledge it. But it is because it is written, it is in the Book, as everyone knows. It is written that it is easier for a camel to pass through the eye of a needle than for a rich man to enter the Kingdom of Heaven. And you can all see that a camel is a bigger beast than a cow! But this is not the whole truth. There is Mr. Bob to teach us. His words, which I read yesterday and which I am going to read again today, are our light. Here they are:

" 'Because to him who hath, more shall be given; nevertheless, from him who hath not, even that which he hath shall be taken away.'

"So it is written. It is here! It is the whole truth, as simple as that. No one knows why; no one can explain. But that is how it is here and now, everyday, every hour. The rich enrich themselves, and the poor are penalized. As for me, I see in this the hand of the Devil; trickery, that's his specialty. It is the hand of the wicked, the finger of the Devil; it is the sign of the furtive. The world is the estate of God, but who is the caretaker? Who is he? He is the Devil! What does the Book teach us? It teaches everything. But what the Book shows to those who can see is

the war of God against the Devil and of the Devil against us.
Against men and women alike."

He opens the Book, searches for what he is looking for, points
to the page and says:

"Just look at this old man Job, lamenting, crying. He complained with good reason that God had let loose against him his
pack of hounds. What was that pack of hounds? Who was in
charge of them? The Devil, it couldn't be anyone else. They
left the old man naked and finished. They put an end to his
wealth. They put an end to his health. They put an end to his
family. They put an end to his honor. They put an end to his
happiness. But they could not put an end to his faith in God.
Because old Job was a hard bone to gnaw. Not the Devil, by
order of God or anyone else could conquer him. I'm not asking
for this for myself, or for us, my brothers; I'm not asking God
to try us that way, to let loose his pack of hounds against us.
No, never. I ask God to save us, to free us and keep us safe.
What I want from God is consolation, cure for our ailments,
assistance in our poverty. This is what I ask of God. We, poor
insignificant wretches that we are, we, God knows, would not
survive the first lap with those terrible hounds in pursuit, biting
us all over, scratching us, leaving us naked, wounded and bleeding."

Xisto reads the effect of his words in the faces of all, and
proceeds:

"The war of God with the Devil goes on here, every day, in
front of us, inside us. Inside me, inside you, deep within each of
us. We are the wretches suffering under the claws of God and
the Devil."

"I exorcize you, I exorcize that twisted truth from you. But it
is the truth. We have to sleep with it, and we have to wake with
it. And it will continue like that until Judgment Day. But are we
going to continue being so soft, or must we harden ourselves?"

He points to another page in the Bible:

"Look, it is written here: 'The day will come when the sun
shall darken. The moon will not reflect its clear light. The stars

will fall from the firmament, and Heaven will shatter into pieces. Then shall come the Son of Man, the Expected One, mounted on a horse of cloud, with all his power and glory, resplendent, the King of Kings, the Grandson of God!' He will come when the enchantment is over. Can the glory of God save us?"

He pauses momentarily, takes a deep breath, but instead of continuing to preach, he asks finally:

"Shall we pray, good people? Now, Perpetinha, how about the one about 'God who shall come':

Lord God Almighty	*mighty, mighty*
He who was	*was, was*
He who is	*is, is*
And shall come	*come, come*

Let's go to the next, Perpetinha. That one about our death fleeing:

Men shall seek death	*seek death, seek death*
They will not find it	*find it, find it*
They will want to die	*to die, to die.*
Death shall flee from them	*from them, from them*
The truth I tell you	*tell you, tell you*
That generation shall not pass	*not pass, not pass*
Without this happening	*happening, happening*
Heaven and earth shall pass	*shall pass, shall pass*
My word shall not	*shall not, shall not*

He pauses again, and when everyone is asking himself whether it's time to go to sleep, he begins to sermonize once again:

"God and the Devil are intermingled and separate. It depends on who is looking at them. One has to know how to look. It is much easier to blend, confusing instead of differentiating everything. In truth, no eye is sharp enough to be able always to distinguish the good from the bad of each thing. What we all see is the endless war and, within it, the two of them at grips with each other. Both, wreaking havoc on each other, so together that one and the other form a single knot, intermingled, mixed up, confused. The sun and the day belong to God, the moon and the night belong to the Devil. But at dusk and dawn they are the same thing: the night wrapped in the day, wanting to be born in it; the day emerging from the night that doesn't want to end. God and the Devil rolled up into one, confused. God and the Devil fighting each other, challenging each other. Fire belongs to the Devil, water to God, but who can live without fire? Whoever tries to will die. Whoever lives without fire is finished. This is what I say to you and repeat, the Devil is there, mixed up in everything. We live with him caring for us, looking after us, offending us, betraying us. That's how it is: if you leave fire unattended, it will burn your house down. But who can manage without fire? Whoever goes into water, with the confidence that it is God's realm, may drown. But who can manage without water?"

Xisto again asks Perpetinha to sing. Solo, she open with "My God, my God":

My God, my God
Why has thou forsaken me?
My God, my God
Why wilt thou not save me?
My God, my God
Wilt thou not listen to my prayer?
My God, my God
Day and night I call upon thee
My God, my God
I call upon thee and thou respondest not
My God, my God
Why Hast thou abandoned me?

They continue singing as a choir. Then Xisto commences a prayer, and they all intone it together. But soon they stop to talk about the Wild Beast that will arrive any day with the major temptation. Perhaps he will arrive in the form of a priest in a green cassock distributing gold beads.

MAÍRA-MONAN

Long ago is the time of the Nameless One and of his belch: Mairahú and Maíra. This, our time of reconstructed men, is the era of Maíra-Monan, God of the Dead, and of Maíra-Coraci, God of the Sun. Each has his own world. That of Maíra-Monan is the world of the living-dead. That of Maíra-Coraci is ours, the world of the living-mortals. Neither can invade the world of the other. Only in an eclipse are they confused, but only momentarily. Then there is the horror. The living-dead start warring with the eternal bats, and if they are wounded, they die once and for evermore. The living-mortals who allow themselves to get involved in this war never return.

The war of the worlds began when Maíra told Micura that it was necessary to confront the Jurupari people, the favorites of Mairahú, the Father-God. It really was necessary because only by force could the night be taken away from them, so one could rest; only by force could the living flute, the piping guan, be stolen from them, so one could dance, which Micura very much liked to do. They would take advantage of the occasion also to obtain manioc and other food that the Juruparis had.

They made plans and departed for the great lake where the village of the great chief Jurupari was located. They spent some time there, listening to and learning the music of the living flutes coming from the depths. They watched the comings and goings of the Juruparis every day as they danced and sang. Eventually, they discovered a narrow channel by which they passed at times from the large lake to smaller lakes.

Maíra then made a living canoe that paddled itself. It was a dolphin whose belly had been emptied out. Maíra and Micura got inside. The Juruparis in the depths of the water saw only an enormous fish swimming around. The fish-canoe went up to the narrow channel and stayed there. Maíra then threw into the water some big fishnets he had brought to catch living flutes.

They waited, very quietly, until the day when the Juruparis decided to dance again out of their lake and entered the narrow channel. Many entered the water, playing flutes and singing and dancing. They were distracted. By the time they realized, three of the living flutes had already fallen into nets and been gathered by Maíra. The Juruparis were splashing water all over the place and causing such a commotion that the strait dried up completely and suddenly filled up wit water again. However, the fish-canoe was really good for navigation and could cope with any tidal bore.

No harm would have been done if Micura had not wanted to hold and play one of the living flutes. As he put his hand into one of the nets, he got a frightful jolt—tremendous, such as the power of ten electric eels together—that threw him, trembling and limp, into the air and then dumped him into the water. The Juruparis, thinking it was Maíra, fell on him to tear him apart. There was such agitation that the water bubbled red with blood! The remains of Micura bobbed up and down, whitish like a soft piece of manioc dough.

Maíra was furious. He ordered the canoe to carry on its own the living flutes to the bank; then he dived into the water right there. The Juruparis went for him like a swarm, not biting but crushing and bruising him with their toothless mouths like sheatfish. Maíra simply grabbed the Juruparis' tongues and pulled. At once they fell dead. He killed a great number of them.

When he climbed out of the lake with the remains of the father of people that Micura had been, all the surviving Juruparis fled, terrified. They dived to the bottom of the water and purely for revenge woke up the night which had been sleeping there since the beginning of time. The night rose in great bubbles exploding in darkness. At once a black gloom spread, obscuring everything, silencing the animals, and frightening the people. Only the toads and cicadas which were formerly mute began to cry out from amazement. There, at the edge of the lake, in the darkness of the first night, Maíra built a little fire to be able to see and to warm the remains of his brother. He began to reconstruct him very slowly. First he worked on one side, then the other. He remade an arm, from the arm a hand, from the hand fingers, and from each finger, a nail. In this way he entirely remade his twin brother, but more beautiful than before. Having finished this reconstruction, he called:

"Micura!"

Micura woke up, looked astonished, and replied:

"I'm here, chief. I've been swimming."

The two then took advantage of the darkness and the fear that had overtaken the Juruparis and dived to the bottom of the lake to look for their gardens. From there they carried away for the Mairuns a variety of trees bearing fruit, seeds, and roots; the best to be eaten raw, boiled, and roasted. The first tree they found was a silky and small kind of palm tree having a soft trunk without branches but with long drooping leaves that bore great clusters of long yellow fruit wrapped in smooth skins, soft and easily peeled off. They are good, sweet-smelling and tasty whether eaten raw as fruit, or boiled or roasted as vegetables. Especially roasted, with meat.

They also found some elegant little plants with knotted gray stems branching, full of knots and of pointed green leaves covered with veins. These plants yield coarse succulent roots from which farina, cassava bread, and tapioca are made. Boiled with fish, they are the best food there is. But be careful, for this species has a twin sister, so poisonous as to kill. Its deadly juice has to be extracted, and the plant has to be well cooked or roasted before it is safe to eat. Some like this kind best in spite of it being so troublesome to prepare.

In the middle of a garden were numerous tall thin plants, green and spiky, with long leaves like sheaths covered with fuzz, offering halfway up the stalks at a height even a child can reach, great ears of grain wrapped in straw. These, too, are good to eat boiled or roasted with fish or meat.

Throughout the Jurupari gardens vivid little green plants grew on little mounds of soft earth. The edible part of these plants consists of the sweet nuts that grow on the roots in shells. These are better than anything for eating raw or toasted, especially for chewing on a voyage or even at home when one is hungry.

So it was that the Mairuns acquired trees and seeds of banana, manioc, Indian corn, and peanuts. The ancient ones liked them very much. We still like them very much today. The foods of the Jurupari are the best, particularly manioc. It lies there, buried, growing. People need only to dig it up when they want to eat it.

Maíra-Ambir, seeing night spread over the whole world, understood what was happening. With great anger, with surpassing fury, he saw what the twins had done to his favorites, the Juruparis. He didn't say anything but started the war right there, sending against Maíra the ferocious hounds that guard his abode on the upper side of the world, at the source of the Iparanã.

Maíra considered things momentarily, and when he had overcome his fear which was great, he sent against his father's hounds his living war clubs. They went flying, directly from drawings in the air, and wrought havoc. Soon there were no more black hounds, flying and snarling threateningly. All of them fell to the ground and were transformed into sloths, making them unrecognizable. The war clubs, having finished the flight, also fell to the ground and were turned into snakes that still slither around there.

Maíra-Ambir did not like this. Now he sent against his son what was most powerful: Jaguarunouí, the Great Blue Tiger, the size of the world. Maíra saw only, in the darkness of the nocturnal sky, that huge blue-black jaguar, growing, sparkling, furious, immense. It spiraled down, descending slowly on the light of the beams that were shooting from its eyes. It came to make an end of him, to make an end of everyone, to make an end of everything. Maíra was crying from fright. Micura was terrified but he begged:

"Hey, brother, save us. You've created all kinds of mischief; now this animal is coming to finish us off. Save your people, brother."

Maíra looked at the people he had just re-created and saw that they merited life. At that moment, he invented the bow and arrow. Quickly he lay on his back, held the bow between his feet, stretched the string extending his legs and pulling his arms in, and shot arrow after arrow into the heights of the sky. The first flew and flew and lodged itself at the top of the head of the sky. The next flew until it hit the end of the first. He shot a third into the end of the second and likewise and so on. Soon one could see a rod of arrows fastened one to the other descending from the heights of the sky. Maíra continued shooting arrows until the pole reached the dancing ground of the village.

He climbed it to confront the Great Blue Tiger of Maíra-Ambir in the sky. Micura climbed after him, enthusiastic at participating in that war, and fearless. He was excessively ignorant! When Maíra let go of the rod of arrows and flew up above the blue tiger, Micura screamed,

"Don't leave me here, brother. I don't know how to fly."

Maíra returned, grabbed Micura by the backside and blew into his asshole until he filled up like a bladder, bobbing in the air like an enormous balloon. While this was happening, the Great Blue Tiger was watching, trying to understand what would occur next. When he saw that huge balloon advancing in a menacing way, he turned to pursue it. Maíra took advantage of his indecision and with a single leap entered the tiger through one of his ears and began to tear at his brains and then to shred the guts of this great beast of God.

The Jaquarunouí of Maíra-Ambir howled with pain, not

knowing what was attacking him. He howled like mad, feeling
his heart, his liver, his kidneys hurting as if they were being cut
to ribbons, as indeed they were.

Micura then entered the fray. He floated near the blue tiger,
turned his back, and began to fart an intolerable stink right into
the nostrils of the divine tiger. Destroyed inside where Maíra
was demolishing his entrails and attacked outside where Micura
was releasing salvos of farts, the blue tiger was losing strength so
fast that he succumbed to faintness and surrendered himself to
space. Maíra then made Micura enter the monster's mouth.
Once he got inside, both of them spilled, all over the earth, the
tiger's blood as redness, its shit as greenness, and its bones, reduced to a mealy powder, as whiteness. So they created the
lively colors that bring so much pleasure to the world.

When this job was completed, all that was left of the Great
Blue Tiger was its great dark pelt with the silvery spots and the
two enormous eyes through which Maíra-Ambir used to look
at the world. Maíra nailed up the pelt in deepest space, and the
silvery spots became the stars. The eyes, which could not be left
there watching the world for the Old One, have served ever
since as the abode and apparel of Maíra and Micura.

Mairahú, the ancestral God, saw that he was beaten, at least
for the time being. He had nothing stronger than the Great Blue
Tiger to send against Maíra. He withdrew then to the lower
side of the world, the side of the Dead, and became Maíra-
Monan, the God of the Dead.

Maíra, the Son, upon entering the eye of the Jaquarunouí,
burst forth into light and converted himself into Maíra-Coraci,
the Sun. He turned his brother Micura into the Moon. The
Mairuns, who were watching from here below and could only
see with difficulty, in the darkness of the night, the war between
God the Father and God the Son, were dazzled when Maíra
became the Sun and drowned the earth in light. They were
afraid of dying from so much brilliance. When night returned
they were frightened even more, thinking they were reduced to
having to remain in the little moonlight of Micura. But dawn

arrived once again. And ever since, day and night have followed each other, the Sun and Moon illuminating and lighting this world of ours. Maíra and Micura move in circular paths, always on the alert for an ambush by Maíra-Monan, who might attack again at any moment.

THE THROAT

At dusk, Isaías walks along the beach with his fishing line and hook and his bow and arrows, looking for something to eat. Quickly he loses two arrows, testing his strength and accuracy. He also loses a hook and half the line on a tree trunk submerged at the water's edge. Hours later, when it's already dark, he returns with a small catfish.

"Not much of a feast, is it, Isaías?"

The feast is realized the following morning. Isaías, who has already embarked, sees at the end of the beach the tracks of a turtle that had come out of the river to lay its eggs and bury them in the sand. They stop, dig up the eggs, wash and eat to their hearts' content those mushy eggs without shells which are good both boiled and fried. They take plenty of them to eat, without salt, as they drift down the Iparanã.

They continue to navigate down the river for days on end, by the throat of the Iparanã. One fine afternoon they eat a turtle with a fat liver and sweet meat which Isaías had found wandering on a beach. But the next day they return to eating hard-boiled eggs and a fish that Isaías had hooked. Days of true hunger begin though every day they have something to put in their mouths.

When they are going down a side channel, the most convenient of the Little Stretch, Isaías notices some thin wisps of smoke rising above the trees near the bank. He looks carefully.

There is no beach. This is one of those places where the forest
comes right up to the water. It could only be the Xaepẽs, he
thinks. It's the limit of their territory. Better not say anything
to Alma.

But they must travel more rapidly. Forget about beaching the
canoe for a while. The Xaepẽs would be there, lying in wait.
Perhaps various bands are hiding there in the forest; they would
give themselves away to the eyes of a Mairun by the little fires
they make, thinking no one can see them. Without those thin
trails of smoke fading away above the crowns of the trees I
would never have known that my death was in hiding there.

They are the Xaepẽs, hunters of men and hunters of metal
tools. There they are, hunting. It is essential to move rapidly. It
is essential to paddle with all one's strength and to keep right on
top of the main current, in the middle of the river. To get
away, get away as far as possible. How many leagues are the
Xaepẽs capable of running along the edge of the forest, keeping
up with a canoe? Keeping up with it, keeping up until it stops?
But he would never stop on the left bank, on their side. If he
had to stop it would be on the right. Fortunately, the Xaepẽs
don't know how to paddle.

I still have half the day to advance. I'll tell Alma that today
we can't stop to look for food. The Mission is not far away.
We'll stop only to sleep and bathe more or less. That way we'll
be able to reach the Mission tomorrow sometime in the morning.

Threads of smoke rise through the crowns of the trees that
lean over the left bank. Below, a small band of Xaepẽs squat
grilling fish caught by hand near the bank. The smoke rising
through the trees describes sunbeams between the trunks and
the vines, making visible the source of the light shining on the
dead leaves on the ground and glowing through the foliage on
the branches. Other bands are camped further ahead, a short
distance separating them from one another. They have crossed
dozens of leagues of forest, walking without rest, to arrive at
the boundary of their territory, to camp there where they can
see, at times, albeit rarely, the powerful white or black men,

wrapped in cloth or leather and armed with thundersticks. Of all the peoples the Xaepẽs know about, none arouses so much interest as these owners of mirrors and sharp cutting tools. Each band encamped there at the edge of the Iparanã will have, in retrospect, exciting stories to tell. About enormous humming canoes without paddles that move rapidly, cutting through the water. About big boats that navigate the river, piled high with a wealth of leather sacks, buzzing loudly. About canoes that go up and down by force of paddles, carrying here and there everything desirable in the world.

A few heroic bands of Xaepẽs have ventured forth and returned, bringing proof of their feats: heavy iron tools in the form of wedges or light ones in the form of fish or biters in the form of jaws. Some have brought empty cans, glass bottles, plastic wrappings. Some bands were actually celebrated because they had succeeded in bringing one or another of those trophies that pass from village to village as supreme examples of exchange.

The Xaepẽs have often tried to approach the strange men. But they know it is almost impossible to come to any kind of understanding with such fierce people. In several years of attempts they succeeded only in increasing the number of victims of the thundersticks that pierce from a distance, killing through small but deep wounds. With extreme care they had managed to capture some whites and some blacks, but these were so violent that they ended up having to kill them. The first captives only served to prove that their white or black color was natural and not painted on as the Xaepẽs had supposed. Later, they captured some children and integrated into the tribe a few women who proved almost useless. They knew nothing about making iron tools or arms. And they didn't even have extraordinary powers.

No Xaepẽ band likes to return empty-handed after undertaking the perilous journey to the Iparanã. Such a failure provokes an unacceptable loss of prestige in the face of successful bands of their own tribe. That is why they stay there as long as possible, until almost the end of summer, seeking an opportunity to fall on someone in a lucky encounter. So it is that they provide themselves with metal tools. But these are so rare and so precious that they are used until they are completely worn down.

In addition to the larger instruments, such as knives, axes, machetes and hoes, they know of hooks, spoons, and forks, a few of which they've collected. One band brought home a pair of scissors which are still the only ones and which gives them enormous prestige. Others brought cloth and shoes which had no use. They also tried drinking rum and eating soap, but found them not good. Salt and sugar seemed better to them. Matches and gunpowder were dreaded and so was anything that resembled them. Many other small things passed from hand to hand, from village to village, without disclosing their utility: spectacles, books, and things of that sort that served only as trophies.

The Xaepẽ band now camped under the shelter of the trees is one of the poorest. They have only a few metal bits and pieces to show for themselves. As a result of this, they have more incentive than other bands to obtain more objects, in any way and at any cost. Their advantage is a white woman and a black boy whose capture had cost the band a war. The hopes of the band rest on them to teach them how to approach and overcome the whites, or, if opportunity offers itself, to exchange them for iron tools. The woman is one of the wives of the chief. Apart from the color of her skin and the texture of her hair, she is indistinguishable from the other women. Like all of them, she carries, inlaid through her lower lip, a thick wooden disc the size of a saucer. The black, in spite of having been a youth when captured, is a Xaepẽ as keen to plunder as any of the others. He is prized for his utility but above all for his value as a trophy—which is especially important for anyone like him who has the status of foreigner, of prisoner of war.

He is standing to one side of the fire, attending to the fish being grilled, moving his enormous lip disc with his tongue, talking to his companions about the best way of attacking the strangers when they are encountered. The others ask him to keep quiet, because they must carefully watch the strangers before attacking them. They must be as vigilant as other bands that had the most success. They must, first of all, watch carefully. Only then would there be any hope of a successful attack.

The old Xaepẽ who is leader of the band goes from group to group, listening to the whispering, recommending silence and care. He repeats to everyone the same instructions, to keep very quiet and to do nothing before consulting him. It is necessary to observe the strangers for a long time before attacking.

Hearing, in the distance, the muffled tock-tock of a stone axe against a tree trunk, and guessing that some Xaepẽ is cutting out a bees' nest, the chief goes off with due care to tell him to stop the noise.

It is the young black who first sees the canoe entering the calm stretch of river. His fright is so great that he shouts involuntarily:

"It's them!! There they are!"

All the Xaepẽs turn around and quickly cover the fire with sand; the tock-tock of the axe falls silent; and everyone crouches in the bushes along the edge of the water, watching the canoe as it descends. At last, everything is in full view: the people in the vessel—one in the bow, one in the stern, both wearing clothes—belong to the tribe of foreign owners of metals. Each group, each man, each woman wants badly for the canoe to come nearer to the bank.

The canoe, however, follows its unassailable course in the middle of the river, borne by the current which opens up into a wide curve beyond the calm depths. The Xaepẽs turn to look at the small Tapera Beach directly below. It is inviting; it is there where, on an earlier occasion, the party from which the woman and child were abducted had disembarked and camped. But the canoe continues down the middle of the river, apparently with no intention of beaching there. Already on the fringe of the little beach where they ran under cover of the bush, the Xaepẽs watch and wait and beg for the canoe to come, to come.

Isaías says to Alma:

"Do you see that cloud of smoke above the trees? Do you

think there are people camped there?" And he himself replies:

"No, no! There's nobody there. Or there would be a canoe drawn up on the beach there. There's no one. Let's keep going. Early tomorrow morning we have to cross the Long Stretch, with the rapids; by early afternoon, with any luck, we will arrive at the Mission of Our Lady of O.

EGO SUM

It can't be memory. I was never there, never. No one was. Nevertheless, I remember it well. I see within myself, I remember with utmost precision that frozen desert and the furious wind shaking the space station. Am I mad? I must be. I was probably always a bit touched, at least since that day when I painted the water supply of the city. Paris green? Potassium permanganate? The result was blue, a methylene-blue, and I very well know how blue that is. Someone said that the kilo packet would be enough to paint the sea. Poison? The water in the reservoir and the pipes—and this I know; as a child I saw and and suffered it—became perfectly blue.

At that time the most complicated and fascinating machine was the locomotive on the Central line. It would arrive every night chugging and whistling, all lit up, its pistons working relentlessly, puffing and spitting fire and steam. It would leave the following morning, all spick-and-span. Ah! To travel by train! Meanwhile everyday it poured out a multitude of people, and the next day it swallowed another, even bigger. They were my people, who went to be Bahians in life, such as I was.

Those were my best years; lacking in grief, they were easygoing, not unhappy. I was the equal of myself and knew myself. Today, who knows about me? I have been partly refashioned out of wood: half of my chest and one arm, the right one, and the whole of my head. I am a leftover. More is known by Jesse who unmade and remade me, taking away irreplaceable parts from the perfect and limitless creation that I exemplified.

Before that, long before, I walked around in different skins, preoccupied with other affairs. Some were untellable, like the voyage in a flying saucepan which I navigated among the stars with Oscar and Heron. There in the dark bottom of that huge flat casserole of political cast-iron, we hunted and were ourselves hunted. We were looking for men without hearts, to bleed them, though much afraid of them, because they could bleed us as well. We took great care not to wound any man with a heart. Our greatest dread, however, was the sphere of memory that flew over our heads, Oscar would say. We needed to know where it was so as not to look at it. Whoever looked at it would have his memory erased.

There are many other cases, more easily told I know. Or they would be if they were worth the trouble. Some seem so authentic now as do all materials of memory. But they get all mixed up in retrospect. A jack tree in the moonlight, the last place where the serenaders in that town of mine stopped. A man who pedals an organ playing Couperin's funeral march and who causes rich and poor coffin stools to rise from the ground. Both are consistent as materials of memory. The jack tree once existed, that is certain, but now it is no more, except in my breast. The man, that one who is not, is I. Both subsist equally in the memory; they are neglected forgettings. He who knows about them is I, and I don't know anything.

But none of this has anything to do with the matter at hand. What is important here and now is to recall how I came to meet Avá, who was a Bororo and who called himself Tiago. That is how I knew him. I saw him once, covering with feathers the tiny bones of his daughter who had died of smallpox. He was much comforted by reciting, with the appropriate cadences, the litany in Latin. Anacã, on the other hand, would have nothing to do with funerals; nor was he a Bororo, but rather an Urubu-Caapor or forest Indian, a dearly beloved friend. He was very short, fat, and cheerful, the closest thing to an intellectual that I ever met among Indians.

He gave information about everything and wanted to know more: "And Uruanta, my great-great-grandfather, did you ever meet him? You saw him? Where?" When I saw him for the first time amid all of those Indians who spoke only Tupi, I was looking for someone who was shouting,

"O quei, boi! O rait, maic!"

He had learned those yells from some gringos who were filming around there. We became and stayed friends, so much so that one day in a gesture of tenderness he gave me some of his blood. It was like this: I was lying in a hammock watching these people living their everyday lives; thinking and writing, concentrating. He was on the other side of the hut, lying in a hammock with a woman. She was lulling him to sleep, searching for lice on him, and cracking them with her teeth. Anacã called out to me:

"E sae, ne e apiay ete." I admitted he was right, that it was true. I was really very sad. We talked: he from over there, I from here. He said that I seemed to be in the house with them, but no. I was very, very far away. Probably with my woman. . . . Soon afterward he came to lie in my hammock with me and showed me, tightly clasped in his left hand, half a dozen of his fattest lice which he nestled in my hair, affectionately.

"They are there for your woman to catch!"

He was a great friend, Anacã. I have so many memories of him. Among others, I see the old man scribbling in my notebook, pretending to know how to write: he wanted to impress his relatives. Better still was when, after months of isolation, my last parcel arrived and in it the *Quixote*. I took the book, threw myself down in a hammock, and started to read, and to laugh like a madman, returning to my old self. When I put the book on the ground, he jumped from his hammock, grabbed the book, opened it and started to howl himself. For Anacã, the book was a laughter machine.

Those months of inescapable living together in the communal

hut almost drove me mad. Only within the four walls of a prison cell have I felt so confined and constrained. Conditioned to live in houses with walls and doors to isolate ourselves, to hide ourselves, we can't stand that ceaseless communion among Indians, day and night, constantly living a communal life. At times I had to run off to search for myself in the bush. The worst was that I would get furious, whenever I found them sending the children after me, fearful that I might get lost. Oh, those times so long ago when I tried to behave like I were them, learning to live the life of others but feeling hopelessly withdrawn into and clinging to myself.

It was then that I felt for the first time the terrible double taste of fear and a desire to die. A pale unhappy man whose only son had just died declared himself *inharon* or berserk. Everyone fled, dragging me with them to leave him rabid and raging alone in the village. He could have set fire to the houses if he had wanted to, killed the dogs, cut off the hammock knots, broken the storage jars, and done all the mischief he was capable of doing until he calmed down. He kicked and screamed on the ground, with his bow and arrows in his hand, ready to shoot. Furious as a warrior at the moment of killing his most hateful enemy.

I, a hopeless idiot, irresponsible beyond belief, I wanted to see his face. I fled and then with the greatest possible care, I slowly circled round behind the houses. As I came out onto the dancing ground, beside a house, to look, I found myself face to face with the *inharon*. I was stunned! So was he. We stood there for a second or a century—I don't know which—staring at each other, enflamed. When my terrified spirit returned to me, I turned around and walked slowly away, very slowly, expecting the jolt of an arrow in my back, craving and at the same time fearing it. Now, I thought, and I would take a step. It isn't now but now it will be. And I would take another. Nothing! So I walked, one step at a time, arrow shot by arrow shot, waiting, waiting, until finally I reached the end of the house. Then I darted from between two of the houses and ran into the middle of the forest.

I stopped around a hundred meters away, frightened by the silence of the madman. Had I completely demoralized the wretched man with my stupid curiosity, my wanting to observe the ferocious hatred of a desperate Indian? At last I became reconciled with myself on hearing the energetic howl with which he resumed his role of furious *inharon*.

His murderous frenzy which terrified everyone, the ferocious madness of a man gone *inharon*, which a man can only exercise once in his life, was a fury bounded by rules. It was a madness of their own. It did not apply to me. That is how he and I, both of us understood it. But I didn't learn. I have continued throughout my life wanting to see people in a frenzy, face to face. Perhaps only so that I will be able to run away in terror. When, upon one occasion in my life, I too had to get furious, I controlled myself and almost suffocated as I was overcome by the vilest grief. But when the hour of fear arrived, the last fear, the ferocious fright of knowing finally with absolute certainty that I was mortal, that I would have to live each day, from that day forward, hand in hand with death; then, and only then did I perceive that the urgent thing is to live. I am learning.

What is there to say? What cannot be said about the gorge of love? Body and Soul of so many altars are drained from my recollections? How many were there? How many will there be? Ten? One? None? Oh, long brief delusions that are as salt to the flesh of life. Hail!

Gratia plena. Ave.

One day I said I would be Emperor, to the amazement of my subjects. They had no idea, the innocents, that my kingdom is of the Holy Spirit, in the old chapel of the Rosary.

Minas, that one, oh Carlos! Still is and so will be, as long as I am. It's a field of memory I'm going to recover, if there still is time. There they shine, I've seen them: baroque, vociferous prophets. One among them speaks to me without pause or end. It is he with mouth burned by the word of God: Isaías.

Oh fierce fires that burn me not! I had wished for the total blaze of absolute truth, I who knew only smoking embers and the bitterness of gall diluted by the sea.

What more did my poor heart insatiably crave? Beauty, perhaps, if it were a matter of free choice, innocent and open. Impossible?

Also and above all, I had wished for glory, like an oxim, a sorcerer. The glory of my lingering after me, for a long time, in the memories of the grandchildren of the son I never had. To endure. But, how! I don't know. What I do know is my enormous envy of the lives in the death of my two most loved friends, Ernesto and Salvador, now no more.

Oh life that trickles away absentmindedly, like sand between the fingers of time, sifting through my hand even the memory of the feel of my past. We endure only, if at all, through the usury of the memory of others until the evening of ultimate oblivion.

MAÍRA AND MICURA

Maíra-Coraci, the Sun, and his brother, Micura-Iaci, the Moon, come down here sometimes to play like people, but principally to experience the world through the Mairun body and spirit.

On several occasions they've come to set aright things that were not going well. One visit was to correct a silly mistake they themselves had made: when they robbed the Juruparis of their jacuis, their living flutes, and abandoned them without thinking. Night had fallen unexpectedly, and having to confront the blue tiger at once, they had not yet decided to whom to give the flutes and the plants. The women very shrewdly, on seeing the plants, the seed, and the jacuis in the living canoe, appropriated everything for themselves.

This created many complications. The women used the flutes to frighten the men and force them to hunt and fish without rest. It is true that they themselves gathered the staple foods from their new fields. But otherwise things were not as they are now. Today a man can go out to hunt, to fish, to catch songbirds, or to extract honey, because the women dig up the manioc tubers and make cassava bread for everybody. Then when he returns from the hunt, exhausted, he can spend a few days in his hammock, resting and eating cassava bread and meat. But it wasn't always like this. No.

In the times when women ruled, everyone was driven to produce like the poor as Europeans are today. The men would have no more of that kind of captivity; they wanted time for relaxation. They wanted to have to go out to work at most only once a day. It could be in the morning or the afternoon, to till the fields, or to fish, or hunt; but let it be one thing each day. And after a great hunt they wanted to rest well, eat cassava cakes and drink tapioca gruel.

The women thought they had a good system and didn't want to change it. Also, whenever they could, they took the most beautiful ornaments. They were the ones who painted themselves most with annatto and genipap. They were the ones who gave orders and relaxed. The men did as they were told and sweated like fools.

All of this took place because the women had the great jacui flutes. The men were not allowed to see the flutes. If they did, the women said, the men would be raped up the ass by the jacui flutes themselves. The poor things, they lived in constant fear.

This state of affairs lasted a long time, a very long time, until the day when Micura, the Moon, decided it could go on no longer, that it had already caused too much trouble. He conspired with Maíra to guarantee power to the men.

Maíra, the Sun, made an enormous buzzer in the shape of a fish which, when swung in the air on the end of a cord, produced a frightening hum. He went to the village, spinning the wooden fish above his head. The women, bewildered by the terrible buzz, stopped playing the flute and singing. Terrified, they ran from the Great House into their own homes. Then the men, who had been alerted, seized the jacuis that the women had left lying on the dancing ground; they took possession of them and of the Great House which thenceforth became the Great House of Men. There, they learned from Maíra how to tame and play the living flutes and how to make the wooden fish-buzzers. So now we men give the orders, have the best ornaments, and paint out bodies most attractively with annatto and genipap.

The women know that they can never again see the living flutes. They know, especially, that they can not nor will ever see Maíra's buzzer. If ever a woman one day dares to look at an anhangá buzzer, she must be raped by all the men until she dies.

The old men sometimes tell of a band of women who have never accepted the rule of men. They had to abandon the villages and roam about endlessly, waging war to get more women to join them, and stealing men. It is easy to recognize them, because to facilitate their use of the bow and arrow they do not allow the right breast to grow. The women they capture are incorporated into their band. They use men to fuck and have children, then they kill and eat them. They also kill and eat their male offspring.

There is no greater danger for a man than to fall into the hands of these warrior women.

It is good to live the way Maíra taught. At times, we think that he likes the Europeans best, but the blame may well be ours. As we prefer to lounge in a hammock or drift with the current, he obligated the others to work hard, without repose, and make things. We were not created for that purpose. We are best at gentle loving and slow fucking. Also we are good for companionship in general as we are not driven by avarice, not given to hanging on to property. We like to give. And we don't overtax ourselves. Women are there for a man to make love to if he wants to. Friends are there to converge, play, and wrestle with. Good food is never missing. Every year the fields yield enough manioc, and there is no end of fish and game.

The best of Maíra's inventions is that children are always

being born for people to play with, laugh with, and bring up with love and patience. It is also very good to paint the body with beautiful colors, to stroll about, swim, dance, drink cassava beer, sing, and make people laugh. This is how we like to live. This is how Maíra likes to see us. As for work, it's not too bad provided it is slow and easy and the sun is not too hot.

Better still is to rest, to have a full belly, and to lie in one's hammock with a woman and fuck slowly, then go out into the bush together for a good shit, and then fuck again, if you feel like it. That's what Maíra and Micura do when they come around here. It's the joy of living of the Mairun people; Maíra gave us this.

THE STOMACH

The little vessel with two souls huddled aboard advances inexorably toward the funnel of riotous waters. Joyfully and vertiginously it descends the thundering stretch of the Choke Rapids. Suddenly it is in the middle of that menacing abyss: the cataract of furious waters, brilliant white, rushing down, streaming along open veins between the rocks, abusive and sparkling. Flat barren land and a whirlpool of sighing waters under the azure light of a tranquil sky.

The tiny canoe leaps free and seems more often suspended in midair than supported by the unstable surface of the voracious current. Alma sits paralyzed as her terrified soul strains to leave her quavering body; Isaías, proud and self-reliant, standing in the prow, holding his bow for no reason, hopes to save them from the inevitable even if that means giving up paddling and leaving it to fate to lead them to safety, leap by leap through the turbulent cascade.

There it goes, propelled by insensate forces. Now it turns

wildly upon itself, maddened in the ferocious vortex of the whirlpool. Stern ahead, it flies violently as if to crash into a thousand fragments against the blue-grained rock protruding from the edge of the mammoth sinkhole.

Alma and Isaías, eyes tightly shut with horror and abandon, can only imagine that the rock must have somehow vanished in thin air or that the canoe bravely vaulted over it . . . or, who knows? Maybe it grazed by, thanks to a masterstroke by a shaft against the rock at the right place, at a precise angle, at the right instant.

They open their eyes in amazement to find themselves miraculously flying along the channel of seething water, rapidly leaving the foot of the rapids, with stem and stern where they ought to be. With the passing of the terror that had left them out of their wits, they try to laugh at the trip and at themselves. Isaías says that the rapids have killed more people than malaria. He soon begins to recognize and point out to Alma old clearings where brushwood had been cut for burning when he was a boy. At last they are arriving.

The voyage had taken many days longer than had been expected; all told, four times as long as Antão had estimated. But they were finally arriving at the waters of the Mission. Just below the Choke Rapids they encounter a boat with four young Mairuns who are paddling downriver, accompanied by Father Cyril. The two canoes meet in the middle of the waterway and continue navigating side by side for some time. The boys, who are returning from a visit to the old clearing, identify Isaías and begin to chatter happily in Mairun.

Father Cyril and Alma don't understand a word but join with zest in the laughter. They even talk to each other a bit. Alma is handed some bananas and honey beans. A little further on, the boats separate, as Father Cyril, being able to navigate faster, wants to go ahead to announce the visitors. He is also very excited to hear the news about the band of Epexãs at Tapera Beach, above the rapids.

In the middle of the afternoon they reach the port of the

Mission to find it deserted. But soon two lay brothers come to greet them; Brother Benvenuto, still young, and old Brother Cipriano, who remembers Isaías. The two carry the baggage. Isaías accompanies his valise to the fathers' house and Alma, her suitcases to the guest room at the sisters' house.

A bed with sheets, curtains, a washbasin, a lavatory, a shower, soap, and a bath towel. It is luxurious. Then a glass of passion-fruit juice, served in the room. Later, tea with cake and biscuits, and the suggestion that they should rest after the hardships of the voyage. In the early evening they will be summoned for talks, she with the sisters, he with Father Ludgero, the director.

Isaías, glued to the window, strains to recognize the old Mission. He had grown up in this house, but the forest has receded quite a ways, and the eucalyptus seedlings planted then are now trees. Everything else has grown too: new houses and a chapel which is now the church of Our Lady of O, or as the old missionaries used to tell the Mairuns, Our Lady of Mosaingar. But it all seems empty, deserted. Where is the crowd of boys who played together back then? He had seen those four youths on the river, and now he counts seven priests walking in a file to the chapel. Could they be the only ones?

He anticipates the probable difficulties of conversing with Father Vecchio who must be very old, almost eighty. How would he start? "Good evening, Father, your blessing." No, too little after too long. "I have returned, Father Vecchio, embrace me." No, that wouldn't do either, it sounds pompous, solemn. Should I simply embrace him and ask for his blessing? No, that's not enough. My God, he thinks, of what importance is all of this? Why should I worry? What matters is our conversation; the explanations can come later. Why didn't I take orders in Rome? Should I speak of that last bitter discussion with the representative of the Order in Brasília? The thought recalled his final outburst: "I'm going, Father, whether you like it or not. It's my land, it's my people, I'm going!" Had any news of this arrived here? Such talk would pain Father Vecchio and also Father Aquino, deeply. What had become of him with his obsession to write and rewrite, year after year, the manual of Mairun ethnology, including more details than any other person has mastered. Did Father Aquino know even half as much about his own Calabrian people?

Isaías kneels on the floor of the room to search inside himself, once more, for what he does not see outside. He wants to consider the sense of his experiences; the years of his childhood spent there; that option—his first premeditated one—to become a priest. What was the sense? Knees on the floor, he begins his habitual rite. First, cleanse the mind with prayer until it is blank. Then, and courageously, open the heart and let unleash the dogs of doubt therein to argue. Since Rome, he has performed the same old ritual ceaselessly; but now he needs a dialogue with God. He and God, together, alone. Without the distance between them, as in the past; communicating in that passion exacerbated by his return.

He wishes and hopes that in this new room of the old Mission, albeit empty, God may be more present than at the foot of his cot in the cell of the Roman convent.

Tremens factus sum ego et timeo
Exsintabunt Domino ossa humiliata

De profundis clamavi ad te, Domine
Domine, exaudi vocem meam
Et clamor meus ad te veniat

Miserere mei, Domini
Quoniam infirmus sum
Saname, Domine
Et anima mea turbate est valde
Sed tu, Domine, usquequo?

Te ergo quaesumus
Ab occutis meis munda me Domine
Et ab aliens parce servo tuo

My Father, nothing here speaks to me of you. Only the trees
and the animals as creatures, because they were created. I too
am empty, alone. I return with the ashes of my ardor; who can I
enflame with these cold ashes? Oh, how I've become cold! I
came to an end, my Father. In truth, I died. I died a long time
ago. I am the shadow of myself, kneeling, self-scrutinizing.
What remains of me? I am only the witness of my failure. Why
have I failed? Perhaps I lack the resilience needed for sacrifice?
No, I had and still have that. Maybe to a fault! What was
lacking in me and is still lacking is passion to serve Thee and only
Thee. Yes, my Father, this passionate fervor I, and only I, know
to be a pretense. A pretense I've continued until today. A pretense that would have emboldened me had I become a priest; a
profane priest. The Word of God would have issued from my
mouth like water from another fountain, water that would
neither cleanse me nor allay my thirst. Would that have been for
want of human desire for happiness? Yes, this too is lacking in
me. I've always thought that a happy man is an idiot. Have I
alone failed, my Father, or have You also failed with me? Are
You not the God who hounds your prey when you want to save
or put to the test? Is it not You, my Father, who hounds relentlessly, especially when You want to lose a soul in order to save it?
Why have You not hounded after me? I have always been eager
to be the fodder for Your divine wrath. I would have sinned
against you, but I would have risen again, reborn, from the
depths of perdition. I have retained my purity, my Father, but
I am dry. I know very well that God laughs at innocents who
despair for love of Him. I am one of those innocents. You, my
Father, saw me sobbing and offered no help. Is there yet time?
Shall I yet be saved? Lord, I feel the stone of the Holy Sepulcher
weighing heavily on my breast. Christ was not resurrected for
me. I am dry, Father, like the fountain that dried up alone in the
desert without assuaging the thirst of anyone. You have re-
nounced me. I too renounce you. My shame, in the past, was my
pride. I thought I bore within my breast, like a star, Your Mark.
You know that I did. My pride, now, is my shame: knowing that

I have always been devoid of You, because that is Your Will. I had little to give; now I have nothing. I was always an artifact of myself. I was my handiwork. Now I know I was a counterfeit coin. My holiness was vanity. My feeling that You needed me, a delusion. Now I know that to You I am worthless. And You, what are You worth to me now? Am I worth anything to anybody? Why continue carving my statue in myrtle? For whom? The truth of man is not sacrifice but pain. No, all pain useless. Even that which is never searched for. Isn't love perhaps the truth? But what is love? The truth of man is his destiny to live. Life has no purpose, but neither does it have a price. Any life is worth the trouble; the important thing is the will to live. To live, paying the tax of pain, of love, of death. To make of life what is offered or what one can offer? But to whom? To You, my Father? What can I give You? I, myself; I, nobody; I, nothing! Not only You, no one needs me, and I include myself. It only remains for me to die. To seek death with my will of a Mairun? No, inside me it says that I must live, that life is the only good. My dying would be another gesture in my dialogue with You, but it would be an empty affirmation, another weak negation. Nothing remains but for me to live, for nobody, for nothing.

Rex tremendae magestatis
Qui salvandos salvas gratis
Salva me fons pientatis

I have only You and myself, my Father, and that is terrible. I am my offering to You. Now I am the one laughing at You; I laugh even as I weep. Here, standing before You, is your work as You have made me. Take it! I have communed a thousand times with Your body and Your blood; now, commune, commune me with myself in spirit. I am not worth the trouble, my Father; I know that. My virtues are the empty holes of vices I never had, nor could have had, even if I wanted. Don't accuse me now of feeding on the pride of my humility. This is all that I have, my Father. I am hollow, hollow and opaque. My soul is obscure, and I have never needed so much to be lucid, standing before You. I need all possible lucidity here and now, my God! Once again I must exercise my choice. A free choice? It is mine; I am responsible! I have everything in front of me, nothing is barred. I can take any road. In this lies my risk. I must judge for myself; I am free to go whichever way I choose. What I lack, my Father, is a goal, yours or mine, that I could achieve in its entirety. I am at a crossroads. All roads open before me. Which is mine? Which is my threshold?

I had twisted my ways through life to follow foreign roads leading only to my distress. Where am I going now? Where are my feet and my will taking me? Martyrdom, if it were offered to me, would be easiest, sweetest, most gratifying. But I don't deserve it. Pastoral work without the hope of martyrdom would be not a road but a routine. Why not be a priest, a minister of God, close to my people—my people, who will go wherever I lead them? Why not follow in the steps of Father Vecchio and, with luck, perhaps create another Isaías like myself? It's laughable. Why did the whole Order take nourishment from me for so long? Perhaps because they saw in me a capacity to eradicate all the rank weeds which Mairuns have in their souls. Those they cultivated during centuries and centuries of heresy. I was full of formulas for loving You, my Father, useless formulas. Here they are on the tip of my tongue. I know them all by heart. My heart is dry.

Ultionis . . . Remissionis . . . Rationis

Now I know, I understand perfectly, that only holy men can strip themselves of everything, even of themselves, and then rebuild. Only holy men can live in destitution. I am not holy, but I am a man. I need help and compassion, even if I don't understand myself. For a long time, I fed on those who were feeding off me. I lived to be their project. This was my project. In that trance, I exalted all my petty virtues. I inflated them to the point of exhausting them. Everyone lived to praise my virtues, but now the wind has been let out of them and they have fallen, wilted. They are equivocal, obvious delusions that don't inspire me to lament them. What will become of me, my Father, what will become of me? Don't abandon me now or unleash Your ferocious hounds on me again. I can't endure it. Bless me, my Father. I don't deserve it, nor do I believe in it, but I need Your grace. More now than ever; now or never. Now that I must choose again before You abandon me, my Father. I am the poor Indian boy, Avá, who left this house so long ago and is once again standing in the anteroom.

Preces meae non sunt dignae

A light tap on the door interrupts Isaías's meditations. It is old Brother Ciano who comes to summon him to see the director. Father Ludgero will receive him in the noble hall of the new building of the Mission of Our Lady of O.

"Good evening, Sr. Isaías. God bless you. I trust all is well with you here?"

"Good evening, Father Ludgero. Deo gratias, I am here at your service. Where is Father Vecchio? I'd very much like to greet him."

"Soon, Sr. Isaías. We must have a talk first. You know that I am now director of the Mission. I would like you also to know that we have heard from Rome about your refusal to take Holy Orders, and from Brasília about your insistence on coming here."

"What else is there to say, Father?"

"Much or little, no one but you can say. I want to be clear and concise. Once again the choice is yours, and I speak with the voice of the Order. You may return to us, to the priesthood. Aware of your virtues, the Order will always be open to you. Or, you may return to the world with your talents: the languages you speak, the studies you have made. It would not be difficult for you to begin a career as a layman. We ourselves, in our colleges, would recruit you as a teacher, with pleasure. Let it be as you wish."

"Everything except the Mission; is that it, Father?"

"No. We are receiving you as a guest. Since you've come, you may stay as many days as you like. You may even, if you wish, go to the village to visit your relatives and return here."

"Thanks, Father. Thank you very much. I shall be a guest of the Mission, as you say, for a few days. May I now see Father Vecchio?"

"We'll go down together to meet him. He spends afternoons with Father Aquino in that alcove in front of the chapel. It should not be too much to ask your consideration, Sr. Isaías, for the age of Father Vecchio."

The reunion with old fathers and some of the older nuns is trying for everyone. But before long, relations improve. On the second day, Isaías sits unselfconsciously with the two old priests in the alcove. They talk about almost everything but say very little about each topic. Matters barely mentioned are not pursued. The only subject never referred to weighs heavily on the three of them: Isaías's desistance and insistence. He appreciates each compassionate gesture. Padre Vecchio performs miracles to demonstrate to Isaías his understanding, his forgiveness, making things more difficult. Father Aquino, in control of himself, his eyes fixed on the emotions of the old missionary, discreetly pushes dangerous points aside.

Sitting together under the passion-fruit pergola, they take tea and biscuits from Sister Canuta. They watch the boys filing into the chapel with Father Cyril in front, and the girls with their governess, Sister Ceci, for evening prayer. So it was until yesterday. Today, as soon as they sit, watching the line of little girls advancing through the flowerbeds to the chapel, they see four old Indian women, in tatters who live on the Mission beach, arriving on the scene and screaming, "Avá, Avá, Uruantãremui!" and they continue to shout violently in their own language. Isaías descends the steps to embrace them and calm them down. One of them crouches, weeping. The others continue their invective. They grab their dry flaccid breasts and shake them. They lift their skirts and run their hands over their skinny thighs, squeezing the wrinkled flesh and scolding. The line of girls distintegrates when the old women start attacking it. They seize two girls who defend themselves furiously while the Indian women tear their clothes off, displaying their emaciated bodies to Isaías, and shrieking the most menacing shrieks in a frenzy.

Alma, who was not to be seen all those days, even at morning Mass, also arrives along with the nuns attracted by the screaming; all are baffled by this incomprehensible scandal.

Father Vecchio covers his ears with his hands, weeping. Father Aquino runs to and fro. Sister Canuta snatches up the teapot and cups as if she were afraid of losing them. The confusion suddenly stops with the crisp orders and forceful gestures of Father Ludgero. Isaías is sent to his room, the others to their houses. There are no prayers. An hour later, the director enters Isaías's room.

"As you have seen, your presence here is unbearable. I must ask you to leave tomorrow. I can have you taken to the village or to Naruai, whichever you prefer."

"I'll go to the village. And Dona Alma, what have you decided with respect to her?"

"She must return to Brasília tomorrow. I am having her accompanied to Naruai. I have already reserved the plane."

"Is that what she wants?"

"She will not stay here under any circumstance. If she wants to go somewhere else, that is not our problem."

THE EXHUMATION

I continue my provisional inquiry with a view to a definitive report on the assignment entrusted to me by Your Excellency the Minister.

Yesterday, I accomplished at last the exhumation of the dead woman in order to examine the body; that is, if one can speak thus of the clean bones that were given to me to put together and examine. But let us proceed by details.

We set out from the post here early in Sr. Juca's boat which is larger and more comfortable than the little canoe belonging to FUNAI. The party included Elias, Sr. Juca, two employees of the post, two employees of the aforementioned Sr. Juca, and myself. We took with us a packet of provisions prepared by Dona Creuza and the tools necessary for digging.

It took us all morning to get to the cemetery. We passed quickly through the village which consists of eight or ten houses rigorously forming a circle around a larger house. According to Elias, the latter is the house of men, a version of an English club, exclusive, aboriginal-style, in which women and children are not allowed. What is most remarkable about this building is that at the ends of the roof ridge—which according to Elias runs exactly north to south—two tree trunks are affixed with their roots exposed. It is a large round hut, thatched with satin-tail grass, whose walls and roof are of a piece. It is supported inside by great posts, some vertical, some inclined, criss-crossing. It is about thirty meters long, twelve wide, and eight or more high. There is no doubt it is large, but above all it is dark and smoky, perhaps because it has only two very small entrances, one at each end, and an opening beneath the roof ridge. Next to this house is a square whose area is more or less that of three or four basketball courts. It is smooth, the ground has been pounded; there the Indians hold their heathen ceremonies.

We traversed the village, interrupted here and there by Indians who approached Elias to greet him and to beg. What beggars these fathers of the country are? Doesn't this reflect something about the national character? A band of children accompanied us from the beach to the cemetery and back, shouting and fooling around. They seemed to find us amusing.

Some adult Indians also came to the cemetery, but they kept their distance, watching the work being done without offering any assistance whatsoever.

Elias said that in their view we were committing a sacrilege and that he himself had misgivings about proceeding with the exhumation. He was doing it only because I considered it indispensable, even as he thought he might be engaging in a violation of tribal customs. I did not agree. Not only was the exhumation indispensable to a criminal investigation, but in no sense were we profaning anything, especially because the case involved the grave of a white woman who had died mysteriously among the Indians. It seemed to me that they were maliciously amusing themselves watching us sweat under the hot sun and denying us help.

Their hostility to Sr. Juca is obvious. I don't know why, but he and the Indians exchanged glances that were far from friendly.

I wish to point out that even though I knew they were savages I could not repress animosity toward their nudity, above all, to that of the adults, the men as well as the women. Elias here also had his say, informing me that they were all dressed according to their fashion. The women wear a tiny pubic covering so insignificant that I could see it only close up when pointed out to me. The men, too, dress according to form. They tie up their genitals with pieces of string, tucking the tip of the penis inside the foreskin thereby forming an unusual bulge.

Men and women alike have no pubic or armpit hair. And the faces of the men are smooth. Elias says that if any hair grows, it is eradicated with hot ashes.

I realize that after the first sighting they no longer seemed to me so indecent. I was truly embarrassed only upon seeing an old man, said to be a captain or whatever that is in their language, wearing only a short striped soccer shirt over his naked body. It was ridiculous, the astounding and innocent presence of someone, who, being a chief, allowed himself to look like that.

Worse still was an old woman who accompanied us. She wore a long, dirty, and tattered dress, but it was discreet. The awful thing about her was that more often than not she would lift her dress to her navel so as to scratch herself.

The general appearance of these Indians is good; they have good teeth—only a few are missing here and there—and good skin, free of traces of illness except for pockmarks. Many of the bigger youths here would make excellent recruits. They are tall and broad-shouldered like the youths of Santa Catarina; their faces are open and pleasant, rendering these youths likable. Elias indignantly protested against the idea of recruiting them; he wants to keep them as savages. It is a pity that nearly all the Indians are potbellied. Even in the children one notices the prominence of the stomach. Here, again, Elias explained, it is the result of their staple diet of manioc flour, eaten as farina and drunk as chibé or cassava beer, which is to them as rice and beans are to us.

Their posture also struck me as strange. The men, who remained to watch the exhumation, spent long periods supported by only one leg with the other leg held and the foot placed just above the knee of the leg they were standing on. I tried to balance myself in this position (here in my bedroom, of course) and found it impossible. Our legs and feet are obviously less flexible than theirs.

As for the women, I noticed that in addition to being potbellied, they have spines that are curiously bent. I mean to say that, when standing, they don't hold their backs straight and erect as white women would. Instead, they arch backward, throwing the belly forward and the shoulders back. When walking, they sway the whole body in a strange manner—not only the buttocks, as the blacks and mulattas do out of coquettishness, but the whole body, as if engaged in a calm and languid dance. The few I saw sitting had a demeanor as discreet as is possible for someone who is naked except for the little thing Elias calls their clothing.

However, let us get on with the disinterment of the nurse or missionary or priestess or whatever she was who wandered in this outer limit of the world and met with disaster, as we know. She was buried Indian style with zealous care, which, according to Elias, is unusual treatment for a civilized person. He adds that the Indians have various forms of burial among which this is the most noble. The procedure, in this case, was to dig two holes about two yards deep and about two yards apart, and to connect them underground by way of a tunnel. Here the woman was deposited in a hammock mounted on forked sticks fastened into the ground. To mark the grave, they placed grids of sticks and leaves over the holes leading to the tunnel and covered them with turf and then with dirt. In this way the deceased remained suspended, without touching the earth.

I saw how the procedure had been followed in this instance. There were two mounds of earth, each adorned with a large clay pot with designs in red on a gray background. I carried one of them with me. We cleared one of the holes, removing the earth very carefully till we came to the grid. I saw that it was still covered with turf preventing access to the tunnel where the body lay in its hammock shroud. Only after the grid was removed could one smell the fetid exhalation from the bottom. In fact, the stench was not as horrendous as I had expected, so I had no need for the eau de cologne I was carrying. I used it only to sprinkle the heads of the girls and women for fun and because they wanted me to.

After undoing the grid, the workers at the bottom of the hole removed first the remains of the hammock with a part of the skull still stuck to it, then the bones which had fallen to the ground, and finally the belongings of the dead woman. These consisted of various vials and tubes of medicines that Elias had given her to distribute among the Indians: iodine, aspirin, ointments, sulpha drugs, and even penicillin. Some were full, others only half full. There were also three skirts and two wornout blouses.

The only thing that demanded attention was an extraordinary necklace of snail shells made by the Indians in the form of exquisitely rounded buttons juxtaposed one next to another along a tube ending with a small idol of black stone. I have this valuable item in my possession. There was also a medium-sized pair of scissors, very rusty. That was all.

The bones were prodigiously clean. Elias attributed this achievement to the termites. There were no signs even of ligaments. Some cartilage, such as that of the ears and nose, had disappeared. The cranium, which I have in possession in case it is needed as evidence, is perfect, with all of its bones intact; the set of teeth was complete, including one gold molar and some white metal fillings.

So it is that the assassination hypothesis proposed by the Swiss is disproved, or at least the presumption of a violent crime in which death was brought about by a fractured skull. There is not the slightest possibility of that. The woman could have died in childbirth, from poison, from an illness, from anything whatsoever (and it is going to be difficult to know the cause), but certainly not from a blow to the head or from violence that damaged her bones. I am confident of this, because Sr. Juca, Elias, and I carefully examined the bones without finding the smallest fracture. It is most probable, in our combined judgment taking into account the known circumstances, that the death occurred during childbirth.

I sought to further my investigations by questioning the Indians about the death, the pregnancy, the birth, the reasons for her going to the beach alone to die. They either changed the subject or would not reply. They even made obscene gestures suggesting how oval, ripe, potbellied she was. They added nothing to that indecency, nor did they speak of the woman with the respect that the agent Elias attributes to them, saying that they call her by a semireligious name, Mosaingar.

Unfortunately, Sr. Juca was of no use whatsoever even though he speaks the Indians' dialect perfectly. The hostility the Indians feel for him made him keep to himself; I believe he was frightened that something would happen to him. I noticed at various times that he took care always to stay in front of me, dragging his lame leg, always to remain under my protection. But his men were much more useful than the workers from the post. Given peremptory orders, they applied themselves to digging, sweated a great deal, and did more than the other two to retrieve and show us all that remained of the dead woman.

Following the exhumation, we hastily reburied the bones that didn't interest us; I had decided to take only the skull with me. Conversation on the way back with Sr. Juca and Elias yielded very little worth recording here. Elias says that I can call him as a witness to testify that she really was pregnant, and was probably made pregnant by an Indian. He remembers seeing her with a belly and can attribute the work to no civilized man. But he insists that I say only that she was *probably* impregnated by one of the Indians. Is he hiding something from me? What could it be? Is it merely unjustifiable fear? Or does it reflect the mania of a protector incapable of pointing a finger at his charges even when they're obviously guilty?

Assessing my observations, I see that, aside from the precise date given by the Swiss and my proof that death was not caused by violence that affected the bones, I have nothing concrete. With the skimpy facts that I have, how can I compose a report for the minister?

In a certain way, my career hangs on this. I don't mean to say that my reputation is really going to depend on the outcome. But my performance in this case could lead to either a promotion or a demotion. It would be good to return with something concrete. I'm afraid of going back empty-handed and, above all, of submitting a report that might make me an object of derision for my colleagues.

Nothing would be worse for me than to run on about tribal customs regarding pregnancy and couvade related to me by Elias in his innocence. But without knowing it, he was revealing relevant facts. He said that, for Indians, women giving birth is an act as simple and natural as defecating and that they can give birth and on the same day continue to perform their household duties. The one who is laid up and who needs looking after is the husband who stays in his hammock taking his time to eat a light meal. The importance of this revelation is that these Indians, accustomed to their women giving birth like dogs or wild animals, did not give any special attention to this white and civilized (perhaps I exaggerate) women about to deliver in their midst. She, perhaps, finding herself suddenly overcome by birth pangs and alone on the beach, succumbed. She was a victim of her own recklessness, having penetrated the forest and allowed herself to be impregnated there. I don't know by whom. Who knows why?

TUXAUARÁ

Sitting on his two-headed bench, the old guide of souls tells of his dream: he has seen Avá, the future chief. He is returning to the Mairuns. He is not returning as Isaías, the priest. He comes as Avá, the chief-to-be. With him comes his woman, Canindejub, the yellow macaw. Even now they are navigating the Iparaná river, heading toward the village.

Nevertheless, no one must go to meet him, no, not yet. For some time yet Avá must journey alone. The guide of souls saw him clearly but says that he was surrounded by the signs of the devils and the juruparis. There are many threats over and around him. But he alone must confront them. Alone, he will save himself. Here are the trials; here are the crossroads. Truth lies in his encounter with himself. Only he can endure the trials and overcome them to purify himself. Only thus will he arrive at how he ought to be. Having triumphed, he will emerge as the future chief of the Mairuns.

Jaguar listens attentively, motionless. It is his uncle then, the true chief-to-be, who is returning. He himself will never have to assume the chieftainship. What a blessing, he thinks, I will now live my life like the other young men. Maybe I will be able to travel upriver to become acquainted with the Mission, or downriver to Corrutela. Who knows, I might end up in Brasília or Belém? I will finally be free from everyone's tireless vigilance. Free from always being accompanied, no longer obliged to say where I'm going.

Teró also smiles with contentment. He opens his mouth to laugh silently, with more pleasure. Avá, my brother-in-law, is arriving at last. He is the one we had given up for lost. But this woman who is coming with him, who is she? What is she like? Can Avá keep his yellow macaw and still marry a woman of my Falcon clan? Inimá! It has to be she. Who, if not her, could I give in exchange for Pinu, if I let Numiá marry Cosó of the Pacu clan? Who will be the mother of the Falcon, my nephew, who will one day be the guide of souls? None of this is important though, Teró thinks. What is important now is to enjoy the good news. What is important is the return of Avá, my lost brother-in-law whom we are getting back. Finally, we Mairuns will have our true chief-to-be and, tomorrow, our great chief himself. We will learn many things from him. We will hear many things from his mouth, many things about the whole world throughout which Avá has wandered, seeing all.

Jaguar leaves the Great House of Men for his mother's house. Then he goes from house to house repeating the news in his own style. The women are eager to learn everything about the Avá who is returning. The older ones who knew him as a boy talk about him as he was. The younger ones who had never seen him inquire.

Jaguar describes his uncle Avá, the true chief-to-be. He is the lost hero who returns with his enormous prick crowned at its base by thick hair thorny as barbed wire, and Jaguar shouts:

"Maité! Maité!" That is to say, it's astonishing, but true. Astonishing!

Maité! Maité! Here comes Avá to fuck all you Mairun women. In a single night he is capable of mounting all of you with his great iron prick. But he never inseminates a woman un-

less he wants to, and he doesn't. He spills his seed only in Canindejub, his yellow macaw.

Soon Jaguar starts another theme, saying that Avá carries an
enormous gun. He's certain. Yes, it's a gun that fires explosive
balls that can blow apart even a house built of stone.

"Maité! Maité!"

He also carries an enormous bow made of steel: "Maité!
Maité!" It was Papahú, king of the Brazilians who gave him this
enormous bow, flexible as a steel snake. When Avá commands
it, the bow goes by itself to hunt for him and comes back with
tapir, deer, peccary, all the best game. "Maité! Maité!" All will
now have to ask permission to navigate the Iparanã. They will
have to ask Avá, beg him, implore him to allow them to enter the
narrow gut that leads to the lagoon.

His woman is Canindejub, the yellow macaw. "Maité! Maité!"
She is coming here with him. She belongs to the most powerful
clan in Brazil, the clan of the great warriors. Her father is the
chief of all the false sorcerers. Canindejub, the yellow macaw,
has an enormous cunt, round and soft, like a sweet potato.
"Maité! Maité!" Her breasts are enormous and spherical like
calabashes. But she belongs only to Avá. Perhaps she has inside
her cunt the sharp-toothed jaws of the piranha. "Maité! Maité!"
These are teeth for biting and cutting off weak, soft little pricks
that might want to enter. Maité! Maité!

Later, the whole village is remarking on the return of Avá.
Now there is fresh news. The oxim, the sorcerer, also had much
to say about his visions. He divined that Avá was returning not
as the chief-to-be but as the anhé: the Anti-Maíra, Lord of the
Litter of the Blue Jaguar that live in the subterranean world of
the nocturnal sun.

He returns as the chief-to-be, of course, but he is returning
also as a powerful otxicom, a sorcerer, the most powerful ever
seen. He is the father of sickness and death, but he causes neither death or illness. He only cures; he only gives life and
happiness.

Avá is carrying two rattles as Teidju can see clearly. They

are enormous rattles covered with callosities made of jaguar skull and filled with blue beads so small and numerous that nobody could count them. Each woman who fucks Avá will be given a necklace of these tiny blue beads. But he fucks very rarely, hardly ever, so as not to spend his strength. Also, he cannot set his feet on the ground; he likes to be carried around on a mat woven of pindoba palm. It is necessary to weave new mats for him immediately.

At night, in the Great House of Men, the return of Avá is the subject of discussion among all groups. The young men listen to stories told by their elders about the past deeds of Avá, about his infancy in the village. They ask endless questions:

"What will happen when Avá arrives? What steps must be taken? What has to be done? Will Sr. Elias remain at the FUNAI post, or will he be sent away? To which house will Canindejub, the yellow macaw, belong? How must she be treated? Who will be allowed to fuck her without committing incest? Whose sister or sister-in-law is she?" They want to know all this with great urgency. Is Avá returning as Lord of the Jaguars? But isn't he also Lord of Mirrors, like the Europeans? Lord of Salt? Lord of Old Knives? As Lord of Guns will he bring one for each of us?

Even for the guide of souls, the old guide of souls; even for the oxim who also had his visions, there are more questions than answers. A great mystery surrounds the return of Avá. Everyone senses this mystery; everyone realizes that there is something very strange about the story of Avá's long-expected return. The guide of souls insists:

"Be calm, be calm, we must wait. Many threats are hanging over him. All is not clear around him. Many juruparis and devils are circling him and his woman. There are many dangers. Many trials. He is in a trance, half-enchanted. He has already passed the worst of his enemies by; he has emerged free from the enormous mill that was about to grind him, to grind him into fine sand. He has passed, passed alive and whole, through the great mill of the false sorcerers at the Mission. Nobody can help him to arrive here, nobody."

Agitated, Remui converses with the dead and later says that all who come are speaking to him about the trials of Avá. Perhaps they are too much for him. Has something disastrous already occurred? Is some calamity still to happen? We must wait, we have to wait and see.

The oxim says much the same. He saw clearly, but did not see Avá as chief-to-be. He suspects rather that he saw Avá as Anti-Maíra, Lord of the Black Sun, Lord of the Blue Jaguars, Lord of the Underworld, the favorite of Maíra-Manon. What does all this signify? What could so much confusion signify? Nothing good, he warns, agreeing with the guides of souls. But no one wants to believe this. No one wants to worry. Everyone wants to enjoy the happiness of the return of Avá, at last.

Among the single men, none leaves the Great House that night for meetings on the dancing ground or the beach. They all remain there in suspense, preoccupied with the new developments, asking questions. Asking and waiting, with imagination freely venting itself. For nothing as important as this has happened among the Mairuns for years, the certain news of the return of Avá. A new door opens. They all want to believe that with the coming of the new chief life thereafter will have more joy, more zest, more taste, more novelty. Who knows, they might even return to making war. There is no doubt about it, affirms Jaguar. Most likely they will revert to raiding other tribes to bring back many new women to the village. They might return to much loving, much fucking and the making of many children, many little girls and many little boys.

The married men have also immersed themselves in conversations lasting well into the night. When at last they go home, they have to relate everything they know and imagine. Each of them talks expansively, lying in his hammock with a little fire burning underneath for warmth. The women, lying in hammocks above those of the men, look down, inquiring:

"Is his prick really very large? Is it hard as stone, never soft-ening? Does he fuck with gusto, and often?"

They end by climbing down into the hammocks of their hus-bands to savor the matter some more.

THE VOMIT

Alma and Isaías are once again descending with the current. They slide down the Iparaná in the splendor of a purple eve-ning about to die in the extended stretches of the Middle Stretch. Isaías paddles now on one side, now on the other, to assist the weak current and to drive sleep away. Alma shudders at each stroke which is stronger than usual, opens her eyes, sees that night is falling, and returns to her dozing. Hour after hour they cut through the water without exchanging a word. Night falls, the moon is born within the water right in front of them, coloring the whole world. Then it rises slowly. Now it white-washes everything, bathing, cleansing all with light. Fish leap out of the water, sparkling. Sometimes a minnow falls into the canoe.

At last, extremely tired, they run the boat ashore and disem-bark on a high dirty beach on the right bank, still at the begin-ning of the Middle Stretch. Isaías throws two hammocks onto the sand. Sitting on these in the light of the moon they con-verse.

"What was that back there, Isaías, what caused that horrible commotion?"

"I'll tell you. And all I want is for you to listen without asking questions. I don't know the causes or the reasons. I only know the facts. You've already seen and heard but couldn't understand. The old women were shouting "Avá." Avá is my Mairun name as you know. They were also shouting "Uruantãremu."

Uruantã is the name of my earliest known ancestor. Remu means grandson: grandson of Uruantã. They were speaking to me in Mairun, as a man, as a Mairun, perhaps even as chieftain-to-be. At first I thought they were welcoming me with ceremonial weeping which is an old Mairun custom. But I soon realized I was mistaken. I understood that the old women couldn't stand something anymore; they were exploding. Do you know what they were saying? It's terrible! "Look," they shouted at me, screaming "Avá, look! Pay attention. Look, Avá! Look at these girls, our girls, the daughters of our people. They're killing them, drying them out. Look closely, Avá. We know what we are talking about. Look, these girls are all dried up, emaciated. Girls grow and fill out only in the hands of men. A man's hand on the chest makes the breasts swell so and give milk. Look, Avá, how dry these girls are without tits. A man's hand on the thighs makes them as well rounded as mine were in my time. Look at these girls with undeveloped breasts, scrawny legs, and dried out cunts." They were pointing at the nuns as they screamed: "Look, Avá, look closely at these wicked women, Avá, these withered and scorched women. They want to wither and scorch our girls too. Did you know they have no breasts? They are incapable of breast-feeding, the fleshless creatures! Did you know they have no thighs, women's thighs? Did you know they don't bleed when pierced by the arrows of Micura, the Moon? Did you know they can't give birth, Avá? They don't give birth, the evil spooky things. It seems that they like Mosaingar very much—they refer to her as Our Lady Impregnated by God, to whom the Mission is consecrated. But they themselves never give birth, the dried out wretches, the miserable infertile creatures. They are killing our girls, Avá. They want to dry them out too so they will never have men and never give birth. You've come Avá; at last you've come. You're here, Avá; put an end to this! Take the girls away! The boys can run away; the boys will run away. But the girls, what will become of them? Here we are, putting up with all of this, only for their sake. Avá, you alone can take

them away. Only you, grandson of Uruantã, can free them
from the old women, save them from the old men. Have done
with these people! Kill those old women and carry the girls
away; kill those men who are not men. Send our boys and girls
away. Let us take them to the village, Avá. Only there where
there are men to love them nudgingly will they mature as women
to fuck, to marry, and to bear children."

"So that's what all that pandemonium was about? The old
Indian women with their skirts up to their chins, feeling and
squeezing their breasts and thighs. It was that? Astonishing!"

"I've summarized it, Alma, translating their words as far as is
possible in another language. I still don't want to comment on it.
Think about it on your own. I too need to think; I need very
much to think about all of this."

"I don't have to ponder anything. It's as clear as day. The old
women are right. They're healthy, mentally healthy. We are
the sick ones, sick from indecency, from our repression of our
humanity, from our rejection of what is natural. We are
abominable. I've learned as much from the old women, now that
you've explained what they said. Thank God for opening my
eyes; I understand at last. The purity of God is not in the
mortification of the flesh. The purity of God, if it exists, if God
exists, is in life itself, in the capacity to fuck, to enjoy, to bring
children into the world."

"Please, Alma, please shut up. Do whatever you want, but
leave me in peace. I need to think."

Isaías continues to plead in a low agonized voice:

"I can't do any more; I can't bear it any longer."

Alma notices that he's crying without shame, tears streaming
down, washing his face. She says nothing more.

Alma stretches out on the sand, wrapping herself in a corner
of her hammock for protection against the cold. Tonight they
don't light their usual little fire.

They remain on the beach for a few days looking at the vast
landscape of the Middle Stretch that one day they will have to
traverse to get to their destination. They eat very little because

there is hardly anything to eat. But they're not worried. They
speak very little—Alma more than Isaías. It is she who searches
for turtles on the fringes of the forest, or for catfish in the
caves. Every evening the sun rekindles the scent of a heap of
sawari nuts and custard apples they've been eating with disgust.
At dusk they sit down to pray. Alma questions herself: What?
I don't need to pray now, or ever, she thinks. Similarly, Isaías;
nevertheless, they pray pointlessly:

Oremus et pro judeis, ut Deus
Omnipotens conferat obcaecatione a . . .
Oremus et pro paganis ut Deus
Omnipotens conferat iniqitátem . . .

They pray sitting in their hammocks, which at last they had
slung, one facing the other. They pray and look at each other,
without seeing and without speaking. Isaías attempts to tell
stories of the old Mairuns, but he is so lacking in enthusiasm he is
unable to continue. Alma also feels that there's nothing to say.
There is nothing in common between their past histories and
these days of waiting for what is to come. What is going to happen? She has a feeling that Isaías is in some way dying and that
she is being reborn, and vice versa. Each of them is transfigured.
Only, she asks herself, reborn as what? Reborn for what? If I
no longer believe in what brought me here, where am I going?
To what end? Why do I persist?

One day, the will to put the little canoe back in the water and
confront the vastness of the Middle Stretch returns to them.
They continue to travel day after day, night after night, day
and night. Isaías, caulking the boat which is becoming leakier
every day, paddling when he has the strength. Both of them
eating what they have, which is not much. They go on and on.
Days later, rounding a bend in the Iparanã leading into another
long stretch, they suddenly see that extraordinary shape in the
distance. Alma immediately identifies it as a flying saucer resting
on a high riverbank in the middle of a burnt patch of forest.
They see but don't believe their eyes.

"Don't be ridiculous, Alma. Flying saucer? But what could it be?"

"Look closely, Isaías. It is a flying saucer. It can't be anything else; it has burnt a clearing in the forest. There it is, round, metallic, flat, shining in the sun. It's a saucer, a flying saucer."

Isaías hurries his paddle strokes, making the canoe rock as he drives it closer to the left bank to see what is there.

It is noon and the sun is beating down on that huge metallic object in the middle of the tract, obscuring instead of revealing shapes here and there. Isaías and Alma wonder if it could really be a flying saucer. It's something; let's go see; let's move closer. It can't be a flying saucer. Flying saucers don't exist, Isaías thinks. But it certainly looks like one, he admits to himself. A kilometer away, half a kilometer, really only a few hundred meters away, they see and discover the wheel of corrugated metal—brilliant, enormous. It can hardly be a house, looking like two plates, one turned upside-down upon the other. Its shape is that of a flying saucer—fantastic, round. Why so perfectly round? And that turret on top, like the hatch of an aircraft? God, what is this?

At last they see a motor launch on a little beach below. It is a metallic, large, and spanking new—but a launch like any other. They relax. It is at least a familiar shape. There must be people aboard, rich people. But what are they doing here in that huge splendid casserole? Closer still, they see a man, a woman, and three children—all fair-haired—appear on the precipice to one side of the disc. They had come out of the disc through a trapdoor and seem to be expecting them. Who are they? People like us? Soon Alma and Isaías calm down upon hearing a cordial greeting uttered in a heavy accent:

"Welcome to our home!"

Alma and Isaías stare at each other: What is this?

"We are North American missionaries," they explain.

Alma, not knowing how to introduce herself, says that she is a botanist on a research expedition. Is that your husband? No,

we are not married. He is an ethnologist. They had lost their
boat and had salvaged very little. Isaías throws Alma a piercing
glance. Why lie like this; what for?

"The house is unusual, isn't it? In fact you could say it is very
rare. A lot of work went into its construction," Bob explains.
"But that was indispensable, given the circumstances."

Sitting inside the house, Isaías and Alma listen to Bob's account. He and his wife belong to a newly formed evangelical
group now working in Brazil. They have been here for a year
and a half and have had to confront a new, tantalizing problem.
They are interested in the Mairun Indians, but especially in the
Xaepẽ and Xitã tribes. One way or another, the word of God
had reached the Mairuns; those who wished to benefit from it
could be saved. But how to reach these wild Indians, lost in the
forest, isolated by their own hostility? The solution they came
upon was to buy this plot of land and build a fortress-house
there, in an area known to be frequented by hostile Indians.
Everything was based on the experience over many years of the
former Indian Protection Service which had tried to attract and
pacify indigenous groups. Dr. Cardozo of the National Museum
had taught them that the basic technique of pacification is to
implant in the heart of the hostile tribe a provocation, a nucleus
to attract their hostility. But it was essential to do so from an
impregnable position.

This is what the principal pacifiers had done. Now they were
doing the same. This explains the use of aluminum sheets eigh-
teen meters long and three meters high for the two flattened
cones that, superimposed on each other, form the walls and the
roof of the house. Structurally, nothing could be simpler: two
superimposed cones, the one above somewhat larger so as to
allow space for air and light to enter. It would be impossible for
Indians to shoot arrows into the interior of the house. It had
been difficult to put up the mosquito screens between the roof
and wall. They succeeded thanks to the skill of a young man in
the Peace Corps.

Inside, the house is hardly less extraordinary. It is very well appointed. Up there is a water tank above a well, guaranteeing a water supply for weeks or months if necessary. Below the tank, between the columns that support it, is a shower on one side and a toilet with a septic tank on the other. Together there are the stove and refrigerator that use gas. There is the radio that works with batteries charged by a small generator.

Bob and his wife show Isaías and Alma all the details of the house: shelves well stocked with canned foods as in a super-market; the bedrooms, separated by curtains; the living room with easy chairs; shelves with books and magazines; and tables all made from the cases in which cargo had been packed.

At last, they sit down to drink canned pineapple juice, to eat cream crackers spread with butter and honey, and to converse. But the missionaries have yet to exhaust their pride in their house and keep getting up to show and explain new details that come to their attention. The walls and the roof are im-pervious to arrows, even flaming arrows. The door, which opens outward by means of a lever, is located up above. Once closed it is so strongly bolted that it resists all muscular human efforts. In the roof are skylights through which firecrackers could be launched—luminous, explosive or non-explosive, but not lethal. As Bob explains, these could be very useful in deter-ring all-too-ferocious attacks by the Indians. They also have powerful loud speakers fixed atop the house through which they could parley with the assailants once it was known what lan-guage they spoke. They would talk to the Indians by way of recordings of a selection of welcoming phrases in various Indian languages. What is crucial is for them to be able to parley from an absolutely impregnable position; "impregnable," Bob repeats.

Shortly thereafter the missionaries lead Alma and Isaías to the other side of the house where they raise a tarpaulin to display, very tidily arranged, a stock of bush knives, axes, scis-sors, knives, beads, and many other things. These were all in-tended as presents for the Indians to appease them in accordance with the best technique, thereby securing peace.

"Everything is calm here," Bob continues, "as we wait for the inevitable attack that will be converted into fraternization. One day or another the Indians will appear. This is inevitable. Perhaps it would have been better to situate the house farther south, up-river, had the Catholic Mission not been there. But in any event the Indians will see this house and it will fulfill its function as an irresistible attraction and impregnable provocation. Now all we need is to wait." That's why they were there: to wait patiently.

"And what about the Mairuns?" Isaías inquires, seated once again, at last.

"Well, the Mairuns demand other techniques. They are the business of my wife, Gertrude. She is a linguist, a graduate of Bright University. She has already made some notes on their language that will enable her to establish its phonetic structure. After a few more months of study she should have sufficient material leading to a better prepared glottology that will help her figure out the Mairun grammar. This will be the first step in our work with the Mairuns. We will then try to produce spelling books and primers to teach the Indians how to read and write. This way they will progressively become accustomed to civilization through the basic instrument of communication, that is, writing. What is most important, however, is that, once this step has been taken, they will have direct access to the source of all true wisdom, the reading of the Holy Bible which by then we will have translated into the Mairun language.

"The whole Bible?" Isaías wonders, surprised.

"Yes, why not? First, some chapters: Matthew, the Acts, Revelation. Afterward, John, the Letter to the Corinthians, and so on until the Bible has been completely translated."

Bob and Gertrude take turns enlightening, explaining how the funds of their corporation are provided principally by pious Americans who want to pay for the translation and printing of the Bible in foreign languages. Meticulously, they inform Alma and Isaías that they consider this task of the greatest impor-tance because they expect the emergence of the Saviour at any moment. And who can foresee from which people he might emerge?

Isaías exclaims: "What? You think that the Awaited One, the New Messiah might come, for example, from the Mairuns?"

"Of course He could! Or why not from among the Xaepẽs or even the Xitãs! Last time, with the Greeks, the Persians, the Romans, the Indians, the Chinese, and many other people richer and more civilized to choose from, weren't the Jews, an unexceptional tribe, chosen? Didn't Jesus come from among them?"

"The effort of our religious corporation to disseminate translations of the Bible and to teach the Indians to read and write is an act of faith. It is chiefly the expression of a desire to clear the road, to facilitate the return of the Savior. Come where he may, there we will await him with our hearts uplifted."

They explain: they are supported by the faithful of a small church in the little city of Plainville, in the center of North America. Each family, whenever it has made a good business deal or has received an unusual sum, deposits as much as it can in the local bank—ten, twenty, fifty dollars—which are then sent to Bob and Gertrude. They in turn have taken on the task of sending to all the pious families of Plainville copies of a chain letter, occasionally with photographs, describing the progress of the enterprise. So it is that the whole community shares their experience and learns from it. The results are encouraging, as much for the inhabitants of Plainville who are enthusiastic about the project as for Bob and Gertrude. When they travel to North America everyone wants to hear them relate stories about the Indians, as much about attacks by the Xaepẽs as about the effectiveness of the Catholic Mission among the Mairuns. It is really very edifying, Bob admits. They always return with their enthusiasm redoubled. They dream of one day being able to report in a brief message to all their friends in Plainville that the pacification of the Xaepẽs has been accomplished and soon thereafter their conversion and incorporation into the fold of Christianity. To this end they spare neither strength nor sacrifice.

The conversation continues into the night. At a certain point Isaías finds an opportunity to say that while Alma is perhaps a trained botanist he is only a dabbler in ethnology. He has never taken a regular course of study at a university, only at a seminary. What he knows about the Indians chiefly concerns their way of life. The first revelation had an explosive effect and needed time to be understood.

"Almost a priest? A Roman Catholic priest? With theology courses completed in Rome, according to what Dona Alma is saying? Bob admits that he himself has taken summer courses to become an accountant. But as to Isaías being a priest, why . . . ?"

"Well," Isaías replies, "these are matters of conscience."

"Please excuse my curiosity," Bob apologizes. Soon he is saying that when he first saw them he had a feeling that in spite of appearances they were special people, unique, cultured Brazilians.

"And Sr. Isaías, as to your experiences or way of living, as you put it, what can you tell us? Have you been among Brazilian tribes? With the Mairuns? Marvelous! What? You are a Mairun? You yourself? Blessed Jesus, he's a Mairun. . . . Wonderful!"

The embarrassment is deep and palpable. Everyone is staring at the ground. Isaías finds a way out by asking Bob to clarify a point he had made about the Apocalypse. Why does he want to translate those texts? Isaías is playing with fire; the fervor of the missionaries is rekindled.

"Yes, this is the main problem," Bob declares. "Don't you know about the bomb? The bomb, well there she is: an announcement of the Apocalypse, confirmed at last. To be sure, it is well guarded by the two chief contenders. But already others are emerging who also have the bomb. Many others. It only remains for someone to set it off. And once that hour arrives, it will be used. Inexorably! Then, according to what is written, there will be plagues, mutations, the beast with seven heads, and everything else. Those who survive will see.

Bob expands on the Apocalypse and continues on the same theme until it's time for dinner, when he picks up the Bible and reads, slowly, so as to absorb each verse:

Days will come when one stone shall not rest on another, which shall not be overturned.

Nation will rise up against nation and kingdom against kingdom. There will be great earthquakes in diverse places. There will be astonishing things and great signs in the sky.

There will be signs in the sun, the moon, and the stars, over the earth anguish among nations in perplexity over the roaring of the sea and the waves. There will be men fainting with fear and by expectation that the world will be overwhelmed, because the powers of Heaven have been weakened.

Then shall come the Son of Man, coming in a cloud with all the power and the glory."

Bob takes a long pause to meditate and rest. Then slowly he turns a clear gaze toward the eyes of Alma and Isaías, and he solemnly recites, scanning the words:

"Because I, the Lord God, take thee by the right hand and say unto thee, do not fear, for I shall help thee."

He takes a short pause and prays solemnly:

"Also I give thee as light to the Gentiles, for beings to my salvation unto the ends of the earth."

As he is finishing his reading the children begin to yawn. Still Bob and Gertrude spend more time meditating while the food is getting cold on the table and Alma's appetite is growing bolder by the minute. There is fish for dinner retrieved from a trap by means of hooks on the line of a system of pulleys between the house and the river.

Alma and Isaías go to sleep late in their hammocks laid out on the ground for want of supports. They sleep amid the echo of the prophetic words of Bob and Gertrude about the coming disaster that is already in sight, inevitable and imminent.

GOSPEL

CORACIPOR

Once again the sun is setting in the vast stretches of the Xaepẽ world. From here on the dancing ground I watch the great globe as it descends. It will shine too brilliantly for other eyes, but not for mine, burnt by all the light that I have seen.

My people, Mairun-Coracipor, the living ones, are arriving to watch the sunset with me. It is sorrowful that my old chieftain, Anacã is not sitting here next to me talking. It is sorrowful.

At the center of the curved row of squatting men the guide of souls is helping the sun to set. On both sides of him, he feels, he senses all the men, kneeling, squatting, sitting, or standing, each man in his appointed place.

Here comes my old woman, Moita, with my dish of steamed fish and yam. My Jaguars are so dear to me, fierce and proud maidens, glowing with sunrise-gold. They walk like stately queens, belching from contentment. Anyone seeing them and knowing no better might think that Maíra is himself a Jaguar. But no, he is a Falcon, a Jaguar killer.

The women of my clan, from the band of this side, will be everywhere bringing things to eat, talking, laughing, smiling. Mine are a very congenial people. No one would think that such

tenderhearted, lovely women could be so resolute, so indom-
itable. It is they who produce the guides of souls with seed taken
from the Pumas; not invariably, I fear, because no other women
are so skillful in the art of fucking.

My relatives, the Pacus, will be sitting there. They are also
members of the Blue Band of the Setting Sun. Friendly people,
good people, discreet and tranquil. They have none of the arrogance of the Pumas, nor any of the disguised haughtiness of
the Falcons. Their defect is that they are so orderly, like people
from Minas Gerais. All that is needed is for someone to propose
something new or to set one foot outside of tradition for them
to utter that great cry, No! But when it comes to good advice
or a salacious bit of gossip, there is no one like a Pacu, man or
woman.

My in-laws, the Arapaimas from the band on the other side,
the side of the Rising Sun, those yellow ones are happy-go-
lucky. They hold everybody up to ridicule; they laugh at even
themselves. What makes them collapse into helpless laughter is
the boasting of my in-laws the Jaguars and my brothers the
Falcons. They associate most with the new clans and often in-
termarry with them.

My Ant people of the Blue Setting Sun are also an ancient
people. But you would never know as they are so graceless and
hardworking. They are always against all plans for festivities,
but when the day comes they give more than anyone. This is
why one says of a larger clearing: it must be an ant clearing!

My Snail family, on the contrary, do not have a reputation
for being diligent workers. They are all the easy life, for lying
in hammocks, for drifting with the stream as the old people
used to say. There are those who think this is because they are a
new clan, but they are not as new as the really new clans. Could
this be why they never start anything and are annoyed when
they find themselves performing a service? The truth is that
they hide from all heavy work. They become impudent in their
displeasure at hard labor. Nevertheless, these easterners are ex-
ceptional for one thing: fishing with harpoons and arrows with

hooks. We Mairuns are water people, but they even more so. In their canoes they are like snails in their shells; they are content and can paddle all day and night without stopping. But don't ask them to set foot on the ground. They won't.

The western clan of Tapirs is not distinguished for anything in this world. The Pumas have the power to command; the Falcons assume the position of guide of souls; the Arapaimas are merrymakers always making fun of pride; the Turtles shape pots and pans and tell stories to make you laugh; the Ants work hard in clearings; the Snails are good at fishing; the Pacus are at least useful in trading. But those Tapirs, what are they good for? Absolutely nothing. They are useless. They are always frowning. It is said that they were good at fighting when there were wars and the enemies were other Indians with bows and arrows. Later they closed ranks, and now they keep to themselves.

My in-laws the Turtles are not like that. They love to laugh and are very friendly and soft-spoken. They are proud of their skill in forging huge urns in immense furnaces like those used for toasting farina. No one is their equal at this. They are also good company, tellers of amusing stories. In the Great House of Men they are always surrounded. While hunting, too, everybody likes to stay close to them, helping them and listening to their conversation. There is no one like a Turtle.

The Coatis from up above are new in the village. They are still being tamed. No one wants to know anything about them, or even to talk to them. Given half a chance a Coati will turn into an oxim, and nearly all of them end up as sorcerers. We have to finish them off or they will do the same to us.

The new Heron clan from that side is not much better. They are also wild. But they have beautiful women; it is a pleasure to look at and an even greater pleasure to make love to them. They are much given to becoming public women and offering themselves. They fuck the men, it is said. In this they are even more gluttonous than my sisters the Falcons. The Herons are also, it is true, very good at throwing javelins and at wrestling. No one can successfully compete with them. The wretches do nothing but train ceaselessly. They don't indulge in amusements. They are like Europeans; for them, to fight is their destiny, an obligation.

There surrounding me will be all my Mairun-Coracipor people, sitting, squatting, kneeling, standing, eating, smiling, talking.

"What are people for, O Carram?"

Jaguars exist to be in the forest, to eat other animals, and to be killed by my people. Birds decorate trees, sing and provide beautiful feathers. Fish are good at staying alive in cold water and waiting for people to come and catch them. But what is an Indian for? Only to stand on one foot, to walk here and there, to work gently, to sleep, to make love, to have children and increase our numbers.

The Indian is finished. Many have died. Now it is necessary to make love, to fuck, and conceive children, to raise them with tenderness, to increase our numbers.

History should be told so as not to be forgotten, so as to avoid extinction. I myself have many things to tell, so as not to forget, so as to avoid extinction. Things of beauty must proceed slowly, without being hurried.

THE ALIEN WORLD

The arrival is a commotion. It is also a quiet, self-contained surprise. The entire village has been descending to the beach to wait, ever since a black dot had been spotted, moving along the great stretch of blue water. When it is close, Jaguar and Maxí, accompanied by all the young men, swim out to meet the little canoe. As each arrives, he touches the canoe with his hand as if it were something magical and swims to one side, then in front of it, then along the other side, to look, to see. They are trying

to guess what the chieftain-to-be and his Canindejub signify in
that guise.

At the place where Isaías and Alma disembark, the people
form a neat circle around them. They remain standing in the
center, motionless, solemn. When that moment has passed, Teró
and the guide of souls, Remui, break through their astonishment
and advance toward Avá. The three men embrace, with their
hands on the shoulders of the others. Forming a circle they
begin to wheel round and round, to spin, raising and lowering
their heads in a slow rhythm.

This continues for a while, but soon they stop and, remaining
in their embrace, they start to sing the ceremonial elegiac chant
of men. Their lament resonates without any tear and is followed
by the wailing of all the women. In conformity with an in-
audible beat, the chanting and wailing suddenly stop. First to
allow the guide of souls to tell of the death and burial of Anacã
in all their details. Later for Teró to recall at great length and
slowly the names of all the Mairuns known to Avá who had
died during the long years of his absence. Everyone is standing
there on the beach, listening. When the discourse is over, the
three men continue to wheel round and round and to lament, all
the while embracing. Their lament is at once for themselves and
for the dead.

Alma, captivated by the curiosity of the children and the
women, finds herself separated from Isaías, first by the circle of
wailing women, then by file after file of people starting to make
their way back to the village. Avá is taken directly to the Great
House of Men and is seated on a stool representing the two-
headed king-vulture.

The hour has come. Avá must now speak at length. He must
be hard and strong as befits a chieftain-to-be. He must talk
about all that his eyes have seen, all that his ears have heard, all
that his spirit has understood, during those long and many years
in the world of the white people.

He himself, however, interrupts the ceremony at an improper
time to request that they wait a little. He goes to find Alma who

is standing stunned on the dancing ground, still surrounded by women and children. She realized that she was not allowed to enter the Great House of Men but didn't know what her attitude should be or where to go. She is worried about a question Teró had asked her on the way up from the beach.

"Are you the wife of our Avá?"

Isaías takes Alma to his house, the house of the Jaguar clan. There he barely recognizes the old women he had left behind, much less the young ones. He introduces Alma in his own language and immediately translates for her: "I said that you are like a sister, that I love you a lot, and that you are to live in our house."

He leaves and rapidly returns to rejoin the ceremony in the Great House where all the men are waiting. He sits, pauses in anticipation of total silence, and starts to talk, haltingly, to allay their curiosity. He speaks for a long time, giving quick accounts of matters he assumes will be interesting to everyone. The ocean which he had crossed going and coming, an immense salt water lake, bigger than the sky; the enormous cities he had visited—Rio, São Paulo, Brasília, and, on the other side, Paris and Rome. He talks about the numberless buildings occupying immense tracts of land and also rising to the sky because houses were superimposed one atop the other. He describes the multitude of residents and the innumerable white people: they swarm like ants from an anthill as big as all the anthills of the world put together. He uses markets as an example: their mountains of food that rise each day to feed all those people. He does not neglect to mention the many who die of hunger, all the same. He speaks of the trains, of the ships, of the airplanes, in which he journeyed by land, by sea, and by air, throughout the world. He describes in as much detail as possible what it means to listen to radios and to watch television or a movie. He comments on the vast number of telephones all talking at once, making contact with people who have never seen and would never see each other. Finally, he speaks about the seasons of the year, dwelling on winter and the whiteness of snow, the piercing cold, the trees stripped of all leaves, and people wrapped up in furs. But also a little about the joys of spring, when tender shoots burst forth in a variety of colors.

After a moment of silence, there are questions which he answers carefully:

"Who is the owner of the salt?"

"Who makes all the tools?"

"Who do all the matches belong to?"

"How do they make glass beads?"

"Who is the Lord of the Mirrors?"

Isaías tries to explain how and by whom everything is made but has difficulty finding expressions adequate to satisfy the curiosity of the Mairuns.

Later, complex questions are raised:

"And as to Maíra, did Avá visit him? Did he see him?"

"Does Avá have any news concerning him?"

"Did he get to see the gods of the white people?"

"Their God the Father, is He the same as Maíra-Monan of the Mairuns?"

"Is his Son, Jesus, Maíra, or Mairaíra?"

"Did Avá visit Him? Did he see Him?"

"Does he have proof that they exist in the form attributed to them by the Christians? Are they very powerful? Where are they?"

"Why did one of them order the death of the other?" Slowly the questions come down to earth:

"As to war, is it true that there is war all the time somewhere?"

"And those rifle cannons that fire bombs capable of wiping out an entire village, how do they work?"

"And those planes that drop bombs from the sky burning or stripping the leaves from the trees, is that true?"

"Did you see the end-of-the-world bomb that Mr. Bob talks about? Does it exist? Is it really capable of annihilating everything including the Mairuns at the snap of a finger?"

"How could that be? Why?"

Hours of storytelling, speculation, and revelation pass. Self-assured now, Avá answers questions calmly and wisely. Uncertain now, he gives the impression of mixing things up. The Mairuns journey with gusto by way of his words, beyond the earth, throughout the great world of the others.

While the men are questioning Avá, Alma, left alone in the house of the Pumas, confronts her fate. Upon arriving, she slung a hammock, with the assistance of Pinuarana, Avá's sister, in the place Moita indicated with a glance. Now she sits there, looking around, feeling scrutinized, not knowing what to say or do.

The Puma women approach her little by little. They pose questions; only a word here, a word there are intelligible in their Mairun phrases. They can make out even less from Alma's long wordy replies. But despite their miscommunications Alma and the women begin to understand each other on the level of laughter and smiles, contact and empathy. They invite her to eat, offering hot cassava bread folded over roast meat and teaching her to drink great gulps of chibé, fresh cassava beer served in a black calabash.

The Puma women are approaching and touching Alma, first her bare arms and hands, which they examine and squeeze gently to see, feel, and admire the color and texture of the skin, the firmness and warmth of the flesh, all in such contrast to theirs. Then they look carefully at her face and hair which they all want to caress and some to fix up, running the tips of their fingers around the delicate design of the curves of her mouth, the structure of her turned-up nose, and the superb arch of her eyebrows, all so different. Later they come to her legs and feet which they scrutinize minutely, their boldness growing with intimacy, shyness having been overcome.

After an hour, Alma naked and feeling foolish is reclining on a mat surrounded by women. As she doesn't want to run away, she prefers to laugh, to fraternize with those people who smile at her sympathetically with suspicion and affection. As much as she can she hides her shame at feeling invaded, exposed, deciphered. But how can she complain about their wanting to see her naked when all these women are themselves in the nude? Why not allow herself to be seen and touched by whomever when they themselves are satisfying her curiosity?

The patches of curly hair under her arms and between her legs are a great discovery for the Pumas, and cause for amusement. The women also run their fingers through and admire the hair on her head, once again comparing it to their own with great zeal. What provokes surprise, almost horror, is their discovery on Alma's legs of hair that had grown hard and stubbly during a month without depilation. Not so the silky, blond cowlicks on her body, which the delicate fingers of the Puma women and girls caress gently, sending shivers all over her. They admire, even praise, the budlike clitoris of her sacred vulva, especially Mbia, who shows Alma her own little cunt and clitoris, pretending to be annoyed, the poor thing, because they are only half the size of Alma's. Her high, svelte buttocks, ample but firm, and her round, taut, elegant breasts please the Pumas to no end. But not her waist which they judge too slender and fragile.

One of the great surprises of this lesson in intimate anthropology is the clean, smooth skin of the soles of her feet which enchants them. All the Puma women want to stroke their faces affectionately against the tender sole the better to appreciate its delicacy which enchants them.

Later, their casual and surprising discovery of a gold molar leaves the Pumas speechless with astonishment. Even Moita comments, talking away with great enthusiasm as she opens Alma's mouth to see the gold tooth better and to stick her fingers in so as to touch and feel the smooth, polished metal.

In the Great House the meeting with Isaías continues. More difficult questions are now being posed. All the men demand that Avá discuss, confirm, or deny, the Mairun version of the world beyond. It is as if they were interrogating the man they had sent to see the other world, the world of foreigners, of enemies. They want an accounting. They follow an argument Isaías had tried in vain to avoid, with Náru, about the end-of-the-world bomb. Is it not the same comet that Ambir Oberá captured to use in the war against the Christians? If not, where is Oberá's captive comet? A Pacu wants to know why Avá had not tried harder to find the famous, touted land of happiness. There, as everyone knows, crops grow by themselves or nourished only by the songs of happiness which the people sing all day. Could there be a more important place to visit then that? A Turtle wants to know what definite news Avá brings about the immortal people who never grow old or die, who only change skin from time to time. There are none? How is that? They don't really exist? How can that be? Has he not seen them; does he or does he not know whether these people exist anymore? If what he says is true, who annihilated them? And when?

A Coati begs Avá to talk about the warrior women with only one breast who hunt men. Where are they wandering now?

The prestige of Avá is much lowered by this trial.

After they all depart in the still of the night, Jaguar walks up to the guide of souls and squats beside him without speaking. Remui understands the mute inquiry. He explains as best he can that to him it is also a mystery. Avá has come so concealed that he cannot be seen. His visible aspect only hides his true essence. It is necessary not to judge him. Not to think for a moment that he is no more than what you see. Within him is the hidden, the recondite, fulfilling the destiny imposed upon him by the powerful sorcerers of the Mission. Through him, within him, some design is yet to be realized. But will it be divine or demoniacal?

Jaguar walks away knowing only that beyond the visible Avá he must continue to see the tuxaurã, the chieftain-to-be, who, when the time comes, in one way or another will reveal himself as he is in truth and as he ought to be: the new chief, tuxaureté.

MY WATERS

The following morning, all attention is directed toward Alma. No one leaves the village, everyone wants to see her. They try to talk to her, using the few words of Portuguese they know. Both the men and the women invite her to bathe with them in the river.

"Isaías, what should I do? All these plying me, people wanting to bathe with me. It's a bit rude, isn't it?"

"Yes. But it would be better to get it over with. You can't live the rest of your life without bathing."

"But, Isaías, I don't have a bathing suit, and in any event I think it would be indecent for me to wear a bathing suit among all these naked people."

"They're not nude, Alma. As you know, both the men with their bá and the women in their uluri are wearing clothing after their own fashion."

"I've seen them, but for me it's not the same; it's too sudden!"

Around midday she makes up her mind:

"I have to deal with this. I'm going out there."

The whole village follows Alma to bathe. Men, young and old, women of all ages and children as well. She undresses non-chanantly. But when she sees all those eyes staring at her, staring at her hairy pubis, she covers herself with her hands and runs as fast as she can to dive into the water. Minutes later the Iparanã is swollen with people. Alma, ever surrounded, yields to the joy of the water, the hearty laughter of everyone, and all the children swimming toward her. She feels at ease. She approaches the beach and, remaining in the water to her waist, calls out to Isaías:

"Come, Isaías, the water is delicious!"

"I can't, I'm naked."

"What are you talking about?"

"I'm not wearing a bá."

"Don't be ridiculous, do you think I have an uluri?"

The first present Avá receives from Jaguar is a bundle of arrows with bamboo tips and an enormous black bow, exquisitely crafted. Isaías smiles, tries the bow, and thanks Jaguar, saying that nowadays he hunts more frequently with a rifle; he has lost the skill for shooting arrows. Isaías reciprocates by giving his nephew his pocket watch with a chain, which Jaguar, content and excited, hangs around his neck.

On the afternoon of the following day, Avá sets out with Jaguar for a two-day fishing trip on the Iparanã and some of its rivulets and lagoons. He settles into the canoe with pleasure, thinking: My waters that will wash me! They are enchanted each by the other: the nephew by his globe-trotting uncle, strange, small, weak, but a master of words, capable of talking about anything; the uncle by his youthful, vigorous, formidable nephew who would certainly assume the chieftainship once the Mairuns realized that he, the uncle, is ill-equipped to command warriors.

They navigate up and downstream and through the lakes, making wide turns. They camp twice, always fishing and talking. Isaías compensates for his clumsiness as a fisherman by telling tale after tale, keeping Jaguar fascinated. But he in turn makes his uncle shut up when necessary so as not to miss harpooning a catfish. They catch many fish, but Jaguar does not want to return to the village without two arapaimas. He would be ashamed otherwise. On the morning of the third day, they succeed in catching the second with a harpoon. Jaguar and Isaías carry them back to the village. Isaías, bent, under the weight of one arapaima, hears compliments from everyone looking on with admiration and congratulating him as if he had caught it. It hurts Avá to know that no one had any doubt that the fish was Jaguar's.

In the village he talks with Alma about the difficulties facing him. It is clear that he is not living up to the expectations of the Mairuns. He explains that this is all the more serious in his case, because he belongs to the Jaguar clan which provides chieftains. This clan needs and must display strength and efficiency. If matters were otherwise, if he belonged, for example, to the Falcon clan and had as his vocation guide of souls, it would be easy for him to be a quiet, reserved man. Even if he belonged to a clan as detested as the Coatis, no one would be preoccupied with his physical deficiencies. People would believe that he was compensating for his awkwardness, if he had any, by transforming himself into a future oxim, a powerful sorcerer. But for a Jaguar, things are different. A Jaguar must be a leader. It will take them a long time to stop thinking that way. He feels all eyes resting on him, perplexed and surprised. He senses that the Mairuns are all wishing for a miracle man, a prodigy to emerge from his meager flesh, from his squalid body. They are wishing for another being: a vigorous Jaguar, mature, wise, commanding respect, the chief they are waiting for.

A few days later they go out to hunt. This time Avá and Jaguar are accompanied by Teró and Maxí. In spite of being armed with a .22 automatic carbine that Bob had lent him, Avá does not fare well. The carbine serves only for salvos to the amusement of Teró, then Jaguar, then Maxí. All the game are shot silently with arrows.

After this second failure, Isaías refuses all invitations to hunt or fish, even as he yearns to relive those first days with Jaguar, when the two of them spent time alone, talking. He had related his experiences to the person he most wanted to hear them. It was as if Jaguar had been there to drink Avá's words so that the former would never repeat or allow to be repeated the foolish acts he had committed, the erroneous choices he had made.

From now on, Isaías converses more with Alma than with the Mairuns. In these talks he unfolds his great project. He speaks for hours on end about the immensity of a clearing he will open in the forest at a certain place that he has shown to her.

"It's a tract of forest on one side of the Black Lake with almost magically fertile black soil," Isaías remarks. "But I don't want it to be like other Mairun clearings with the plants all mixed up, growing as if in the wild." His clearing will be arranged. Corn, beans, and peanuts will be grown separately so that everything will be in order to facilitate bumper crops. The cultivation and sale of produce will allow for the purchase of many things for distribution among those who most participated.

The best feature of the plan is the innovative idea of exploiting the sport and ceremonial impetus of the Mairuns, converting it into a productive force. To this end, the clearing will be divided into a red half and a blue half, in the same way that the village is divided in summer for the great wrestling competitions and the javelin-throwing matches. This sport-based division into northern and southern halves will ignore the matrimonial bands and clan divisions, permitting the reunion of Mairun men and women, regardless of where they live, in the same working groups. The idea is to channel the Mairun zeal for sports into productive activity. The Mairuns, Isaías explains, apply all their physical and intellectual resources—which could lead to progress—to a superelaboration of social, ceremonial, and sports etiquette. The thing to do now, he continues, is to induce them to divert those motivating forces to the economic sector so as to promote development. No one can imagine the lengths that a Mairun goes to to observe a ritual precept or to bury an old chief with honor; it is astonishing. What they don't understand is how to enter the game of real, practical life with the same vigor. This is partly the fault of certain religious beliefs, such as the conception of a heaven accessible to all after death, and the illusion of a land without evil that awaits the hopeless, like a road that is always an option, open to those who have the temerity to confront hardships.

Alma thinks that Isaías is only complicating matters:

"As far as I am concerned the Mairuns have already made a revolution achieving liberty. Among them no one is rich or poor; when nature is unkind, everyone gets thin; when it's generous, everyone gets fat. No one exploits anyone. No one orders anyone about. Their liberty to work or play as the spirit moves them is priceless. And what's more, life is varied; no one is a drudge, a beast of burden. For me, the Land without Evil is here and now. No one quarrels with anyone. Only the men with the women in their momentary fits of jealousy. Leave these people in peace, Isaías. Don't complicate things."

MAÍRA: REMUI

Maíra-Coraci, the Sun, spins unceasingly in the immensity of celestial blue. He gyrates in a fixed path as though tied to the end of a cord. Isn't he like an immense rhombus that the Mairuns spin in the sky? But he doesn't buzz or roar; he only gives light and warmth.

Sometimes he also tires of his perpetual gyrations and wishes to descend just for a moment to his remade world. Once again he wants to see greens, reds, yellows. He wants to smell the odors he himself put into things. He wants to clothe the bodies of men; he wants to feel the pleasure of the women of his people, the Mairuns. He also wants to become emotional through sentiments of happiness and sadness, nostalgia and melancholy, disillusion and hope that enliven the Mairuns.

Now I am going to visit once more my old guide of souls. He thinks he will be the last, the final one: the end of the series of so many guides that I have known. He wants finality. It is sorrowful; my little light who still illuminates the Mairun spirit. There he is, Remui, sitting on his bench which reminds me of the heads I took from the King Vulture; there he is shaking his rattle. He is making it buzz and is murmuring something to his beloved dead.

How can you continue living in that body, Remui? It's worn out from so much use. You can hardly see shadows. You can hardly hear voices and the sound of your rattle. As to your sense of smell, perhaps you can still catch the sweet stench of a human carcass. You could well eat grass thinking it was meat. My old guide of souls, I can't allow you to rest yet though I understand how much you want to come to an end. Speak, little old one; speak, guide of souls; speak to me.

Avá arrived and has not arrived. He who has come is not the true Avá. The one I awaited, he whom I saw traveling by land and by sea, day after day has not arrived. That was indeed Avá himself, through and through. He who has come is what remains of my son, Avá, after the most powerful false sorcerers of the Europeans has robbed his soul. He goes about half asleep, lost to himself and to us. Behind his eyes there is a cloud, the blindness of those who no longer have souls to die. He is no longer a living mortal, one of us. He will never be one of the living dead. He is outside of our worlds. We don't see him yet for what he is. Already he doesn't see us. He is lost, asleep, enchanted, bewitched. Who can wake him?

This Avá was my hope. He must have saved us from imminent perdition. It was always he who would return, bringing us all the great secrets of the Europeans. He who would uplift the whole Mairun nation. But he came empty. He brought us nothing, not even himself. With him we have lost our chieftain-to-be who was to have become our chieftain. He returned empty, drained. It is as if he had been taken out of his skin. It is as if he had been turned inside out. But what they did was worse. They took away his spirit. He who is here is what remains of a man who has lost his soul.

Now, I have no more hopes; it only remains for me to die. To die from having waited so long. To die from lack of appetite for a life I find disgusting to live. Only to die, to die! Die while the earth may yet want to putrify my body as it putrified that of my chieftain Anacã and those of so many before him. It may well be that tomorrow the earth itself will beg you for repose, Maíra. It may well be that it will say: I am tired of eating putrid flesh. And you will have to listen, you will have to attend to its plea.

We, the Mairuns, are becoming extinct, and along with us, Maíra-Monan, Mairahú, and Maíra-Ambir, Our Creator. You yourself started all this, Maíra-Coraci. You wanted to be alone. There you are anew and renewed everyday, as you were yesterday as you will always be. Who will save us? What will become of old Maíra-Monan, castrated by you? Our ancient God who died for us, perhaps He, and only He, can save us now. Not you, scoundrel God, who could have helped us at any time but never wished to do so. Who knows if perhaps the Old One, the Nameless One, will send another of his belches to enter some other Mosaingar? Then the twin sons of the Lord would be born for everything to start all over again.

Here and now, nothing can be done. All that remains for us is to wait. To wait to see the end, to know how it will come. As for me, all that sustains me here is my displeasure, my obligation, my destiny of being guide of souls to the dead. Without me, what would become of them? There is no one else to be guide of souls. Only Teró perhaps, or Náru. I don't wish that for my nephew Teró. But so it must be, if I am not to be the last, the final guide of souls. Is Náru, a Pacu, up to the task? I doubt it.

How sorrowful that my true son Avá cannot be guide of souls. He could never be: he has been stripped of his soul. He has walked far too long with the wicked for him ever to be able to speak to the spirits. His being a Jaguar, his being born of my woman Moitá of the House of Jaguars, is perhaps not the greatest impediment. The obstacle lies in the loss of his soul. He walks about with his body empty, his eyes glazed, his mouth speaking the words of another. A guide of souls cannot be nurtured where there is no soul. He is nobody. There is nobody behind his eyes. How would he be able to speak to the great wheel of the Mairuns of all time?

The great wheel turns to arrive here every evening bringing two, three, sometimes more souls from each house to talk and listen to me. Without me, the wheel would continue to rotate; I would then be in the middle of it, lost like one more speck in the dust storm of the sky. But the wheel would revolve for nothing, without an axis, in a great house of men such as this, without a guide of souls to listen to the past, to speak of the present, and to divine the future.

I don't want to imagine—nor am I capable of imagining—a world without souls, a world deprived of spirits who would be flying around in space without a fixed, immovable point as their center. Will things survive the death of the spirits? Can the world balance itself without a fixed, immovable point to support it like this great house? Can time proceed with yesterdays, todays, and tomorrows together but separated like grains on an ear of corn if there is no fixed vantage point on the ground of the world from which the Mairuns can take account of the sun? Who can guarantee that the sun will rise, reach its summit, and set every day?

I am tired, the Earth is tired. Perhaps even the Sky is tired and wants to collapse. Only for you, Maíra, is the bright clarity not a burden. Aren't there hours, though, when you also wish for eclipse? It surprises me that birds and children enter the world wanting to live life with joy and resolve. Why? I am tired. The Mairuns are tired, tired of living. And who knows, perhaps even the dead themselves are tired of whirling about. Only the two of you, Maíra and Micura, in your bodies of fire and light, illuminating the new world, the world of the white people by day and by night, are not tired.

This old guide of souls is decrepit. I want to touch and hear young people. People who believe, or, if not, are at least alive: people who enjoy living. Remui is nothing but melancholy. I need to measure the despair of Teidju, to experience the sadness of this Avá. How is my young Jaguar, with all of his muscles and firmness? And this European woman, who is she? What is she doing here living among my people? What is to become of her?

THE COLT

The population of Corrutela dwindles at the beginning of summer. The cowboys leave to look for work herding cattle in the backlands. There, they prize the roundups, driving the cows about to give birth and the yearlings to the recently opened pastures along the Iparanã. These are long journeys, slow and easy so as not to tire or maim any of the herd. But they are also entertaining: for a good cowboy there is nothing like a cattle drive. It is not as good to return with old cows and premature bulls that need to be revived and fattened up in the winter pastures. During these journeys provisions are meager. There is much work and little pay.

Corrutela becomes populous again when the cowboys return from the interior with money in their pockets and hunks of sundried beef, or with purchases from backwoods towns: brilliantine for little girls, a piece of cotton cloth for a prospective mother-in-law, prerolled cigarettes, a bottle or two of rum.

This is when the time of temptation begins for Xisto. Not until their ardor is dampened by the heavy rains do the young men leave off buzzing around the girls like a swarm of bees. Every night there are serenades with guitars. Every week there is dancing to the music of accordians in the houses of good Catholics. With rum not available or sold, there is not much danger; but it is necessary to be on the alert. The Devil himself is there, deceiving, tempting.

Squatting in the shade of the church, Xisto preaches to his flock:

"Look, there goes Tião Comboieiro and his pack. You need only look to see and understand. From within him, God is making him stronger to bear the load. From without, the Devil is weighing him down. Poor Tião is sweating from the strain. The Devil takes it easy, sitting atop a heap of rubbish. That's how it is with everything, not only with business."

Xisto pauses, takes a draw on his pipe and continues:

"The Devil likes to get into everything, but what he likes most is to get inside people, to interfere. He is always looking for a horse, his horse, for a mare, his mare. Or for his colt, the greedy one. Who is free of the Devil? There is where the real danger lurks because the body of each is his sanctum. The body is the house that God gave us, a blessed abode for us. When the Devil enters that house, all is lost. Not only that unfortunate one, but many more are also lost. How can we know if the words of the horse of the Devil are his or the horse's? Are the words of the mare of the Devil his or the mare's? Are those of his colt his or the colt's? She is the colt who is the Devil. No one knows. Things are as they are. The world is full of temptation. He emits flames to set the thicket on fire. We ourselves are the thicket. Ah, my brothers, my sisters, here, in this mouth of night, in threatening darkness, are some men, women, and young virgins. We are all here under the protection of God with our hands pressed together, praying for deliverance from the Devil. Now let us sing, brethren."

They sing the refrain, clapping their hands to the rhythm Xisto sets. Their enthusiasm and fervor grow as they sing, sometimes standing still or jumping with arms raised, or swaying and dancing.

Halleluja! Glory! Hosanna!
May God save me, may God uplift me.
We are of the Lord Our God,
God is our abode.

Xisto stops singing and proceeds:

"When the Devil enters someone, what can be done? Nothing at all. There is no solution. The person is finished but still living, a tempter, one of the damned, an eater of the souls of others. That is the law, my brethren: a law given by God for those who know how to see, a law good for those who live in conformity with God, good for those who accept the severity of the will of God. But it is a hard and deceptive law for those who fall into perdition. It is a law without a judge or anyone sworn to judge. It is the law of only our Lord Jesus Christ.

"He is up there above us, at the feet of God the Father, watching. He is watching His hunter down below, the Devil. He looks and sees the Shameless One hunting souls among the little people who compose the flock of God. The will of God is mysterious. The Devil himself was the Black Angel, the Silent Angel, the Angel that He used to love best. But the Devil was the one who complained most, who wanted most to assist in the work of God. Was he not the angel that God lost? Is he not the Fallen Angel? The Devil who is within us lying in wait, is the huntsman of God. God and the Devil are intermingled. The will of God is mysterious, recondite, obscure. God is like the light of the sun that shines everywhere, including the shady side of the chapel: here it is dark, but the light of God still delineates each face and figure. God penetrates even the pure heart of blackness that is the kingdom of the Devil. God is like the air which is everywhere, in the light as in the darkness. I even think that air is the exhalation of God. When he blows, there are gales, tempests, hurricanes. . . . All the world sees and is frightened, discovering that the world is full of air. The air comes from God, but also from the Devil, excommunicated, the brother of the angels, the creature, fallen, torn, and disgraced. When we suffer from lack of air as in the affliction of the final hour before death, it is the Devil who is clogging our system, suffocating us as he fights for that soul. The huntsman of God is everywhere, hunting sinners who have already sinned and sinners who are about to sin. The Devil is no cowboy; he does not eat what he himself has raised. Nor is he a farmer; he does not eat what he himself has grown. The Devil hunts what is not his own. He catches any fish he can. Whose is the game he hunts and the fish that he fishes for? They belong to God. They are the little creatures of God, like me and like you, Perpetinha. The Devil wants me, Xisto, you, anyone. Anyone, good and bad, can be a home for the Devil. Why is everything like this so difficult? It is the mystery, and the mystery is what has not been revealed. God is the Father. God is good, but God is the law, severity, virtue, purity. God is the mystery. He found this as a way of sifting his people, separating the grain from the chaff, as it says in the Holy Book, to find out who is who. To separate those who are useful from those who are useless, the damager from the damaged. That is why we need to be like game, like the coati, labba, tapir. We need to sleep with one eye only, keeping the other half-open, vigilant. We must be ready to bolt when the dangerous one, the mangy one, arrives. Only perspicacity can save us from perdition. Mysterious is the mystery of the Lord."

THE BLOOD AND THE MILK

To the rhythm of the Mairuns Alma lives a season of long blue days. Every day she feels more strongly the beauty of living, the joy of existing, that she learns from them. She participates in everything, seeing with her own eyes and hearing through the ears of Isaías. So she attends, trying hard to understand, the great feast of the presentation of the nubile girls after their first menstruation. Ecstatically, Avá admires through the eyes of Isaías the girls wounded by arrows from the moon, so beautiful in their nudity. Alma gazes at the young bodies shaped by the hand of God.

The girls had been secluded for months in cabins set up inside the houses, without seeing or speaking to anyone, without being able to go out for some sun. Now they are coming out, lovely, fresh, resplendent. The whole village has its eyes on their charms. They wear on their chests, giving distinction to their budding breasts, the solar necklace of gilded feathers that each of the girls carefully made by herself to demonstrate her skill as a maiden. They have limpid smiles on their faces. Their bodies are painted with happy stripes of red annatto and black genipap. They are wearing enormous alluring, blue-black headdresses with fringes long enough to cover their mouths. Their legs are bound with cords, are swollen and baroque. They carry proudly calabashes of cassava beer and gourd cups in their hands.

"Would you like some of my milk?"

All afternoon the Mairuns, sitting in a circle on the side of the setting sun, watch the nubile girls serving their cassava beer to the men whom they are going to fuck. The people look and smile, gossip and comment joyfully on the form displayed by each of the girls as they enter womanhood. Buds, the sprouting of life renews.

"Did you see, Jaguar, did you see how Inimá's breasts stick out? Who has been going around squeezing them? Maité! Maité . . . !"

"Look at Araruama's thighs," Jaguar replies, "see how plump they've gotten. Have you snared her yet?"

"And Anurá, look at that little tummy of hers. She must be already pregnant! What charm. Is she about to give birth? Who is the father?"

"No, brothers, Yupti is the only pretty one. Look at her carapuá, warm and round. My goodness, I wish they'd give me that little yam!"

"Boys, there is Tumií. Looks how she walks, the shameless creature, waggling her behind like a white woman. She must have learned that from Canindejub! What a beauty!"

The girls walk about, talking, laughing, flirting with their future young men ceaselessly. Future? Who could tell? They go to their houses to get more cassava beer and return to serve it and to let themselves be seen, to exhibit themselves. They smile and prance, spin around and pause, and start to flirt once again with their favorite young men.

"Aren't you having more of my milk, Jaguar?" inquires Inimá, offering him another gourdful.

The women smile and remark:

"Look Calu. Look at that Inimá, she is going to fuck for her whole life."

"As far as I know," says Anoã, "she started to fuck long before she was wounded. You'll see how she won't be able to have children because she was fucking so much even as a child."

"None of that," Piti says. "You were fucking and fucking a lot long before you began to menstruate, and you have many pretty children."

"Lie, that's a lie! I never fucked before I was wounded, never. Nor did I fuck while I was secluded. Only once. Afterward, yes. You were the one who always had no shame; you were the one always doing it. Weren't you the one they caught with the late Anacã in your seclusion hut?"

The men are also commenting. Teró shows Matipu and Cosó how bashful the two young Tapirs, Suiá and Mati, are in front of Araruama:

"They both want to marry her. Which one will it be? They are going to have to take turns for a long time. Now, in my time . . ."

The old woman Camãi is irritated and remarks tartly that life used to be much better. At the feast of her first blood there was food in abundance. The men had gone out to hunt and to fish and had gathered great quantities of game and grilled fish. It was a good feast with lots to eat. "I offered my cassava beer with one hand and at the same time gave out slices of meat and fish folded in cassava bread with the other. Things weren't what they are now, with only a little beer and everyday food. The men today are so lazy. Life is different. It is because we don't have a real chieftain to make these lazy ones work?"

"Yes," replies Moitá. "We are all old and tired. But it is always worthwhile to live. It's good to see these young girls coming out every summer, so lovely. Even walking by Canindejub they seem to have good figures. They are almost as pale as the yellow macaw."

Pinuarana, Teró's wife, and her daughter Mbiá, Náru's wife, who are sitting with Moitá, agree energetically. Smiling, Pinu points to Inimá.

"There goes one who eats jaguars. Be careful with her, she is going to rob some from us."

MAÍRA TEIDJU

I need another descent to get a feeling for these people of mine. Together with them I want to see anew this little world of mine down below. Whom will I assail today? How about that oxim, that sorcerer? I need to feel what it is like to be what Micura created by spitting into his mother's womb. I clearly remember that my brother invented that oxim when the other one, Tapiir, turned into a very powerful evil sorcerer. I am entering him . . . how disgusting, what a vile body this is. It doesn't see light and shade very well; nor can it distinguish colors. What gives the joy of life to this lunar creature of my brother Micura? The only good thing about him is his desperate lucidity. It is this light burning in the night of his life that hurts him so much. Speak, oxim, speak to me:

"Oh, I, Teidju! I already, not now, nothing! No one: nobody. Not I, not I! That Avá, yes: he is doing poorly, perhaps worse than I. He began by looking in my eyes, laughing, smiling. Smiling at me, face to face, as if I were like the others. I am not. Later, he started coming around. Now he comes every day. Is it because of the meat that I give him? It could not be to hear me converse. I'm not much given to talking. Ah! that's it, it's true: he comes to have someone to talk to. What he wants is an ear to listen to his foolishness. I don't know what's the matter with him. He seems to want to be a kind of oxim like those false sorcerers upriver, a black oxim. For this he has been preparing for many years. He has returned and he is not an oxim or anything else. He should have been the chieftain, but he won't do for that. You can see in his face that he's twisted. Never, never will he be a chieftain.

That scoundrel—his cousin, Jaguar—he really demonstrates what it takes to be a chieftain. Who, looking into those eyes and at that hatred that springs from them, is incapable of divining Jaguar's destiny? He is a born warrior. I don't look at him face to face any more. Before, I used to stare at him, and he would lower his eyes. But for some time now he has been giving me a look so hard and unwavering that I bow my head, and I hide. And he is still only a youth.

This is true not only of Jaguar. I feel this repulsion in all, except Avá. In some, it is loathing, principally loathing; others, fear, principally fear. But the effect is the same. I am the one who should be frightened. I ought to disappear, vanish. Yes, that's what I ought to do! But that is what they want; that is what would please them. Another thing, if I were to leave here, where would I go? Am I to plunge into this forest to live like an animal among animals? My life would probably be worse than an animal's. But I am not an animal, I am a person, I am a Mairun, I am one of Maíra's people. That is what I am, whether they like it or not. I am a Coati, or Teidju, a true Mairun.

"What is fluttering around here? Go away, animal; go away, wretch. Whose was that cold tongue of a bat that licked my neck? Go away! Are you one of the sempiternal bats attacking me again? Go away, wretch! Go suck the neck of your mother."

I need to think. I know very well that nobody wants me. But they can't get along without me; they are afraid of me. I see the fear growing; I like to see it growing. It makes me afraid, but truthfully, it makes me more happy than afraid. I like to see I have a little power that inspires respect. The trouble is that I know only too well how it will all end. I saw that when they finished with Tapiir. Any day they will turn on me. But for now no one has the nerve. How would they manage without an oxim? The Mairun don't know how to live without eating the flesh of game. And they cannot eat impure meat. Meat in itself is the abode of putrefation; it is a danger, a vice. How much meat have I purified for them, meat capable of putrefying the whole population: poisoning, destroying, killing it? Meat capable of melting bones. I have never seen, but I have heard stories of people without an oxim. They become deformed, even transformed into sacks full of soft bones rattling against each other. So it is; that is what happens to those who eat impure meat.

No one before has ever wanted to live with me, an oxim, to hold conversations with me, to laugh with me, to drop by every day. This one must be sick in the head; he must really be badly off, this Avá. Or perhaps he is extremely sane, who knows? Does he ignore the fact that nobody forgives an oxim for being an oxim, although nobody can get along without one? Otherwise, why would he dare, as opposed to all the others, to come in and talk to me? And I, why do I run the risk of increasing their hatred of me? Will it make matters worse? Won't they say that he, too, is an oxim? Is he an oxim? I don't know.

"What is that owl doing here? Is it the great black owl? Or is it the vulture with an eye in the asshole of its head? Is it some animal trying to tell me something? What is it, who is it? Am I raving? That's not true. There is an animal fluttering. Something is fluttering here. What could it be?"

I never wanted to be the oxim. Who would? It befell me, like destiny. It is worse than being short, fat, and ugly. Maybe that's precisely why. Ever since I was a boy I have been round and plump, flabby, ungainly, and ugly. I couldn't be with the others; they all made fun of me. I continued to grow, becoming self-conscious and hiding. Only my mother would have anything to do with me. While she lived, she would search for me; she could always find me wherever I was hiding. She would come and give me a piece of meat and cassava cake, every day. It was she who told me that one day I would end up being an oxim. She said this without sadness as if she had always known, as if she had brought me into the world to meet that destiny. I trembled with fear and shame; I became an oxim with my rattle in one hand and my feather whisk in the other. It was old Tapiir who made me into an oxim to relieve my attacks, the foaming at my mouth, of which I have never been completely cured.

"Whose is this croaking? Where is this acrid stench coming from? The sweet stench of the decomposing flesh of the chieftain ceased long ago. Is it the stench of an exhumed corpse? Who would die and remain unburied and smell so vile? It smells like the stench of Tapiir, but he has been dead for so long! Could it be the reek of my own flesh rotting there in the forest that I am already smelling?"

When Tapiir was treating me, I myself took up the rattle and the whisk and played with them for hours to get to know them. I continued learning, learning. One day the rattle was already an extension of my hand; I could no longer feel it. I felt only its absence when I was without it. The same was true of the whisk made of seriema feathers; if I mislaid it the feeling of loss would be awful, as if my fingers had been cut off. Ever since, the rattle in one hand and the whisk in the other have been part of me. My two hands serve me this way: to shake the rattle and to wave the whisk. The whisk and the rattle speak more often and better than my mouth.

That was until this black oxim, this false sorcerer from the white people, Avá. With him, when he is here with me, I just shake my rattle, slowly, slowly, almost like Remui: chuá . . . chuá . . . a fine chaca-cha. Sometimes he stops talking and stays there listening to that little chuá . . . uá, silently. It is like a fluttering of wings, of the wings of a beetle, but it can get as loud as the mother of all cicadas and much louder, even as to become deafening.

One day, before the death of Tapiir, someone came to beg me

to cast a spell, but I wouldn't. Later on, somebody else with
very polite manners, came and asked to be cured: I cured him.
Ever since I have continued to cure people and to grow. My
mouth learned to speak to the ministering spirits who were
flying over there. I believe I was apprenticed by them; I am
their adept. One by one they came and entered me. I trembled
from fright, without reason, simply out of ignorance. It was
difficult for me to discover that they only wanted my eyes and
my mouth to see and to sing with. Thus I continued learning
until I became a good singer that the whole world likes to listen
to. Today I sing with the voices of all people and all animals:
plaintive and frightened, terrifying and ominous, or soft enough
to lull whomever listens to sleep. My mouth also learned to chew
tobacco and to smoke many trembling, nervous, vibrant leaves
that hide over there. The last thing I learned was to blow smoke
and to suck on the little things, dead or alive, that get into
people, provoking illnesses and pain.

One day I woke up as a new being. I had learned that with the
rattle, the whisk, and smoke I could go out flying into the
world. At first, I used to journey in the neck of an anum bird;
but later I mastered a quenquém, a leaf-cutting ant of the forest. Now I fly in anything that flies, even airplanes. You don't
believe it? Neither do I.

Things were this way for a long time until, already living
here in my little hut, I had the courage to look at Tapiir face to
face. Before, I couldn't; no sooner would he see me than he
would start pointing at me and fall into helpless laughter: Oxim,
oxiii . . . m!

After he died, the old chieftain himself, Anacã, arrived here
at my hut one day, carrying an enormous stag on his back. He
came doubled over under the weight of the deer. I knew what
had to be done. I cut it open and peeled off the skin from the
stomach (it was a white-tailed deer) just as someone would skin
a man he was going to eat. I took out all the entails. I took the
liver which was very thin. I cut the meat into slices; I bit into
slice after slice, returning everything. I took nothing for my-

self, not even a shoulder; I took nothing for myself, only the dry liver. I didn't cut the stag into four and take a quarter as Tapiir used to do and as I now often do. I was a fool lacking courage, without anger. I was a real fool. Now it is different.

But I only purify game and heal the sick. I don't kill anyone; I don't injure anyone through sorcery, never. I have never wounded, poisoned, weakened, hit or killed anyone. I only purify and heal. When meat goes bad or a sick person dies, it is not my fault. Only I don't know why the hunting of wasps' nests for honey should always be so poisonous. Could that be why they don't like me? Or does that happen because they don't like me? And the people who die in my arms, why do they die? But why should everyone have to live? I can't go on, I don't have the power; at least, I don't have enough power. All I do is use my rattle and my whisk to heal, to purify, to divine the future.

I don't prophesy as much nowadays. It's not as it used to be. Nobody comes to me anymore to ask for advice about where it is best to hunt or where it is best to fish or when it is good time to leave on a journey.

Nobody asks me anything anymore. Nobody comes here to complain about aches I might be able to relieve. They come only if dragged by someone else, their faces twisted by fear. Seeing death already in the eyes of many of them, I say at once that I won't shake my rattle. Like the guide of souls, I say that the person has already danced Coraci-Iaci, but they implore, they beg, they entreat. They know that it is my duty, my destiny, to heal. The discourse of the guide of souls is his alone. Only he can say calmly to someone that the hour of death has arrived, because he considers it is better to die than to live. They expect an oxim to be able to cure anyone all the time. If someone dies, or another gets worse, they all think that the oxim has killed or bewitched the person.

I never used to provoke as much fear as I do now, and this in turn fills me with fear too. It seems that everybody thinks I can do anything, can hand out life or death, make people enjoy themselves or suffer, at my whim. For many, I am like the old oxim of long ago. Perhaps many are thinking that I am all-powerful like the otxicom, the evil sorcerer, of ancient lore. But I . . . I can do nothing. I am nothing.

"Again the fluttering of an owl, a weird sound, that stench. . . . Are they coming from within me or from outside?"

The anger of many of them came from knowing that I used to fuck the women in the family of each person that I had treated. But if this had not been so, I would never have fucked a single woman. I had had enough of masturbation. But that awful anger I saw on their faces ended up frightening me. I stopped that a long time ago. Now I'm back to masturbating. But even so the anger grows ceaselessly. Their anger at me, and mine at them.

It was worse than ever after the affair with Iapu and the curse I brought upon his head. I came across the wretch as he was about to finish shitting in the forest, and I couldn't avoid seeing the pile of stool he had dropped. It was fat, dark, robust, typical of a man who has eaten a lot of meat. Iapu understood what I had noticed and realized that I knew that he had been going around in the forest, eating the game he caught. He was completely humbled. All I could say, or what escaped from my mouth was: "Your bowels are going to fall out!" And didn't that very same thing happen? Iapu is no longer able to shit without a hand's span of gut popping out. Everybody knows the reason: My words, really, my curse, the power of my curse. They describe many cases, some true, others less so, all of which involve something I did or said. These stories account for my notoriety, my bad reputation as the evil sorcerer that I don't want to be, the sorcerer that I am not.

Is that true? Here alone, I question myself:

Isn't it true? "Isn't it true that I want to kill without knowing, that I wish for the death of people I can't cure, that my ill-will toward someone has the power to destroy him? No, it is not true; otherwise, half these Mairuns would be dead, finished, or crippled. I can't continue being subject to the capricious repugnance, the gratiutous anger, the irremediable fear, provoked in everyone. I can't.

"What is it that is fluttering, chirping, stinking all around me? Or is it within me?"

Is it better to live with this ever increasing dread than to die? Yes. I want to live with or without fear. Were they to leave me in peace, contempt would soon follow; and I value being someone who is frightening. This is how it will be. What is there to do? Terrifying fear will grow as much as possible in them and in me, in both of us together. On the day when it finally explodes and I am done away with, they will remember and fear me for a very long time, not as a poor, ugly lout, nor as the healer, a nice man. I will live on in their memory as the otxicomigin, the evil sorcerer of ancient lore. I will become the Teidju who, while he lived, was capable of anything and dared everything. And not only will I die in the arms of these wretches, I will be reborn to possess their spirits as terrifying dread. After my death, who will wander from the village at night? Who will dare to watch nightfall at the edge of the Black Lake where I will be in the company of Old Tapiir?

THE SEED OF
THE GUIDE OF SOULS

Isaías sits on the dancing ground near Teró, chewing a stalk of grass. They remain there not speaking for a long time watching the sun go down. Teró moves closer until his shoulder touches Avá's, and he embraces him affectionately. Isaías thinks: our habits of bodily contact, our masculine intimacy, are so typical of us, so Mairun. He puts his arm on Teró's strong high shoulder, thinking: he is older than I am, perhaps ten years older, but he is incomparably stronger. This Teró is a real Mairun. He is precisely what a Mairun should be. He is destined to replace the guide of souls, but, for now, no one sees in him the future guide. Things will probably continue like this for the next ten or fifteen years without his revealing a mystical sign or giving an indication that he is destined to be the one who will put the living in communication with the dead. But when the hour arrives, there will be no doubt; he will fulfill his role. He was born for it. His clan, that of the Falcons, is the one that produces the most people capable of this miracle, this leap at the exact moment that will transform him from man to guide of souls, from an ordinary person to an intermediary and a bridge between the world of the living and the world of the dead. The day will come; everyone knows. It might be soon or a long time from now. Teró will probably go into the forest with his bow and arrows, as he has done all his life, simply to hunt. But he will see the forest changed, transformed. The tree trunks will seem to be made of translucent green resin, the leaves of vibrant glass. Then the forest will open up exposing the sky from which will descend upon Teró a numberless flock of golden parakeets coming by the thousands from every side. They will descend on him for him to kill them with a glance, to disappear there in front of him, vanishing in the air, taking a leap from being live birds, fluttering in flight, to being invisible spirits returning to their sunny, aerial world. Teró will emerge, resplendent, from the forest. Everyone will see that he is enchanted and be-wildered. But no one, not even Pinuarama, will say anything. Nor will anyone look when he picks up Remui's rattles and starts getting a feel for them. That's how it will be.

Sitting there, embracing Teró, Isaías is thinking and feeling that he can no longer delay this matter. He needs to talk; he needs to discuss it with Teró. He can no longer keep it to himself.

"Teró, my brother-in-law, I realize that I was wrong."

"What are you talking about, Avá. In what were you mis-taken?"

"Oh, Teró! You know very well. That clearing which required so much work from everyone is foolishness. You were entirely correct when you told me that the season was not right, that the rains would be coming. They came. I mistook an early dry spell for summer. All that work wasted, days and days. And how they all worked! There I was, kindling their spirits, urging them to work harder, thinking some were lazy. Why did they help me, knowing that it was all foolishness? Teró, why?"

"Because they wanted to. They like you, Avá. And how could you have known that the rains were about to fall? You'd been away for so long."

"Yes, Teró. For you, I must be like a child."

"That's unimportant. Forget it. What is important are the seeds and the seedlings. How did you get them?"

"Well, I brought some from the post; Mr. Elias lent them to me. I bought others on credit from the gringos in the House of Mirrors."

"That is the point, Avá, it's serious. You could get them only because you are you. Only the chieftain can incur a debt without upsetting the whole world. We know that we cannot have debts. It is very important that you pay for what you bought on credit immediately. It is most important. This I beg of you, go to the post, then go to the House of Mirrors and ask them squarely how many dried arapaima you must pay for the seedlings and the seeds. How many? They must tell how many. There is still time. We're going to make an effort and we're going to pay. It is very important. We need to pay."

"Ah, Teró, I understand. I'll leave today for the post, and tomorrow I'll talk to the gringo. I'll find out what I must pay in arapaima. Now I understand."

"Don't stay with such a sad look on your face, Avá. Don't you know that we Mairuns are a people of laughter? Laugh, it's good for you. Laugh, man! Shall we?" The two are laughing, at first discreetly, then they are howling louder and louder until the laughter spreads to all the people squatting in the vicinity.

"Now that we've laughed with gusto I have a matter to dis-

cuss with you, my son-in-law. A matter I have kept to myself
for some time. The hour has arrived: next year we're going to
open a great new clearing only for jurupari plants which will
yield everything in abundance, won't we?"

"Of course, we will. A clearing like mine, very big, isn't that
true?"

"No, not exactly, no. It will be a good clearing, a Mairun
clearing, a big one. A clearing for ourselves. A clearing to yield
plenty of food for the feast of your marriage to my neice
Inimá."

"Inimá, Teró? But why Inimá?"

"Yes, my son-in-law, precisely Inimá, my niece, the little
Falcon. It is she who must be your wife, the woman who will
bear your children."

Isaías falls silent; he remains for a while embracing Teró,
almost trembling. Later, he goes for a walk, bewildered, thinking painfully: to marry, to marry that child. . . . He recalls
slowly the beautiful image of Inimá, swaying, a sorceress with
her long black hair with the bangs that had grown to her mouth
during her seclusion. He sees her, a seductress, giving cassava
beer to Jaguar. (Don't you want any more of my milk,
Jaguar?) Inimá must be my wife. Why? I must inseminate her,
Teró's successor. But why me? Who else? I, Avá? No, that's
not the reason. He only wants from me the seed of the guide
of souls in my sperm. Despite everything I am the chieftain-to-
be of the Mairun people, the heir of Anacã, the living Jaguar,
the father of the future guide of souls who will be the father
of the chieftain of my grandsons.

Wandering about, Avá comes upon the Great House of
Men. There, he moves from one group to another listening to
the news, conversing a little here, a little there, with people
from different clans. In one hand he holds a bible Pastor Bob
had given him and under his other arm he carries a box of
woven straw his sister Pinuarama had given him in which are
kept the ornaments of the chieftain. He wants to fix a frayed
diadem of feathers. At last, he sits in his proper place, right in

the center of the Great House of Men. He pokes a small fire there, opens the straw box, takes out the diadem, and starts to reattach the loose oriole feathers to the headband, using a mixture of resin and wax, then tying the feathers in place with minuscule knots. Evidently he lacks the skill this delicate work of coordination requires. He is already running the risk of undoing the whole diadem when Náru, the husband of his niece Mbiá, sits down beside him. He takes the solar headdress to mend it himself and starts asking questions while Isaías chews straw:

"Avá, tell me, Avá, why are the false sorcerers disputing among themselves, each with the other?"

"How is that, Náru? What do you mean?"

"The false sorcerers of the Mission and those of the House of Mirrors are always in disagreement. What is it they don't know? Why do they have to argue?"

"Ah, yes, now I understand. The Catholics and the Protestants? It's complicated. It's as if one side were saying that Maíra is more important and stronger than Mosaingar, and the other side were saying, no, Mosaingar is stronger and more important.

"But that's ridiculous, Avá. Everyone knows that Maíra is strong and that Mosaingar has no importance whatsoever. Maybe you've committed a foolish mistake. It seems as if you've engaged in nonsense by siding with the false sorcerers of Mosaingar at the Mission. Wouldn't it have been better if you had sided with the others? Are they not stronger? They say those people in the House of Mirrors are good at war."

"Yes. I myself don't know. Perhaps it would have been better. But I think that in the end it's all the same. I am going to finish my days here, here where I am now. Aren't you glad I have returned?"

"Ah, Avá, don't ask me that. I am extremely glad. How couldn't I be? The entire village is happy. It is our joy to have you here with us. Don't you see that our women there in your house, your mother, your sisters are happy? So are we all."

THE BROAD LANDS

Greatly agitated, Juca gets up, walks about, sits down. He rises again to his feet and walks some more, all the while talking to himself in a barely audible voice.

"What a masterstroke! Only the senator could have done something like that. Who ever heard of such a thing?"

"What's the matter, Juca? Are you talking to me?" Dona Doca inquires, troubled by the excitement of her husband, usually so taciturn, distrustful, and moody but today so talkative. Is he going mad?

Juca goes from the porch to the living room, then through to the bedroom. He stops at the kitchen door. He retraces his steps, dragging his lame leg, talking and talking:

"There's nobody like the senator. Have you ever heard of such a thing?"

He needs to walk and talk to think clearly about the new horizon opening before him: wealth at last, the real wealth of the truly rich.

"It was God, maybe? Who knows? It was God Himself. My time has come. Now or never."

He doesn't hear his wife's question, nor does he see the children who, astonished and terrified, are looking from outside through the open window. He continues to pace, shouting and gesticulating.

"This time I'll pull my feet out of the mud. Ah, yes, I will!"

Then he sees, blocking the doorway, the burly figure of Manelão who has just appeared and, noticing the agitation of his master, stands motionless, wondering what has happened.

"Hey, Manelão, I sent for you hours ago. Where have you

been, man? Grab Boca there in the yard and go caulk the big boat right away. We are leaving very early tomorrow morning."

"What's this, Boss? Didn't you tell us that we were going to spend a week here resting?"

None of that, Manelão. Get to work. We are leaving before daybreak tomorrow."

"What about my girlfriend, boss? She's the daughter of your crony, Aprígio; she's your own god-daughter. I promised that I'd pop the question tomorrow."

"Forget that! Leave marriage for later. Anyway, my god-daughter is still a little girl. Let her wait. We're in a hurry, Manelão. This voyage will take months, Manelão, so be prepared. I want to make the most of the rest of the summer, in the service of the senator."

They depart in the cool of the early morning, in the big boat loaded with supplies and towing a canoe with a spare motor. This time, in addition to a little merchandise to exchange or sell, Juca takes a lot of gasoline, some carbines, and a box of ammunition. Manelão feels with pleasure the weight of each of the three .44 rifles. He checks them and sees to it that they are in perfect order. He begins to dismantle them, one after the other, to oil them. There is no better work for the hands and eyes of a hood from Monção.

They travel up the Iparanã, powered by the motor, avoiding strong currents. But even near the banks they feel the force of the water rushing down river. The motor strains all its horsepower to make headway upstream, throwing up a backwash. Juca gradually explains the purpose of the trip to Manelão, always insisting that it is a matter of grave responsibility requiring total discretion: the business of this senator, it's most confidential stuff. At first he is scarcely forthcoming with what is indispensable to plan the project. He explains that they are going to the Mission of Our Lady of O; from there they will journey up the Iparanã to Ebemporá-de-Baixo where their buddy Pio was living. As they proceed they will pay particular attention to the tributaries emptying on the right, that is to say along the left bank of the Iparanã, where upon their return they will have to disembark frequently.

"You must be joking, Boss! And the Epexãs, those horned beasts?"

"To hell with the Epexãs, Menelão. Why do you think I've brought those three yellow stocks along? This time they learn or we burn them with hot lead. They're no longer Indians. They are *invaders* of the land. We have to eradicate the whole race of them from here."

He explains that they will travel up each stream, channel, or opening by canoe or on foot to estimate its length and depth as well as the direction from which it originates. The task is to take note of the power of the water and especially the names of all the rivers, creeks, and backwaters on the left bank of the Iparanã.

"We have Boca here for that," observes Manelão, "he knows the river like his back yard."

Juca adds that they will also have to note the approximate distance from one mouth to the next and how far they penetrate each, but he concludes by saying that will need not have to make any maps whatsoever.

"The senator has already ordered that this entire area be photographed from above, from an aircraft. He needs only the names and anything else I can say about the characteristics of the water and the land so that the topographers can draw the maps.

The voyage continues monotonously for days and nights as they ascend against the current. The new motor coughs, sneezes, stops whenever the propeller falls off, but it continues to push them, further and further up. Each day they rest only when night falls. Then they rise early the next morning to proceed with their voyage after gulping down a few broken biscuits left over from the previous night.

Juca slowly reveals the project. He talks about the senator's secretary who had come to Creciúma expressly to see him and to deliver a letter describing his assignment.

"He's wise, an astute man, that one. He opened my eyes so that I could see what was right in front of my face, but what neither I nor anyone else would ever have figured out. I learned from him that the only true wealth of the Iparanã lies in this great world of endless expanse. When it has been completely deforested and converted into pasture, it will be the largest single cattle raising area in all of Brazil. Just fronting the Iparanã are already more than sixty leagues of land with high and low forest, foot-clear or overgrown, not to mention the natural savannas and palm groves, the stretches of coarse tall grass in the clearings and dense brush along the river edge."

Juca remarks that until now the savannas had appeared to him as wounds, open sores in the great forest. In fact, they are the best part. Already on the native grasslands of the Epexãs, one could begin to raise cattle with hardly a bit of work. Prompted by Dr. Clovis he had started to imagine enormous zebu bulls grazing and tending the zebu cows. There would be vast herds of cattle hidden in the lush pasture of tau forage grass, their whereabouts revealed only by the configuration of horns glistening in the sun. In the end these lands would have their rightful owners, lands abandoned until now, lands they had passed and observed and were now passing on their return, measuring distances, noting directions, recording names. That entire world of virgin expanse will be the ground someday of incredible estates belonging to those eminent landowner sons-of-bitches from São Paulo and to the gringo associates of the senator.

"And to me," Juca adds, "to me, oh, yes!" he repeats to Manelão, continuing, "I was very clear to the doctor-secretary and clearer still in the letter that we wrote jointly to the senator and that I signed. I will risk my life to carry out his instructions, promptly and discreetly, down to the last detail, just as he urges, according to what that Dr. Clovis tells me. But I trust and expect that the senator will do me the same justice and defend my rights. Mine and those of my father, as the true trailblazers of this whole wilderness which in truth we discovered for Brazil and have civilized all by ourselves without any help until now."

His parcel of land, Juca claims, will be the size of Belém. A pity he could not take possession of the chestnut groves behind Prainha de Tapera, but the senator had already promised that area to Father Ludgero for the new house of the Mission. Perhaps it is better this way, because there would always be the risk of attack by the Xaepẽs even if the high banks were cleared of forest. Better not get them accustomed to slaughtering Juca's cattle, thinking they're some new kind of game.

Throughout the long voyage, especially during stopovers, Juca prattles on, sending Manelão into an ecstasy of admiration for the perspicacity of the senator. As Dr. Clovis has said: he is a true statesman. And as I say, he adds: the senator stands out; he is a great sorcerer, an otxicom, and one son of a bitch of a landowner. Under his wings anyone can get rich. It is only a matter of proving worthy of it without proving unworthy of it.

Dr. Clovis had told Juca, who now repeated it, how he had set up the whole business in accordance with the instructions of the senator. The first thing they did was to get the old maps of the concession of lands to the Mission of Our Lady of O from the state archives. Then, with the help of the American Embassy, they obtained a plan of the parcel of land bought by Mr. Bob. With these possessions, the great and the small, they flew from this side to that side, over everything, making photographic maps. Now, all they need are the names of the rivers, the lakes, and the backwaters, and some information about the terrain, to divide and register natural plots in the name of the Iparanã Colonization Company, headed by the senator's son-in-law.

However, certain selected parcels of land were already assigned to various friends, such as especially Dr. Clovis and Juca, who has a right to prior consideration. Also deserving consideration were some entrepreneurs from Rio and São Paulo, friends of the senator. These people, in any case, would pay well for their land and would endorse the immediate commencement of deforestation and raising of livestock, which in a short time would make the whole region even more valuable. For them, there would be no problem; the government finances whatever rich people want. But Juca estimates that the sale of a small plot of his Belém-sized share would bring in enough for him to start clearing the rest and to breed cattle.

"I'm rich. It's now or never!"

Compulsively he repeats to Manelão that anything is easy for those who have vision and power, like the senator. Once the land has been properly divided along rivers known and well traveled, like those of the Mission—whose map he has laid out there on the sand—they are going to expand the perimeter of more and more plots so that each will face the Iparanã and run inland for three or four leagues, always in between rivers. In the future, after the demarcation and registration of all the parcels of land along the Iparanã as far as its source, the senator will request another strip of territory in the interior and will proceed into the forest, colonizing the bush deep in the heart of Brazil.

MAÍRA: JAGUAR

Maíra-Coraci dives once again from the summit of the sky, this time to fall into the innermost soul of Jaguar: his is certainly a Mairun body as it should be. For him, the world is splendid, marvelous. That is how he sees it, magnificent under my light: technicolor, sparkling, luminous. Light where it is supposed to be clear, shade where it is suitable. Through his eyes I see the blues and greens I created from the excrement of the Blue Jaguar of my father. Those scarlets from the blood spilled by the Angel of the Lord. Oh! those yellows. . . . But better still is the joy of Jaguar's mouth. This fierce appetite for peppers, for sweet and sour and salty foods. Now the ears: let me hear, Jaguar; the world hums beautifully, melodiously, in your ears.

The body is all aglow, well prepared, ready to attack. The

head erect, intimidating, watchful on a towerlike neck. The torso swings freely on the legs, the arms open with pleasure; the hands and fingers are good for feeling, caressing, and squeezing. Oh, the sensation of the heat and the cold, the delight in warmth and coolness that all of the skin of this massive body feels. Oh, my young Jaguar, this is the way to live.

But the best things I gave him are these balls aching with desire, that pikestaff always ready for fucking. Touch it and it stiffens with pleasure, so hard it hurts from being so good to fuck with. Enjoy it, my boy, enjoy it. Bulge in those rags. They are not proper clothing for people. It is a fantasy of the Europeans that Mairuns are naked. Careful! I must be careful! I am frightening you too much, Jaguar. You might go mad. Calm down, my son, calm down. Speak now. Speak, my son-in-law, speak.

"I was idling around the dancing ground, walking from here to there, until I felt his presence. It was before sunset. He was sitting in the middle of some men in that little place of his there on the dancing ground. I saw that he was looking at me; he wouldn't take his eyes off me; they followed me wherever I went. At a certain moment he looked at me with determination; he looked at me eye to eye, and I drew closer to him like a cunt to the mouth of a serpent. He grabbed my watch machine that my uncle Avá had given me, and pulled me slowly down and down until I was kneeling, hunched over in front of him. Then he let go of the chain and remained staring at me for a long time. He stared and said nothing. I thought of standing up but his eyes paralyzed me. I continued to squat, at last resting on my heels, in his position, arms on crossed legs, hands holding suspended knees.

"He looked deeply into me; he looked right into my eyes. I withstood his stare as long as I could, but then I was unable to and lowered my eyes. What to do? I respect the old guide of souls. Then he gave me that order, silently, and I untangled myself from my rigid position without being aware of what I was doing: I lowered my arms; I surrendered myself to him! I then noticed that the whole circle of people had come and were watching what was happening. But no one approached to listen. Some even went further off, watching from a distance, pretending they were not.

"It took time for the guide of souls to start talking. He began by recalling the black puma, the one that I had brought, but he called it a jaguar. He said it was a perfect jaguar, mature and ferocious. That would heap glory on any hunter who brought it to the house of the clan of the Jaguar.

"But it was you, Jaguar, a jaguar who killed your uncle."

I didn't say anything, I stood there, conjecturing, worrying. I thought, I thought a lot; my mouth uttered nothing. What to say to the guide of souls? Did he think perhaps that I should not have killed that puma and brought the pelt with the head and claws still intact? I, too, knew that this was a challenge to the men of other clans: to bring an entire jaguar pelt to our clan. But why can't a jaguar by the name of Jaguar himself bring a tiger to his house? And my jaguar was not just any jaguar. It was an enormous black puma with silver spots and green eyes shining like lanterns. Come to think of it, it defied me with its very existence. And why was it born, why did it live, killing and eating animals and even people, killing indiscriminately . . . why, if not to stand face-to-face that day and challenge me? Its destiny was to confront me in a life-and-death struggle. My destiny was to confront it in a life-and-death struggle.

For three days I had pursued that puma. It was mine when I killed it. It was mine even more when I skinned it with my arrow whose point was an old knife blade, casting the guts aside and spreading the red flesh there in the bush, as I thought about the treaty between Maíra and the king vultures: there is your carnage, friend, I thought, I was hungry, but it never entered my head to grill even a little piece of the meat.

That jaguar was mine . . . even as my sister Mbía was mine before she began to menstruate. That jaguar was all mine when, for two days and two nights, I walked under the weight of its pelt, the weight of its claws, the weight of its head. And I was almost his, chiefly when thoughts of its strength and glory entered my head, of how it had killed other animals by breaking their necks, one by one, including that of a white hunter.

I know, inside myself, that I am Jaguar even more, the jaguar of the jaguars, now that I am the living puma. But how can the guide of souls understand these things? I could tell him what I dreamt that night when I went to sleep dead tired, after I had left my Jaguar sister there on the dancing ground, covering the cave of Anacã. I could tell the old man the dream I had. In dreaming about him, about the great black puma, I dreamt about myself. I saw myself penetrating the forest to its ultimate depths. I heard the curupiras rhythmically beating the great roots girding the trees to announce to the whole forest that it was I, the Lord of the Jaguars, the Jaguariara, who was entering and advancing there. It was I, the Lord of the Forest, the Caariara who was advancing upon it.

The old guide of souls could never know, nor could anyone who did not undergo the experience ever understand, that I was that jaguar, that that jaguar was I as I carried its pelt dripping blood throughout the depths of the forest, during days and nights, until I reached the village.

A long time passed there on the dancing ground while I remained quiet, thinking intensely, but without opening myself to the old guide of souls. I was afraid that he would possess my mind. He, too, shut up for a long time and was so quiet that I picked up the watch machine only to change the position in which I found myself, as I thought of getting up and going away. Perhaps the guide of souls had nothing to say to me. But then he spoke, and said,

"Be careful! Don't trust your eyes. Never trust your eyes. Avá is as I could see him. He is strong, he is handsome, he is wise. He is not as you see him, like that, a sickly wretch. This is what remains of a man whose soul has been robbed. Of any man. Perhaps your jaguar could have been any tiger whatsoever."

I left my watch machine alone and put myself again in the

same position the old man was in, hands holding unsupported knees. I was just squatting there. I could see the veins on the forehead of the old guide of souls as he thought hard and deep. At last he spoke again. He spoke and said,

"You, Jaguar, you will be the first chieftain to tie up his own member."

This was exactly what the guide of souls said to me. But what does a guide of souls know about being a chieftain? He is the guide of souls, lord of the souls of the dead; the chieftain is lord of the bodies of the living. I armed myself with courage and said:

"The chieftain will be my uncle Avá, or whoever, not I!"

I thought hard and deep about what the guide of souls had told me. My uncle Avá, the real one, is invisible, bewitched. The Avá who is not pathetic, the Avá only the guide of souls knows, will appear before us one day. We have to wait. When the spell on him is broken we shall have the chieftain.

I don't want to think about or understand, I don't want to remember, I don't want to know any of that. It is true that no one but I could see a chieftain in Avá. Nor can I see him well, nor can I imagine the strength of a chieftain there inside him. The old guide of souls asked why I, Jaguar, had killed that puma. Why? he asked. Why did he call that tiger *jaguarun*? Why did he say that that tiger, the great black puma, was my uncle and that I had killed my uncle? My uncle is Avá, the only son of the guide of souls who is alive and well. Now I know this with absolute certainty, because my grandmother, Moitá, told me that she never fucked anyone but Remui, that Avá is the son of the guide of souls and no one else. I don't know why he is or seems to be of a different clan. No one knows. Perhaps Avá, my uncle, whom I see, whom everyone sees, is not bewitched. Perhaps he is like that, weak and cowardly, as are many old men. But even so, he could be the chieftain. There won't be any wars, at least not now. If there is one, I am here to be reckoned with. Why can't a man like him be the chieftain? The old guide of souls told me there on the dancing

ground, his last words. He said, as he stared into the depths of
my eyes, chilling my very brain,

"Né tuxauareté ypy, rancuãi ibá."

These were the words of the old guide of souls. It was not
an order, he can't give me orders. Neither was it advice. How
could a guide of souls advise a chieftain-to-be? I am not a chieftain, but I will be one. What am I supposed to do? Will I really
be the first chieftain to tie up his own prick? No! But if I don't
tie myself up, who will do it? Also, I doubt very much that
Avá would dare to tie me and all my other companions, turning
all of us into his young warriors. Here we are dressed in these
Christian trousers to hide our cocks that grew in the midst of
our pubic hair. All of us are going about naked, and that
shouldn't be. But the old chieftain didn't want to tie us up.
Perhaps he was awaiting the arrival of Avá, which all of us had
anxiously awaited for so long a time, who knows? I, Jaguar, will
I tie up myself and then my companions? With what kind of
guise? Everyone knows that one day I shall be chieftain. But
that will be very much in the future. It will be a day when I no
longer will call myself Jaguar, because I will be called by the
name of my first son. Until then, until perhaps my third son, the
chieftain will be anyone. Not me!"

Inside Jaguar, Maíra smiles impudently, like someone asking:
"Is it such a shame?" Jaguar relaxes his tense muscles and re-
views with delight his main pleasure. Ah! There's no one like
Canindejub, the yellow macaw. She is extremely jealous. At first
I was afraid that she thought she was half Jaguar because she
lived there in our house, and she was furious. But her fits of
passion are really caused by jealousy.

I like Inimá very much too, but she's different. She also dies
of jealousy, protesting that Canindejub is teaching me many
lewdnesses. And she calls her one of the public women.

When I'm inside Canindejub, I feel sucked, squeezed by her
white and hairy cunt. Then comes that spurt of joy. I rest, and
then I mount her again, the way Maíra mounted the peccary. I
crouch upon her and invoke her passionate fury, as the whole

world becomes my prick going in and out of the slippery softness of my yellow macaw.

With Inimá it's something else altogether. She is my little canoe flowing with the current downriver, in no hurry, with me inside unaware of time. I can't go two days without the refined cunt of my Canindejub, and even less without my little Inimá, with her nestling cunt, warm, intimate, secret. Rooted in my lover.

THE DRIVEL AND
THE HARD CASH

I saías ambles throughout the village and ends up in the house where cassava is prepared. There, in a corner, he watches the women at work squeezing the mass of manioc in a large tubular basket woven from palm fronds, then toasting the foodstuff, now free of its poisonous juice, in a great, round, earthenware oven. He listens with relish to their gossip. Now and then he participates in the conversation.

Old Anoã of the turtle clan likes to ask Avá many questions.

"Tell us, my son-in-law, how the whites manage to have so many children?"

"Well, my mother-in-law, that's not exactly the case. The women there are like the women here. Only a few have more than two or three children; four at the most."

"I'll have none of that. You're trying to fool me. How can people who give birth infrequently have so many born among them? Do they have many twins? Two, sometimes as many as four at a time, isn't that so? And they like to fuck a lot, all day and all night, isn't that right? The white people who came here in the old days, they liked to fuck a lot. Later, these false witch doctors and white-assed sorcerers who are good for nothing arrived. Tell us in plain words what fucking and childbirth are like over there. Did you get to see?"

"Yes, of course I saw. But what I saw was very much the same as here. I think that Mairun women raise their children better, with more affection, don't beat them rabidly, and do all they can to make them happy. That is what I see here with my own eyes every day. But I never saw it there."

"What are you talking about, Avá? you must not see very well. There are women and women here. A few are as you say, others not at all. And there are some who are wicked vipers. Look at my granddaughter Panam, she has no patience at all. Every day she stuffs my great-grandson's mouth with pepper to wean him and to stop him from getting into other mischief."

"Ah, Grandma, don't say such dreadful things! That's enough! Haven't you noticed that Naí has already been talking for a long time now and walks by himself all over the village, and that his little brother is almost here? How can I let Naí go on sucking milk that belongs to his little brother?"

"But it's as I say, there's no lack of bad women here. Or men for that matter. My sons-in-law are good for nothing. There is not one of them who can look after himself. They all want to bleed their children with scarifiers every other day, the excuse being that this will make them grow up strong. No sooner does one of those beastly fathers see his little tot playing happily, growing up nicely, than he approaches it with a piranha's jaw to bleed it. But I don't allow that. My grandchildren from the house over there, the little Turtles, only bleed themselves during the heat of blue summer days."

Meanwhile, Bob walks worriedly all over the village dampening conversations. Wherever he pauses to give a greeting with his gravelly accent and a smile, or even when he stops just to look, the murmur, so Mairun, of rustling voices, with trills and tremulous warbles, comes to a stop. As he starts to go away or to take his eyes off them the singsong of happy female voices returns only to die down again if it seems as if he's coming back, to listen, to scrutinize.

He searches for Isaías everywhere, with the urgency he puts into everything he does. In the end, he finds him in the cassava house. The two converse under the weight of the silence of words unsaid by all those women.

"Good afternoon, Bob, what's the matter, you seem worried."

"Ah, Isaías, I've been looking for you all over the village for the longest time."

"Well, here I am at your service, Bob. Let's go sit down. There are no chairs, but this mortar for pounding manioc will do. What do you want?"

"It's simple, Isaías. Very simple. You are helping Gertrude, my wife, talking to her for hours and hours. This is very important for us Americans. But, having adapted to Brazilian customs, I myself came to have a word with you personally."

"Well, man, what is this about?"

"Isaías, it's just that . . . we want . . . we need to pay you. It's not right for you to waste so much time with my wife without some remuneration."

"Don't be silly, man, don't even think of it. For me it is a pleasure to collaborate with you, with Dona Gertrude."

"I *do* think of it, if you'll allow me to say so. We have even calculated your pay. We verified that a worker at the post earns, more or less, thirty cruzeiros a day. As to the amount of time that Gertrude works with you, that's at most eight, ten mornings or evenings each month, about twice a week. If we were to pay you a little more than the salary at the post, we would be giving you three hundred cruzeiros a month. I think that's about right. I know it is not much, but we are not pretending to be able to pay what you are really worth. We want to pay a reasonable minimum, and this according to our calculations is here at your disposal."

Bob takes an envelope out of his pocket and tries to put it in the hand of Isaías who refuses it emphatically.

"No, Bob. You just go back; go back there and tell Gertrude that she doesn't owe me anything. Also tell her not to come here any more to talk with me. I was doing that as a favor. Since I've declined your offer, I am under no obligation to deal with either your or her."

"Isaías, Isaías, I believe I have offended you. I see that I've offended you. I'm always the same; a disaster with Brazilians. I've never known how to do these things. Please, Isaías. I'm going; Gertrude will come, she herself, to talk to you. She'll come to converse with you tomorrow. Tomorrow."

Isaías walks straight home to look for Alma. He wants to tell her of the gringo's offer. Alma is astonished:

"What's wrong with them paying? Is it that it's too little? Tell him . . ."

Isaías tries to explain that that is not the problem.

"Don't you understand that exploitation is another thing altogether. It's plain abuse."

"Abuse or not," says Alma, "be what may, I would have accepted. Now, if you don't want to work with her any more, if you don't like her (I myself can't stand the sight of her), if you don't get along with her, don't work with her. But if you work for that fool, let her pay. Take it in the form of merchandise, Isaías. If they don't exploit you too much, you should get something out of it. It's better than nothing."

Isaías is irritated by Alma's lack of comprehension of his reasons. But she insists: "Do as you like. But my opinion is this. I can't deal with that Gertrude. The other day we quarreled. Can you imagine? She came here and kept following me around, asking if she could do something, if she could help. Finally, I exploded, I told her yes, that she could help, and that the best way would be by bringing medicine. Do you know what she asked me? 'But aren't you afraid of making out prescriptions? You're not a botanist?' The idiot! I felt like pissing in her face. So let her have it: 'Yes, I am afraid,' I told her. 'I am afraid of seeing those children bleary-eyed wtih conjuctivitis and no collyrium available; of seeing men dripping with the gonorrhea, which is so common here, and no penicillin to give them; and of seeing all those sick women and you there with a house full of medicines. That's what I'm afraid of. No, not afraid, ashamed.' She is so barefaced she did not anticipate my reprimand in the least. She didn't bring any medicines. All she wants to give the Indians is her biblical drivel."

"You're happy here, aren't you, Alma?"

"More than ever, I admit. I believe I am really a Mairun. Do you know what I'm feeling today, what is troubling me? This white skin of mine, this head of hair, these blond hairs all over my body. My deepest desire is to possess a real Mairun face. And what about you, Isaías? What is good for me is difficult for you, isn't it? I can see that things are not as you would have them. Right? Don't answer me. Let me speak so you can know what I'm feeling about all this. Look at me, Isaías: you're in a bad state; I can see it in your face. But wouldn't you be just as badly off anywhere? I can't imagine you feeling good under any circumstances whatsoever. Not even as the false sorcerer to the Coatis. Even if that were possible, you would be any better off? I can't see you succeeding at anything: a teacher in Rio or a parish priest in Pindamonhangaba. That's how it is Isaías. My advice is that you relax and become reconciled to your fate. Rid yourself of your obsession to screw and unscrew yourself. You are going to live here your whole life, man. Calm down, take it easy, or else you'll go off the deep end. Don't take everything so much to heart."

"Alma, I'm going to get married."

"Married, you? Are you crazy? Not to me!"

"To Inimá."

"That little girl? Ah, yes, I know. It has to do with those complications of your people, with the clans, isn't that so? You are obligated to marry her, right?"

"Who knows?"

THE OPOSSUM AND
THE PUBLIC WOMAN

Months accumulate upon months. Clear blue days and luminous nights pass, leading to cloudy days and murky nights. The whole world has become enveloped in mist. The sun rises, red and enormous, and sets, larger still and crimson during the opalescent evenings. The moon also surges, resurges, revealing and hiding itself, at times huge, full, silvery. Mysterious, miraculous, in the middle of the hazy sky.

In the first light showers we found our ultimate joy. With the coming of fresh waters, wabray and lukunani fish came quickly to the surface, describing canals with the resplendence of their blue and golden scales.

But soon, the heavier rains fall, raining for many days, weeks, and months. The world then seemed to dissolve under the mantle of widespread water. Black clouds darken the horizon; as they break, rain pours in white curtains onto the thatch of roofs, mud onto the dancing ground. The people, consumed by sadness, huddling around little fires, now are eating dry cassava bread or roast or boiled potatoes, almost always without meat or fish, and are drinking nothing but plain cassava beer. Mosquitos come out and multiply. Fierce midges, gnats, and punkies sting, annoy. They are the lords of the world. The beaches disappear, inundated by the cold and turbid water of the Iparanã. With them, fish, birds, and large and small game also disappear.

So it was for months until little by little the joyfulness of summer began to return. This year the first to arrive were the spotless white ibis and the dusky herons, serene in flight, perching on the crowns of trees, afraid of dirtying their feet. Then came the toucans and their cousins, the toucanets, and finally, flocks of macaws and parrots. All life renews itself. At last clear blue days, blue waters, blue skies, open and luminous, return; infinite beaches are reborn. The air is full all of a sudden, first with the precise colors and indecisive flight of all the butterflies, then with the chant of the cicadas and the shrill noise of the grasshoppers.

Alma lives the life she wants. She loves being Canindejub. She thinks of herself as a yellow macaw. She traverses at will from the post to the village and from the village to the post. There she has coffee with Elias and converses with Dona Creuza. They spend hours gossiping. Dona Creuza complains about their life; Alma tells her about village intrigues. She always returns to the village with medicines and a little something else that Elias has gotten for the Indians.

It is in the village that she feels free and easy. She wanders along the beaches, enters the river, bathes, now wearing only panties she keeps for these occasions. She has a horror of visitors, who, fortunately, are rare. Dressed in the few clothes she owns, she ambles about the village with complete abandon.

She feels like a Mairun woman amid the Mairun people, and she is proud to speak the language better than Gertrude. The Indians laugh when they hear her pronounce certain words as a man would, words accented differently by women. She learns to make dolls in the Mairun style, but she creates them with such mischievousness that Elias recognizes them at once and always buys them all. He says that in the future people will talk about an artistic revolution among the Mairuns. But nobody will know that it was inspired by a certain Dona Alma.

She continues to live in the house of the Jaguars with Avá's people who for a long time now have been more hers than his. She works with the women of the house, making flour, cassava bread, and assisting in all the other tasks that have to be done. The only work she doesn't like is going to the clearing to search for manioc roots and corn. In everything else she is a Jaguar woman among all the others. One afternoon she finds herself with Isaías in the house, and they are startled each by the other. She inquires:

"Where have you been? I haven't seen you in ages. Where were you? In the house of your little Falcon woman? At the side of the oxim? Or with the believers?"

"I've been wandering about. But I've returned. I came to visit my Jaguars. But, that aside, don't you think it's ridiculous for you to walk around with those black stripes of genipap on your body, and those red circles of annatto on your face?"

"Ridiculous? No, you are ridiculous. Why are you meddling in my life? Let me live it in peace."

"Who will talk to you if I don't? You are very much enjoying being the Canindejub of the village. You are already the mascot of the Jaguars. Be careful!"

"I won't stand for that, Isaías. You are the one who is miserable and ill-tempered. Do you know what the boys call you? Micura Sarigüê, which is to say: 'Father of the Opossums'. That is your name, Isaías! The girls are walking around saying that you are Father of the Opossums—Sarigüê, with a diaeresis over the u!"

"Alma, let's be serious. Stop the foolishness. I only want to help. I am from here, and I know my people"

Together they walk toward the river, silently for a while. Alma resumes the conversation, saying that for a long time she had wanted to talk to him. She wants to talk to him concerning many things she knows nothing about, does not understand. She speaks now in a different voice. She stops, talks, gesticulates, without waiting for him to answer.

"You shouldn't try to understand everything, no. This is all very complicated. There are more rules of etiquette here than in the white world."

"That's all right, Isaías. But I want you to explain things to me anyway. Today, for instance, I got up and went out in the morning. Everyone was watching me with malice, both men and women laughing from ulterior motives. Any day they might greet me with stones in their hands. Why? I have the impression that everybody knows that I slept with Teró. How could that be? Did he go around talking?"

"No, Alma. Things here are at once simpler and more complicated. Everyone knows. There's no need for anyone to say anything."

"What do you mean? How do they all know? If they know, it is because he told them! So if I give someone a tumble in the darkness on the dancing ground everyone will know that I've been fucking?"

"What a coarse expression, Alma. Let's see, try to understand. You are wearing this snail-shell necklace. Everybody knows the necklace. Everybody sees that it's yours. In this world of ours, things made by any person are as immediately recognizable as handwriting is to you. If I pick up an arrow or a basket or a necklace, anything whatsoever, and show it to someone, that person will be able to tell me at once who made it. This necklace of yours was made by Teró. That's obvious. In addition, it can be known or guessed that he gave you the necklace at night, yesterday. I could even tell you how!"

"Well?"

"You met each other at night on the dancing ground. He put his hand on your back . . ."

"Yes, he did and I said 'Good evening, Teró. How are you?' "

"You didn't have to say anything, no. All you had to do was to crouch, bend over, and fornicate."

"What's this 'fornicate' shit, Isaías? To lie down and fuck, yes. What a mania for sinning, for fornicating? I don't fornicate with anyone! I lie down, I fuck. So what? You believe he didn't have to seduce me. That it was enough to tap me on my back for me to get down on all fours! Are the women here like that? Good! I have some friends in Rio who have never eaten a woman. They live sex-starved because they lack both the guts and the spunk to get fucked. Here, I suppose it's enough to pat a girl on the behind for her to lower herself, get on her knees, hoist her ass in the air?"

"Alma, have respect. Let me explain. You are here, living among us in our world, according to our customs. In a manner of speaking you are a mirixorã."

"And what the hell is a mirixô . . . rana?"

"A mirixorã is a public woman, a class of women who don't marry and don't have children. They are always available, so to speak."

"So that's what I am. Mirixorã means whore, a whore for the Indians! Is that what you've reduced me to, Isaías, to a whore for the Indians?"

"No, this has nothing to do with being a whore, Alma. A mirixorã is a highly appreciated person. She is even consecrated in a ceremony. You are not a real mirixorã. They are selected and prepared for their function in such a way as to be superior to ordinary women. So much so that Mairun women are hardly ever jealous of the mirixorãs who can fornicate at will with their husbands. So you see, mirixorãs—who are autonomous women, free of clan obligation, without husbands to look after—resemble you. That is the reason for confusion. It is likely that my sister Pinuarana, Teró's wife, said to him: 'Go see Canindejub on the dancing ground; she will give you joy.' That's how it must have been because Pinu is still suckling her latest baby and cannot have intercourse with Teró."

"Isaías, that makes everything worse. I've come to this: a whore for Indians. Understanding what you've said has been very painful, but I'm no fool. I understood. At last. It also hurt me to understand your attitude toward me when we arrived and you took me to your house. I never thought that being a guest in your house meant that you were rejecting me, treating me as a sister."

"But Alma, there was nothing equivocal about that. Our relationship has never been anything more than fraternal. All that I was obliged to do was to take you to my house and ask them to treat you as a sister."

"Yes, but at that time I didn't understand that what you were doing was rejecting me, that the whole village thought I was a Jaguar, and that, being Jaguar, all the others, from other side, could make love to me. That is why that crowd followed me for such a long time while I was in the dark. And you were the one who had arranged things. In effect, you told everyone: "Look, here is fresh food that I've brought for you!"

"Yes, it was more or less like that. I don't see anything bad in it, at least not in my intentions. You are your own mistress. Do as you wish . . . freely."

"The worst is yet to come, Isaías. You know. Already you know of my affair with Jaguar?"

"Ah! But Jaguar . . ."

"Of course. When you took me to your house, it was a rejection, a fraternal rejection. And as for Jaguar, when we started to see each other, there was also a rejection: he refused me his fraternal friendship, didn't he?"

"Yes. He likes you in a different way. As you are not really one of the Jaguar clan, there was nothing incestuous about it. There was no reason for him not to be with you."

"You are all opportunists. For one reason or another, fathers and sons can fornicate with me legally. Mirixorã. That is what I am. Now I know: a whore for Indians. I'm going down to the beach for a walk; I want to be alone. How ridiculous! Forget the beach. Do you know what I am really going to do? I'm going to the house where cassava is prepared to work with Pinuarana. That one, she is a real woman. A lady. Stop this foolishness, little Alma. Don't let this mirixorã business—about being a whore who is not exactly a whore—upset your little life. Good-bye, Isaías-Avá, here goes Canindejub to make farina and to fuck as is the will of God."

MAÍRA: AVÁ

From up here, tracing this sky without beginning or end, I look and see. I see everything. From below, everybody looks at me and sees me with the light that I give them, reflected back.

Who can exist save under the weight of my radiance? I look and
see my little world down there. I see the water of the rivers
and of the seas. I watch them down below, my little Mairun
people.

Today I want to enter someone to sense the world again with
the body and the spirit of living people. I want to see with the
eyes I gave them. I want to think with their minds. I want to
smell and taste and listen and touch. Once upon a time, this gave
me more pleasure. It still pleases me, but not as much and less
every time. Something is lacking in those creatures of my father
whose lives I did so much to improve. Something is lacking;
what can it be?

There is that Avá who so much wanted to be Isaías. I am
diving into him: this shit of a body, worn out from such abuse.
It is a tube: at one end, the mouth through which it passes food
inside, without enjoying its smell or taste; at the other end, the
asshole through which it shits, again without enjoyment. Had I
known they were going to be like this, I would have left the
people as my father made them. Speak, wretch. Speak, Avá.

Here I am in my little Mairun village which I longed for so
much. But how different, how different it is, my God. Everything is so different from what I had expected. It is true that
neither am I the same. I see nothing through the eyes of bygone
years. But look how everything has changed! I know I, too,
have changed. But, unfortunately, we have not changed together; nor have we matured. I am not what I should have been,
for myself or for anyone else, and every day I pay the price.
They also have changed rather than progressed; they have declined. Why do I say they instead of we, as I should?

These, my Mairun people, this village, have all deteriorated.
The houses are not as they used to be. Not that their dimensions
or style have been altered; but formerly, long before houses
became full of cobwebs and cockroaches, the people would set
fire to them and move to a new village that was ready. Also, the
people were better looking and stronger. No one had rotten teeth

as now. They are all on the decline. Not they; we. All of us, I too: I recognize.

Only in the young men and children can any exuberance be seen. My nephew Jaguar and his companions exhibit vigor and beauty that excite envy. But this joy proceeds from youthfulness rather than from their own nature. They also try hard to maintain their looks by accentuating their youthful beauty: painting themselves with annatto in shocking sanguine stripes which—between stripes of blue-black genipap redrawn every week—they retouch everyday. Well painted and adorned, they live as if every day were a feast day.

Thus they go about here without doing anything. They concern themselves only with living, with living pointlessly. They appear to be waiting. They are the new warriors, who are ready for a war that does not, will never, come. But against who will they fight? Against the whites, against the Christians who are our enemies, it should be. But how to confront them? Meanwhile, the Mairun warriors are waiting there pointlessly. They do nothing. They are warriors in a war that does not now nor ever will exist.

They occupy themselves by engaging in capricious hunting or by staging fishing contests every week affecting great prowess. The other day the whole village roared with laughter at seeing them arrive, sweating from fatigue, carrying a live boa constrictor tied to a cabbage-palm trunk. The snake was writhing around the palm, opening and closing menacingly its enormous mouth. It was an enormous snake; everyone looked on and was vastly amused by the young men who pranced about the dancing ground with the pole and the snake of myriad colors, running after the girls, threatening to stick the snake into them. They soon tired of this sport and went outside the village to let the snake loose so that it would live in fear of humans far from the dancing ground. Is it normal for such robust youths to waste their time on such pranks?

Today, they brought a live cayman with its snout tied up.

They arrived pulling the animal by its tail and making it dance all over the village as they shouted:

"Call your people, cayman! Let them come! Let the caymans come! Let them come!"

Every day they do something like this: bogus hunting or fishing. Stupid, self-indulgent pranks. Meanwhile, they are waiting for the war that has not nor ever will come. As for real work, only grownups and the elderly do any work. And only a little at that. Except, perhaps, for the adult women who bear on their shoulders the burden of life, the responsibility for looking after and feeding so many lazy warriors.

The girls are more interested in painting their bodies and faces and indulging in licentious liaisons than in hard work. Even so, they do more than the young men. They are proud of the baskets they plait, the hammocks they weave, and the pottery they mold. In truth, they work more to show off their skill than to be useful. It could be said that utility is not a concept that preoccupies anyone here. Each one of those baskets, hammocks, or pots absorbs ten times the effort necessary to make it adequate for its everyday function. But if whoever is making them is shown to have the slightest lack of taste or skill in her workmanship, she will redouble her efforts. This is why the most ordinary baskets for carrying manioc tubers from the clearing to the village, the simplest pots for settling cassava pressings or for cooking are of a perfectly useless perfection. Where will the time and energy for the serious tasks of life come from if so much vigor is wasted on useless exhibitions? A desire for beauty? A will to perfection? The time has passed when I saw the Mairuns as latter-day ancient Greeks. Greeks, my foot! Perhaps all that the Mairuns and they have in common are sodemy and prostitution which are both rampant around here.

Not only the youths but everyone else here has become a carouser. These people make fun of even the holiest things. The other day I was asking about the old stories of creation, which I remember with so much respect, and I could neither listen to nor tolerate the ridicule with which they told or greeted each story. They were having the most fun in the Great House of Men; everybody was laughing mischievously at the feats of Micura and the follies of Maíra. Worse still, they laughed at Teró's rude imitations of all the persons and all the animals referred to in the stories, as much for his voice as for his mimicking antics. It was insupportable.

Here I am in my village, restored to it but not restored to myself. It is becoming more difficult every day for me to feel that I am a Mairun inside my skin. I pass my fingers through my hair, which is thinning, as happens to white men. I wash the eyes of my spirit with prayers as I used to do in the old days, in the hope that they might see better when clean. But no, every day I feel less at ease within myself, and the others are getting tired. Many people pass without looking at me; and if they look at me, they don't see me. Only my nephew Jaguar, when he sees me, stops, laughs, smiles, greets me. He speaks, proudly holding up with his right hand the watch I gave him, which he wears on a chain around his neck. I very much like his attitude toward his trophy-ornament, the old watch of my long Roman hours. At times I feel a certain nostalgia for them. Except for Jaguar, the rogue, no one else wants to know about me.

To the old guide of souls, my father, I pass unseen or seen all too much. He pierces me with his eyes to see beyond me the man I know I'm not. I don't even know who that could be. Is it my soul? I have to be sociable with him; I approach him, I squat in front of his little bench in the Great House. Sitting on my heels I wait there for hours for him to say something to me. But the moment I address a word his way, it seems that all the dead suddenly come flying up to him, hovering hovering, demanding his attention. Frightened, he looks to the right and to the left, he looks up, he looks down, and to each soul he says,

"Wait, I'll talk to you right away. No, no one knows, no. No, I said nothing, I told no one."

The weather here has changed too; game is becoming scarce.

Days pass without our eating meat. Soon the rains will come and there will be many new leaves, green leaves, red leaves.

I remain listening, waiting. Listening to the conversations of the guide of souls with the dead and to the buzzing of his rattle. Waiting for him to tell me something. But nothing. I end up exhausted from waiting.

I try to follow someone who might want to talk to me there in the Great House of Men. But no one wants to. I end up at home, in my real house, the house of the Jaguar clan, swaying in a hammock and watching Moitá, Pinu, and Mbiá and the rest of my family engaged in their endless sweeping, cooking, weaving, suckling, and talking to each other. They don't talk much to me, but that is as it should be. Mairun men have little to say. The women are the ones who talk a lot, as much among themselves as to their husbands—Inimá has nothing to say to me, because we have nothing to talk about, but the others do converse with me every now and then. They are very fond of talking to their husbands at night and in hushed tones. Wives and husbands have much to say to each other. In the houses, at night, there is an endless murmur.

Not even Alma gives me much attention. She is always extremely busy, going from here to there, from one house to another, giving aspirins to one, sulfa drugs to another, treating whoever is sick, whoever asks for or is in want of assistance. It seems that when she cures anyone, she comes across as an oxim, poor soul. I ought to tell her how she will be slaughtered as an oxim if she does achieve glory. Now I'm being wicked. Could it be that I resent her? She is doing what she can. Am I?

My only friend in the world is the oxim, but he hardly ever speaks aside from official pronouncements. When I arrive, he gets excited, happy; he gets up and sits down again and gives me boiled or roasted meat. He must get an abundance of meat from everybody to be able to give so much to me.

I talk mostly with Dona Gertrude, who comes two or three times a week in the motorboat to work on the dictionary and the grammar book. At first she used to ask questions and make notes concerning what I said. Now, she doesn't. She leaves me pencil and paper, tells me what she wants me to write down, and goes away. At times, without reason or authority, she becomes angry and demanding as if I were her servant. And am I not? When she comes back, she seems to want me to have done whatever she has invented I can do. I never said yes, I never said no. I don't do everything she tells me, but I always do some of it. We work together. I converse much with her. She is the one who gives me the cigarettes that I smoke or give away, and the matches. Also, she gives me her husband's old clothes to wear. I go about ashamed of my nudity as a Mairun and as a European. The pubic string is not enough to cover me. It never was. That is why I am always doubly clad: wearing, as a Mairun, the string that I have tied my member with and, as a Christian, a well-buttoned pair of pants.

My only friend is Teidju. I pay the price of listening to his diagnosis of my ills, but I learn from him a great deal about the Mairun spirit. Nothing here, it is true, occupies me more than Teidju's theology. Is that a vice that sticks with me after so many years of Roman speculation? Or is it the result of my impotence to live life from day to day? Without Teró, who also takes meat and fish to the house of his clan, his niece would have thrown me out of there. Why does Inimá accept this marriage invented by her uncle? And I, how do I endure this celibacy?

Only intellectual life offers me any nourishment here, even reduced to the aridity of grammatical geometry with Gertrude and the demonic exuberance of Teidju. It is curious, this contrast between the voracity of my spiritual hunger and my hopeless lack of carnal appetite. Lack of appetite? I am in awe and envy of the voracious thirst for living exhibited by the Mairuns and Alma as well, this capacity for dedication to and enjoyment of the mosaic of harmonious relations between one and another. I don't have any such talent. I am just a miserable machine for thinking and praying for God to help me.

NEGLECT

Once more I am noting in this draft the facts of the events that will inform my report to Your Excellency. For two days I have been a guest of the priests and nuns at the Mission of Our Lady of O. During the last two nights I slept peacefully for the first time since I left home: in a clean bed with mosquito netting, in a whitewashed room containing a window and a fly screen.

The treatment I receive is royal. What a difference, compared to the FUNAI post. For one thing, the buildings are large and solid; the house of the fathers, the house of the sisters, the house of the catechumens, the house of the boys, and the chapel which is as big as a church. These are all located within an extensive garden and form a little square, well designed and maintained.

It is true there are very few Indians, but what a difference! These are marching toward civilization, without Rondonian romanticism; they wear clothes and shoes, and are clean. The girls even have a certain charm despite their obtuse, uncultivated little faces. And if there are only a few Indians here, there are even fewer at the post. They are numerous only in the village, which exists merely as a result of the obstinacy of FUNAI and the interplay of reciprocal interests (who knows if these are unconscious?) between the protected and the protectors—a game in which the latter are the true beneficiaries.

Not that the priests have told me this; their discretion is exemplary. They have nothing but praise for FUNAI and for Elias as well, even if he is a Protestant. They go so far as to say that they could have done nothing, that their work would have been impossible, without the understanding of the government and the support of FUNAI.

"Look at all this!" And they add, "One day it will bear fruit, one day it will bear fruit."

How? What can poor Elias do with his caged chickens, which we ate those days when we were there? Those chickens were the only manifestation of civilization at the post, caged as they ought to have been just like the Indians.

This is what I said to the priests, and they were greatly amused by the paradox. They agree that the strategy of FUNAI is to freeze the Indians in their customs and thereby protect them from degeneration. But they don't believe that this is being done to its best advantage. There are doctrines, they say; but what doctrines?

I have also made some progress in the case that preoccupies me, though less, to be sure, than I had hoped. And much less than I need.

The woman's name was Alma das Neves Freire. She entered the region in the company of the aforementioned Isaías via a C.A.N. plane that landed at the Naruai strip on May 1, 1972. She arrived at the Mission on the 19th of the same month, staying here only three days. She was not a missionary, nor had she any ties to this or any other mission. She was, so to speak (in my words, not those of the priests), an adventuress in search of new experiences. She may have been religious, they say, but mainly she was confused. She wanted to embrace a religious career in the same way as she had indulged in psychoanalysis as a cure and as an escape from a dissolute life (the commentary is mine). As the priests said, she was an unfortunate girl, as so many are today, confused and needing care and understanding.

Her relationship with Isaías was, for all intents and purposes, accidental. They were traveling companions on the same flight; thus they became acquainted and proceeded together, as best they could, to the Mission. From here they continued toward their destination, which was the indigenous post. Now comes the fundamental observation, the argument that matters most to my report: as far as the priests are concerned, the fact that they both went to the post means that they effectively became the responsibility of the federal government.

Isaías, detached from his order since he left Rome, deeply
convinced of his own unsuitability for the sacerdotal vocation,
was returning to his former life. For this he needed assistance
from FUNAI, which owed him as much protection as was
due any Indian. It is true that he could have stayed at the
Mission where he was offered a post as a teacher, there or at any
of the other houses maintained by the Order throughout Brazil.
He declined. He did not want to work, though he is now working (notice the contradiction!) for the North-American Protestants—the same people I found living in a bizarre house
between the post and the Mission. I shall have the opportunity
to come back to them later. The aforesaid Isaías, I have been
told, is now assisting an ethnologist whom he is initiating into
the secrets of the Mairun dialect and into the mysteries of their
tribal customs. It is honest work, the priests say, though I de-
tected in them a certain embarrassment. It could not be otherwise, with a lost sheep, after so many years of sacrifice expended
on him.

But it is the woman who is the nucleus of the case. And now
comes the fundamental point: her presence in the Mission was
formally forbidden. Note well what Father Ludgero told me:
"This is not the place for people of that ilk. Not among us,
nor among the Indians who are in our care, especially not
among them. We could be exposing them to who knows what
disgraceful familiarities." These were his words.

Why didn't FUNAI respond similarly? Knowing of her presence in the village, Elias did nothing. As if the Indians were
not his pupils, protected by the government, the wards of
FUNAI! Here is evidently a case of neglect, so characteristic
that I am unable to gloss over it, however much it hurts me
to do harm to Elias or worse still, to poor Dona Creuza. But,
how to excuse his shocking lack of concern for the fact that
a strange woman (whose habits, in the very least, he could not
answer for) had installed herself in the village and was living
three as if it were her home? Naturally it benefited the Indians,
but even more so Elias, because with her in the village dis-

cause with her in the village dispensing medicines he didn't have to preoccupy himself with even that.

The death was apparently accidental. There is a complete lack of any evidence of violence in all that I have seen thus far. And the absence of any disputes that may have given rise to a crime is also noteworthy. Nor is there any indication of possibly conflicting interests. Who could gain anything from the death of this woman? In all probability her death was caused by her having given birth to twins in adverse circumstances, among Indians who know nothing about proper hygiene or many other things that a civilized woman needs during her delivery.

In all of this, what is most prominent is the incontrovertible fact of the ineptitude of Sr. Elias, one that borders on total neglect. In addition to exposing the Indians, in their innocence, to influences that might be undesirable, he exposed a white woman (to be sure, she was an eccentric) to the imminent risk of her life, resulting in her demise. For now, I don't wish to say that Sr. Elias is a criminal. His case is one of administrative rather than criminal neglect. But I cannot overlook this neglect, because it has led to a death; or rather, three deaths, if one includes the twins.

I could return to Brasília from here; the priests have offered to place all their resources at my disposal. They could make a request by radio for a C.A.N. plane to land next Friday on a nearby airstrip. They themselves could take me in their launch to the settlement at Naruai. Unfortunately, however, I am still not in a position to close my investigation. I will have to return to the post, and perhaps to the village. I should add that it is always a good thing to leave by the same door through which one has entered: I dread the risks that could be incurred by all these changes. What would not advance the case would be to stop and see the Protestant missionaries. I talked with them on the journey upriver. Their Portugese is weak, and they are badly informed. They really have nothing to add to what they have already told me. The fact that they gave shelter and work to this Isaías has no great relevance to our case.

What I am afraid of is being unable to bring this assignment to a definitive conclusion, as is my professional duty.

The facts given to me by the missionaries have at least enabled me to be precise about the identity of the deceased woman and the date of her arrival here. Added to the facts provided by the Swiss, these details constitute the only concrete evidence of what occurred, taking into consideration—of course—my own observations during the exhumation of the corpse. And finally there are my own inferences with which I shall flesh out my report. A major effort will be required for it to be a complete document, since I cannot deliver a criminal of proven guilt into the hands of justice. This is unfortunately quite impossible.

I have only two concrete issues to attend to, and that is why I must return to the post. The first involves the only possible defendant: Isaías. Certainly, he is hiding evidence that could be useful in elucidating the crime and his involvement in the case. The other is the undeniably compromised position of Sr. Elias. I need to have a talk with him to help me characterize the accusation of neglect, if in fact that is what occurred, even if he should deny it with evidence. Was it a matter of the functional neglect of savages who are wards of the state, placed under his care? Or possible criminal neglect, leading to the risking of life that was fatal for a representative (good or bad is irrelevant) of Christian civilization?

THIS BONE

The days roll by and life continues to be sweet or bitter depending on who does the tasting and when he does it. Every afternoon—as it has been in the past, as it should always be in the future—the men sit on the dancing ground to watch the sun set. The women bring food and leave it at the feet of their husbands and unmarried brothers. Some sit together nearby to chat for a while. Sometimes they eat there with the men, too.

Alma squats next to Isaías, right behind him, and starts saying:

"Isaías-opossum, your wife is playing around too much. Did you know? Or perhaps that is unimportant? Could it be that only the turquoise honeycreepers are screwing her? This is becoming a scandal, boy!"

Isaías looks straight ahead without responding, chewing his stalk of herb.

"Look, Isaías, I think there is a lot of fucking of Inimá going on around here. Open your eyes, man, incest is rampant here."

Isaías concentrates, chewing his stalk, silent. Inimá arrives, bends down—as the watch she is wearing on a chain around her neck sways—and gives her husband something to eat, a gourd of fish and mussel stew. Without so much as a word, she leaves after Avá has thanked her warmly in Mairun, Portuguese, and Hebrew:

"Muhĩ, cuñataẽ. Obrigado, Lilith. My little Lilith, thank you."

"You think I'm abominable, don't you, Isaías? Abominable or not, right now she left to fuck. You know with whom, don't you? With your nephew, the son of a bitch."

Isaías eats quietly, looks at Alma, gestures at her as if to say that he is not paying attention to what she has been saying. His indifference irritates her even more.

"You yourself are to blame. It even seems as if you have contracted the castration complex of the Mairuns. Jaguar told me the story of the woman whose cunt had teeth like the mouth of a piranha. Stop guarding your prick, man. No one is going to bite it off. No woman has teeth there. Only in the mouth of her head. What Inimá wants is to fuck; what she likes is prick; if you don't sleep with her she will end up fucking everybody."

Standing up, Isaías responds:

"Yes, Alma, the priests were right. You should never have set foot here. Now listen carefully; I think the hour has come for you to leave here. Go away soon, once and for all, while there is still time. I am not going only because ... because?"

"Forget it, Isaías-Avá. Who are you to give me advice? I have nothing to do with the world outside. Everything I have is contained in my little life here. I will not throw this bone away, no. My life is here. I've realized myself here. Now I am going to live here. Man, you're the one who doesn't belong here. Don't Indians suffer from being cheated on? Whenever I like someone, I can die of jealousy."

Alma walks away toward the houses. She awaits nightfall so she can return to the dancing ground and to her adventures as a mirixorã, come what may. Nevertheless, she walks about in a troubled state of mind, shrugging her shoulders and shaking her head. She is preoccupied with the indifference (or who knows what?) of Isaías. He knows better than I what a cuckholded husband must do here. Give this errant wife a sound beating! Without inflicting much injury, of course, because her brothers might be offended. But a good spanking is indispensable, if only to prove that the woman has a master who is jealous, and, above all, to make up afterward in the hammock, with a tearful fuck. But Isaías is not one of those men. Will he ever sleep with Inimá? He is quite capable of just remaining a virgin. Isn't he? Or will he finally fall for her, the jerk!

MICURA: CANINDEJUB

Micura spins about the sky spying on the dives of Maíra. He sees immediately what is going on and laughs; nostalgia for our time as humans among humans. What mischief! Micura decides to play, too. "It's been so long that I hardly remember visiting my little people there below, so ungrateful!" He dives and hovers over the village, musing to himself.

That one over there is my oxim who knows everything and ignores everything. He doesn't even know that I made him from spit. But he doesn't interest me. Now that woman . . . yes! I will enter her: Oh! She's a white woman. But she likes being the Canindejub. She likes being a mirixorã even more. It was Avá who brought her here, but he never fucked her, the fool! Be quiet, girl, keep still! I am entering you up here through your head. This idiot is trembling all over. She feels as if she were being fucked in the head.

Oh, what a fair and joyous body. A mouth that delights in all tastes. A rich voracious mouth. Oh, what a nose to smell all odors, stenches, and fetidness. Are you depraved, woman? She is hard of hearing; her ears are damaged but are good for listening to music. They are so full of rhythm and melody! This woman is an ocean of music.

And these pointed, sensuous breasts, breasts that have never given milk however much they may have been sucked. You are tense, woman. Relax! It is enough only to make her feel her breasts to make them swell and harden like pikes. Life avidly lived. I am now going to the most intimate attraction of your cunt. Here: how good it is! Sweet pussy! I would like to remain here inside forever, whole, in this cunt of cunts. What a hot little cushion under this bush! An almond-shaped and bearded cleft with a clitoris like a bird's beak. Immense. It expands and contracts like the mouth of a catfish, like the cunt of a dolphin: water nymph.

Oh, lascivious woman, you live off your juice. With your whole body you take pleasure; you take and give it too. This smooth skin covered with fuzz, with its bush of pubic hair, is so lovely. Good and wiry, that hair should be enough to cover my entire face. Skin with absolutely sensitive hairs and pores, made to feel breezes and to delight in other bodies. Be quiet, woman! I really want to stay here in the warmth of your womb, which is begging for a child. I could give you that; of course I could. But no, speak now, speak so I can hear you. I've come for this, to listen. Speak to me, my love."

"What am I doing here? I don't believe anymore in what brought me. That illusion of mine was an illness, I think. And I've cured myself here. The anguish is over. I take pleasure in the life I lead. I don't want to save anyone; that is no longer my ambition. I simply want to live; to live this lazy rhythm of Mairun life, swinging in the hammock and drifting with the current.

Every day I take care of people who want and need me. Every night I give myself to men, fucking whom I like and whoever desire me. And who does not like the paramour Canindejub? Only Isaías! But what the devil does he expect of me? I was not made like him. Thank God, I have yearning, ardor, desires. But they are no longer important to me. I know with absolute certainty that I am playing an important role here. I was most offended when he told me I was a public woman. I don't know why, but I was very offended by the idea of being a whore for Indians. That doesn't matter to me now. It is a function, not a profession like those of librarian, social worker, or dentist's receptionist. No, it is a function, a religious vocation. Yes, that's it.

But if one day I were to tell these things to anyone, to Fred for example, he would die of shock. I can well imagine, I can even see, the expression on his face upon hearing me say that I feel like a priestess, a priestess of love, of free love, of joyous love. He would sit there pissed and preoccupied, thinking: she's mad; she's lost her head. And I, never so sure of my own judgment.

What I like best is the good work of each day, especially when I help these people sick with influenza, measles, mumps; people who require my attention; people who like me, who use my abundant energy. But I confess, I could not have managed without the other aspect: the daily love of Jaguar and my nights as a mirixorã—the adventure of discovering who is about to mount me. Who is there, crouching on the ground, his legs under my thighs and his thing inside me, quiet, for hours without moving, neither he nor I. Until no one can stand it any more and there is that explosion—he inside me—chua . . . I with myself: aaah!

Who would think upon seeing these Indians' little pricks all rolled up in strings that when the knots are undone they would grow so much and so well! They are hard and exactly my fit. Also, I greatly enjoy giving pleasure to Jaguar, though I am hardly ever satisfied. He is like a rooster. He undoes his string, puts himself inside me, and gush . . . ! It's all over. I go away content, feeling his thick come dripping between my thighs. We rarely fuck here in the house, very rarely. I sense that it upsets him too much. And we never fuck on the dancing ground as I do with so many others. We usually do it on the beach behind a sand dune or in the mangrove swamp near the village. For a long time, we used to go the banana plantation. He would look at me and I would know at once; I would get up and start walking there. But we stopped because the little girls of the village discovered the place and would go there waiting to see and to laugh, giggling while we enjoyed each other. There was no harm in this, but it is better not to be a spectacle. Now, we vary the place: one day here, another day there, and it's always like this: he looks at me that way that I recognize, and he walks ahead, as if nothing were happening. I follow him, dissimulating. What are we? Lovers we're not. That's what I was with Fred who supported me. Sweethearts? Engaged? Perhaps we are one of those. But whatever we are, it is very complicated for Jaguar. Apparently we are breaking clan rules. It's a form of incest; perhaps that's why it is so enjoyable. I am very afraid of his being worried. Do Indians really have worries? Of course not! These people are free of stupidities, except those who are half-civilized like Isaías. That one is not so inclined. Jaguar and I are not engaged in clan incest on this level of things because I am as if suspended in the air above classifications, or beneath them, I don't know which, but nonetheless free from them, although not to the point that Jaguar would want to tumble with me on the dancing ground. Once a youth came; the night was pitch black and I thought it was Jaguar. Soon I discovered it wasn't when I wanted to kiss him as I had taught Jaguar, mouth to mouth with tongues outstretched, coiling and uncoiling—slipping —around each other.

What is this that excites and upsets me so? Nothing, nothing at all! I was only thinking of the true joy of living, which, at last, I have found here. The only thing that worries me now, even if not much, is the decline of Isaías. But I know I cannot help him. Everybody here is attentive to him, helping him to do I don't know what. For the Mairuns, Isaías is fulfilling some mysterious destiny I know nothing about. As I understand it, they all believe that through him something or other would occur were it not for something or other. I can only intuit, guess, or invent the rest, who knows? And why do I have to know? Especially I, who am ignorant of everything? Isaías is here, it seems, to witness something shocking that will happen, something staggering, miraculous, I don't know what. Did he come to witness this thing, to witness whatever it is? Perhaps he is the new apostle who will bear witness with absolute and un- deniable certainty—and with all the terrible consequences of this—that God exists in reality or, at least, wants to exist. What do I, who am ignorant of everything, know about this? My God, why am I rambling on like this? Am I crazy? Who is thinking with my head? Who is speaking with my mouth?

Here, only some looks I have received disturb me. That of the frog of the oxim pierces me, making me feel cold all over. The vague and distant gaze of the guide of souls gives me a feeling of uneasiness. He seems to be asking me a question I don't understand. Is he maybe asking me what I am doing here? With all the others, I am at ease: with the men, the women, the children, even with the pet animals and the dogs in all the houses, who know me and like me to scratch them.

I fear that this cannot last. The people there at the post find my presence odd. Though it seems that they've calmed down, as well they should! I am doing all the work of a nurse without charging them. Sr. Elias says he is looking into an appointment for me. What he has been doing for a long time is putting money in his pocket. What do I care? What I want is to do what I have to do here, and there is more than enough of that. And as for love, thank God, there is no lack of it for me."

"This is it, my love; I'm going to leave you now, playing at being a mirixorã and an oxim. I have a lot to do up there. Any night now I will return. And then, who knows, I may leave a seed."

What is that, my God, am I losing my mind, talking to myself without meaning to, alone, getting excited and enjoying it? And now I am hearing voices. I, an oxim? I beg you!

ARMAGEDDON

Dressed in a half-grimy gown of coarse cotton, Xisto prays, squatting against the wall of the little chapel. He scratches his beard, flashes his sparkling eyes, and says:

"God is our Lord, our salvation. In God we trust. We praise Him. But the road of God is not easy, no. The road of the Devil would be easier. God himself said: 'If you want to follow me, shoulder my cross and come!' Whoever thinks of saving his life for worldly pleasures is already lost. But he who loses his life for God's cause will be saved. Whoever believes in God, including the dead, shall be resurrected.

The devil of it is that we know very little of God. We are ignorant of much more, though not of His Son—only-begotten until now—who came to earth to save us. But even He only revealed himself to us disguised as an ordinary person and as a lamb. I don't know anything, but at times I have the notion that this world of ours, or that which appears to us, is an eye looking at the universe. The eye of God? We, firmly held in the pupil of that eye, see only a tiny piece of the kingdom of the eye and have to guess the rest. Is this heresy?

The sky, the azure firmament, with its flocks of walking clouds and its display of sparkling stars: is this not the white of the eye of God? The earth, with its stones and hard surfaces, its sweet and salt waters, with its pastures and its forest: is it not the pupil of the eye of God? An egg-eye without eyelids to blink, always vigilant. What is He looking at so attentively? A heresy, Sr. Cleto?"

"It seems so to me, if you will pardon my bad judgment, Sr. Xisto. Do you now remember that we promised not to stray from the revealed word? What is written is written. We have only to read to make the spirit understand. We know not, and must be silent about what is not in the Book. It is a mystery."

"It is and it isn't, Sr. Cleto. God is on the loose! Be careful! He is a bull, not a castrated bullock like one of yours. He is a bird of fire, the Holy Spirit, whom no one can tame or govern. God is God, the giver of gifts. And if He gave me this gift of speaking with clarity, then no one can gag me. No one. But who am I to be obstinate with the Word, my God? I will not lose sight of the terrible reprimand that He gave Job. It is I who say and proclaim with my mouth: "Blessed be the Lord of the World. It is I, a son of man, conceived in sin, born of woman between feces and urine; it is I who admire the grandeur of creation and exclaim, wondrous! My spirit there inside me does three pirouettes and asks, replying: Who wakes the day every morning with His lights, enabling us to see the work of the Lord in all its splendor? Who, in the evening, lets the curtains of darkness fall and enflames the moon and the stars in the sky? Who distills the rain and makes it fall upon the earth to renew all greenery? We know these are the works of the lord of the Universe, of Him who gave us his eye as our abode. There, perhaps, he lives, sees, talks and associates with others. Who are they? Gods? Creatures? Is there a God of Gods? I entreat you. Apostasy! I already know, I recognize anathema! At times, I think we are no more than mosquitos annoying, by flying around, the principal creatures of God, sucking divine honey, the sweet blood of our celestial fathers. Who is it that knows? What we know is nothing, no. Only a jot. Is it more knowledge than is possessed by an elk which knows so much: how to procreate its kind, how to feed and care for itself alone in the bush? Our wisdom affords us nothing that enables us to look after ourselves so well. But it allows for speculations, abortive schemes such as those I am indulging in here and now, I realize. But what is there to do? We are clay modeled by the hand of God. Inquisitive clay.

Sr. Cleto, preoccupied, remarks to the companion at his side upon the exaggerations of the pious mystic:

"He becomes more exalted every time. May God help us!" Xisto puts an end to the murmuring, saying:

"God is great, perhaps too great. Does He pay any attention to our praise, our lamentations, our prayers, and our hymns? Perhaps not. We don't know. We only know, with complete certainty, that he abominates our sins. And we know this because it is written in the Book of the breath of God. Look at this:

"*'For God there are no distinctions. He will condemn sin wheresoever it manifests itself.'*

"Which is to say that God will punish the Jew as well as the Roman, the Indian and the Christian, the Catholic and the Protestant, the black and the white, the rich and the poor. He will punish us for all our sins, the sins we have already committed and those we shall commit in the future, and He, the Omniscient, is tired of knowing. He has already noted them. Debited them. No one can escape from that fact. God himself has said that whoever boasts of not having sinned is sinning by speaking falsely. We were made by God to be sinners, badly resisting temptation with the feeble forces of our lamentable wills. Not for love of God, nor for fear of Him, but from dread of eternal perdition. At the final hour, we shall know. He will be among us, disposed to seize our souls by the scruff of the neck and drag them to the weighing in and the final judgment, while our bodies

are still floundering, warm and pliant. He will cast the lost for
evermore into the depths of the dark abyss. He will elevate the
saved in glory to the heavenly heights, to the celestial peace we
have been promised. I can already see myself there, together
with Sr. Cleto, both of us dressed in blue cotton gowns, each of
us receiving six sheep to raise in the pastures of heaven. Once
every ten thousand years I shall shout to Cleto, asking him how
many sheep he now has. His response will come thundering:
'The very same six, Sr. Xisto!'

"My hand shuts my mouth. My hand will not allow it to
blaspheme anymore."

Xisto stops, rises, stretches lazily, heaves an agonized sigh,
squats again, and continues in a tired shaky voice:

"Many of you people hereabouts are affiliated, wanting to
pray, wanting to sing. As I have already said, there is a time for
everything, even to sin and to lose oneself, even to die; what
will be the use of praying and singing then? Why should someone who doesn't know what to ask from God, or how to ask,
want to pray? Only the Holy Ghost, only He, spreading His
wings over us, can inspire us with ardor to pray in such a way
that God will listen. Without that sacred fervor not even the
Psalm of Psalms can be sung with devotion. Today, I am speaking words from my mouth as they come, without censorship,
without shame, all the words that rise from the depths of me
because they have been inspired by the breath of the Lord God."

"Sr. Xisto," Perpetinha interrupts, "speak to us again today, if
it move you, of the shape of things to come: of things to come."

"I shall speak of that; all I beg God is to speak through my
mouth. I am very much afraid of the future with its stories of
what will be, with its remembrances of things that have not
but will occur. The future is at the end of the Holy Scriptures,
concluding the Revelations. It is the word of John of God, the
Apostle-Prophet, condemned to wander, speaking from the
harshness of his exile. John begins by saying that he is the voice,
that what he speaks are the words of God. He tells how, while
he was resting in his house, the Lord called him from the other

side of the door for the final revelations. He said He might return any day; it could be right now, this minute, this very instant.

God the Father will return to judge us. He will return with thunder and lightning, terrifying to behold. He will appear on His throne surrounded by the four principal beasts—all-seeing and praying—who are God's executioners. But the prophetic beasts will have to recede before the decapitated lamb that will come bearing its own head with seven horns—on each there will be seven eyes, and in each eye a name of blasphemy—howling, echoing, mantled in darkness. The lamb of God will come to tear the seven letters, break the seven seals, blow the seven trumpets, mount the seven horses, loose the seven fiery angels, burn the seven disloyal churches, and raise to glory the seven pure spirits He will meet. At the commencement, says John of God, only the vulture king, soaring with its great wings in the heights of the heavens, will be seen, and only its first screech will be heard. Then the sky will open, making way for the angel on a white horse, who will come brandishing a bow with no arrow. With his hand to his brow shading his eyes, this Navajo angel-Indian will watch. If there are no cowboys in sight he will signal a second Indian to descend, mounted on a red horse and armed with a broadsword. Behind him will descend, at a gallop, the Indian upon the black horse, bearing the scales of justice; and then the yellow-bay horse ridden by Death and Fate, one facing forward, the other backward. Here below, the slaughter of the just and of the sinners will begin, and the struggle between Death, wanting the cadavers, and Fate, wanting to herd the flock of souls off to Gehenna. The people will clamor for justice but will see only the missionaries, martyred by the Indians in the backlands of Brazil, ascending to heaven in their white vestments. Only they will be saved from the mortal panic which will descend upon the world before it is finally shrouded with the black mantle of the great silence. But the silence will be broken by the sound of the copper trumpets of the angel-sergeants who will return to finish off whatever remains. One will burn the forests and the pastures with napalm. Another will cast the moon into the sea which will boil and, converted into blood, will kill all fish and sink all ships. The third will unleash the bomb-of-the-end-of-the-world which will extinguish the sun and the stars. Only the vulture king will escape, soaring in circles above the ruined world, to screech three more times. Then, the bottomless pit of hell will open and a vast cloud of smoke will spread over the world. From the midst of this cloud will issue a plague of preying locusts to suck the juice of mankind. This will mark the end of the end of all life. Nothing that up to then was still alive will escape asphyxiation in gases or the robot-locusts. But don't think this will be the absolute end. No, my brothers, this will only be the start of the New Era, the gateway to the New Jerusalem of the living souls that will be inaugurated with great feasts by the chosen souls who will live there eternally, for a thousand years, this first year of the future millenium. The curse will then be lifted, and spirits without sin will live, surrounded by flowers of crepe paper, in the garden of the Lord, where no cactus will grow, where no thorns will ever be seen. That is how it will be, it is written. This is our future, which will come, which will come!

CORPUS

MOSAINGAR

How sweet it is to sway in the hammock of the House of the Jaguars, and of my own Jaguar. I feel too wonderful. I would even say—if I had anyone here with whom to talk nonsense—that I'm happy. I must seem quite idiotic, as befits the look of a happy woman.

But I'm also worried. Absolutely! This pregnancy! How I enjoy this seesaw, this swaying. It is almost a caressing. Better still it would be if Jaguar were here on top of me, with the in-out, in-out of a sweet little fuck. We only made love in the hammock a long while ago, when I first arrived, at night. Who would have thought that I was going to stay here for more than two years? That time has already been lived. How much more is my lot?

Old Moitá looks at me from her corner as mysteriously as ever. She is the real head of this house. Here the men don't give orders. Perhaps they do in their Great House. But inside this house, here, it is the women who are in charge, who make decisions, propose and dispose. The brothers, it is true, are somewhat important because they bequeath their positions to their nephews. But they come here mostly to eat. To eat food they never bring. What they catch, while hunting and fishing, they take to the houses of their own women. Those who bring food here are the husbands of the various Jaguar women. A husband here is not in charge of anything. It is a world of women. A Mairun husband is a species of lover. He is the one now fucking so-and-so, or who, having fucked her so much that he got her pregnant, and ended up father of the whole brood. He could leave tomorrow and no one would care. Husbands here must do whatever strength requires. They must fell trees the whole year and burn their clearings there in the forest. They have to bring meat or fish almost every day so as not to lose face in the eyes of the women and of the children. Their right is to come every night to fuck and to sleep, and to sit on the dancing ground every evening, waiting for the women to bring them their food, which might be fish and potato stew, which might be some meat with whatever else they have around from the afternoon. For example, today we ate very well. Teró brought a tapir for Pinuarama. She gave a lot away but we got the best of it. With this exploit Teró surpassed Náru and Souí who still showed pride in their faces for having caught a stag with fine antlers.

Moitá is the oldest woman in the house. Her prestige comes from this. Not from the fact of being married to or having married Remui, the old guide of souls. As far as I can see, he has not come to this house for years. He lives in the Great House of Men. Moitá is the grandmother, great-aunt, mother-aunt, of all the women in the house, if she is not great-grandmother or great-grandaunt. I am, for her, some kind of surplus or supernumerary. Not that this is inconvenient. I am very attentive toward her and all the others; I give them an abundance of aspirins. As soon as I guess that someone has a little headache, I rush to offer them aspirin. Apparently, what Moitá can't admit to me, what makes her watch me so suspiciously—especially when I am swaying in the hammock—is her being unnerved by the fact that she cannot see my cunt and must guess where it is. She has a burning awareness that under my dress I am naked and hairy. She will never get over the thought that a woman is going around without the uluri. I could take off my clothes, expose my whole body, and no one would bother to look. Except they might look at me as some sort of extravagance because I am white, foreign, and hairy. What I do know is that, dressed as I am, in their eyes I am now naked.

Is it worth the while to try again to wear the uluri? No, it is useless. Sometime ago I had tried, as a way of approximating their fashion more closely, when I saw what a scandal was caused by my going about naked under my dress. Soon I understood that I would have to shave off my pubic hair, and continue to do so for the rest of my life. I am not an Indian woman. They have practically no body hair. When even a hair grows, they remove it with hot ashes and it doesn't grow again. We don't do that. I gave up. Now, it doesn't matter to me, inasmuch as I know that the men like me as I am. With me, apart from me as a person, they are fucking the white woman, the foreigner, the bushy naked one. I swear that Jaguar likes to lie with me more than with any other woman, including Inimá. I swear it!

I need to discipline myself, to leave off thinking about naughtiness and concentrate on the serious things of life. Listen, Alma, pay attention! Be careful, there is danger in sight. You are pregnant, woman. Impregnated by an Indian. By one? By many? Who can tell? You are going to give birth in this Mairun village. Have you thought about it? Think well. Is there a midwife? Of course not, nor much else. A maternity ward? I am not worried. For centuries upon centuries, Mairun men have been fucking Mairun women and getting them pregnant, and the women have borne the children with smiles on their faces. I don't ask for any more than that. If my child has half the charm of the children here, I will be happy, and it will be, too. What I feel inside me, and feel with great joy, is the force of life growing, budding, blossoming, renewing itself. I feel that what is growing inside me, my son or my daughter, is growing with all my help. My child is my work; I concentrate entirely on him or her. To tell the truth, what I feel instead of fear is enthusiasm. Alma dear, be careful, you are going to give birth to a very masculine boy or a very feminine girl. Stop exaggerating, woman: whether you give birth to a boy or a girl is unimportant; what matters is that you are going to have a baby. A very beautiful baby child that I am going to raise playing and smiling in that open world of the Mairuns. Isn't it beautiful?

For a long time I felt afraid and uncertain. I had stopped having my period, but I kept going into seclusion like the other women. Later, I felt the seed sprouting roots running down my body into my legs. I liked the feel of a hand resting on my stomach. I felt my breasts hardening. It was only then that I saw my belly swelling and faced the truth. I am pregnant. What should I do? This has happened so many times to so many women, thank God. Now it is my turn. I am pregnant. I am making a little baby. I am going to give birth. It won't be long before the little devil starts kicking in my belly.

All the Mairun women already know. Araruama, who has also been mounted by Jaguar—perhaps thinking that the child was his (and why not?)—was the first to let me know that she knew of my pregnancy. We met in the farina house; she came very close to me, smiled, and passed her hands very slowly over my belly, toward the sides. While doing this she looked at me as if she were envious. But her smile manifested joy, if I understood it correctly, and she said,

"Is another little Jaguar going to be born?"

Which of all those men is the father of my son or daughter? Only God knows. Maíra and Micura, too. But something deep inside tells me that the father is Teró. Is this because he is mature, as a father should be? Is it because I like him as a lover? But why couldn't it be Jaguar since I fuck him the most? He is young but very much a man in spite of his anxiety. I felt his abundant juice entering me more often than that of any other man. Why couldn't it be his seed that has entered me, thrived, fertilized me, and is now growing?

What will my son or daughter be like? Will it be Mairun as I want it to be? Or will it be white, a European, in the sense of someone civilized and Christian, as I was, as I used to be, as I still am in spite of myself? It will be born here, and I would like it to be Mairun. The norms of these people are strange: although the Mairun male obviously plays an important role in reproduction, he hardly has a function in the upbringing of the child. Here, a child belongs to its mother and is of the clan of his mother. It will respect its uncle but never its father. That is why this child of mine, despite being Mairun as much as it is, is my child, is of the clan I lack. The man it will venerate has to be a brother of mine, and I don't have one. My child will have no one; will be alone; will be here in the Jaguar house. Will it have a little Jaguar in it for all that? But it is very bad for a person to be only a small part of something. He will remain suspended between two worlds, like that poor Isaías, or like myself. I live here in the house of the clan of the Jaguars for a reason alien to this world of theirs. I am here because Isaías brought me here. I am here now because here I feel appropriate and because, I think, everyone here likes me. I also believe that all the other Mairuns think of me as a Jaguar, or almost one. In truth, I am a mirixorã, as is the fate of the women of the new clans, of people who have arrived here recently (here, recently means within the last few centuries). But I arrived much more recently, and as such, I am not really a paramour. To be one I would have had to have participated in the initiation ceremony of a generation of women, which never happened. I have never served anyone butternut beer! Or cassava brew!

I behave like a paramour. I enjoy it; but I cannot truthfully say I am a mirixorã. What am I really? I don't know. A candidate to be a FUNAI nurse, an ex-missionary, an ex-friend of the ex-Isaías: these comprise my identity. But I was never more a person among other persons; never more a part of a community to which I belong, that knows and wants me as I am and for what I am. Compared to what I am here, where I am nobody, I was nothing in Rio where I was much more. There, all

who are aware of themselves should realize that they are nothing: annulled by such false, stereotyped convivialities as "Good
morning!" "Have a nice day!" and "It's a pleasure." Dispos-
sessed of talent, even if it be that of a famous singer or a soccer
idol, which very few people are. Deprived of the knowledge
that so much has grown and multiplied in form that no one
knows anything except bits of information and irrelevancies.
There is no longer any wisdom. Dehumanized in front of the
typewriter or loom, tapping out what others have written or
weaving the designs of others. I want none of this. At the same
time, I don't want to Mairunize myself completely. I want to
stay here as long as it gives me pleasure and gives them joy.

The devil is this pregnancy. Formerly when I was menstruating, I would remain, a few days each month, sequestured, closed
in, with the wounds of Micura's arrows. Not because I was
ashamed of my period, as bothers the Mairun women. For them,
the flow is the blood of the child they should have had and did
not. They were good, those days of conviviality, of the delicate
curse, of open laughter. They were useful, too, because they
gave the men a feeling of security, assured them that, when I
wandered the dancing ground at night, I was pure: perfectly
fuckable. It terrifies a Mairun to touch with so much as a finger
blood from the wound of Micura's arrow. I also enjoyed the
sequestration, because I am totally enchanted by my coexistence
with the Mairuns. I like enormously to feel that I am one of them.
I especially like to feel that I am a woman among the women here.

But, my dear Alma, what you really like among us—speaking frankly—your greatest pleasure is to fuck Jaguar, as you did
yesterday, toward the end of the afternoon, in the dunes down
by the Iparanã. We went there in his canoe, steering downriver, describing a long curve to reach the far bank. Once we
arrived, while I was arranging the sand as I used to do in
Ipanemã Beach, back in Rio, he cut some banana leaves to cover
our bed of sand. I loved the gesture of affection. I loved it even
more because it freed me of my apprehension that by making
love on the beach sand might get inside me. There we stayed,

lying close together with our heads raised, looking at the river and at each other. For the first time, he was, so to speak, completely nude in front of me. In the light of the sun he took off the pants he always wore without covering himself with his hands, ashamed, and allowed me see his muscle emerging from the foreskin, swelling and growing into the fullness of prick, by now already in my hand. I didn't dare to kiss it. What would have happened if I had? I succeeded in getting him to linger in me much longer on the second time around. Not by stopping altogether as is the Mairun papa-mama custom, but by entering and withdrawing, sweetly and slowly, as though he knew at last how good it also was for me to be fucked by him. I went on lovingly to caress his whole body from head to foot, thinking with all the force of my mind: I want this child growing inside me to be exactly the same as Jaguar.

Later we held each other, our heads raised and our bodies curved on the leaves lining the hollow in the sand. Downstream below us, the dune continued its curve. In front, it entered the waters of the river to emerge on the other side as a sandbar that continued further on as thicket which converted itself into bush and then into an endless horizon of forest turning from green to blue as it changed into sky. From there, it continued to arc itself and to ascend slowly as infinite curved space of the deepest blue above us. Then it proceeded with tranquility, bending and descending until it converted itself, behind us, into another horizon of forest and sky completing the curve of the world. And it continued to arc across the thickets and sands finally to support our heads on top of the dune covered with the green leaves of wild banana. High above us, Coraci the Sun was watching us while completing his daily task of tracing his long curve along the rails of the sky. We two, relaxed, each with a hand on the sex of the other, were at once the knot and the noose tying and pulling in the world.

I had never before had this feeling of the world as a nest. I could have had it nowhere but here, where people exhaust their eyes looking ahead, staring ahead, seeing only the forests and the skies of the original creation devoid of any mark of the human hand.

But the best thing about that afternoon of mine was the innocence of our nakedness which, at last, had our mutual consent. A guilty innocence, enjoyable, because in truth I had a strange feeling, essentially Mairun, of absurd modesty about lying there exposed to the sun, so hairy; and a shame about touching Jaguar, completely nude, reclining next to me. I learned yesterday that nudity is the most intimate and secret state between a man and a woman who, alone in the world, reveal themselves before each other for love and contemplation.

MAIRAÑEÉ

The endless murmur rises for me. It is my people down there begging for the miracle: the exception. They want to continue to exist as they are.

If this world is made for change, why should only these Mairuns remain unaltered?

So much love for the lives without distinction of my chosen people. Why? My most beloved yet unfortunate people.

They can see, with dsimay, the wave growing. They have a premonition that they will be engulfed. Which wave among others will merit them? Which wave of the river or the sea guards in its bosom the face, the name, the life-style?

There is nothing so good, I suspect, as being always an I, unique, alone, self-contained, self-satisfied. Omnipotent. Who might it be?

If all the others were to unite, they would lose the face, the name, and the mode of living. Why is it necessary for my people to persist?

If at least they knew how, were able, or had the will slowly to change their mode of living so adequately that one fine day they would take on another identity without wanting to or knowing? Who will contrive it?

No, not they. These Mairuns of mine love themselves only as they were made, remade. Well made, they will be undone.

To love themselves like that, as they are, with so much obstinancy, isn't that the chief manifestation of their love for me who made them?

No. Unless their being my chosen people obliges me to be a captive: a tribal God. Under constraint. Like the others, I too am ecumenical by vocation.

God of the Indians and the blacks, it is true. But equally, God of white and yellow men. God of Brazilian mulattos. Brown God. Universal.

There they are reliving their past: constant, content. They beg only for everything. They want me to return to help them in their obstinate desire to remain as they are. They ask only for this: to remain unaltered, stewing in their own juice. Forever. Who can do this?

Not I! I am not alone. I am not unique. Nor am I only theirs. It is they who are uniquely mine. There are others and now they are wanting to come and go. To merge.

What to do? If I submerge myself and converge, I will emerge with the rest, confused. I will stay. If I stagnate, I will distinguish myself in an instant of glory, but I will be finished. I will pass on. Forgotten? Ignored?

There were times, long ago, when I could perhaps have won this war. But I did not fight. Now it is too late: all that I can do is conform; all that my people can do is join the rest.

Who knows, perhaps I made them for this unwittingly? They are my seed, thrown to make everything else piquant. For them—a grain of my joy of living—I must remain in the world.

Without them, who would remember, who would praise me? My people whom I remodeled, breaking the mold of God the Father.

It was I who made my father. But who made me?

A world deprived of the Mairuns, would not it, pitiably, be deprived of me, too?

What is now the greatest risk? To win this war? To lose this war? So many wanting to create suns to extinguish me. How can I persist?

In the blackness of the world in which I will have been extinguished, what light will shine? Who will know of me? When there are no Mairuns, can there be a Maíra?

No, Mairahú my father, I am not begging for peace. A truce, perhaps. How to avoid the inevitable disaster that will inundate them and perhaps me as well, perhaps all of us? What kind of a God am I? A mortal God?

PASTORAL

Bob is upset about what happened in the village of Corrutela. The disgrace had occurred in precisely the most pious family. Who can figure out the designs of Satan; who can uncover his strategems?

Sr. Cleto is a quiet man. His wife Dona Gueda is also very discreet. As to their own daughter Perpetua, the victim, no one would ever say that she was possessed by the Devil. Small, thin, pale, and taciturn, excessively shy, she was always hiding in corners. Bob himself remembers her only for her fine ear for music and for the clear voice with which she used to sing the psalms with such feeling and purity.

Hear, O ye gates; call out, all ye cities
Acclaim ye the Lord; Worship ye the Lord:
The Lord is good.

Well, she was the victim. With her the tragedy was consummated. Of that there is no doubt. Nevertheless, no one can explain what happened. According to what they say, they were praying and singing as they did every night, led always by Xisto, when everything happened all of a sudden.

This minister Xisto is such a fanatic, Bob recalls. If he had his way, no one would work, only pray. He is also somewhat confused: he cannot get the idea of calling the Messiah Saint Sebastian, the Phantom Tornado, out of his head. Other than that, he is a pure and devout man. He has done more than anyone to rid Corrutela of boozing and prostitution. He put an end to drunkenness by sending the people to smash, one by one, all the bottles of rum being sold by Sr. Melchior. As for the whores, they were put on board a boat with enough to eat and drink and were made to paddle down river to Creciúma.

Who will throw the first stone? Who will accuse Xisto? It won't be me, Bob thinks, as he descends the Iparanã in the launch at full speed. He feels the rending force of the wind on his face and on his chest which are bare to the sun. Throughout his arms and hands—which are resting on the motor—his legs, his whole body, he feels the tremor of the water, turbulent under the launch which flies through the air over all the agitation, leaving in its wake a foamy, undulating wake.

On my last visit, when I distributed Bibles to the new converts, I couldn't help but notice that Xisto was wearing a long robe like a priest's cassock but made of a coarse bluish-white fabric. I remember well that the minister had let his sparse beard grow and was carrying a shepherd's crook. I even warned Sr. Cleto, Bob consoles himself. We talked that night after prayers, and we agreed that it was nothing more than a bit of harmless extravagance. There was not the least suggestion that he was a priest, nothing of the sort. The man was a believer, faithful to the Holy Bible and everyone trusted him. Excessively. I myself ended by agreeing. It was better to leave him alone, treating the matter as whimsy.

An illiterate congregation, incapable of reading even the

Holy Book for itself, needs guides. The only people available there in Corrutela were the very dour Sr. Cleto and the very fanciful Sr. Xisto. But only they knew how to read fluently and had some idea of the revealed word. Sr. Xisto, with his mania about Saint Sebastian, wanted to convert the birth of the Awaited One into a reincarnation. What is worst, he seemed to believe that the reincarnation could befall anyone, including himself. But he also used to say that He would come only when everyone was free from sin, purged of all impurity; when everyone was leading a holy life, an innocent life.

Bob chooses carefully from a collection of fishhooks, testing them one by one on his thumbnail to find the best. He casts his lines and recasts them behind the launch. I have never crossed this stretch without hooking a pacu or a lukunani or two. Today too, I want my fish.

I need to concentrate now on what happened. What a tragedy! I still think that the cult only contributed to the sanctification of life, the purification of sins. Everything was done for the deeper penetration of the Word of God in all. Who should throw the first stone? I? Never! I admit that the songs were somewhat outlandish at times. If I had not imposed order one night, I don't know where they would have gone with those exhortations: lead me, Lord! Save me, Lord! Hosanna! Hosanna! There were too many hosannas. I also remember that on two occasions I had to insist that they stop stomping their feet and swaying their bodies in unison, dancing (in essence) with arms outstretched to the skies. Would they pray like this every evening? Isn't the hand of the Devil discernable in all of this? They reminded me of our pentecostal sects with their exclamations, their fervor, and their anointments. What to do? Should I dissuade them from following the path of the Lord because it is dangerous? How could they accompany Christ any other way? Who would advise them to reject the way of the Lord for fear of the traps of the Devil?

The only abusive doctrine was the insistence of Sr. Xisto on disenchanting the enchanted as if some Antichrist were impris-

oned in someone or in something from which it could be freed.
But Sr. Xisto understood well what this could lead to. He himself saw that there was a risk of giving more strength to the
Devil than to God. He understood perfectly well that only
prayers extracted word for word from the Holy Bible are the
doors that lead with certainty to salvation.

Another outlandish doctrine was that with the coming of
the Son of God there would be, at last, not only peace over the
ruins of the final war, but also, he insisted, plenty for all. This
was all very well and good, but not the insistence that the
abundance would result from the redistribution of land which
would all be returned to God, its only owner. Also, cattle, said
Sr. Xisto, would be divided among everyone. Other goods as
well. Everything would be shared so that each family would
have its own clearing, cow, and horse.

How could one question the naïve dreams of abundance running rampant among such simple and poor people?

Bob lengthens the voyage as he circles the backwaters of the
Otter Reach. He wrenches from the launch all the speed of
which it is capable, making the boat leap through the air. So it
is that he calms down and resumes the journey, but soon he is
demanding anew from the motor its total power and speed at
maximum horsepower, riding in circles over the agitation he has
caused in the waters.

He continues to dwell on his preoccupations beneath the sun,
in the midst of the cloud of spray suspended in the air. He recalls that Sr. Xisto not only spoke of those things but also pro-
cured support for them from the Bible, which he read and
reread, tirelessly, to those people

The loud, deep voice of the minister returns to echo in his
ears:

They have built houses and live in them
They have planted vines and eat their fruit.
They have not built for others to dwell
Nor have they planted for others to eat.

It would be better, I told him, also to read the following verses:

The wolf and the lamb shall graze together
The lion shall eat straw with the ox.

How can one hope for wisdom from so much ignorance? Or require fidelity to what is wisest if understanding the sacred text presupposes a capacity we lack and that only the Holy Spirit can give us? The Word of God is fire. But only it purifies and saves. How can one leave the children of God without support?

What can be done now that the terrible news of the death of Dona Gueda's own daughter has arrived? The soldiers came down from Creciúma and took over the village of Corrutela. They themselves buried Perpetinha who had lain there for days, unburied, without her tongue, which Xisto had pulled out to save her from demonic possession. They arrested Sr. Cleto, who in a fit of fury to avenge his daughter had wounded Xisto and fled into the bush where he was found, completely mad. Xisto has vanished. Nobody knows where he has run off to. Dona Gueda, who sent for me, must be devastated. What can I do?

Bob traces in circles, increasing then decreasing his speed. He sprays water with the launch, now tilted to the right, now to the left. In the midst of the course he wonders in anguish: What can I say to those poor people of Corrutela, stricken by this tragedy? What consolation can I give that afflicted mother?

I saw an evil, evil tongue. I saw a holy tongue.
Deliver me from bloodguiltiness, O God.
Thou God of my salvation. For thou desirest not sacrifice.
But why boasteth thou thyself in mischief, O evil tongue?
Thy tongue deviseth mischiefs, working deceitfully.
Thou lovest evil more than good, Se'lah.
Thou lovest all devouring words, O thou deceitful tongue.
I saw, I saw, surely I saw

The mouth of the just bringing forth wisdom:
but the forward tongue shall be cut out.
And out of her mouth goeth a sharp sword:
the fierceness and wrath of Almighty God.
And she hath on her thigh a name written:
King of Kings, the Lord of Lords.
And I saw the beast, I saw the beast.

THE SEMEN OF THE SPIRIT

The days run freely without spiraling into weeks; the weeks run loose without adding up to months. Reduced to a pair of threadbare pants, Isaías ambles by himself about the dancing ground, his hands clasped behind his back, his head bowed. He no longer goes to the port to see the canoes coming and going. Nor does he go to the post to visit Elias and to drink coffee with him. He doesn't want to deal with the gringos except to ask for things for Inimá. Alma herself avoids him for fear of his brusque moods and fits of anger.

His only friend now is the oxim. He sits with him for countless hours of conversation, either at the back or the front of his hut, depending on the position of the sun. He also eats there frequently. He feels more at ease with the oxim than at the house of Inimá, the Crested Falcon, or at the house of Moitá and the other Jaguar women of his Jaguar clan. He even avoids going to the Great House of Men. He no longer receives the attention he was given formerly; he no longer excites curiosity. It is rare for anyone to sit down beside him and engage him in conversation. It is even rarer for the Mairun men to invite him to join one of those groups, jostling each other in some corner of the Great House, telling each other tales or recounting shameless stories, rubbing against each other and laughing joyously with contentment.

Everyone is cordial, escessively so. He is treated as if he were merely a visitor who would one day go away. A welcomed visitor even if he should have long ago departed.

Inimá, his wife, lives as if she were free, a single woman. The most she does is to bring him food every evening on the dancing ground, food which the other Falcon women have probably cooked. She herself never sits down to talk or to eat with him. She delivers the bowl of food and leaves without saying a word. Where does she go? Every now and then they must at least converse? As for Avá, what more does he expect of her?

Sometimes Alma approaches him, wanting to talk for the sake of good manners, but it is difficult. Each time, he becomes more closed, refusing to facilitate contact. What is going on with Isaías? she wonders. Is his marriage finishing him off? Or is his vocation really that of a martyr, a sufferer? Isn't he living the destiny of a martyr, which I once yearned for, in the simplicity of this humble and humiliating life? The Mairuns do not seem to regard him as a frustrated failure, a cuckhold. For them, apparently, Avá is meeting a destiny. Which? Is he the Divine Martyr himself, or only a martyr suffering the pain of being a cuckhold? I don't see in him a martyr burning for love of God. He lacks the fervor, the contrition, the sanctity, for this. Neither do I see him as being passionately, painfully in love. For this also he lacks the ardor.

The friendship with the oxim began like all the others and developed as a result of the oxim's curiosity for news of the great world outside. Later, it deepened because both were interested in the same things. Teidju's great worry is to know if the priests there in the outside world are guides of souls, like old Remui, diviners of the future and friends of the dead. Or if they are oxims, sorcerers like himself, sanctifiers and healers. Isaías is incapable of explaining such ambiguities. He tells him that there are priests who claim to know about the other world, that there had been saints who performed miracles, divined the future, and brought about cures. But they were all very different from the guide of souls and the oxim. Teidju insists on asking questions, forcing Isaías to explain—in terms of the Mairun way of life— all that he knows about priests and sorcerers, saints and demons.

One subject to which he always returns is that of the great sorcerers who are chieftains at the same time in the underworld, in the subterranean world of the Black Sun. He asks Avá if he has seen them, if he has known anyone who made the great journey to the end of the world and returned from the other side. He wants to know if anyone there outside has ever seen the great sorcerers hunting in their mantles of black jaguar. Anxiously, he inquires, "Why didn't you bring back a great crown of real macaw feathers? The kind that burns the head from so much heat but gives total power to whomever wears it. This power," he wonders, "isn't it the real source of the energy of the sorcerers that enables them to command the jaguars and to govern the underworld?"

Avá admits that he knows something about that. But that it isn't exactly as the oxim supposes. He explains that the sun spins above and below the world, always shining. But its position is really fixed; what turns is the earth. Teidju despairs at these ridiculous absurdities. On many occasions he wonders whether Avá knows little or nothing at all. How can the position of the sun be fixed if everyday he sees it moving in the sky? How can an airplane keep on flying without ever reaching the end of the sky if Maíra shot an arrow that stuck in the bottom of the sky?

Avá becomes demoralized as a source of religious knowledge even as the oxim gains authority and confidence in his own knowledge. And he convinces himself even more as to the truth of the Mairun tradition in which he had always believed. This Avá is an idiot, he talks only foolishness. Even so, and for this reason, their friendship grows. It is consolidated even further by the means through which Teidju gains ascendency over Avá and assumes before him a protective attitude that gives Teidju great satisfaction. He does not dare to treat Avá as a sick person, but insinuates that there are problems, serious problems, of which Inimá is the least. Grave problems that perhaps he and only he could solve. Avá listens to him attentively. The oxim diagnoses slowly, day by day, revealing his reasoning a little at a time. Today he says something that he will deny tomorrow and will later affirm and deny once again, until he dominates the argument. Thus he paints, for Avá and for himself, a picture that is an attempt to explain why he, Avá, is what he is: so peculiar.

His basic idea, defined at last, is that Isaías suffers from a fundamental ambiguity. Probably because his mother, Moitá, had fucked too much with too many men, mixing various semens. Those men did not remain for the couvade when he was born, and this made him weak, skinny, and confused. Some of the donors of semen had probably even already died. Avá, carrying the various semens all mixed up inside him, was born and grew up full of contradictions. On the one hand he is a Jaguar-man and, as such, should be strong, vigorous, and brave. On the other hand, he is Micura-man, and, as such, is skinny, pallid, and preoccupied with spiritual matters.

The problem lies in separating these two psychic substances, making one of them—that which lacks the strength to grow—die, and the other—that which has the greater possibilities—emerge, revitalized. This is, in the opinion of the oxim, his lunar part, his Micura heritage, his anti-Jaguar nature. Which comes closest to the oxim himself.

In order to invigorate the Jaguar side, Avá would have to abandon everything and leave immediately, leave now, this instant, on his own two feet, in search of Ivimaraẽi, the Land without Evil. He would have to face the hardships of the struggle against Maíra-Monan to force him to acquiesce in his return to and integration in the world there below. But, for this, Avá does not have the necessary daring and strength. Does he?

If he doesn't, he will have to take the opposite road, beginning now to prepare himself to assume the role of sorcerer someday. As Avá will always maintain a little of his Jaguar nature and a shadow of his power as chieftain-to-be, he will always be able to remind the Mairuns that the true authority, the true command, is his. This opens for him the unique possibility of being at one and the same time a most powerful sorcerer, and a chieftain. Which is to say, he could be a kind of master sorcerer ruling the world up here. A chieftain is a little Maíra: an oxim is a smaller edition of Micura, but a master sorcerer is not Micura, or Maíra. He is a being pertaining to Maíra-Monan, to the Old Ambir of the Black Sun. This is the most that Avá can aspire to. And it is probably what he should be if he does not want to become sick, to become paler every day, vomiting bile and blood until he dies. This will be his destiny from which he cannot escape.

Some time after completing the diagnosis-prognosis, the oxim already notices how Avá's fingernails are turning purplish and his lips pale, as he takes on the appearance of a sick person.

He repeats incessantly that he alone, the oxim, can prepare him for the transfiguration. It would suffice for Avá to desire it. It would suffice for Avá to beg a great deal for it. But, for this, Avá must renounce everything and everybody and must go live in a little cabin built next to his, in the shade of the House of the Coatis. He will have to stay there a long time, always in his hammock, never setting foot to ground. He will have to live there the whole time, enveloped in smoke from special cigars made of tobacco and dried fish that the oxim will blow on him. On certain occasions he will need to remain immersed in smoke from pepper and roots, crying and sneezing to rid himself of the poison inside him, to release the nature of the tormented oxim of Maíra-Monan that is suffocating within him.

When he has been sufficiently purified and strengthened, the second phase of the treatment and apprenticeship will begin. There will be a long period when he will be bled every morning, but bled with scarifiers made from the jaws of iguanas. First on one arm, then on the other. On the chest, then on the back. On one leg, then on the other. Only at the end will his face also be scarified.

The last phase of the treatment—the most difficult and dangerous—will be that in which he will finally have to accustom himself, little by little, very slowly, very gently, to support in his hands, the weight of the two rattles. And, with the rattles held very firmly, to parry the attacks of the devils, who will all come to assault the cabin and the village. Perhaps they will kill people. At the very least, they will bring about calamities—all of this so as to hinder a Jaguar, a Puma, from holding in his hands the omnipotent rattles, more powerful than those of the Coatis, which only a Coati can clutch. It will be very risky. He might even die on such occasion. But, if he stands fast, he will have the help of all the powerful and mysterious spirits. He will then be recognized as the first master sorcerer, of the side above, challenging Maíra there under his light, with power perhaps to do anything he wishes. Not merely in the little world of the Mairuns, but in the whole world of the Red Sun. Avá listens again and again to the interminable recommendations and prescriptions of the oxim. He is the most docile but also the most slippery of his clients.

One day, Teró goes to look for Avá to talk. They leave together. Teró asks him about that unusual friendship. Avá tries to explain to him and to himself how careful one has to be. The truth is not to be found in only one place. And it is not a single thing. It is everywhere; it is multiple, dispersed, and contradictory. God created man to know himself, seeing himself reflected in the deceptive mirror of human minds. That is why I need to look very carefully. Only by looking beyond people will I be able to know God and decipher His designs. Only this way can I have hope of achieving what I want most as a man: simple things that are within the grasp of others, but which for me are almost unattainable.

Teró tries to smile, to understand. In the end he leaves Avá, promising to come look for him someday to go fishing on the Iparanã while there is still time.

HÉ MUHERE TÉ

I was strolling about the village, watching the women coming from the fields bearing firewood, cassava, potatoes, and corn; watching the men coming up from the river with their fish or returning from the forest with game and going to the house of the oxim. I also saw Isaías, poor unfortunate thing, pacing from here to there and back again. At last, I came across Jaguar. Sitting under a sawari-nut tree at the edge of the trail, he looked at me, smiled, and in front of everyone, he made a gesture for me to come and sit next to him. It was almost the same kind of gesture a Rio playboy might have made in the old days. I liked it so much!

What was it about? I swear he knows I am pregnant. I swear he thinks he impregnated me. We talked a lot. Dusk was beginning to fall, and up to the moment we had to rise to go and join the others to watch the sun set, he continued to talk. He talked about serious things, and this time, it was not I who spoke in my mangled manner. He did most of the talking. He talked, explaining things in his lovely way.

I love to hear his voice as much as to feel the tenderness of his effort to make me understand everything. He spoke very slowly, repeating, explaining. When he first began I thought he was going to tell me a dirty story. He used the word "hole" and pointed to my vulva, saying that that was the hole of life and that it has the same name as a certain basket something or other, full of little bones covered with feathers, that is the hole of death. Through one you are born into this world, he said, through the other you are born into the other world. This is why, he said, the corpse here is the child there, and the child here is the corpse there, and they are also called by the same word. The matter was absolutely serious, and there was no chance for me to squeeze out of him as much as I wanted to. Or could it be that he was talking about child-bones-corpse and hole basket-vulva because that is a father's way of speaking to the woman who is going to bear his child. What do I know about how these people think? What do I know about those Mairuns? He has talked to me on many other occasions but never with such concentration and seriousness.

Nowadays he talks to me much more than to Avá. He barely smiles at him. I found it difficult to understand. He smiles in a superior way, almost as if he were being protective: a terrible smile to see on the face of a boy when directed at someone older. I asked him what he thought of Avá. He didn't answer me. I insisted, and he tried to explain to me that Avá could not be seen, could not be discerned. Perhaps only by the guide of souls; perhaps not. Nobody knows how to see Avá because Avá does not exist: he is becoming. He is emerging from his skin, he said, like a snake that changes its skin every year. But a snake changes its skin to become even more a snake. Not, Avá. He is changing his skin to become the other, and nobody knows yet who the other will be. But as he is already the other, nobody sees him for what he is. What does all this mean? It is another mystery of this Mairun world, which I understand imperfectly.

I only know what I see, and in Isaías I see nothing but frustration and failure. It hurts: Inimá doesn't even pay him any attention. Here, in this world of his, I feel so good! In fact, I have never felt better than in this world of his in which he feels he has no place. I have adjusted perhaps as a result of the mutual respect with which I treat the Mairuns and they treat me. I don't want, I don't imagine, nor would I ever conceive or desire to make them my equals. I don't imitate them. I am I, they are they, and we understand each other.

The trouble with Isaías is that he is ambiguous. To be and not to be. He is neither Indian nor Christian. He is not a man nor can he leave off being one, poor thing. To be two is to be neither, nobody. But it is also beyond his strength. He cannot stop participating in a we with me that excludes the Mairuns and that nearly offends me. Nor can he feel in himself that he is only a Mairun among others. The poor soul never stops racking his brains, at once progressively clarifying and confusing things. Take this marriage to Inimá. Could it be that he possibly likes her? It was an enormous shock to him when I told him yesterday, in passing, that I was pregnant. He didn't say a word. He opened his eyes wide, looked at me as if he were stunned, spread his limp arms like a doll in a gesture very typical of him as of late, and went off toward the house of the oxim.

The other day I was behind him for a long time on the dancing ground, mixed in with all the people who gather there at sunset to eat and talk. It was very noticeable that he spoke to nobody and nobody spoke to him. Not even Inimá. Then I heard, I heard him well, muttering to himself. I edged a bit nearer and heard better; it was a litany in Latin, like those of my father:

Tra-la-la, ora pro nobis
Tra-la-la, ora pro nobis

Now that it is night and I am swinging in my hammock, let's see if I can forget others so as to think of myself. I need to concentrate on my problem. I intended, but without success, to think about it the whole day. It has been like this for some time now. It even seems as if I am no longer capable. Is it the pregnancy that makes me languid? Where does this lassitude come from? I am pregnant and I don't know by whom. I am going to give birth here among the Mairuns, this is the problem. If this is in fact a problem . . . because it could very well be a solution. With a child growing up as a Mairun, would I be integrating myself better into this world I'd like to make my own? Becoming the mother of a little infant, would that be for me what it would be for a man to be its father? The men here change their names when they father a male child: Maxihú is the father of Maxi. Teró was for a long time Jaguarhú. Would I be

Iuicuihí if my daughter were called Iuicui? Or Mairahú if my son were to be called Maíra? Is that possible? It would be better if it were a little girl: Iuicui. I could bring her up to be a mirixorã like me. We would start a new tradition of paramours from the Jaguar clan. Our descendants could even end up being the most beautiful, preferred by all the men for lovemaking out of pure pleasure. This is what I want, a very womanly daughter, Iuicui, to become a most feminine mirixorã.

Foolishness, I'm talking nonsense. This is no time to play! I have a problem, a big problem. Above all, this giving birth. I saw Mbiá, the beloved daughter of Moitá, have her baby. I saw how she gave birth here, in this very house. When she indicated that the hour had arrived, her husband Náru and her brother Jaguar who were waiting there, at once began to dig a hole in the middle of the house and covered it with plantain leaves. She waited only allowing us to see her contractions from time to time. At last she rose from the hammock in which she had been sitting and, assisted by Náru, walked over to the hole. There, with her back to him, she put one foot on each side of the hole and squatted as if she were going to urinate, supporting herself with her hands. I could see then that she was straining to give birth without being able to, her forehead sweating, and was letting us see that her strength was dwindling. Then Jaguar came to her aid. He stood in front of Mbiá who stood up and put her hands on his shoulders. Jaguar held her wrists tightly as Náru put his arms around her belly and, with fingers interlaced, squeezed down on the bulge of her belly forcing it downward.

I myself was in absolute agony as I looked on, but I saw that Moitá and Pinu, despite what was going on, appeared calm. In her state Mbiá began to half-moan, murmuring a drawn-out aaaaaah, more a bleat than a cry. Immediately she squatted over the hole to give birth with her knees apart. Náru was supporting her by her armpits, turning his head nervously from side to side, obviously suffering.

Suddenly Mbiá started to give birth: I could see the little

pointed, wrinkled head at the opening of the hole. A moment
later the complete body was suddenly emerging, with the cord
and the bag. With little delay the tiny baby was there, the little
pagan on the leaves, screaming. Mbiá herself cut the cord with
a sliver of bamboo that was there for that purpose and made a
knot separating it from the afterbirth, which remained red and
bleeding atop the green plantain leaves. During the entire birth,
Náru had been supporting Mbiá by the armpits, visibly agitated.

Having given birth, Mbiá rose rather shakily, turned to face
Náru and said: "I have given birth." He replied: "I have given
birth, too." She went to sit in the hammock with her little son
and remained there resting and watching Jaguar who was filling
the hole with earth and smoothing it over, looking very serious.
When the ground was smooth once again, Mbiá rose and left
with Moitá, Mbiá carrying the child while the old woman
carried the afterbirth and the umbilical cord to wash and bury.
It was Náru who went to the hammock with the gravest expression in the world, taking it all badly. He murmured in a
complaining tone:

"Hẽ muhere té. Hẽ muhere té. Hẽ muhere té."

He meant "I myself am dying." He remained there in the
hammock for days and days, drinking a little turtle soup now
and then, eating some fish scales and other light repasts lovingly
cooked for him by Mbiá. He was in couvade. Even now,
months later, he hobbles slowly around as if he were con-
valescing after a serious illness or recovering from a grave disaster. Everybody says that hard work, displeasure, a fright, an
extravagance, anything like that, could be very harmful to him
and to the child which is growing very nicely. His name is
Uruantã, and that is why Náru is now called Uruantãhú.

Well, now I know what giving birth is like among them. I
saw! Now I have to think about my own parturition. Who will
dig the hole, as I have neither a husband nor a brother? Who
will support me by the armpits? To whom shall I say "I have
given birth"? And who, recognizing himself as the father, will
say to me: "I have given birth too"? Who will lie in couvade

to protect the life of my child? And, above all, Alma my dear, little daughter of Sr. Alberto from Cosme Velho, above all, my dear little Alma, you are not a Mairun! Who will guarantee that just because you are here you will give birth as easily as they do? The births I have heard of are terribly traumatic events with screams and frightful sufferings. Even today the divine plague still weighs upon us: one must give birth with pain.

It would be better, Alma, my friend, little companion of the Jangadeiros, it would be better if you left here quickly, with the help of those gringo friends of Isaías's. To go and knock on the door of Fred's consulting room, saying, "Dear, I've come a little pregnant from the bush into your arms!" Don't play with fire, woman. Think seriously. Who will be the father in that hour? Where will you go to give birth?

Go on! I'm putting myself through enough anguish. Everything arranges itself in this world, especially here. Tranquility, little Alma. Tran-quil-i-ty: keep going so that God may help you. This business about the father is foolishness. About the couvade, even more so. Am I going to allow some man to snatch the glory of my having been big bellied for months? Or to steal my role of giving birth? I am the mother of my daughter Iuicui or my son Mairaíra, and the father as well. I alone! No, I and God!

AVAETÉ

The Iparanã, confined with difficulty to its bed, runs vertiginously, vibrant and red like a puma. The turbid waters flicked by the breeze, tremble and undulate, moaning in the air, running riot on the banks and reverberating, crackling, against the drum of the bottoms of the canoes. The great dunes, still visible, are no longer naked. Here and there tufts of goat's beard and crabgrass are appearing, beginning to dry out. Green bushes with blue and yellow flowers await the rising waters that will drown them.

Stuck in the skin of Avá, Isaías walks along the dunes. He is unaware of the sand beneath his feet and of the opaline light of the sun in the midst of the sky darkened with purple and scarlet clouds. He wants nothing more than to retreat to the intimacy of his hole for his argument with God. He prays monotonously about his sadness as a living man who loves, suffers, and feels.

O God, my God of Light, source of flowing waters. Rock of ages, ice-cold crag. Lord, what will become of me without Thy love?

Lord, here I am once more, lacking Thee, lacking Alma. In vain I humiliated myself, supplicated, wept. The words froze in my throat. My eyes dried up. But my heart throbs, sighs, and keeps vigil. What will become of me without her?

Lord, only Thou canst save me. My afflicted soul dies outside me, in agony. Inside me, how will I live without Thee or her?

Lord, here I am, dead of fright at myself, of the pleasure of my longed-for death. I live nourished by this disillusioned love. What will become of me; what will become of her?

Now I know, at last I have understood that love is stronger than death, and that jealousy burns more than the flames of hell. What will become of me, Lord without Thy love?

Lord, here I am at Thy feet, contrite. My God, secret fount, hidden clarity, silent voice, present solitude. Give me, Lord, the love I yearn and have no hope for.

Give me, Lord, through the Virgin Mother, impregnated by the Divine Word, give me Thy love, even if it damns me.

Give me, Lord of Babylon, the forbidden fount of my salvation and my perdition.

Give me, Lord, my fount which has been promised me and which is sealed only to me; my wife, my loved one.

Day and night it flows, Lord, it flows and sings, gallant and content, indifferent only to me.

Day and night it flows and sings—secretive and wise, in light and darkness—the fount that is mine and prohibited only to me.

Give me, Lord, the love of my loved one, impassioned with her loved one.

Our Lady, Mother of God, do not deny me the ardent miracle of my anxious adventure; to gain the love of my loved one.

Our Lady, only Thou, Divine Word Incarnate. Only Thou, our Lady, whom Heaven permits to be incarnate among spirits. Only Thou, Holy Mary, canst give me the love of my loved one.

Lord, my God, the Chastiser. Lord, my God, the Savior. She is my cross, which I deserve; give me her love, for my eternal perdition, give it to me.

Her love, O Lord, is the only paradise I aspire to. If I am lost with it, without it I do not wish to be saved.

Give me, Lord, my unfortunate love. Even if it comes surrounded by all the scorpions of jealousy. Even if it costs the eternal damnation of my passion-ridden soul.

Give me, O Lord, Her love or my death.

THE SAVAGES

Eduardo Enéas Indian Post
19 April 1975

His Excellency Sr. Colonel
Augusto da Matta Celeste,
DD. Director of FUNAI

Sr. Director,
   In accordance with my duty as a functionary I am communicating to Your Excellency, by means of this private report, an unfortunate occurrence which has just taken place in the zone under my jurisdiction, in an area contiguous to this the Eduardo Eneas Indian Post of the Mairun Indians of the Iparanã River.
   One day last week, which must have been between the 8th and 10th of the current month and year, the death of two persons and the wounding of a third occurred at Tapera Beach, in an event probably related to an act of war by the Xaepẽ Indians. The news was brought to this post on the 14th last by the pastor Robert Toddy who told us that at the Evangelical Mission, otherwise known as the House of Mirrors, he had found a man called Manelão, seriously wounded.
   He added that the aforementioned man related that he had been camping at Tapera Beach together with his employer, José Jaguar de Oliveira, nicknamed Juca, and another employee called Boca when, before dawn, they were suddenly attacked by a band of untamed Indians, probably the Xaepẽs. In the attack, his two companions lost their lives, struck down by blows from a club. The victims referred to were Sr. José Jaguar de Oliveira (Juca), a merchant of Creciúma, a town downriver in

the state of Pará, and the other, an employee of the same man, an individual of humble status, a member of the Epexã tribe, named Boca, and regarded as mentally defective.

On receiving the news, I set out at once toward the aforementioned beach where, given its distance from this post, I arrived on the 16th. I was able to verify, firstly, that the Mairun Indians, inspired by their natural generous inclination, had covered the two corpses with sand to preserve them from the vultures and armadillos. I was also able to verify, at the same time, that the tracks and prints made by bare feet—attributable to the Mairuns—were so many, all over the beach, that no evidence could be obtained from them.

Having disinterred the bodies, I was able to ascertain that both had had their skulls smashed by blows from a club. I could not confirm the presence of any other wounds, because the bodies were in an advanced stage of putrefaction. My immediate concern was to give them both a Christian burial on an elevation at Tapera Beach where we found some solid ground, marking the site with two crosses.

Previously, on the voyage upriver, I had made contact with the wounded victim and reporter of the incident, Sr. Manuel Gão, verifying that his wound—a cut in his right pectoral muscle —had been properly treated by Sr. Robert Toddy, and that he was already recuperating. I then took his statement, from which I was able to reconstruct the episode in the form that I've transcribed below:

The three men had been sleeping on the aforementioned beach, Sr. Manuel Gão in the boat, the other two in hammocks slung in an old abandoned house (hut) that is there. When the attack occurred, the first two were killed immediately, but Sr. Manelão (alias Manuel Gão), awakened by the noise, untied the boat, and was able to slip into the river channel, thereby distancing himself from the area of danger. As a result of this opportune act and the darkness of the early morning, he was shot by an arrow that was not fatal, its trajectory having been slightly deflected.

On the return voyage, I resumed my talk with Sr. Manuel Gão, who had nothing to add to his previous statement. His condition as victim of this serious assault being evident, I authorized his return to his port of origin. He left at once with the boat and its respective merchandise which consisted almost entirely of the pelts of ocelots and otters (whose hunting is illegal but not part of my duty to prohibit, in accordance with Instruction 257 of December 1964), to return it to the orphaned family to whom he would also have to report the sad news of the tragic death of their head of household.

As much from the statement of the victim, who is the only eyewitness, as from my own on-site investigations, I was able to ascertain that the two deaths and the wounding are quite probably the responsibility of the Xaepē Indians, of unknown linguistic affiliation (allophylian). This hypothesis may be supported first by the above evidence and second by the evidence provided by the presence of a club which, though rough, has the typical shape of the Xaepē variety.

It may be worth observing, nonetheless, that the Mairun Indians do not accept the hypothesis that the deaths were caused by the Xaepēs. They argue, with some sense, that these Indians have the custom—never belied—of leaving a club behind for each man killed. They do this as much to mark the number of the dead as to determine how many, and which warriors have the right to change their names to designate themselves war heros. The Mairuns allege that the club does not appear to them to have been made by an indigenous hand, because of the carelessness with which it was fashioned. And that it is even more unlikely that it was made by the Xaepēs, because as they, the Mairuns, see it, the club was carved with good, well-sharpened tools, and it is known that the Xaepēs have very few of those, and what they have is in poor condition.

I did not wish to refrain from mentioning here these considerations, but I must note at the same time my judgment that the Mairuns are by nature very skeptical and are always questioning everything. I can attest to this, for I have lived with them for more than ten years.

The investigation having been completed, I took the post's launch along the left bank of the Iparaná River fifty kilometers upstream and downstream, respectively, from the place where the tragedy occurred to see if the presence of the Xaepēs could be confirmed. Unfortunately, not a sign could be found indicating that these Indians were still anywhere in the vicinity. This being the case, it can be assumed that if they were the perpetrators, after completing their attack, they fled into the forest, returning to their tribal territory some hundreds of kilometers inside the jungle.

In the absence of a better-informed and clearer judgment, I am of the opinion that the episode should be considered closed without further ado, as it was probably the result of an act of war on the part of wild forest dwellers.

If I were given the opportunity to express my thought on the matter, I would opine that it would be worthwhile to reinitiate, as has been done before, a policy of pacification of the Xaepē Indians, with allocation of the necessary resources and in compliance with official instruction, carried out by a man experienced in the backlands. Only thus will an end be put to the decades of bloody conflict during which they have made victims of many people up and down the Iparaná and during which they have themselves been victims of innumerable acts of violence, including those perpetrated by the servants of that José Jaguar de Oliveira himself, who met his death at their hands.

Awaiting instructions, I certify that I am, your obedient servant.

With republican salutations,
Elias Pantaleão da Silva
Agent 17—In charge of Eduardo Eneas I.P.
of the Mairuns, in Rio Iparaná.

OTXICON

It is afternoon; the village is paralyzed by fear. The whole morning Corĩ screamed with pain in the house of the Pacus. All the women are sobbing from horror.

This afternoon she started to moan and to swell up. She is enormous, her fattened fingers spread out into swollen hands. Her huge fat arms rise above the glands of her armpits. Her legs and feet have been softened as if they were the legs of a rotting turtle. Her belly is a bladder about to burst.

She stopped moaning. Now only a foam oozes from outside of her mouth. She dies.

She was Corĩ, the little Pacu girl, so talkative, as happy as could be with her habit of daintily licking her fingers like a squirrel. Early in the morning she had gone with her mother to gather firewood and had seen an armadillo run into a hole. Her mother screamed at her not to—it was too late—for brighteyes had already stuck her hand in the ant nest. There inside, a rattlesnake bit Corĩ's hand fatally: what a shriek she let out!

Later, at home, they suck Corĩ's hand. They burn it with hot cinders. They do everything, but in vain.

Finally Epecuí arms himself with courage, lifts Corĩ, dead but still warm, onto his back, and accompanied by all the Pacu clan, carries her toward the hut of the oxim.

They find the house closed with a thick stake across the doorway. They force it open and enter. There inside, in the dark, is the oxim, sounding his rattle and waving his feathers from side to side. Epecuí lays Corĩ down on the beaten earth floor in front of him in silence. The oxim slowly raises his eyes and looks at all the Pacus one by one. He shakes his rattle in such a way as to recreate the sound of a rattlesnake. They all become excited, their eyes aflame with hope. But instantly the oxim sounds his rattle louder and louder. It is no longer the sound of a rattlesnake, it is the sound of horror. Fear returns and fills all their faces.

"This is Corĩ. Cure the rattlesnake bite there in her hand," Epecuí shouts.

The oxim continues to shake the rattle to simulate the sound of a rattlesnake. He begins to move his head from side to side, backward and forward, from right to left. Epecuí repeats:

"She is for your to cure, oxim. Ask what you will."

The oxim remains seated on his legs, swaying, waving his feathers, shaking his rattle. But he begins to make a more definite sound, higher, louder and louder until the house is vibrating in a deafening way, piercing the eardrums of everyone. Then suddenly the oxim stops and, in that screaming silence, shouts:

"She is dead. Take her away. She is dead!"

When the shock wears off, they all leave crying. Except Epecuí; he bends down to lift Corĩ up in his arms. He rises from the ground, slowly, with the little girl in his hands. As he turns to leave he turns his back on the oxim; and kicks him twice, knocking him over, all tangled up in his feathers. The rattle falls to the ground and splits open, spilling its abundance of seeds, beads, shells, and little turquoise pebbles.

Everyone leaves behind Epecuí and the dead Corĩ, the happy one. They cross the dancing ground to get to the house. There the Pacus remain, the others going on to their own houses. Inside the Pacu house, the Pacu women begin to intone a lament. The other women, each in her own house, start to wail. The whole village sings, lamenting the pain caused by the death of Corĩ, under the light of the evening sun.

Then it was that the howl was heard. A deafening noise coming from the river bank. They all turned to look. They guessed: it must be the young men who are coming with some new joke. Joking at a time like this? The shouting rose in volume as they entered the dancing ground, and with them came a strange stench. They have brought six opossums in a round basket which they roll along the ground, kicking it like a football. The opossums fart, stinking so badly as to kill. The young men laugh and shout.

"Hey, Micura, come here. Come here, Micura."

Nobody knows how it was, nobody saw him. Nobody knows who came among them and spoke. Only a boy was seen darting to one side with the basket of opossums on the end of a pole, to cast it into the river. The young men run to the other side in single file, silently, directly toward the hut of the oxim. They break into the thatched hut from all sides at once. They grab, lift up and dismember the oxim on the spot. With only their bare hands.

What was seen later was the group leaving with the tattered remains of the corpse that used to be the oxim, rolled on the ground, trampled and kicked along the paths of the forest into the interior to its deepest part.

The village is now silent. Nobody is crying now. Painted all over with annatto, with bunches of flowers all round her, Corĩ has been laid in a new cotton hammock. In the distance one can hear the sound of men digging two deep holes and a tunnel connecting them. There in that dark space, in the bosom of the earth, isolated from everything, Corĩ will sleep in her hammock slung between two forked branches, with all her belongings around her. Corĩ-Coraci, color-and-sun. Joy.

KYRIE

The Mission of Our Lady of O. Two old men are conversing in the shade of a trellis. Neither is looking at the other. Each speaks while sitting in a chair turned to one side. Father Vecchio looks at the chapel which he never tires of admiring. He looks without seeing. He looks, inside there, at the chapel he was able to see before he contracted glaucoma. Father Aquino looks outward, looks at the river, waiting for a canoe that never arrives. Like every afternoon.

A nun and a priest issue from the conventual houses through two opposite and symmetrical doors. She in front of the girls. He in front of the boys. They walk at the same pace, with almost the same rhythm, until they find themselves in front of the door of the chapel. They stand in front. The boys look down. The girls look at the boys. They enter. Outside, four old Indian women, kneeling on the ground, are grumbling. Like every afternoon.

High above, another Iparanã seems to run along the roof of the world. A mirage? No sky is more ample, more open than this boundless, anguished sky of the late afternoon. A tenuous white line marks the west, describing a raveled ribbon loose in the wind. Obedient to one rhythm, all together, moving at the same time, the great white wings slowly open and close. It is the herons that are leaving. One of them momentarily abandons the file, and they all appear to waver, to tremble insecurely. But soon it returns, resumes its place, and the world is in balance again.

Si iniquitátes observáreris, Domine,
Domine, quis sustinébit?

FATHER VECCHIO: "Our angel has left, Father Aquino. How that feebleness cloaked in virtue deceived us! In the end, he had the strength to break with us."

FATHER AQUINO: "Isaías is neither weak nor strong: he is innocent. And is not theirs the Kingdom of Heaven?"

FATHER VECCHIO: "Nonsense! This is a case of moral irresponsibility."

FATHER AQUINO: "Like ours, my brother?"

FATHER VECCHIO: "You are always returning to the same theme, Father Aquino. Have mercy. Didn't you promise me? For how many years have we been discussing this to no end?"

FATHER AQUINO: "I disagree. We've accomplished something. At least we have exchanged roles. Now I am the rock of the scandal."

Sister Canuta arrives with tea and pastries. Fat and smiling, she puts everything on a little table between the chairs in silence: she is deaf and mute. After serving the tea, she steps back two paces, checks that all is as it should be, and returns to the kitchen, content. Like every afternoon.

FATHER VECCHIO: "She is the one who is most reasonable in our discussions"; he points with his chin to the sister. "She maintains her smile affixed to her face and has never lost a drop of tea or a single biscuit. How many years has it been since she came?"

FATHER AQUINO: "Don't change the conversation, my father. I have spent the night with that swirling in my head. We must talk."

FATHER VECCHIO: "You were always too ambitious. Ambitious vis-à-vis yourself. Ambitious vis-à-vis the Order. Ambitious vis-à-vis the Church. Even vis-à-vis the whole world, Father Aquino. I am not. At least I try to be humble, tolerant. I live small with my truths, without vehemence or heroism."

FATHER AQUINO: "Small truths, little doubts, it's all the same. Perhaps you are right. Perhaps it's not worth discussing. In fact, that debate began way back in 1560: with one fishhook he converted them; with two, he unconverted them. Do you remember? This after years of catechism, provided by the secular arm, in a state where the Church reigned supreme. What can we say?"

FATHER VECCHIO: "Your conclusion is the total impossibility of conversion, isn't that right, Father Aquino? Even if we were to arrive at the certainty that it is impossible, it would still be worth the trouble to try. It is always worth the trouble to till the fields of the Lord, even knowing that only he can cause faith to flower. That is what I think. Without any certainty. And perhaps I think this way because I cannot withstand doubt. Doubt that is gnawing at you. Behind all this is the malignant idea of the futility of our work: we have built up on sand. Forty years of work in vain."

FATHER AQUINO: "It's true. We both have come to this like those who came before us. But you have gone back on your own argument, Father Vecchio. You don't want to face up to the responsibility of using your own judgment, to think before God about our work. It is impossible to run away. What disturbed me all night was an idea that is not new but whose aspect I have never properly examined. Formerly, I, too, accepted, without much effort, the idea that we till the fields for the harvest of God: the conversion of the gentiles. Now I see that the true crop is not the Indians. Is it God? We here, should we be ardent for love of Him? This idea—as I have understood it for some time—would make us irresponsible. Here, we would be only as witnesses to a miracle, if one were to occur. But now I ask myself: Are we here for love of Him? For love of the Indians? Or for love of ourselves exclusively? I am very much afraid that we labor in this garden not for the salvation of the Indians. Nor to praise God. We are doing it for ourselves, for our own puny salvation, the martyrdom we long for, the sanctity we covet."

Smiling, Sister Canuta collects the crockery and stops for a moment to look at the two old men. They laugh, they smile with her, imbibing the sweetness of her piety.

Subvenite Sancti Dei,
ocúrrite Angeli Domini
suscipientes animam ejus
offerentes eam in conspectu Altissimi

FATHER VECCHIO: "That was not a typical reflection on your part, Father Aquino. So, did we also fall into the pit of egoism? Are we ourselves our only cause? That thesis is too provocative to be humble. But I acknowledge it as being suffered and sad. Too sad for arrogance. Let us continue thinking. What made you take this leap, Father Aquino? Isaías and his drama?"

FATHER AQUINO: "The drama is ours, more ours than his, my father. You know that I trusted him; how many times during so many years did I argue that it wasn't a matter of quantity but of quality? I thought we had given the Church a pure priest, a virtuous, aggressive missionary. How was it possible not to think that way in those days? The idea was sufficiently compelling for us to take it before the Mission with hope for success. During my last visit to Rome I spent days and days talking to him, after I had completed the revision of *Mairun Ethnology*. He never deceived me. He remained virtuous and energetic. Despite his uncertainty regarding his vocation; despite his anguish at not being able to find himself. It was terrible to feel that he saw no light ahead of him yet continued to burn with faith. It was we who believed we saw the light for him and for us. We saw what we wanted to see, because in truth the light never did shine. Isn't that so, Father Vecchio. Neither for us, nor for him. God never gave us, nor does he now give us, any sign. Not that I wished or prayed for one, thinking I deserved it. It's just that I can't any longer: *Kyrie eleison*.

The two fathers interrupt the conversation to listen to the organ and accompany, from where they are sitting, the service sung by the choir. Outside, the afternoon—long, rosy, lilac—closes in peace. Within them, the whirlwind. They remain silent for a long time listening to the music while oblivious to the prayer being sung:

Requiem aeternam dona eis, Domine
Et lux perpétua luceat eis

Dies irae, dies illa
Solvet saeculum in favila

. . . .

Lacrimosa dies illa
Lux aeterna luceat eis, Domine
Cum sanctis tuis in aeternum

. . . .

Te decet hymnus. Deus
Kyrie, eleison. Christe, eleison

FATHER VECCHIO: "How is it that I still have hope? Or do I suffer from weariness? Weariness from thinking, afraid that I might have to start all over again. I am seventy-eight years old; and you just turned seventy, didn't you? We have one foot here, the other in the grave. These buildings, this chapel, which is so beautiful: our work. They are our mark on the world. Better than that first thatched hut we constructed. Better than the second. Better than all of them. Better also than the Tuscan village where I was born."

FATHER AQUINO: "Better also than the Mairun village we found here?"

FATHER VECCHIO: "Let that be, brother. I wanted to say that my greatest fear in life was to be sent back to Tuscany to grow old and die among my own. You know how it is."

FATHER AQUINO: "It is the same with me. That is why we decided to write the *Mairun Ethnology*. We held on to that to escape the sentence of having to return, wasn't that so?"

FATHER VECCHIO: "It's true, but what I don't like to recall is the wisdom of the general. He understood our anguish. Then he sent that letter guaranteeing that by the will of the Order we could live and die here if we wanted to. And we did, thank God. It was the greatest act of charity in the life of that holy man."

FATHER AQUINO: "We are closing the circle once again, like every afternoon. We talk about the general, repeating charity and holy man. You are in the hour of death, my father. Both of us—like the deceased Sister Ignês whom God summoned yesterday—have nothing more to give. We are even incapable of saying anything new to each other. Today, like every afternoon, we are repeating ourselves."

FATHER VECCHIO: "Can we not think of alternatives? Was there an alternative that would have been better? Are there any other alternatives for those starting out now? These new priests, these new sisters. What advice can we, who are at the end, give to those who are beginning? There I go again."

FATHER AQUINO: "Let that be, my father. We are becoming feebleminded."

Ite missa est. Alleluia, alleluia

The boys file out of the chapel with Father Cirilo; the girls with Sister Petrina, the new sister, a very good organist. Like every afternoon.

TUXAURETÉ

The guide of souls did it all with only two or three orders. No, not orders, appeals, because this is the Mairun way of commanding.

The young men return from the forest, exhausted. They bathe for a long time in the Black Lake, under the light of the moon, to prove to themselves that they are not afraid. They advance in single file, Jaguar following the others. In this formation they enter the circle of houses in the middle of the night, with the moon very high in a cloudless sky.

They stop, afraid: the silence is terrifying. It is much quieter than on a normal night. Not even the dogs, which are usually so noisy, bark or snarl at the file of young men arriving from the band of the Rising Sun.

Some of them, those who are from the clans on that side, go to their houses to find out what has been going on. But soon they return, running, having seen that they are shut, the doors barred with stakes. They reunite once again, forming a circle around Jaguar. What should they do? What is all this about? A curse of the oxim? In the houses, there were only the dogs, growling, grumbling.

They turn toward the Great House of Men and see, with even greater astonishment, its illumination in the middle of the village. It is a solar light, of a red sunset, that shines through the straw making it look as if it were on fire. The old Great House of Men is an enormous lamp incandescent in the middle of the night. They all run to it and, at the entrance, are frightened by the sight of all the Mairuns inside. All the people, the men without exception, the women, yes, all the women and even babies still being nursed. The Mairun people, the Mairun village, have invaded the Great House of Men on an ordinary day. Why? There they all are, standing or seated, pressed against the walls, under the torches of burning pitch that give off light. The silence is total as is the effort to clear a space at the center of the Great House, around the columns of cedar where the guide of souls is sitting alone, the old guide of souls, his rattle buzzing very quietly.

What could this be? It might be some connivance on the part of the oxim. What are all the people doing here? As the young men enter the people recede, creating a space around them that forces them to move forward, nearer to the guide of souls. They advance reluctantly, mistrustfully, looking from side to side, recognizing someone here, another there, everyone. They try to read what has happened in the faces of the people: they want to know their intent. They also look at each other uncomfortably and turn around, searching for an explanation in Jaguar's eyes. No one understands anything, but they all move forward. At last they are all standing, forming a semicircle around the bench with the two-headed Vulture.

The guide of souls then looks into the eyes of Jaguar who thereby understands that he has to advance to the middle of the file and face the old man. Then the guide of souls stops shaking his rattle, unwinds a thin cord from around his wrist and hangs it around his own neck. At last, he rises slowly, bearing in his palms a small mat made of green burite fronds which had been under the bench. Laid out on the mat, side by side like little snakes in a row, are eleven cords of the whitest cotton. Jaguar sees and comprehends. He throws the old guide of souls a piercing glance. He wishes to speak but can't find the words. Then he makes up his mind: he steps forward, takes the little green mat with the cords from the hands of the guide of souls, and holding it in his palms, cries out:

"The old guide of souls must tie me up. I shall be his warrior!"

The guide of souls is frightened, but understands the order. He picks up one of the cords—the one in the middle—with trembling fingers, and puts it on his own wrist. Then he bends down in front of Jaguar, undoes his shorts, and slowly pulls them down to his feet. With his feet Jaguar helps to take his shorts off. At the same time, the other young men undress, taking off their shorts and throwing them behind their backs, standing naked. Naked in front of the guide of souls, naked in front of everyone. The old man bends down, takes Jaguar's member in his hands, compresses the shaft into its skin, and holding the foreskin with one hand, ties a knot around it with the white cord he has been carrying on his wrist. He rises to the fullness of his height and looks Jaguar in the eyes, maintaining his gaze with mirth. It is as if he were taking pleasure in testing the strength of the new chieftain. Having executed the tying of Jaguar, the old guide of souls takes the green mat in his hands and walks to the first young man in the file. There, with solemnity, Jaguar forces the member of each man into its skin, pinches the foreskin, and ties the knot. So he makes warriors, one by one, out of these ten men, from the first to the last.

All of this occurs amidst the silence of everyone. Mothers shut with a hand the little mouths of the babies they are nursing. The bigger children know everything, if only by being present in the illuminated Great House of Men, or they assume that this is a most solemn moment by the mysterious air about everyone. With the tying ceremony concluded by a buzz from the rattle of the guide of souls, the men squat in a circle around the old man. He sits on the two-headed Vulture bench and speaks: "He who ties a man is a chieftain. We have a chieftain. The tying is what makes a young warrior. Now we have new men: Mairun warriors. Now and always. The tying is done in the light of the sun, in the middle of the dances of Coraci-Iaci. That is why, here in the Great House, it is now daytime. Tomorrow the chieftain will give word to commemorate our happiness with a great Coraci-Iaci."

They all leave, jostling each other, talking, commenting. The young men remain on the dancing ground with the other men. No one returns to the Great House of Men. The women return to their own houses, with their husbands and children.

The next day the sun rises, makes its journey across the sky, and dies, as if it were an ordinary day. But all the women are menstruating when they awake. Even the little girls, wounded by the arrows of Micura.

CODA

Dóia, I'm going to tell you something. Perhaps it will make you sad. Do you know what I saw today? The skeleton of the deceased. Blessed Virgin! Didn't I say so? I knew Quinzim was dead, ever since the day he disappeared. Since that day, here inside me, I knew that he would never come back. Where did you find his skull? Quite near, as I was returning from the

saltwater lake. The bones were there on the ground! Those of
the dead man and of an otter. Both skeletons right there, gleaming. I buried him as best I could in the sand, with the point of my
bow. I had no tools with me. Nor was I getting anywhere.
There was no good meat to be had. Could you tell how he died,
Sr. Xisto? It could have been anything, Dóia. A snake, who
knows? It was not a jaguar. No! A jaguar breaks a man's neck
and does great damage to the skull. It may have been a fer-de-
lance. Virgin Mary! A fer-de-lance! Three days ago I killed one
here. It had been warming itself in the sun on Sr. Manelão's new
woodskin. Little innocent Antãozinho had been playing
nearby. Virgin Mary! *I'm coming, Jaguar, I'm coming. I already know, Jaguar, I know that what you want is to go to the
sand dunes. It's only there that you like it, right?* Ooh! Major,
don't tickle me. The colonel almost saw us yesterday. One of
these days he'll come in and catch us fooling around. Don't
tickle me, darling. Tell me . . . tell me about that girl, that one
among the Indians; was she pretty? Did she really die in childbirth? What, Aninha, my love? Didn't you read my report?
Ah! Major, well, yes, since I typed it, of course I read it. I was
talking nonsense. It was very well written; I liked it a lot. But to
tell you the truth, it didn't enlighten me much, no. Tell me,
Nonato, was she pretty? Of course she was. What do you
think? That I would brave the bush for God knows how long,
searching for an ugly dead woman? Was it only from childbirth
that she died? What do I know? It was more from madness and
from bad luck. That woman was very crazy and very unfortunate. When did you ever hear of a white girl, blonde, beautiful,
and educated, going out there and giving it to the Indians to the
point of getting herself pregnant? Was she prettier than I?
Aninha, my little animal, no one could be prettier than you.
Impossible! But you aren't thinking of going out there into the
bush to tame Indians, are you? May the Lord deliver and protect me! I'm not crazy. Aninha, my flower, I want to tell you
the only good story I heard on that trip. It's about that grumbling old bitch, the wife of the agent at the FUNAI post. Ah

yes, I know, the one who was careless. Well, one day when the old woman was complaining bitterly of a migraine headache, Elias threatened her: Be careful or I'll tell the major what that German said to you. And he related that the woman was complaining a lot about her pregnancy, and Curt remarked: You are absolutely right, ma'am, absolutely right. The fate of women is very disagreeable. Women should not have to be pregnant, nor suffer birth pangs alone. This is all so unjust. It would be better if they just laid eggs. In times of crisis, they could be eaten; in times of abundance, incubated. Doesn't that seem good to you, Aninha? *Sure, Inimá, I'm a water animal. I only feel at home when I'm there. Shall we go?* The voyage was very profitable, Dona Coló. The yield of ocelot pelts was no big thing, but the otters made up for that. However, the best part was the transporting of goods for the senator and for the other estates that are now being opened. It was such good fortune. It gave me a lot of prestige in the eyes of that rabble of riverbank dwellers, and a little money to boot. We are going to pay our debts, Dona Coló. You'll see. And we will even have cruzeiros left over to buy a few more heifers this year. I knew it, Sr. Gão, my beloved deceased couldn't have done it any better than you. The children and I would have been lost if God hadn't sent you, Sr. Gão. It was God who sent you. Which is to say, Dona Coló, that you don't regret having married me, do you? What? After all you've . . . I am glad to be so satisfied. Thanks to the Virgin Mary! May God keep Sr. Juca down there under his protection, but he was far too violent a man. I think it was the Indian blood in his veins. At times I even fear that one of the children will grow up like him. Don't be afraid, no, Dona Coló. Don't be afraid. I am here. This year I'll put young Juquinha behind the counter; you'll see, ma'am. *I'm coming, Jaguar, I'm coming. Wait until I've finished picking off your ticks.* Hello! Hello! PYB 371 Mió calling PYB 173 Micê. Over. Hello! PYB 173 here listening. Over. Hello! Micê, this is Father Cirilo: *The director wants news of the little Indian girl who was returned. What happened? How did it happen? Why did it happen? Over.* PYB 173 this is Brother Faria replying: As to the Indian girl, Teresa, await a letter with details. Over. Mió here, Father Cirilo, replying: Letter received and read. It explains nothing. Father Ludgero wants an oral explanation by phone. Information, please. Over. This is Faria PYB 173 replying: What does he want me to do? The wife of the deputy returned Teresa by means of the carrier; she didn't come here herself. She only sent word that she never wanted to see an Indian girl in her house again. Over. Mió here, Cirilo speaking: Give a better explanation, Faria, I want to understand you. Terê, who was so charming, why was she rejected? Why was she beaten? Why was she accused of cannibalism? Over. Micê here, Faria speaking: I can only relate here what I can prove and that is very little. Teresa was brought back crying by the deputy's chauffeur. She continues to cry but does not complain about anyone. The chauffeur was the one who told us that the deputy's wife had struck her in a fit of anger. A sudden blow, without significance. Over. Cirilo here: Recount in detail the story of cannibalism. Over. Faria, Micê here with your explanation: There was no cannibalism. Only that the deputy's wife, on seeing the Indian girl kissing her baby's little feet, feared that the girl had reverted to the old custom they call anthropophagy. She set upon Teresa and gave her a dreadful beating. Over. PYB 371 Mió here, Cirilo speaking: I understood very little and badly, practically nothing. Tell me now about the accusations of prostitution. Over. Hello, Micê here, I'm speaking: There is nothing about prostitution. Only that the deputy's wife doesn't want to be responsible if, by chance, Teresa should fall into it. But she hasn't fallen. Not yet. Over. *You say you are coming but you stay here, Inimá, endlessly hunting for ticks. It's true that you catch them very well and crack them beautifully. But you don't want to come with me to the place I like.* Creuza, my old woman, this whole story is going to explode in our faces, you'll see. And what have we to do with that? The girl died there in the village, and if the major didn't uncover how she died, whether from childbirth or not, what has that to do with us? Sr. Juca died at the hands of the savages; it was the savages

who killed him, not we! You aren't here to bother with savages!
No, thank God, you are the agent of the Mairuns. And about
that lizard Teidju, who is going to know about his death? Leave
that matter alone, Elias. Nobody will even notice. I'm not talking
about that, woman. All I'm saying is that the stick breaks the
weakest knees. That major is going to do me in, he's going to
get me fired, you'll see. How, I don't know, but I'm sure of it.
Look, Elias, the major is too much of a gentleman. Fool! I'm
telling you, woman, I'm telling you. Be prepared for it. There'll
be a transfer, and it won't be a promotion. And if it were only
a matter of that, things would still be all right. That man is
going to put an end to me . . . put an end to us, Creuza. Don't
be so pessimistic, Elias. Your pessimism only gets us in more
trouble. Speaking ill of the major, such a fine young man. *Don't
you like me stroking your hair? Ingrate! You used to love it. I
know, everything is nostalgia for the Canindejub. She was the
one you liked best. Those things, you learned them from her.
Inimá, my love, tell me; don't you like it? So much!* I am going
to do as you order, Dona Gertrude: I will translate as you wish,
word for word. But I can guarantee that this way no Mairun will
ever understand a word of Matthew. Please do as I say, Sr. Isaías.
These are the instructions I am giving you. I gave them because
they are the ones that I myself received. I haven't mastered the
Mairun language. At least, not sufficiently yet to do the translation myself. This is why you are assisting me. But the moral
responsibility for the translation is mine, and mine alone. And
this I will not yield. All the more because this is not just any
translation. It is a translation of Matthew; and if I cannot follow
the translation word for word, I cannot accept it. As I can demonstrate, Dona Gertrude, the words are the most exact and the
most appropriate and the most comprehensible. In the plays of
phrases and words, in questions of syntax, I have slightly altered
what we produced together. They are modest alterations made
with care and judgment. Each people, you know each people
thinks within the frame of its own idiom. Unless the translation
is put in the frame of the Mairun idiom, no Mairun is ever going

to understand a single word of the Holy Bible. It can't be as you wish, word for word, noun for noun, verb for verb. I don't want to get involved in that, Sr. Isaías. But I think it should not be forgotten that of the three of us the only one who knows linguistics is Gertrude. She is getting her doctorate. Now you, too, Gertrude, must respect the integrity of the language of the Indians. What is the use of a perfect translation if none of them understands it? Of course I am not an idiot, nor am I as dense as you seem to think, Bob. What you don't know, what you don't want to understand is that Sr. Isaías is not merely putting it all into the Mairun syntax. No. In addition to words, he is adding phrases and images. And that is inadmissible, abominable. The Bible is by itself the main source of images for all literatures. If Sr. Isaías is going to begin our collaboration by introducing some new images, how will that turn out? *Shall we go? Ah! Jaguar. I'll go because you want me to. But it seems best to me here. This is where I like it best, in the hammock that I wove for both of us, and it's so lovely here.* Thank you, Sister Petrina, God will reward you. I know I have no right to be pleased. I know very well that everything you do, you do for the love of God. You are right, Father Ludgero. We are all here to serve the Lord. But I can't hide the satisfaction your words give me. I don't know what would become of us without you, without a nun so well prepared to assume with such competence the directorship of the convent. I never imagined that Sister Canuta, being deaf and dumb, could fail us like this. It was necessary for you to assume the directorship for order to be restored to the houses and for everything to proceed as it should. May God reward you for your words, Father Ludgero. The convent is renewing itself, Sister. The Mission is coming to life again. God has removed the oldest of the workers from among us. May God keep and protect them: Father Vecchio, Father Aquino, Sister Canuta, Sister Ignêz, Brother Ciano. But God gives us the joy of seeing that we are younger now. The average age has fallen considerably. And it was necessary because Senator Andorinha had quite raised my hopes. Ah! Father Ludgero, the

news has already spread through all the corridors of the House.
You should have seen the happiness in the faces of all the new
nuns and young priests. There is a contentment that no one can
hide or wants to conceal. Well, yes, Sister Petrina. Yes, it makes
me certain that we shall soon be assigned to pacify the Xaepēs.
In addition to being given land for the new Mission, we will have
the privilege of being charged officially by the government to
pacify the Xaepēs. We and only we will have the honor and the
difficult task of summoning them to live in peace with the
Brazilians and of leading them into the bosom of Christianity.
Only one thing saddens me, Father Ludgero. And permit me to
recall it to you once more; please forgive my insistence. We have
had a number of visitors recently: the senator often comes, and
with him many politicians and businessmen whom we have to
put up in the Mission. Couldn't something be done about that
horrible shack of the old Indian women's, down there on the
beach? Would it not be possible to send them back to the village? This is a problem that requires much patience, much wisdom, Sister Petrina. But we are already on the way to a solution,
with the help of God. I have myself given instructions to the
kitchen to start giving them food to eat at lunchtime and dinner, something we haven't done for a long time. As a result they
will become once again dependent on the house. Later on, we
might find a discreet room for them here inside. Then we will
be able to remove that from the beach of which I, too, am
ashamed. *Little Inimá, my darling, let's go right away. The
Iparaná is weeping with nostalgia for you, let's go. I'm coming,
my sweet, I'm coming.* Good afternoon, Pio, old man. What
brings you here? A message from Sr. Manuel Gão de Araújo?
No, sir, no, Sr. Tonico. I came only to see how things are
around here. Any news? Well, yes, Pio, we are finishing the
construction of the big new estate house that will receive the
senator's guests. The landing strip is ready; today it will be used
for the first time. You'll see; these pastures of the Epexãs' here
will soon abound with herds of livestock to make your mouth
water. The first herd is already on its way: six hundred cows

and more than fifty little bulls. All are beauties, brandless. They are coming from Uberaba along those trails. Within a month more will come. And the Epexãs, pardon the question, Sr. Tonico. What did you do with them? Those marginals—those dropouts, as the senator calls them—what a disgraceful lot. They didn't want to cooperate, the miserable fools. They wanted nothing to do with work. The solution was to call in a battalion of the Third Regiment and evict them as squatters on the senator's estate. When the troops arrived and the Indians saw the soldiers, they fled. I doubt they will ever show up around here again. The news I received was that they crossed on foot the distance from here to the Maruim River, penetrating the depths of the forest. They must be there. That's where they belong. They could have worked. I have a surplus of work to be done. But these half-breeds from the back country prefer to keep their distance from work. You're absolutely right. The Epexãs are a very strange people; in truth, very evil. Brutes, they are. Very backward. All the people who live along the banks of the river are afraid of them. Whenever I pass them, going upriver or downriver, I'm apprehensive. It was enough for us to stop paddling for an instant, and stones would rain down on us. If anyone approached nearer, he would be met by arrows. They are a tough people to put down, those Epexãs. Only the senator with a troop of soldiers could do anything with them. That's how it is, Pio. It's as you say. It is high time civilization arrived. It is Brazil that is now finally coming into its own, incorporating this river. You'll see all that will remain of that valley of the Epexãs will be their name: Fazenda Epexã. That's what the senator calls it. But now, Sr. Tonico, what about a little work for me; have you arranged something? Ah! Old Pio! I have. But the Senator's instructions are precise: there is to be no stealing men from Sr. Manuel Gão. And nothing, nothing whatsoever to do with any man who is in debt. And you, I know already, you are under the weight of a frightful debt. You settle it with your boss; if he sends me word, you have a job. Adequate work, of course. I have work for the whole world. *Come with me, you naughty little Falcon. I want to dwell in you the rest of my life. I'm coming, my great Jaguar, I'm coming now.* Hello? Who's speaking? It's me, Fred. This is Queco, a friend of Alma's, do you remember? All to clearly, Queco. Did you also see the picture of the major with her skull in his hand? I was stupefied, Fred. Who could have imagined such a thing? Little Alma, dead. I'm horrified. So am I, man, what a terrible death, alone in that wilderness. But what do you think really happened to her, Fred? Have you any idea? Well, I think it was what the paper said: a double birth. Twins, man. It's like that English joke: Wait while I go into the bush to have twins; I'll be back before you know it. That woman was mad. Look, Fred, I telephoned *O Globo.* I spoke to a friend of mine there to see if I could find out something more than what appeared in the account of the interview with the major. But no, my friend told me the same thing. I feel like going to talk to him. What are you going to do, Queco? Are you going to talk to the major? Better leave this business alone, or you'll end up as father of the twins. Yes, I was thinking of it. But I'm not going to get involved in that affair. I'm not going to, no. What can we do, Fred? Listen, buddy, death is death; and definitively. No one can do anything. That's true; but I think about what I could have done and didn't. That's what I think about. Look, Queco, leave it alone: if I, who am a shrink and was—as you know—very fond of her, can't do anything, imagine the little you can do. Forget it, I tell you: living is dangerous! She knew. That's how it is, Fred. You did what you could. It is I who don't really know if I did all I could. I read the papers and was devastated. I still am. Me, too, Queco; I confess that I didn't want to listen to any patients today. The first person I've spoken to is you. And it was just as well, Fred. If I had gone looking for the major, what could I have said to him? You could only have asked for her skull to bury, am I right? *Inimá, little Inimá, my sweet honey bear, why are you so naughty with me? Let's go lie in my little canoe, my darling. We'll drift with the current and make such love.* Doctor Ramiro, have you read Major Nonato's report? I haven't read anything, man. I'm not going to waste my time with that. You read it, didn't you, Noronha? Well, of course: I read the whole thing, Dr. Ramiro. It's very interesting. The man had an incredible voyage throughout the Amazon world. A real periplus, as he said. It made me envious. Not that I ever want to undertake such a mission. I wouldn't wander through those forests if you paid me. Lots of traveling, but nothing clarified; am I right, Noronha? Did he clarify anything? I read the statements in the newspaper. Adding insult to injury: that the death was accidental, the result of childbirth; nothing criminal. So what else is new? We deduced as much without leaving this office! The whole trip, costing the government a bundle, was entirely unnecessary. The expenses he incurred were considerable, Doctor, that's true enough. But what you ought to see in the report is how he buried that FUNAI agent. That poor man will never raise his head again. The major invented some sort of functional-criminal negligence, or administrative-criminal something-or-other, with at least two hyphens joining and separating the words, which is going to put an end to the career of that agent. He's all washed up. He'll be fired. *Inimá, porã tebĩ, ne tebicua he rancuãi sururuc potare eté. I'Jaguaroui, hebĩ catú hebẽ xeremymbotá apõ. Heteti rereco hebĩ xebi. Inimataĩ, cuña tebĩ, ne tebiroeté carapuáhẽ'ypy sururucatú.*

ABOUT THE AUTHOR

Darcy Ribeiro was born in Brazil in 1922. A distinguished anthropologist, he specializes in the indigenous peoples of Brazil. He has also served in government: he was Minister of Education and personal adviser to President Goulart before the military coup of 1964, and he was recently elected Lieutenant Governor of Rio de Janeiro. Forthcoming in English is his second novel *O Mulo*, which was also an international literary triumph.